CW00642372

THE KEY TO THE ABYSS

BOOK TWO OF THE DRAGON-MYTH CYCLE

JOSEPH FINLEY

TARASTONE PRESS

The Key to the Abyss
Copyright © 2018 by Joseph Finley

Published by TaraStone Press
First Kindle Edition: November 2018

Edited by Carolyn Haley
Cover Design by Jessica Bell
Map by Jeff Mathison
Interior illustrations by Streetlight Graphics

ISBN: 978-0-9884108-0-0 (print)

This book is a work of fiction. Names, characters, places, and events either are products of the author's imagination or are portrayed fictitiously.

All rights reserved. No part of this book may be reproduced in any form or by any electronic or mechanical means, including information storage and retrieval systems, without written permission from the author, except for the use of brief quotations in a book review.

The Scripture quotations contained herein are from the New Revised Standard Version Bible, copyright © 1989 by the Division of Christian Education of the National Council of Churches of Christ in the U.S.A. Used by permission. All rights reserved.

❄ Created with Vellum

A NOTE ON PRONUNCIATION

Because the novel is set throughout tenth-century Europe, it contains a few Old Norse, Old French, and Gaelic names that can be a bit difficult to pronounce. The following is a rough pronunciation guide for some of the trickier words.

Aurillac—OHR-ee-YAK
Alais—AH-lay
Charon—KER-uhn
Ciarán—KEER-in
Columcille—KULL-im-kill
Évrard—eh-VRAAR
Gerbert—ZH-eh-RBeh-R
Jarl—YArl
Jelling—YELL-ing
Jörmungandr—YOOR-muhn-guhn-dahr
Jorundr—YOR-uhn-dahr
Maugis—MO-zhee
Nimue—NEE-moo-eh
Poitiers—PWA-tee-ay
Tuatha dé Danann—Thoo-a-haw-day-dah-nawn

When the thousand years are ended, Satan will be released from his prison and will come out to deceive the nations at the four corners of the earth, Gog and Magog, in order to gather them for battle . . .

—Revelation 20:7-8

Castel Sant'Angelo

St. Peters

Castel
Sant'Angelo

TIBER

Pantheon

Leonine
City

CAPITOLINE
HILL

Forum

Colosseum

PALATINE
HILL

CAELIAN
HILL

AVENTINE
HILL

Lateran
Palace

Porto
Di Ripa

RIVER

Rome   A.D. 998

PART I

In later times some will abandon the faith and follow deceiving spirits and things taught by demons . . .

—1 Timothy 4:1

THE EXORCIST

I n the Year of Our Lord 998, a week after blood rained from the sky in Aquitaine and many feared the End of Days, the abbot of Saint-Pierre needed an exorcist.

The abbey loomed over the tiny village of Solignac, where men claimed a foul spirit had possessed one of the hundred and fifty monks within the monastery's thick stone walls. The afflicted man's howls pealed from the abbey's highest window like the call of a rabid wolf. Yet not even the village dogs answered those howls, for there was something terrifying and unearthly in the madman's cries that sent the poor beasts cowering in their masters' hovels. By dusk, no villagers or animals could be seen in the pastures or pathways around the cottages that stood in the abbey's shadows when three unlikely travelers arrived at the abbey's gatehouse.

The first of the travelers, Brother Ciarán mac Tomás, wore a threadbare habit dyed Benedictine black with a broad cowl over his head. The garments had belonged to a poor monk felled by an arrow at the battle of Brosse, but Ciarán had patched the arrow's hole and scrubbed out the bloodstains, making the clothes a tolerable replacement for the Irish cowl and habit he lost in Córdoba. In his right arm, the young Irish monk cradled a slender object four feet long and wrapped in sackcloth, its top shaped vaguely like an altar cross within a Lenten veil. The object would prove vital when confronting the possessed man. But judging by the grumblings of his two companions, Ciarán suspected he was the only one who believed in this plan.

Another horrid wail sounded from the abbey, and Khalil al-Pârsâ gave Ciarán a black look. The Persian poet wore his unease on his handsome face, his lips pressed together between his sculpted beard and mustache. "This is unwise," he said, gripping the hilt of the sheathed scimitar hanging from his sword belt.

"It's the only way," Ciarán replied. "The enemy is searching for the Key, and this demon may know where they're looking."

Khalil grimaced. "So you would seek guidance from a demon?"

"Guidance?" Ciarán shook his head. "No, but maybe a clue." He started toward the abbey's oak gate, when Alais called out behind them.

"Maev's too scared to move," she said. The young widow caressed the mane of their pack mule, whom Ciarán had named after the defiant Queen Maev from the old Irish legends. "Look, the poor creature's shaking." Concern lingered in Alais' storm-gray eyes and the pout of her lips; though as hard as it was, Ciarán tried to ignore her misgivings. She remained the most beautiful woman he had ever known, even as she stood there in a simple gray dress and a hooded cloak that covered her raven-colored hair. Their cause this evening, however, was greater than his feelings for any woman, so he reminded himself of his mentor's old saying: *Lad, remember your vows.*

"We'll tie Maev up out here 'til it's over," he told her.

Alais sighed, and glanced at Khalil.

"There must be a better way than speaking with this demon," the Persian insisted.

"Ciarán, he's right," Alais added.

Ciarán glared at them, muttering a curse under his breath as he rapped on the gate.

A peephole slid open and a pair of flinty eyes stared back, only to wince when another raving cry raged from the abbey's top floor. *"Sancta Maria, Mater Dei,"* the gatekeeper muttered in Latin, before a long sigh. "Who are you, brother, and why of all places have you come here?"

"My name is Ciarán mac Tomás. We heard rumors in Limoges that your abbot seeks an exorcist."

"Are you one?" asked the doorkeeper in a desperate tone.

"Of sorts," Ciarán replied.

The peephole slid shut, and behind the door a key rattled in a lock. The door opened, revealing a Benedictine monk with a gaunt, pock-marked face. He clutched a wooden cross that hung from his neck, while his eyes darted between Ciarán and his two companions. The monk's gaze grew wide at the sight of Khalil with his Moorish complexion and a scimitar sheathed at his side, but even wider upon seeing Alais, who must have looked to him like the image of the Blessed Virgin.

"C-come inside," the gatekeeper stammered. "We can put your mule in the stables."

Ciarán dragged Maev by her reins into the abbey's muddy court-yard. No geese or goats picked through the mud, though from the nearby stables came the fretful whinny of horses. At the courtyard's far end stood the abbey, a cluster of buildings three stories tall. A lonesome church spire rose over the abbey's gabled roofs, where stone gargoyles perched like hungry crows. The gatekeeper helped stable the frightened mule, then led them through the abbey's front door into a cramped vestibule dimly lit by tallow candles. "I'll fetch the prior," he said.

He returned, accompanied by an older monk with a sullen face and tufts of white hair above his ample ears. The prior, who wore a finely wrought silver cross, cringed as another ghastly howl echoed through the abbey's halls. "Brother," the prior said, trying to regain his composure. "How can I help you?"

"Father Prior," Ciarán replied, "I'd like to speak with the abbot about the man who's been afflicted."

"That will be a problem," the prior said, his hand fidgeting with the silver cross. "You see, our dear abbot is the man who's been possessed."

5

Ciarán raised a brow; he had not expected that answer.

"We found him five days ago, unconscious in the graveyard," the gatekeeper added. "When he awoke in his bedchamber, our Father Abbot was stricken with the spirit that has claimed him."

"Then it seems your abbot's need for an exorcist is quite personal," Khalil said.

The prior pursed his lips. "Brother Ciarán, I do not know who you are, or why you keep company with a Moor and a woman, but you cannot help, for we are under God's curse."

"Curses can be broken," Ciarán said, glancing at the object he held wrapped in sackcloth. "You just have to use the right tool."

"We've tried everything, I assure you," the prior insisted. "Just four nights ago, Brother Denis tried to expel the demon by reading to it from the Book of Revelation and warning of our Savior's return at the end times, when He will cast every demon into the Lake of Fire. But the abbot tore the book from his hands and ripped the very pages from their binding. He near choked the life from poor Brother Denis before we bound the abbot's arms to his bed frame. Yet I fear those bonds weaken by the day."

"And two nights ago," the gatekeeper said, "Brother Lucas took one of our holiest relics, a rib bone from Saint Eligius, and used it against the demon. Yet the abbot seized the bone with his teeth and snapped it in two! Brother Lucas tried to save it, but the abbot bit him so hard he nearly tore off poor Lucas's hand."

"Is he all right?" Alais asked.

The prior nodded. "He near bled to death, though our infirmarer bound the wound, and by God's grace Brother Lucas now rests in the infirmary. Yet after that, our sacrist, Brother Jerome, tried to fell the evil spirit. He wrote the opening passage of the Gospel of Saint John on fresh parchment, then scraped the words into holy water and forced the abbot to drink it. But he retched the blessed water back up, and the vomit scalded poor Jerome's skin like hot lamp oil! He lies in the infirmary, at death's edge, I fear. So I don't know what tool you plan on using, Brother Ciarán, but nothing can be done. 'Tis a sign of the end times, just like the blood rain over Aquitaine."

"The end times are far from certain," Ciarán said. "But what matters now is your abbot's condition, so take me to him."

The prior ran a hand over his bald head. "If you insist, but once you confront him, you will be beyond the power of our prayers."

They followed the doorkeeper and the prior down a short hallway lit by rushlights where a narrow stairwell emerged from the shadows of an archway. "Where is the rest of the brotherhood?" Ciarán asked.

"Holding vigil in the church," the prior replied, "praying their psalms drown out the abbot's wails."

They climbed the stairs as another ravenous cry erupted from beyond the top of the stairwell. The prior made the sign of the cross and stepped into a shallow passageway that held the stench of a dung heap. At the end stood an oak door, though its face, and even the surrounding stone, was covered with a festering black mold that spread in every direction like a spider's web.

Khalil recoiled at the smell of it. "What is that?"

"I'm afraid it's been spreading ever since the spirit took hold of the abbot," the prior said, covering his nose with the sleeve of his habit. "The door leads to his bedchamber. There, you will find him."

"Are you certain you want to do this?" Khalil asked Ciarán under his breath.

"Aye." Ciarán winced at the stench, but strode past the prior and grabbed the door handle. The iron felt warm to the touch.

"Be careful," Alais said behind him.

"I will." Ciarán steadied his nerves. *This is not an exorcism,* he reminded himself, *but an interrogation. And I have the power to make this fiend talk.*

Ciarán opened the door and stared into darkness, inhaling a breath of the rancid air. As he stepped into the chamber, he heard a hiss, then around the room a score of candles burst to flame as if lighting themselves before settling into an eerie glow. Along the walls crept more of the thick black mold, while torn parchment littered the floor surrounding a once lavish four-post bed heaped with soiled blankets and the husk of a leather bookbinding. In the bed, half covered by the blankets, lay a bloated and balding man as old as the prior, with dark circles beneath his bulbous eyes. His outstretched arms tugged at the pair of bedposts, where they were bound by tangles of leather cords.

Ciarán made the sign of the cross. "Peace be with you, Father Abbot."

The abbot's lips widened into a grin, revealing a mouthful of brown and bloodstained teeth. "There is no peace," he hissed, "and there is no abbot. Only me."

Ciarán stepped toward the bed. "Who are you?"

"My name is Legion," the abbot said.

"You lie."

The possessed man sneered. "And you are no exorcist, Ciarán of Hibernia, son of heretics."

A chill crawled up Ciarán's skin. *It knows my name.* He drew a sharp breath and placed his left hand on the object, curling his fingers under the sackcloth. "Your brethren are searching for the Key to the Abyss. I know why they seek it, but where are they looking?"

The abbot let out a chilling cackle. "They shall find it, but not you, son of heretics. No, not you."

Ciarán clenched his jaw. "Tell me where they're searching."

"Who are *you* to command me?" the abbot growled.

"I am the keeper of Enoch's device." Ciarán tore the sackcloth off the object, revealing a sheathed longsword with a cross hilt and a round gemstone embedded in its pommel. He slid the sword from its scabbard; its steel blade glinted in the candlelight.

From the doorway, the prior gasped. "You'll kill the abbot!"

Ciarán glared at the prior, then raised the blade. "You know what this is and what it will do," he told the abbot. "So I suggest you start answering my questions."

The abbot's eyes narrowed to slits. "You're too late," he said between huffs of breath. "The Morning Star has awakened, Gog and Magog heed his call. The sacrifice is ready, the heir of Constantine shall fall!"

"Answer my question!" Ciarán leveled the sword's tip at the abbot's neck.

The abbot thrashed forward, straining his bonds. Behind him, wood cracked. Ciarán could not risk the man breaking free. He leaned over the gemstone in the sword's pommel, focused his will, and whispered a word born of the language of creation. *"Eoh."* Power surged through his arm as a ghostly white flame hissed down the blade.

The abbot cringed. "The Prince of Rome," he said through clenched teeth, "holds the path to the key."

"Who is the Prince of Rome?" Ciarán pressed.

The abbot gave a defiant growl; his veins bulging, his face reddening.

"Answer me!"

A look of madness flashed in the abbot's eyes. "You're too late!" he screamed. "The pillar will be broken, the Watchers shall be freed!" With a roar, he ripped free of his bonds and lunged at Ciarán, clawing for his neck.

Ciarán slammed the flat of the blade into the side of the abbot's head. Where the steel struck, flesh sizzled and the abbot let out a bloodcurdling cry. White fire flared from the blade, and within its sudden glow, Ciarán glimpsed a visage of pure hatred—manlike and hairless, with eyes like embers and a maw full of fangs. With a blast of heat, the spirit disappeared like a flame blown from a candle, leaving only the abbot in its place.

Ciarán exhaled. *It's gone,* he knew, for in the short time he had possessed Enoch's device, no demon had survived its touch. He let the fire die on the sword's blade. "Father Abbot?" he asked the man.

Huddled against the broken headboard, the abbot breathed heavily, a dazed look in his eyes. He touched the side of his face, seared and swollen where the blade had landed, and shook his head. "The Prince of Rome holds the path to the Key . . ." he muttered. "What does it mean?"

"I'm not sure," Ciarán said. "But I pray you can help me figure it out."

2

THE DEMON'S WORDS

The abbot of Saint-Pierre hunched over one of the long wooden tables in the abbey's refectory, devouring a bowl of porridge and a loaf of dark bread. "By God, I've never been so famished," he told Ciarán between gulps of spiced wine. "I feel as though I could eat a whole hog." He licked a dollop of porridge off his thick fingers. "I know our good Saint Benedict forbade us meat under his rules, but I doubt he was ever possessed by a foul spirit, or else there would be an exception, don't you think?"

"I'd reckon so," Ciarán said, not mentioning that he too had once been possessed, in the old Roman amphitheater outside Poitiers. His mentor, Brother Dónall, had saved him from the demon, but he had slept for a day afterward and woke up in the infirmary of Saint-Hilaire-le-Grand as hungry as the abbot seemed now. At the time, Ciarán had remembered nothing of the spirit that possessed him, though his affliction had lasted mere moments before Dónall wrestled the demon free of Ciarán's mind. The abbot's possession, however, had lingered for days, and Ciarán hoped the fiend's tenure had left a memory or two burned into the abbot's mind.

He glanced at the refectory's entrance, where the prior and the gatekeeper looked on like a pair of nervous field mice. The prior had insisted the abbot go to the infirmary, but the abbot would hear none of it, even though the side of his face was red and blistered where the flat of the blade had struck. To appease the prior and treat the burn, Ciarán had whipped up a salve of butter and marigold petals, which glistened on the abbot's face as he wolfed down another fistful of bread.

"Father Abbot," Ciarán asked, "may we begin?"

The abbot drained his cup of wine. "I'll tell you what I remember, Brother Ciarán. But first I would like to know who the three of you are, and why you came here."

Ciarán looked to Khalil, sitting on the bench beside him. The Persian gave him a nod.

Ciarán thought about where to begin. Four months ago, he had been no different from the brothers in this abbey, believing he would spend his life in monastic devotion, illuminating manuscripts in Derry's scriptorium. But then a black-robed bishop had arrived to accuse Dónall of heresy, and ever since, Ciarán's whole world had turned upside down. He wondered how much of the story the abbot would even believe, and decided it was best to begin with a question. "Father Abbot, do you believe the Apocalypse to be imminent?"

The abbot bit off another hunk of bread, answering while he chewed. "Half the Church believes so, for the millennium draws near, a thousand years after the birth of Christ. A week ago, blood fell from the sky over Brosse, as surely you've heard, just as it's written the Book of Revelation. The first angel blew his trumpet and there came hail mixed with blood and whatnot. Since then, an evil spirit has bedeviled me and terrorized all of Solignac, so of course I believe. The angel has sounded the first trumpet, and I fear we stand less than two years from the brink of Armageddon."

"What if I told you the End of Days could be averted, at least for the next thousand years?"

"I might think you to be mad, Brother Ciarán. God has set the wheel in motion, and no man can stop it from turning."

Ciarán set the sword on top of the table. "Unless God gave man the means to stop the wheel."

The abbot narrowed his gaze. "Where are you going with this?"

"Back at my monastery," Ciarán said, "in the north of Ireland, I learned of a book written by Maugis d'Aygremont, one of the twelve paladins of Charlemagne. The book spoke of a secret prophecy about the End of Days, one that if fulfilled could avert the Apocalypse at the end of the millennium. That secret led me and my mentor, Brother Dónall mac Taidg, to the home of the Lady Alais of Selles-sur-Cher, who sits with us now."

The abbot's eyes widened. "The cousin of the Duke of Aquitaine?" He wiped a smear of porridge from his chin. "My lady, had I known . . ."

"It's nothing," she said. "When we arrived, you were hardly in a place for a proper introduction."

"Quite true," the abbot said with a sheepish grin. "Brother Ciarán, please go on."

"Like the Book of Maugis d'Aygremont," Ciarán said, "the paladins of Charlemagne had preserved another secret, kept safe by the lords of Selles-sur-Cher since the time of King Charles the Bald. The secret was a copy of the Book of Enoch, an ancient text that elaborated on the sixth chapter of the Book of Genesis, which told the story of the time before the Great Flood when the sons of God went into the daughters of men. The text told of a great and glorious device that, according to Maugis' tome, could help prevent the End of Days. We sought out the device, and our quest led us to Córdoba, where we met Khalil al-Pârsâ." Ciarán gestured to his friend sitting beside him. "Khalil is a renown poet among the Moors, but he's also a scholar of Fierabras, a Moor himself and another of Charlemagne's paladins who knew of the device. And with Khalil's aid, we were able to find it. That device is the sword which freed you from the demon, and more particularly, the gemstone in its pommel. The Bible called the gem the Urim, and etched in its center is a symbol of the one true name of God."

"Sweet Jesus," the abbot said, bearing a look of utter astonishment. "Are you saying that with that weapon, you've averted the End of Days?"

"No," Ciarán said, "but if that's ever to be achieved, we must find one more relic, and that's why we came to you."

A spark of remembrance flashed in the abbot's eyes. "The key . . ." He rubbed his temples as if trying to summon the memory. "When the spirit was inside me, I heard it speak with another. A ghost in the darkness. Whispering, conspiring, talking of terrible things. The ghost spoke of a key to a bottomless pit . . ."

"Aye," Ciarán replied, grateful the abbot had remembered, but concerned about this mention of a second spirit. It reminded him of Brother Remi's old warning back in the crypts of Saint-Germain-des-Prés. *The enemy has servants that hide in the shadows . . . and not just men.* But that concern would have to wait.

"It spoke of the Key to the Abyss," Ciarán told the abbot. "It's referenced in the Book of Revelation, the key to the prison that holds the fallen angels who rebelled against God when war broke out in Heaven. At the abbey of Saint-Martial in Limoges, we found a copy of a commentary on the Apocalypse written two hundred years ago by Saint Beatus of Liébana. He portrayed the Key as an object as long as a man is tall and crooked like a dog's hind leg, forged of black iron, with an L-shaped head and three prominent teeth. We know the enemy is searching for it, and we know we have to find it before they do."

"The enemy . . ." the abbot said gravely. "It said the Morning Star awakens. Brother Ciarán, you know what that means, do you not?"

Ciarán nodded. "It's from the Book of Isaiah. *'How you have fallen from Heaven, O Morning Star, son of the dawn. You have been cast down to the earth, you who once laid low the nations.'*"

"A reference to Lucifer, the Prince of Darkness," the abbot said, clasping his hands to his chest. "And you know what Revelation says about him. When the thousand years have ended, Satan will be released from his prison. Do you think finding this Key can stop that?"

"I don't know," Ciarán said, "but what I do know is if the enemy seeks the Key, then stopping them from getting it might be the next step in preventing the End of Days."

The abbot's head sank into his hands. "The spirit and the ghost . . .

they want the Key more than anything in this world. He looked up, wide-eyed. "They believe the way to find it lies with someone called the prince in Rome."

Ciarán glanced at Khalil; he could tell from the Persian's eyes that his mind was churning.

"You mean the Prince *of* Rome," Khalil said. "That is what the spirit said, one of several things. When you put them together, they form a verse:

> The Morning Star has awakened, Gog and Magog heed his call.
> The sacrifice is ready, the heir of Constantine shall fall.
> The Prince of Rome holds the path to the Key.
> The pillar will be broken, the Watchers shall be freed.

Ciarán stared at his friend, reminded once again that the poet's mind was sharper than his scimitar. Alais, however, shook her head. "It's more like a riddle," she said.

"The spirit spoke in riddles," the abbot admitted, "as if only he and the ghost knew the secrets behind their words."

"Then we'll have to unlock those secrets," Ciarán said, confident his plan had worked. When they arrived at Limoges, the notion that the enemy would seek the Key was but a theory, and a vague one at that, for they had no idea where the journey would take them. But he had forced the demon's words from its mouth, and it had shown him the way.

The abbot stared at them, his face ashen. "What will you do now?"

"The only thing we can," Ciarán replied. "Find the Prince of Rome."

By morning, the abbey's courtyard had returned to life. Chickens and geese pecked through the mud, while two massive hogs wallowed in their filth and goats trimmed the grass around the abbey's curtain wall. A burly monk filled a trough full of oats for the horses in the ramshackle stables, as another chatted with the gatekeeper at the entrance to the gatehouse. Despite the gray sky and the occasional splatter of rain, every soul in the abbey acted as if a dark cloud had been lifted over Solignac.

Ciarán had no trouble coaxing Maev from the stables into the courtyard. He had laden the mule with the few things they owned: blankets, cloaks, a spare change of clothes, and the plain-looking canvas sack concealing two coats of armor. The first was the polished mail hauberk that once belonged to Maugis d'Aygremont, which Orionde had given him inside the tower of Rosefleur. He had never felt comfortable under its weight, and knew that, despite what he'd done at Brosse, he was still a monk, not a warrior. Also, he much preferred a monk's robes to the heavy chainmail, even if they were dyed Benedictine black instead of the natural gray wool he wore as a monk at Derry. The second coat hidden away in the sack belonged to Alais. It was a close-fitting tunic made of feather-shaped scales given to her by the sisters of Orionde. Alais had only worn it once, but it made her look resplendent, like one of the beings who created it. Folktales and myths called them the Fae, the faeries of legend. But Ciarán knew the truth. Orionde and her sisters were refugees of the ancient war in Heaven, angels who left their celestial home to explore the wonders of this world. But unlike the Watchers—the fallen angels condemned to the Abyss—the Fae committed no mortal sins on the earth, earning them clemency instead of imprisonment. Orionde and her sisters were gone now, slain in the battle outside Rosefleur, while men waged war at Brosse. As he secured the sack to the mule, Ciarán wondered how many of the Fae in this world still survived.

He tucked Enoch's device, wrapped once again in sackcloth, between the sack and the leather packs carrying their cloaks and clothes, making sure it was secure. Maev looked at him with her big brown eyes, and Ciarán gave her a pat on the neck.

"I suppose we're supposed to wait for both of them in the rain," he told the mule.

He was brushing raindrops from Maev's coat when his friends emerged from the abbey's oak doors. Alais pulled her hood over her long raven hair, while Khalil strode toward Ciarán. The poet had a serious look in his eyes.

"What's wrong?" Ciarán asked.

"I have thought about it all night," Khalil replied. "I do not think Rome is the right place to go."

"How can it not be?" Ciarán asked with a frustrated sigh. "The demon said the Prince of Rome holds the path to finding the Key. A map of some type, perhaps, and if it's in Rome, that's where we have to go."

"Why do you think we can trust this demon's words?"

Ciarán clenched his jaw. He knew he should not easily dismiss the Persian's views, for at the age of thirty, Khalil was nine years Ciarán's senior and near as learned as Dónall had been. Yet he was new to the prophecy, whereas Ciarán had benefited from Remi and Dónall's counsel for months before the Persian joined their quest. *If only Dónall was alive to lead us,* he thought with a pang of sorrow.

"This demon's words are all we have," Ciarán replied. "If not Rome, where would you have us go?"

Khalil wiped the rain from his brow. "To one of the great libraries in Constantinople, or to Baghdad, or perhaps back to my home in Persia. We found Enoch's device through what we learned in the Great Library of Córdoba, in the writings of the magi. The wheel of prophecy is older than Christianity or Islam, even the faith of the Jews, and in the last millennium, when the wheel came full circle, it was the magi of Persia who fulfilled it. Surely they would have recorded their knowledge to aid the generation burdened with this task in the millennium that followed. I would find far more comfort in their words than those of this demon."

Ciarán shook his head. "You don't know if the magi wrote down their secrets. And if they did, who knows if those writings even still exist? Maugis didn't say a thing about the magi in his book."

"Perhaps Maugis did not know of their role. But if you are correct about this Key to the Abyss, it means the magi possessed it a thousand years ago. Beatus of Liébana wrote of the Key, and you trust his depiction of it. Yet would you not seek out the knowledge of the magi, men who once held its cold iron in their very hands?"

"Ciarán," Alais said, "he has a point."

Ciarán threw up his palms. "So let's see, we're supposed to embark on a tour of the greatest libraries on earth to search for some thousand-year-old text written by a cult of Persian magi whose followers —if there happen to be any left—are nowhere to be seen this time around. Meanwhile, some bloody 'Prince of Rome' is searching for the Key to the Abyss, bent on unlocking the gates of Hell."

"I have been to Rome," Khalil said. "I assure you there is no monarch, and no prince."

"Maybe the demon was speaking figuratively," Ciarán pressed.

"Or perhaps he was lying," Khalil snapped. "It seemed all too eager to expose the secret of this supposed prince."

Ciarán looked Khalil in the eyes. "I could be wrong, but what if I'm not? Every time I think about this, I remember the first time Brother Remi told me about the prophecy, in the crypts of Saint-Germain-des-Prés. Dónall was being his usual stubborn self, doubting the prophecy's existence, yet Remi put it to him plainly. The price of being wrong, he said, is unimaginable, for the horrors of the Apocalypse will rain down on us all. So if there's a chance this Prince of Rome exists, and if he does have the power to find a key that can free the fallen angels, don't we have to go?"

Khalil turned to Alais. "My lady, what do you think we should do?"

She closed her eyes for a moment, as if deep in thought. "I suppose, being the only woman means I'm the most sensible one here. So even if we decide to go to Constantinople, Rome is on the way. I suppose there's no harm is going there first. Then we can decide if there's a better course."

Her words made Ciarán smile. "She's right, let's be sensible about this."

Khalil sighed. "In every story you have read, have a demon's words been anything but lies?"

"In many a lie, there's a kernel of truth," Ciarán said, taking Maev's reins. "And God willing, we'll find that truth in Rome."

3

THE SAXON POPE

N early three hundred leagues southeast of Solignac, an army gathered outside the walls of Rome.

Thousands of horsemen claimed the front ranks with a legion of archers and foot soldiers assembled behind them. An array of banners snapped in the breeze: the blue and gray diamonds of Bavaria, the gold and crimson stripes of Carinthia, the black lion of Meissen, the white horse of Tuscany, the red hawk of Breisgau, the silver wheel of Mainz, and the standards of every bishop in Northern Italy. At the center of the front ranks fluttered the golden banner of Saint Michael, and beside it a crimson flag adorned with crossed keys, one silver, one gold: the banner of Pope Gregory the Fifth, Vicar of Christ and the man who would reclaim Saint Peter's throne.

Gregory rode beneath his banner, gripping the *ferula,* a hardwood staff topped with an ornate golden cross. A crimson cloak draped over his open-front cassock and the *triregnum,* the triple crown of the pope, covered his close-cropped blond hair. From the saddle of his steel-gray stallion, he gazed upon the Porta Flaminia, a massive arched gateway in the Aurelian Walls barred by heavy wooden gates and flanked by crenelated towers. At twenty-six years of age, Gregory's eyes were sharp as a falcon's, and even though the army remained well beyond bowshot of the walls, he could count the archers on the battlements and even recognize the two men standing in its center beneath the defiant banner of the marble horse.

"The villains are watching us," Gregory told his cousin Otto, the seventeen-year-old king of the Germans and Lombards, and Holy Roman Emperor of the West. "Crescentius Tyrannus and his consigliere, Naberus da Roma."

Otto sat proudly atop his white charger. His polished mail hauberk gleamed in the sunlight, which glinted off the gold crown encircling his helm like a halo around his smooth and delicate face. He peered at the Aurelian Walls. "They dare defy me?"

"Are you surprised? This man was bold enough to break his oath to you, chase me from Rome, and install an antipope on Saint Peter's throne. I warned you not to underestimate him."

"I've not done so," Otto said, regarding Gregory with the soft, brown eyes that reminded the pope of Otto's Byzantine mother. "This is not my first battle."

"No one has underestimated anyone," called a voice from behind them. Gregory turned to see Otto's chief counselor, Gerbert of Aurillac, amble his roan mare beside the emperor. Gerbert wore a black tunic and scapular that hid his slight frame, though it did nothing to hide the monk's enormous opinion of himself. He was twice Gregory's age, a fact the man noted often when boasting of the wisdom of his years. The balding monk looked up at them with his aquiline nose, his ginger beard, and his usual smug expression. "Your Majesty," he said to Otto, "Crescentius could never hold the city against an army this large. He has not enough soldiers to man all twelve miles of the Aurelian Walls. Besides, for weeks now our loyalists inside those walls have been urging the city guard to surrender. Soon, Your Majesty, you shall ride through those gates, and"—he turned to Gregory—"Your Holiness shall be returned to the Lateran Palace."

"Crescentius will never surrender," Gregory replied with a bitterness in his voice born of his fourteen-month exile.

Gerbert waved a dismissive hand. "Behind us stands the might of Germany and Italy, united under Saint Michael's banner. Otto is the

Holy Roman Emperor, ruler of the citizens of Rome, like Caesar Augustus before him, and born of the noblest Greek and German blood. He will command the Romans with eloquence and grace, and they shall love him for it. Crescentius may proclaim himself prefect of Rome, but he lacks the divine right to rule. He will not stand against us long."

Gregory pursed his lips. *The old man fancies himself as Cicero!*

"You honor me, Gerbert," Otto said, touching his counselor's arm. "See, cousin, it's only a matter of time."

"It will take more than eloquence and grace to defeat John Crescentius," Gregory said, annoyed by Gerbert's overconfidence and Otto's gullibility. Neither had been there when Crescentius's men stormed the Lateran Palace crying, "Down with the Saxon pope!" They sought to imprison him in Castel Sant'Angelo, where so many of his predecessors had met their end. Only by the grace of God and with the aid of his papal archdeacon had Gregory escaped the palace and fled to Pisa, where he learned Crescentius had installed the traitorous Greek, John Philagathos, on Saint Peter's throne. John the Greek now ruled the Holy See as John the Sixteenth, making a mockery of the papacy. Otto and Gerbert had never known such humiliation, and it lingered in Gregory's soul like a festering wound.

He grew more restless as the hours passed, as did the emperor's army. Like Gregory and his cousin, most of the cavalrymen had dismounted, while archers unstrung their bows and spearmen sat sullenly on the grassy field or leaned on their weapons, griping to the men around them. Gregory's stomach ached for food, and he suspected the legions behind him felt the same. "We should make camp soon," he suggested to Otto.

"Perhaps," his cousin said, unable to hide his disappointment.

"Or perhaps not, Your Majesty." Gerbert pointed at a man riding toward them on a black destrier. A full beard flowed beneath the rider's iron helm and his long, kite-shaped shield displayed a black lion on a mustard field, the heraldry of Eckard, the Margrave of Meissen.

Eckard reigned in his war-horse. The German's eyes betrayed

THE KEY TO THE ABYSS

nothing of the news he brought, and his battle-hardened face bore a serious expression.

"Your Majesty," Eckard said as a cunning smile cracked his lips. "Our loyalists inside the walls have taken the Porta Salaria. They're prepared to open the gate as soon as we can get there."

Gregory's spirits soared. "Eckard, you've done well!"

"Which gate is the Porta Salaria?" asked Otto, his face aglow.

"The next gate to the east," Gregory replied.

"Ironically," Gerbert noted, "it's also the gate by which Alaric entered the city when the Goths sacked Rome."

A determined grin spread across Otto's face. "Unlike King Alaric, we're here to liberate Rome, not plunder it." He raised the lance he had carried with him since they left Aachen. The weapon had been forged by the Emperor Constantine, who centuries ago had enshrined the spear's tip with one of the nails that had affixed the Savior to the cross. The Holy Roman emperors had protected the relic since the days of Charlemagne, and now the youngest of those emperors used the Holy Lance to rally his legions.

"Margrave," Otto commanded, "ready our men!"

Word spread among the army and a chorus of cheers soon filled the air. Archers scrambled to string their bows, horsemen mounted their steeds, and spearmen fell into ranks. Otto climbed onto his charger's saddle, and a page helped Gregory atop his own mount. He gripped the reins and felt a surge of excitement as the army began to march toward the Porta Salaria. Then behind him, some of the cheers turned to cries.

Gregory turned in his saddle. A horseman charged from the ranks, his mount's hooves of pounding the turf. The rider aimed his spear straight at Gregory's unarmored chest. "Death to the Saxon pope!" he cried.

Gregory gasped. His stallion darted right, but not fast enough to avoid the blow. Then something flashed by his eyes. The rider flew back in his saddle, a lance protruding from his gut. Margrave Eckard clutched the weapon and roared as he hurled the attacker off his horse, causing the frenzied animal to bolt.

Gregory struggled to regain his breath. He gazed down at his would-be assassin. He was more boy than man, of northern Italian stock judging from his fair hair and long limbs. The boy clawed at the lance jutting from his stomach.

"Explain yourself!" Otto screamed, his face burning with sudden rage. He thrust the Holy Lance an inch from the boy's chin.

Blood trickled from the boy's lips as he choked out an answer. "The thousand years are ending . . ." His eyes widened as he spoke. "And when the Savior returns, no foreigner shall sit on Saint Peter's throne . . ."

Otto stared at the dying boy, then regarded the scores of horsemen gathering around the scene. "He's mad," Otto told them, "and mistaken about the end times. Your Holiness, tell him why before he faces God's judgment."

Gregory's hands were shaking; he had to take a deep breath before he could utter a response. "Because of the prophecy of Daniel, Your Majesty."

Otto spread out his arms as if to draw the attention of his army. "And tell us, what did Daniel, the prophet of scripture, foresee?"

"Daniel foresaw that before the End of Days, four great empires must fall," Gregory said. "The last of those is the Roman Empire, which you preserve to this very day. So long as that empire stands, the world shall live."

"See?" Otto yelled, raising the Holy Lance. "We have nothing to fear!"

A triumphant cheer erupted from the surrounding warriors. Otto leaned toward Gregory. "The Crescentii and their assassins shall not harm you, cousin. I swear it." He turned to Eckard. "Margrave, the poets shall sing of your deeds here today. Now, let us retake Rome!"

Eckard wheeled his mount to face the army. "Column formation!"

As the warriors assembled, Gregory looked down at the boy, who stared back, life fading from his eyes. "I *will* reclaim Saint Peter's throne," Gregory promised. "And when I do, Crescentius and John the Greek shall meet your fate and taste God's judgment."

4

ALL ROADS LEAD TO ROME

Alais' father had always warned her about the old Roman roads that crisscrossed France.

Many were impassable in places where the forests had reclaimed the land and grown over the flagstones, and most were marred with broad potholes where men had plundered the stones, making them treacherous for carts and mounts. Yet the true danger was the roving packs of wolves and the wild boars that could gut a man with their tusks, and worst of all the brigands. As a child, Alais would never travel the roads unless accompanied by her father or uncle and a score of their armed men, for neither wolves nor brigands were bold enough to attack an Aquitanian lord and his mail-clad horsemen. Even after her marriage to Lord Geoffrey of Selles-sur-Cher, she always had her husband and his men-at-arms to protect her. But since Brosse, her only traveling companions had been an Irish monk and a Persian poet, hardly the type of escorts a French noble-woman ever expected to have. Then again, few things in her life made sense anymore.

She had gone from being the cousin of the Duke of Aquitaine and the lady of Selles-sur-Cher to an outcast accused of witchcraft by Bishop Adémar of Blois. Although the accusations were false, made by the bishop to cover up his own sins, the monks of Selles-sur-Cher had seen all the evidence they needed to assume the accusations were true. That evidence came in the form of a key, shaped like an Egyptian ankh, which unlocked a book shrine her late husband's family had kept secret since the days of the first Carolingian kings. The shrine contained a copy of the lost Book of Enoch, a tome sought by Brother Dónall and Brother Ciarán, and ever since then she had witnessed things that would cause even the most devout priest to question his beliefs about angels and demons and the End of Days.

A day after leaving Solignac, the three travelers and their pack mule followed the road that would eventually take them to Bordeaux, where Ciarán hoped they would find passage on a ship to Rome. Despite Khalil's misgivings, Ciarán seemed confident the Eternal City was where their pursuit of the prophecy must take them. Alais too felt certain they must go there, though not for the reason she gave Ciarán and Khalil at the abbey of Saint-Pierre. For ever since Brosse, Alais had seen Rome's ruins in her dreams.

She recalled them vividly: triumphal archways and towering pillars, bathed in the light of a full moon, supporting the crumbling remnants of once glorious structures. They stood amid a sea of rubble overgrown with grass and shrubs as if whole palaces had been ripped from the earth, leaving only their foundations and the columns that once adorned their grand entranceways. The images seemed so real it was as if she had been there before, even though she had never traveled south of Toulouse before their voyage to Córdoba a few months ago. She felt certain these ruins must be Rome, for her father had been there once on pilgrimage and told her many stories about the old Roman Forum, a place so awe-inspiring it was as if giants had built the monuments before men and time tore them down.

Each time, the dream ended at a grassy hill pocked with warrens. Atop the hill stood the cavernous vault of a ruined temple, with the crisscrossed pattern of a domed apse still visible in the reddish stone. Its porphyry floor, adorned with patterns, looked the same as it must have a thousand years ago, and there, amid motes of fireflies winking like tiny sparks, danced a woman in a silky white dress. Tall and slender, she moved like the flowing waters of a stream, her silvery hair billowing around her head. Her beauty was unnatural, for she looked like Orionde, as if somehow the Fae still lived. The woman sang as she danced, crooning a haunting song in a foreign tongue that beckoned to Alais. But Alais knew the dream could not be real, for she had seen Orionde die on the fields of Brosse.

Each time Alais awoke from the dream, she was reminded of Orionde's cryptic words in Rosefleur's great hall. At the time, Alais thought she was the one chosen to find Enoch's device, for between her and Ciarán she was the only one born of Charlemagne's bloodline. Orionde, however, had dispelled that belief. "You have yet another role to play," she told Alais. If only Alais knew what that role was. But she had a strange feeling it had something to do with her dreams of Rome.

"Are you all right?" Khalil asked her.

His question woke her from her daydream. "Just fine," she said with a smile.

In the brief time she had known him, Khalil al-Pârsâ had shown himself to be perhaps the most refined man she had ever met, and the most fascinating for certain. He had been a famous poet in Córdoba, a master of six languages, and a lover of the late caliph's wife, who was rumored to be the most beautiful woman in Al-Andalus. He had also been as wealthy as a Spanish lord, but sacrificed all of that to aid them in their quest to find Enoch's device. His devotion to the writings of Fierabras, an eighth-century Moorish poet who became one Charlemagne's paladins, had led him to a verse concerning the device that was identical to one hidden in the Book of Maugis d'Aygremont. Since then, Khalil had believed his own fate was as intertwined with the prophecy as hers and Ciarán's.

Alais glanced at Khalil, then realized Ciarán had fallen behind, trying to maneuver Maev around a mudhole where the flagstones had been pilfered from the road. The woods encroached on the road's edge, so Ciarán had to guide the mule around a birch tree before she was back on the path. "You think whoever rules these lands could have had a bit more respect for this road," Ciarán said.

"How do you think these French lords get the stones to build their castles?" Khalil replied, waiting for Ciarán to catch up.

Alais patted Maev's neck. "It's like that everywhere in France. Father used to say the stones were too precious to keep in the dirt. I suspect it's the same in Ireland."

"We don't have any Roman roads in Ireland," Ciarán replied.

"Why not?" she asked.

"Because the Romans never conquered it," Khalil said.

"True," Ciarán added. "They thought the ancient Irish were too wild to be conquered. The Irish fought naked, you know, howling like banshees with their swords and shields. The Romans thought they were madmen."

"Naked?" Alais blushed. "They must have been mad."

"Back home, we have a saying," Ciarán said. "Why did God invent mead?"

Alais raised a brow. "Do tell."

"To keep the Irish from ruling the world," he replied with a grin. "But at least it kept the Romans away."

Khalil lifted his chin. "A maxim, I suppose, about the Celts and their drink."

"We do make a fine mead," Ciarán said. "Which reminds me of another saying from back home, one Dónall was fond of: An Irishman is never drunk so long as he can stand on two feet."

Alais smiled. "That sounds like something Dónall would have said."

Ciarán grinned back, but Khalil just sighed. "Would you look at that?" The Persian gestured down the road. Ahead, the trunk of a dead oak had fallen across the path. The surrounding woods were thick with birch and pines, and it was clear they would have to go into those woods to guide their mule around the obstruction.

Ciarán held up his hands. "Whoever rules this land *really* dislikes his roads. Not to worry, though, old Maev can get around it."

Alais did not like the shadows pervading the woods. Even though the leaves had not returned to the white limbs of the birch trees, the dense canopy of the pines only allowed slivers of light from the gray sky above. She followed Khalil, who stepped off the road onto the earthy duff and made his way around the jagged remains of the fallen tree. Its sprawling branches were gone, and Alais imagined the treetop had snapped off in a storm long before the rest of it died.

She glanced back at Ciarán. Maev stood stubbornly before the moss-covered log. "Come on girl," Ciarán urged, patting her neck before tugging the reins. The mule did not budge.

"Let me try," Alais said. Back in Selles-sur-Cher, she and Geoffrey had never lacked for livestock and she'd always had a knack for working with animals. She caressed Maev's mane, then brushed her fingers across her face. Taking the reins from Ciarán, she whispered in the mule's long pointed ear. "Follow me, Maev." The mule let Alais lead her off the road.

"I think she likes you more than me," Ciarán said.

"She just needed a woman's touch." There was enough space between the trees for Alais to slowly guide the mule around the shattered tree trunk and back onto the road that cut through the woods. There, Khalil greeted them with a look of alarm.

"There's a stump on the other side," he said. "This tree didn't fall, it was cut down."

Ciarán cocked his head. "To block the path?"

Alais tensed. Her gaze darted through the woods, just as the first man stepped from the shadows onto the road. A chill of fear surged up her chest as a second man emerged from the forest. Both wore thick beards and stained green cloaks over broad shoulders. The first man, with a cruel, blunt face, gripped a short sword, and the other, a hook-nosed brigand, menaced with a spiked club. Behind them, two more cloaked figures appeared from the woods.

"G'day, brother," said the blunt-faced swordsman. "There's a toll on this road, even for clergymen, and we come to collect it. We'll kindly take that mule and all it carries in exchange for your safe passage through these woods."

"And the girl too," said the fourth man, who loomed taller than the rest. Alais could see the pockmarked skin of his beardless chin jutting from the shadow of his cowl. "I want me the girl."

Alais tried to steady her nerves. Her right hand fell to the slim dagger she kept belted around her waist, a keepsake she had claimed on the battlefield of Brosse.

Khalil glanced at her and Ciarán. "Let me deal with this."

"There are four of them," she said under her breath.

"Then it might be a fair fight." Khalil slid his curved scimitar from its sheath, its blade gleaming in a sliver of sunlight seeping through the pines.

The brigand shook his blade. "Don't be stupid now, you bloody Moor!"

Khalil spun and struck in a flash. The brigand tried to parry the blow just as the scimitar sliced through his arm. "I'm Persian, thank you," Khalil said as the man's sword clattered on the flagstones.

With a roar, the second man swung his club, its spikes aimed at Khalil's head. The Persian ducked and spun, cleaving his blade across the second man's ribs. Alais watched awestruck as Khalil moved with the grace of a dancer, whirling and slicing his blade. His first two victims lay in the road, clutching their wounds, while the third swung a woodsman ax in wild arcs, trying to keep his attacker at bay. As Khalil's scimitar caught the axman across his forearm, the fourth man let out a piercing whistle.

The woods came alive. Leaves rustled and birch limbs swayed as a dozen more brigands rushed from the shadows. The pockmarked man charged, a long knife in his grip.

Alais pulled her dagger from its sheath. A week ago she had stuck a spear in the back of Adémar of Blois, and she would not hesitate to stick her dagger in this brigand right now. Her heart pounded as the brigand reached for her arm, his brown teeth clenched in a voracious grin. He caught her left arm, but never saw the dagger in her right hand until she plunged it deep into his gut. The man gasped in pain. She ripped the dagger free, and backed away, holding the weapon outstretched.

"You bitch!" he growled, clutching his stomach. He staggered back at step, blood seeping through his fingers.

"I'll stab you again!" From the corner of her eye she glimpsed

Khalil, fighting six men, while even more sneaked toward him. *He'll be overwhelmed!*

"Ciarán!" she cried.

He was rummaging through the packs strapped to Maev's back. An instant later, he pulled the ancient blade free. Ciarán put its pommel to his lips and whispered into the embedded gemstone. Then he thrust the sword into the air as a cry burst from his lungs. *"Columcille!"* Blazing light exploded from the blade like the fire of a thousand torches.

The brigands turned and stared into the light. Their hostile expressions melted into looks of pure terror, like sinners in a mural of the end times cowering in the fire of judgment. She had seen the same look in the face of Fulk the Black on the fields of Brosse, for Enoch's device struck fear in the hearts of men.

Her assailant recoiled in the blade's light, his mouth open in a silent scream. Ciarán lunged toward him. "By God's bones, stay away from her!"

The brigand backed away, holding his bleeding gut, while his comrades broke and fled like rats from a burning barn. The two wounded brigands crawled from the road into the woods, leaving bloodstains on the moss-laden flagstones.

"Are you all right?" Ciarán asked as the light began to fade from his blade.

"Yes," she replied with a nod, then she searched for Khalil, who was wiping the blood from his scimitar on the hem of his cloak.

"That device does come in handy." Khalil gestured to the sword in Ciarán's hands. "Whatever you're calling it now."

"Caladbolg," Ciarán replied. "This sword has had a lot of names over the years, so I chose its Irish one."

"Then thank God for Caladbolg," Alais said. The tension in her nerves began to ease, replaced by the weight of exhaustion. "Let's hope the next village is not too far down this road."

"I don't think the brigands will return," Khalil said. "Men like that are cowards at heart, and we've shown them we're not meek travelers on the road."

Ciarán clapped Khalil on his shoulder. "That we have."

"Still," she said, "I'll feel much safer when we reach Bordeaux."

FOR THE NEXT FIVE DAYS NOTHING DARED TO THREATEN THEM ON THE road. Perhaps the wolves and boars sensed the presence of Enoch's device and gave it wide berth, while the brigands had already learned their lesson. Still, Alais felt relieved by midday when the road began to border rows of grapevines near the bank of the Garonne River, and she glimpsed the first cathedral spires rising above the city walls of Bordeaux. The road ran near the harbor where scores of cogs, cora-cles, and fishing boats crammed the wharves and riverbank, their masts swaying with the tide. Moored somewhere within that crowd of vessels sat a cog named *La Margerie*. She was the same ship that had taken Alais and Ciarán to Córdoba and back, and Ciarán's plans now hinged on another voyage, if he could convince the ship's captain to sail to Rome.

At the harbor, they left the main road for a pathway that led to the Jewish Quarter, a small settlement built outside the city walls. Its streets were relatively free of refuse and its homes looked well kept, many of which had small herb gardens and chicken coops. The Jewish Quarter held warm memories for Alais, for it was here where she, Ciarán, and Dónall had gone after fleeing Poitiers when the Bishop of Blois accused her of witchcraft. They were taken in by Josua, the nephew of Isaac ben Ezra, the rabbi of Poitiers, and in the few weeks she had lived there, Alais grew fond of Josua's wife Aster and their children.

Josua and Aster's home was among the larger houses in the Jewish Quarter, one of the few made of stone blocks instead of wattle and daub, with two chimneys and a slate-shingled roof as opposed to the thatch that topped most of the quarter's homes. The house was a testament to the success Josua and his older brother had enjoyed as merchants, trading wine and olive oil between Aquitaine and the Moorish caliphate of Al-Andalus. Yet Alais feared that sadness lingered within those well-made walls, for Josua's oldest son Eli had died on their last journey, slain by a Moor's arrow while trying to save her life. As the three of them approached the house, a pang of apprehension settled in her gut, reminding her that Eli's death left a wound within her that had not healed.

"It was not your fault," Khalil told her, as if sensing her unease.

She shook her head. "He fancied me, and wanted to protect me. Had I not put myself in danger, Eli would be alive today."

"You feared for Ciarán, and were it not for Eli that Moor's arrow would have pierced your heart. I believe it was kismet that you lived, even if Eli had to sacrifice his life. There is a reason you are with us."

She gave him a weak smile, but his words reminded her of Orionde's. *You have yet another role to play . . .*

Three paces ahead, cradling Caladbolg wrapped in its sackcloth, Ciarán approached the front door. Its frame was adorned with a mezuzah, one of the tiny scrolls inscribed with Hebrew scripture the Jews affixed to their doorposts. "Let's pray he's home," he said, then rapped on the door.

A slender man with a head of curly hair that tapered into a wavy brown beard answered the knock. "What is it—" he said, before his eyes flew wide. "You ..." Josua blinked twice. "But there are only three of you?"

A mist gathered in Alais' eyes as Ciarán replied, "Isaac and Dónall fell."

Josua gazed at them dumbstruck.

"I was with them," Khalil said. "They gave their lives outside Rosefleur to stop Dónall's rival, who was trying to unleash a terrible evil."

"*Rosefleur* . . ." Josua shook his head in disbelief. "Is this why you've come, to bring me this black news?"

Alais placed a hand on Josua's shoulder. "No." He embraced her and buried his head in her hair. He sniffed back a tear, but she let her own tears flow. "I'm so sorry," she said, "so terribly sorry for your loss. Not a day goes by I don't think of him."

Josua pulled away, trying to regain his composure. "Why have you come?"

31

"We need passage to Rome and have little money," Ciarán said. "You and Évrard are our best hope."

Josua folded his arms across his chest. "I still have a wife and three children, I cannot risk another of your quests."

"Have you already forgotten the importance of that quest?" Ciarán pressed.

"This prophecy you chase?" Anger rose in Josua's voice. "This cause that claimed my son's life, is it anything more than the same fear being spread by all these Christian priests? It's the same message at every church in Bordeaux: wars and famines and blood raining from the sky, all they say are signs of the end times, one thousand years after the birth of your Christ. Even Jews I know are getting scared. But the rabbis believe none of it!"

"Your uncle did," Ciarán insisted. "And I dare say he was the wisest rabbi you ever knew."

Josua threw up his hands. "All you Christians seem touched in the head!"

"I am no Christian," Khalil said, "yet I believe as firmly as anyone. The prophecy is older than Christianity, even older than Abraham. And if you had seen the things I have, my friend, you too would believe."

Josua rubbed a hand across his face, then gave a long sigh. "Come inside."

He led them into his sitting room, where embers crackled in a stone hearth and the aroma of stewed chicken wafted from an iron pot hung over the fire. "Where are Aster and the children?" Alais asked Josua.

"At the market, with my brother and his family."

On a table near the hearth lay a broad sheet of parchment bearing a map of the trade routes between Bordeaux and Al-Andalus. Khalil glanced at the map. "Are you planning another voyage?"

"The last one cost us more than my son," Josua said bitterly. "We must avoid Córdoba now. Al-Mansor has spies looking for our ship. We'd be fools to sail up the river, so our coffers are running dry. My cousin Abir hopes that by summer it will be safe to return, but I have my doubts. Évrard has a notion to go to Barcelona, thinking trade may be good there, but I'm not so sure."

Alais felt a thickness in her throat as she listened. *This is all our fault. All my fault.*

Ciarán removed the sackcloth and laid Caladbolg on the table. Celtic patterns adorned its leather sheath. "Our last journey had a terrible price," he admitted, "but it led us to this."

Josua blinked. "Is that . . . ?" He stared at the gemstone in the sword's pommel. "Is this the gemstone my uncle longed to find?" The awe in his expression reminded Alais of the first time she had set eyes on the gem.

Ciarán nodded. "To Isaac it was the Urim, the gemstone etched with the one true name of God. But it's part of this blade. They're one and the same."

"I don't see how," Josua said. "My uncle said it was the gemstone from Aaron's breastplate, the one he would use to talk with God."

"I found it hard to believe too," Ciarán said, "until I saw it with my own eyes. In each millennium, the device has taken a different form. In the age of Moses and Solomon, it was just a gemstone. Yet when I found the device, it was in flux, its form changing from a staff, to a stone, to a cup, and to a sword. When I took it, its form held fast as this weapon, its incarnation in this age."

Josua rubbed the back of his neck. "So what does this mean? Just because you found this device, am I to suddenly believe all of these apocalyptic fears? Religion drives men to madness. How do I know my uncle was not stricken with this disease, as you may be too?"

"I'll show you," Ciarán said. He drew the sword from its scabbard. Josua recoiled from the blade, which gleamed in the lamplight. Ciarán put his lips to the pommel and whispered the now familiar Fae word —"*Eoh.*" The gem sparkled, then flared, like hot coal erupting with flame. A fiery glow danced down the length of the blade. Josua stepped back, his jaw slack.

"This weapon," Ciarán said, holding out the sword, "has existed since the days of Enoch, before the Great Flood, and it's needed once more as the cycle of prophecy nears its end."

Josua shook his head. "When you told me this before, I am not sure I ever believed it all. Yet this light …" His gaze was fixed on the glimmering blade.

"It is true," Khalil said. "I assure you. After we took leave of you and Évrard at La Rochelle, we traveled to Brosse and found the gateway to Rosefleur. When we arrived, the tower was under siege by an army led by pale-skinned giants like nothing you have ever seen, as if the legendary Goliath had returned with all of his siblings. These were the Nephilim, the race of Gog and Magog, which we believe has lived in secret since the Great Flood, descended from those created, according to your Book of Genesis, when the sons of God went into the daughters of men. Outside Rosefleur, a Nephilim priest and a coven of sorcerers sought to unleash a terrible evil from the depths of a great chasm, but your uncle, Dónall, and I fought to stop them. At the edge of that pit, I could hear the voice of the thing trapped inside, in the depths of the Underworld. It was the voice of the one we Muslims call *Shaitan,* the one the Hebrew scriptures call *Ha-Satan,* and the one the Christians call the Dragon in their Book of Revelation. The Nephilim were seeking to free him from his prison. But your uncle and Dónall felled the Nephilim priest, though it cost them their lives, a sacrifice made for the noblest of causes. So I assure you, the prophecy and the legends surrounding it are very much real."

The gravity of Khalil's words settled over everyone at the table. The light in the gemstone began to fade, and Ciarán sheathed the sword. "Even though they failed at Rosefleur," he said, "the Dragon's servants are still working to free him, and to bring about the event that will cause the End of Days. They seek the key to the bottomless pit, the device that will unleash the fallen angels imprisoned since Enoch's time. At Limoges we found a description of this Key to the Abyss, forged of black iron and as long as a man is tall. Then at Solignac we learned the existence of a map of some sort to find this Key, and it lies in Rome."

Josua sighed. "So you want Évrard and me to take you there?"

"We have nowhere else to turn," Ciarán said. "And consider what's at stake. It's the same cause for which Eli gave his life, and Dónall and Isaac too."

Josua closed his eyes and let his head sink into his hands. Alais wished Ciarán had not brought up Eli's sacrifice, all in the name of this cause. *It almost blinds him,* she realized.

A moment later, the front door flew open. Everyone looked up as a rotund man strode into the room. His sweat-soaked hair lilted over his broad forehead to the base of his protuberant nose. "I smell Aster's chicken stew!" Évrard announced, his jaw jutting as he spoke. He glanced at the three travelers, then his broad smile beamed. "Milady! Brother Ciarán, and Khalil, my Persian friend!"

"Évrard!" Alais rose and embraced the old captain, catching a whiff of sherry when she kissed his cheek.

"They want us to take them on another voyage," Josua told Évrard.

"To where?" Évrard asked.

"Rome," Ciarán replied.

Évrard cocked a brow. "Rome, eh? May I ask why?"

They offered him a seat at the table and a cupful of wine as Ciarán repeated their tale. As a Christian, Évrard seemed more willing to embrace the story's apocalyptic implications, yet he became more subdued as the tale went on, and grew misty-eyed when he learned of Dónall and Isaac's sacrifice. Then Ciarán told him about the exorcism at the abbey of Saint-Pierre, and of the demon's words. "So that's why we must go to Rome," Ciarán said. "To find this prince and the map he holds."

Josua shook his head. "I am certain there is no monarch in Rome."

"That is what I have been telling him," Khalil said.

Évrard took a long sip of wine; his normally ruddy face looked pale. "He's not a true monarch," he said, setting down his cup. "He calls himself prefect, and the duke and count of the Romans. But he's known by many as the Prince of Rome."

Alais' skin chilled at his words.

"So he's real?" Ciarán said.

"That I can promise," Évrard replied. "He's the head of one of the oldest Roman noble houses. His name is Crescentius—and he's the most dangerous man in all of Rome."

Alais glanced at Ciarán, and then to Khalil, who shook his head. "Perhaps the demon spoke the truth," she said.

Josua held his head in his hands, then glanced at his partner. Évrard nodded back.

"If everything you've told us is true," Josua said, reluctance lingering his voice, "we will take you there. May Aster and the children forgive me."

Ciarán took his hand. "You have my thanks. None of us chose this journey, but we must take it, for the sake of your wife and children, and everyone who has already given their lives for this cause. Their sacrifice shall not be in vain."

Alais nodded, though she realized she felt none of Ciarán's enthusiasm, but rather a weight in her chest. Perhaps it was Évrard's revelation or maybe Khalil's conclusion. But whatever the cause, she suddenly had a terrible feeling about this journey to Rome.

5

DARKENING DREAMS

An easterly wind filled *La Margerie's* sails as she glided past the Rock of Gibraltar, a massive limestone promontory that jutted from the ocean like the dorsal fin of some titanic sea beast. The cog's seven-man crew stood on the main deck gazing at the towering rock, while on the forecastle Ciarán wondered how high the rock must rise to its green-encrusted peak. "More than a thousand feet, don't you think?" he asked Khalil, who leaned on the wooden rail, his dark hair rustling in the salt-tinged breeze.

"I have no doubt," Khalil replied. "The Moors call it *Jebel Tariq*, the 'Mountain of Tariq.' In antiquity, it was one of the two Pillars of Hercules."

Ciarán had never seen anything from antiquity before, though until recently he thought he would never venture beyond the emerald dells and cliffs of Ireland. "Dónall told me that Plato wrote of them."

"In *Critias*," Khalil said. "Each one had a cauldron of flame burning at its peak, making them beacons, much like a lighthouse. But according to Plato, they were also the gateway from the Mediterranean to the island of Atlantis, before it sank into the sea. We could be sailing over it now."

Ciarán glanced over the rail. The cog's prow splashed through the dark-blue sea, which betrayed no sign of what secrets might lie beneath its surface. He thought about King Arcanus, the legendary ruler of Atlantis who, if Maugis' writings were to be believed, first discovered Enoch's device at the ends of the earth. "I wonder what Atlantis was like?"

"I have always imagined a city on the sea," Khalil said, "with a harbor filled with ships, their prows curved like a heron, and columns beyond the wharf soaring into the sky. Poets and philosophers would grace its streets and hanging gardens, while gulls soared above a great pyramid with its tip crowned in gold. At the city's center would be a plaza with a library, larger than that in Córdoba, or even the Great Library of Alexandria. A center of learning and music like no other, and with no zealous clerics seeking to burn it down."

"I would've liked to have seen that."

Khalil nodded. "As would I." He glanced sternward, where Alais had emerged from the cabin, looking troubled. "She did not sleep well again."

"No," Ciarán agreed.

"I should go talk with her."

"I'll do it." The words jumped from Ciarán's mouth. Khalil had grown closer to Alais, and Ciarán knew how much it bothered him, despite the monastic vows that should have kept him from such thoughts.

"Do the monks of Derry have much experience when it comes to a woman's moods?"

"Perhaps not most women," Ciarán said, "but I've known her longer than you."

Khalil narrowed his gaze as Ciarán turned away and descended the short flight of timber steps to the main deck. He gave a nod to Mordechai, a Jewish lad with a muscular build and hooked nose whom Josua had recruited to replace Levi among the crew. The soft-spoken Jew nodded back, before calling up to Bero, one of the Christian seafarers who manned the crow's nest.

Across the deck, Alais watched a seagull skimming over the water, searching for breakfast. As Ciarán approached, she glanced up. A melancholy look lingered in her storm-gray eyes.

"You were talking in your sleep again," he said.

Her eyes widened. "Was I?"

"It was more like mumbling, but your secrets are safe. I couldn't understand a word you said."

Alais smiled briefly. "Do you remember how Isaac had dreams during our voyage to Córdoba?"

"Aye," Ciarán said. "He dreamed of Rosefleur."

"Well, ever since Rosefleur, I've been having strange dreams too. They begin the same each time, but the end sometimes changes, revealing a bit more than the time before."

"You think these dreams are like Isaac's, portending the future?"

She ran a hand through her long raven hair. "I don't see how that could be. He was a mystic, and I'm surely not one. Yet I'm certain I've been dreaming of Rome."

Ciarán shook his head slightly. "How do you know?"

"My father described it to me many times. The great columns and archways, a hill with the remains of a palace, and a great amphitheater, which he called the Coliseum. I've dreamed of them all. Not every night, but enough to know that's where we're going."

"At the abbey," Ciarán realized. "Is that why you chose my plan over Khalil's, because you'd been dreaming of Rome?"

She glanced down. "I thought it might be a sign for where we should go. But now I'm not sure."

Ciarán frowned. "What do you mean?"

"Each time, I dream of a ruined temple atop a hill. The temple's roof is gone, but its floor is intact and on it stands a tall and graceful woman with hair like silver."

"Like Orionde?"

"Just like Orionde. She dances beneath the light of a full moon, singing a haunting song, while fireflies flit around her. But then the moonlight dims, swallowed by the clouds. The fireflies surround Orionde, yet behind her all I see is darkness. My heart begins to race, for I sense there's something dangerous in that darkness. I cry out to warn her, and then I wake, but I'm certain she was in peril."

Ciarán thought for a moment. "Maybe you were thinking about Orionde, and in your dream you're trying to warn her because you know she dies."

"She died on the fields of Brosse, not in a ruined temple," Alais said. "Yet what if she's trying to warn us from beyond the grave—about some danger in Rome?"

"Just because it might be dangerous doesn't mean we shouldn't go," Ciarán insisted. "The demon's words are all we have, and Orionde never said the journey would be safe."

"You would ignore her warning?"

"Aye." Ciarán clenched his jaw. "So many have given their lives for this cause. Dónall and Isaac, Brother Remi, Eli, even the parents I never knew. I'll not let their deaths be in vain, so if there's any chance this Prince of Rome can lead us to the Key, I don't care how dangerous it might be."

Alais shook her head slightly. "I see your mind is set on this point." She spun and strode toward the forecastle, where Khalil stood, glancing their way.

As he watched her go, Ciarán felt a burning in his chest. *To hell with a woman's moods,* he told himself. Her dreams were just dreams. He felt certain Khalil would tell her what she wanted to hear, but they would both be wrong. For Ciarán knew they were following the right path. Without Dónall to lead the way, the demon's words were his only guide, and there had to be a reason for that.

No matter what awaited them in Rome.

A WEEK LATER, *LA MARGERIE* TACKED NORTHWARD UP THE WHITE COAST of Al-Andalus. Alais had not spoken further to Ciarán about the purpose of their journey or the dangers it might pose, and perhaps she was wise to take her mind off such things, for ever since they entered the Mediterranean Sea she had slept soundly through the nights. As days passed, her dreams of the ruined temple and the haunting woman in white became but memories. Alais felt a sense of freedom, eased of these troubling thoughts, allowing her to marvel at the deep blue waters of the Mediterranean and the palm-lined beaches that stretched along the Moorish coastlands. At the port city of Alicante, she and her companions dined on a stew of shellfish and rice yellowed with saffron, a Moorish spice, and chased the meal with red Spanish wine that Josua procured from the city's Jewish Quarter. She laid down to rest in the ship's cabin, her body warm with wine, and closed her eyes. Yet when she thought she woke, she found herself far away from the wharves of Alicante.

Alais stood atop a grassy hillside, watching a lavender butterfly dance in the breeze. She followed the butterfly until she spied her sister, Adeline, darting behind a corner of the palace walls. Her sister wore a violet ribbon in her dark-brown hair, the one Mother had given her on her tenth birthday. Alais sprinted after her. "Adeline," she called in the cheery voice of an eight-year-old. "I found you!"

Adeline looked back, cocking her head. "It's me, silly—Julia."

Alais blinked. *Your name is Adeline.* She glanced down at her bare legs. Beneath the hem of her kirtle, her left knee still bore the scab from when she'd skinned it on the stairs of the old Roman amphitheater outside Poitiers, the last time she and her sister played hide-and-seek.

Her sister gestured Alais to follow. "Come on, Father and Mother are at the games."

Alais blinked again. In the valley beneath the hill stood a titanic arena. Thousands of people filled its marble grandstands built into the cliffs, cheering and screaming as a half-dozen horse-drawn chariots raced around an oval track, spewing dust behind them. Banners of red and white, the same colors worn by the charioteers, snapped in the breeze surrounding the track, where spearlike obelisks of sandstone and porphyry rose proudly in its center beside giant statues of rearing stallions.

"Father and Mother are in their new box," her sister said, pointing to a pillared and covered structure in the center of the grandstands.

Flanking the box stood two massive crimson banners bearing a golden eagle above the letters "S.P.Q.R." to indicate *Senatus Populusque Romanus.*

Alais scratched her head. *Our family's banner is a crimson lion . . .*

"I bet Maurus wins," her sister said. "Father said he's the fastest charioteer to ever race in Circus Maximus!"

In the arena below, a red-clad charioteer edged past one in white for the lead. A roar erupted from the crowd, for a moment drowning out the pounding of hooves and the cracking of whips. Among the crowd, people waved red and white ribbons, and Alais found herself lost in that sea of color until she felt the disturbing touch of another's gaze. She glanced left and noticed an unusually tall man standing at the entrance to the palace gardens. Clad in a black cassock, the man had a pale face and a pointed black beard, but it was his eyes that frightened her the most. They were feral—and disturbingly familiar. Alais gasped. *Adémar!*

Her sister tugged on her arm. Adeline's eyes were wide with fear. "Run!" she screamed.

Alais darted after her sister. Glancing behind, she saw the black-clad man start after them, gaining quickly with his long-legged strides.

"We can hide in Father's temple!" her sister cried.

Yet ahead lay only ruins. What had once been a marble temple with towering columns was a heap of crumbling stone strewn with vines and moss. Each of its columns had been toppled or severed, and the remains of what may have been the temple's roof blocked the stairs leading to its terrace. Adeline ran on undeterred, dashing around a corner of the ruins. Alais followed; behind her came the huffs of her pursuer's breath.

As she rounded the corner, she saw her sister flying down another flight of stairs that must have led to a cellar beneath the temple. She glanced over her shoulder. The black-clad man was just yards away.

She lost her sister in the shadows. "Adeline!" Alais yelled as she rushed down the stairs. Beneath her feet, a stone gave way. She fell forward down the stairs, and cried out. A pair of gigantic hollow eyes stared back, carved into a stone archway shaped like the gaping maw of a bearded giant. *She's inside there!* Alais scrambled to her feet and ducked beneath the jagged fangs of the giant's mouth—and then she fell again. The stairs were gone, as if she had stepped off a cliff into a chasm. Her screams echoed around her as she plunged into the darkness.

Alais bolted awake, gasping for breath. She glanced around, wondering where she was, then gave a relieved sigh. *I'm in the cabin.* She staggered to her feet and walked out to the deck. She ran her fingers through her hair as the cool salt air washed over her face.

"You're having nightmares again," said a man's voice. She turned to find Khalil leaning against the ship's rail, the lights of Alicante behind him.

She nodded as he wrapped his arms around her. "It will be all right," he said.

As her heartbeat settled, she drank in the scent of his skin and looked into his almond-colored eyes. "I fear something terrible awaits us in Rome."

"If that's true, then we shall not stay long. But my hope is it was a nightmare, and nothing more."

In the warmth of his embrace, she prayed he was right.

6

PONTIFEX MAXIMUS

P ope Gregory sat restlessly in his litter, peering through the screen-slatted windows, searching for any sign of the mob. Save for a few herdsmen watching their cattle graze on the rubble-strewn pasture that once was Circus Maximus, all he could see were the half score of foot soldiers clad in mail tunics, scarlet cloaks, and crested helms, all brawny Saxons or fair-haired Lombards who were among the fifty men-at-arms that guarded his litter. Although he knew that a dozen horsemen rode ahead of the litter, leading the procession from the Lateran Palace to the imperial fortress, Gregory wondered if he should have brought more of his papal guardsmen. For while there had been no further attempts on his life since the emperor's army reclaimed Rome, the mob could gather quickly and had grown unruly of late toward the Germans occupying the city.

He turned to his papal archdeacon, who sat on the plush seat beside him. "Rumeus, do you think these Romans will ever accept a Saxon pope?"

Rumeus furrowed his brow, though his face still looked cherubic, despite the bags beneath his eyes and the baldness of his head. The portly Roman was almost twice Gregory's age, but unlike the syco-phantic Gerbert, the pope had grown to appreciate the archdeacon's advice. "That is a difficult question, Your Holiness," Rumeus said with a clever look in his eyes. "A third of the Romans believe Crescentius will ride from Castel Sant'Angelo and drive you again from Rome, while another third believes John Philagathos is the rightful heir to Saint Peter's throne. As for the final third, I hold out a sliver of hope."

A hint of a smile formed on Gregory's lips. "Can't you ever say anything just to put my mind at ease?"

"I find there's magic in the truth," Rumeus said with a shrug and a smile.

"How can I win over the rest?" Gregory ran his fingers through his short-cut blond hair. "My goals are noble, are they not? To restore the papacy to its rightful place and help rebuild this forsaken place. Why wouldn't the Romans embrace this?"

"Because they are proud. Rome was once the greatest city in the world. It ruled the people from your northern homeland, considering them 'barbarians'—their word, not mine—so to this day many Romans cannot stomach the idea of living under the rule of Germans and Saxons. And besides, for more than a hundred years, they've had the Crescentii and the old Roman families to feed and protect them. Who needs a pope when you have a Prince of Rome?"

Gregory clenched his jaw. "*Crescentius Tyrannus.* Have your sources found any link between him and the man who tried to kill me?"

"We know there are others like him. They call themselves the Brotherhood of the Messiah. They're convinced of the coming Apocalypse, and determined that when the Messiah returns, a Roman pope will be there to greet him. Yet we still don't know whether they're beholden to Crescentius."

"I wish you'd find out. It would be helpful to know if I am fighting one enemy or two. Popes who fail to master their enemies tend to be short lived these days."

Rumeus shrugged. "Pope John the Fifteenth reigned for a full ten years, and only died of a fever."

Gregory rolled his eyes. "Leo the Fifth lived but six years, and Stephen the Seventh barely lasted two. John the Tenth was suffocated, and so was John the Eleventh, while Stephen the Eighth was mutilated, Benedict the Sixth was strangled, and John the Fourteenth was poisoned. Half of them spent their last days in the prisons of Castel Sant'Angelo, and all died at the hands of the Crescentii or their kin. By God, Rumeus, I refuse to end up like them. We must kill Crescentius. Then the Romans will have no choice but to embrace me."

Rumeus placed a gentle hand on the sleeve of Gregory's white cassock. "Be mindful, Your Holiness, of the words of our Lord Savior: 'He who lives by the sword, shall die by the sword.'"

"Perhaps, but my sword shall be swung for a just cause."

Rumeus gave a slight frown. "Of course, Your Holiness."

Gregory felt the litter ascend the Aventine Hill, and soon he spied the stone towers of the emperor's fortress. The litter came to a halt before a papal guardsman opened the door to the cool morning air. The guardsmen formed two columns with a pathway down the middle, ending at the fortress's arched gateway. Before the gate stood Margrave Eckard with a score of his mail-clad Germans, their kite-shaped shields bearing the heraldry of the black lion of Meissen. Heribert, the Archbishop of Cologne and Chancellor of the Holy Roman Empire, stood at Eckard's side. Just three years older than Gregory, Heribert was a tall man, and handsome, with a shaven face and strong jaw. He nodded at the papal litter, his hands clasped at the waist of his scarlet cassock.

Gregory smoothed his crimson shoulder cape and adjusted the gold cross that hung over his cassock before Rumeus stepped from the litter to announce the pope's arrival.

"All hail Gregory, *Pontifex Maximus, Servus Servorum Dei,* Vicar of Christ, and Lord Pope of the Apostolic See of Rome!" Rumeus bellowed as Gregory appeared before the chancellor and the Margrave of Meissen.

"Welcome, Your Holiness." Eckard bowed to kiss the Fisherman's ring on Gregory's outstretched hand. "And thank you again for the casks of wine. That was most generous."

"Eckard," Gregory replied, placing a hand on his shoulder. "You saved my life. The least I could do was send you some of the Lateran's finest."

Eckard grinned. "Shall I take you to the emperor? He's on the terrace."

Gregory exchanged brief pleasantries with Heribert, then followed Eckard through a pillared audience chamber with mosaic-covered walls. One depicted Hector admonishing his brother Paris. Another showed Hercules fighting the Nemean lion, while others portrayed dancing nymphs and prancing centaurs.

"Has my cousin added to his titles of late?" Gregory asked.

"You mean in addition to The Servant of Jesus Christ and His Apostles? Then yes, he now claims the titles Consul of the Roman Senate and People, and Emperor of the World."

"The whole world?" Gregory lifted an eyebrow. "My, how Gerbert's flattery has gone to his head."

Eckard shrugged, then pushed open the double doors that led to the broad covered terrace. Thick marble columns spaced ten feet apart lined the terrace's far end, and between two of them stood Otto the Third. He dressed in a blue silk tunic and wore a coronet of golden oak leaves atop his head, making him look more like a young Caesar than a German king. In his right hand, he held the Holy Lance of Constantine as if it were a plaything.

"Cousin!" Otto said, beaming.

"Shouldn't you keep the Holy Lance in a chapel, where it might be closer to God?" *And safer.* All Gregory could think about was Otto dropping one of the most sacred relics in Christendom over the terrace and having it shatter on the hillside.

"Nonsense. I am God's chosen on earth, it belongs with me. Now come look." Otto gestured toward the city as Gregory strode to the edge of the terrace. "She was once the greatest city in the world," Otto said. "Together we can make her that again. *Roma Aeterna.*"

From the terrace, however, Gregory looked upon a city of ruins. Beyond the Palatine Hill rose three towering pillars, all that remained of the Temple of Castor and Pollux, amid a quarry of wreckage that once was the Roman Forum. Near the triumphal Arch of Septimius Severus, the colossal columns of the Temple of Saturn stood proudly, but the rest of the structure had long ago collapsed. Around it, stray pillars and the crumbling remains of statues lined the path to the once great Coliseum, which itself had been turned into a tenement house for those too poor to live near the river. *Sic transit gloria mundi,* Gregory thought. *Thus passes the glory of the world.*

Otto pointed the lance toward the Palatine Hill, topped with grass and trees surrounding the ruins of the imperial palaces. "Augustus lived on that hill, and on the remains of his palace, I could build one of my own, a new palace for a new Rome."

"A noble vision, cousin, but we have more pressing concerns." Gregory pointed west, beyond the vineyards and pastures in the Field of Mars and the cramped homes, shops, and churches clustered on the riverbank. Across the Aelian Bridge, the hulking edifice of Castel Sant'Angelo stood like a gigantic round tower guarding the entrance to Rome. "Crescentius remains safe inside those walls while his loyalists roam the streets, poisoning the mob against us."

"The people of Rome have no stomach to fight my army," Otto said with a wave of his hand. "Besides, I have hundreds of men surrounding the castle and no one has left its gates. Crescentius will run out of food and he'll have no choice but to surrender."

Gregory's jaw clenched. "*He* may be inside those walls, but his assassins skulk about this city, and need I remind you that one of them tried to kill me? There's also talk that Crescentius has been sending messages to Emperor Basil in Constantinople, who I'm sure does not look kindly upon your new title of Emperor of the World. And all the while, the antipope, John the Greek, takes sanctuary somewhere in Italy. A third of Rome believes *he* is the rightful pope, for God's sake. So long as he lives, the man undermines my claim."

Otto frowned. "John Philagathos may not be pope, but he's still my godfather."

"He was supposed to be a devout priest, yet he shared your mother's bed! And by claiming the papacy, he defies your will." Heat flushed up Gregory's neck. "Have you heard from Count Berthold?" he asked, referring to the German lord sent to hunt down the false pope.

"At last report, he and his men were riding toward Campagna."

"John the Greek can be elusive. Let's pray Berthold is up to the task. But there's no reason to delay with Crescentius. He's a hundred times more dangerous and his continued existence is an affront to your authority."

"You want me to lay siege to Castel Sant'Angelo? They say it's impenetrable. No one has ever taken it in battle."

"But," Gregory said, recalling some of Gerbert's finest flattery, "you are no ordinary man. You are the Holy Roman Emperor, the heir to Constantine and Charlemagne, the grandson of Otto Maximus, chosen by God to rule the West. Mere walls will not defeat your holy purpose."

"I am . . ." Otto slowly nodded. *"Emperor of the World."*

"Then who on earth could oppose you?"

"He's just a Roman," Otto muttered. "Not a king or an emperor."

"He is but an oathbreaker, while you are Christ's anointed avenger."

"By God, you're right." Otto spun toward the doors. "Eckard!" he shouted, summoning the thick-bearded German. "It's time we take this battle to Crescentius, to the walls of Castel Sant'Angelo."

"Aye, Your Majesty." Eckard raised a brow to the pope.

A ghost of a smile crept across Gregory's lips. "In the words of the psalm, let them go down into Sheol, for evil is in their homes and in their hearts."

And by God, he prayed silently, *let them suffer.*

7

THE ETERNAL CITY

On an April afternoon, under an easterly wind, *La Margerie* glided into the sprawling port of Marseille. Fishing boats, long-hulled knarrs, and potbellied merchant cogs crammed the wharf as the cries of circling gulls mixed with the chatter of the fishermen who crowded the piers, mending nets or sorting the day's catch. After mooring the cog, Évrard left to speak with the harbormaster, while Josua and Mordechai disembarked for the market, hoping to trade olive oil and pickled fish cheeks purchased in Barcelona for enough provisions to last until they reached Rome.

Onboard, Ciarán watched Alais and Khalil from the sterncastle. She stood at the railing, close to the Persian as he gestured toward a fortified abbey on a hilltop south of the harbor, never failing to lay a hand on her shoulder or the small of her back. The sight of it hardened Ciarán's stomach, even as it called to mind Dónall's admonition: *Remember your vows, lad.* But whoever wrote those vows had never known a woman like Alais. Still, his abbot had always taught that jealousy was a sin, and Ciarán did not need the weight of that sin bringing him down, especially given the importance of their journey and the tidings Évrard brought when he returned to the cog.

Khalil and Alais joined Ciarán near the mast to hear what the captain had to say. "It seems the young pup of an emperor marched on Rome," Évrard told them, "and restored his cousin, the pope, to Saint Peter's throne."

"The German emperor?" Ciarán asked.

"Apparently, he took damn near every German and Saxon lord along with him, as well as half the lords in Lombardy and Tuscany," Évrard explained. "They say the army was ten thousand strong, so the Romans gave up without a fight and opened the gates, and now the city's overrun with stiff-necked Germans."

A wave of apprehension churned in Ciarán's gut. "What about the Prince of Rome?"

Évrard shrugged. "I asked, though the harbormaster didn't know his fate. But the pretender pope, John the Greek, fled for his life, and the Germans are hunting him like a wounded boar."

"I hope your prince has not absconded with this Greek," Khalil said, "or we've sailed all this way for nothing."

Ciarán grimaced. "Let's pray not."

In the days after they left Marseille and sailed into the Tyrrhenian Sea, the thought that Crescentius could be off hiding somewhere in Italy with a false pope troubled Ciarán even more than the relationship between Alais and Khalil. A morning after passing between the mainland and a small isle that Évrard called Elba, they reached the mouth of the Tiber, where on the river's southern bank stood the ruins of the ancient port of Ostia. No ships moored in the port, which was nothing more than a decaying husk of a town half buried in silt. "Why did the Romans abandon it?" Ciarán asked Évrard, who stood with him on the forecastle.

"Heard it was a plague that wiped 'em out," Évrard said. "They call it the 'Roman fever.' You know how our northern lords and bishops like to make pilgrimages to Rome to go kiss the pope's ring and all that tripe, eh?"

Ciarán nodded.

"Well, it's said 'bout half of 'em that stay through summer drop dead of the fever. Which is why I tend to avoid Rome. Plague is bad for business, I always say."

Ciarán's eyes widened. "When did you think it'd be a good time to mention this?"

Évrard puckered his lips. "Well, if what you told me about this prophecy and the end times is true, we've got bigger problems than risking a little fever."

"Suppose so," Ciarán replied, though he could not help but wonder if the danger Alais sensed from her dreams might be all too real.

"But all things considered," the captain said with a wink, "when we get there, you find what you're looking for just as fast as you can. I'd rather not stay through the summer, if you know what I mean."

Ciarán swallowed hard and prayed that Crescentius was still in Rome. Otherwise, *I've led them into danger, and all for naught.*

By midday, *La Margerie* sailed up the glistening Tiber, skirting a narrow green island where white swans glided by its shore. To Ciarán's delight, Alais stood with him at the ship's rail, watching the swans and several braces of ducks that gathered among the tall reeds at the river's bank. He thought it best not to tell her what Évrard had said about the Roman fever, for he could tell by the look in her eyes that she was still wary about entering Rome. Less than a half league past the island, the river turned sharply northward, where a trio of turtles basked on a moss-covered log, and then snaked eastward for a time before meandering northward.

As the river curved east again, Ciarán spotted the first sign of Rome: a massive tower that stood at the corner of equally massive walls, as imposing as any he had ever seen. Lined with arrow slits, the Aurelian Walls stretched north along the river with stout square towers every hundred or so feet. Spires and rooftops peeked above the walls' crenelated battlements, and from the depths of the city's legendary seven hills clanged scores of church bells ringing in the holy hour of Nones.

"Those walls look twice as high as Poitiers'," Alais said.

"I've never seen anything like it," Ciarán replied, gaping at their sheer height, which must have been more than fifty feet above the Tiber's bank.

They sailed alongside the towering walls until the river flowed through a break in the barrier, with each bank flanked by another square tower, topped with a golden banner. Passing between the towers, Ciarán noticed the links of a gigantic chain drooping from a portal in each tower wall into the Tiber. That chain, he imagined, could be raised when the Romans wanted to seal the river from enemy ships.

Inside the walls, the city came more clearly into view. Trees edged the river's muddy banks where rows of narrow houses and shops, many two or three stories tall, crowded around the Tiber, and beyond them churches and towers rose atop two nearby hills. On the river itself, men fished from sandbars, while others dragged nets from small fishing rafts. A score of fishing boats, skiffs, and cogs were moored on the west bank, but only two vessels seemed as large as *La Margerie*. Beyond the wharf stood ramshackle sheds and a stairway that climbed to a stucco building topped with a clay tile roof adjacent to a square brick tower. Yet that was it. The wharf was vastly smaller than the sprawling port of Marseille or the crowded harbor of Bordeaux. A thousand years ago, Roman ships had ruled the Mediterranean, so Ciarán had expected a much grander port than the one before him.

Mordechai tossed a line to a pair of olive-skinned dockworkers who helped guide *La Margerie* to a wooden jetty that reeked of rotting fish. Évrard disembarked first, climbing down the gangplank to greet the dockmaster, a stooped man with a haggard gray beard who spoke rapidly in a thickly accented Latin. Évrard, whose Latin was never good, gestured for Ciarán and Khalil to join him. Khalil translated the dockmaster's demand for a dockage fee, which Évrard reluctantly paid, then Ciarán asked the question that had gnawed at him since they reached Marseille. "We're looking for a man named Crescentius. Do you know if he's still in Rome?"

The grizzled dockmaster gave them a curious look before a smile cracked his lips, revealing teeth as brown as his sunbaked skin. "You came all the way from France to see Crescentius? Your timing could be better, no?" the man said with a chuckle.

"Is he still here?" Ciarán pressed.

The dockmaster nodded. "Oh, yes, he's still here."

"Where can we find him?"

"If your friend has two more denarii in his pocket," the dockmaster said, "I'll show you."

Khalil gave the man two silver coins. The dockmaster bit one of the denarii, before stashing the coins in a belt pouch and leading Ciarán and Khalil to one of the smaller skiffs. From *La Margerie's* railing, Alais held up her hands, as if to ask where they were going.

"Don't worry," Ciarán called back. "It'll be all right. He knows where we have to go."

He joined Khalil and the dockmaster in the skiff, which sat low in the water. The grizzled Roman unmoored the skiff and began rowing upriver.

"How far are we going?" Khalil asked.

The dockmaster gave another throaty chuckle. "Not far, you'll see." He rowed toward a bridge with six stone arches that spanned the river. Moss clung to the stone piers and up the ends of the bridge, where shrubs grew on the west bank, flush against what looked to Ciarán like a church with another clay tile roof. The skiff glided under one of the archways, to emerge heading toward a boat-shaped island where a basilica stood with a tall square bell tower adorned with triple archways, one stacked atop the other. A small village surrounded the basilica teeming with fishermen hard at work, while several black-robed monks joined in the day's labor. Fishing baskets and eelpots floated along the island's shores, and a small fleet of fishing boats anchored along ramshackle jetties. Two arched footbridges connected the island to each side of the river, where more two- and three-story structures rose from the riverbanks.

"Is the whole city built along the river?" Ciarán wondered aloud.

"Everyone lives near the river," the dockmaster said. "It's the lifeblood of Rome."

"That's because the Roman aqueducts that brought clean water to the city from the Alban Hills are no more," Khalil added. "Most of the ancient city is now fields and ruins. For many, the river is the only source of water."

The dockmaster grunted his acceptance of Khalil's explanation before guiding the skiff beneath the archway of the bridge connecting the island to the west bank. Soon, they approached another pair of towers flanking the river where the Aurelian Walls met the riverbank. The dockmaster rowed toward the gap between the towers where the links of yet another great chain drooped beneath the water.

"We're leaving the city!" Ciarán exclaimed. "I thought you said Crescentius was still here."

"Calm yourself," the dockmaster said. "We are heading for the *Civitas Leonina*."

"The Leonine City?" Khalil said.

"Yes," the dockmaster replied. "Pope Leo's city houses more than just Saint Peter's Basilica, but also the stronghold of the Crescentii."

Ciarán's nerves eased, but he wondered if he could trust the old dockmaster as the man rowed alongside another stretch of the Aurelian Walls that curved with the Tiber. In time, the dockmaster brought the skiff into view of a second set of crenelated walls that extended west, perpendicular to the Tiber. As he rowed past the thick Leonine Walls, where the river bent to the northeast, Ciarán's jaw dropped. For within the walls stood the largest castle he had ever seen. Circular in shape and surrounded by a fortified curtain wall, the hulking structure towered above the city, and atop its crenelated battlements a huge standard of a marble horse fluttered in the breeze.

Yet surrounding the castle stood a veritable forest of siege engines.

Timber siege towers, taller than the curtain wall, ringed the castle's west face beside catapults and a triangular-roofed battering ram, all standing amid a sea of banners: some with blue and gray diamonds, others with gold and crimson stripes, some bearing black lions and others with red hawks or white horses, all rippling in the breeze. The siege engines stood out of bowshot from the castle, but nonetheless looked imposing and dangerous. On the castle's east face, a three-arched bridged crossed the Tiber to the Aurelian Walls. Scores of soldiers manned the bridge, hoisting more banners, the most prominent of which was a huge golden standard bearing a winged angel with a flaming sword.

"The Mausoleum of Hadrian," Khalil muttered upon seeing the fortress.

"Now it's known as Castel Sant'Angelo," the dockmaster said, "the Tower of Crescentius."

A lump hardened in the pit of Ciarán's stomach. "It's under siege."

The dockmaster gave them a brown-toothed grin. "Although these Germans seek to besiege it, the fortress is impenetrable. The Prefect Crescentius and his stout Roman guards will pick off these invaders with arrows like ducks sitting in a pond, and when victory is won, they will chase these Germans out of Rome like the vermin they are. And I hope they take their Saxon pope with them."

Ciarán shook his head in disbelief. "With an army surrounding the castle, how are we supposed to get in?"

"Heh!" the dockmaster huffed. "That is a problem, no? But I know someone who can help perhaps."

Khalil's eyes narrowed. "Who?"

"They call him Charon," the dockmaster said with a wicked grin. "And he knows the underworld of Rome like the ferryman knows the rivers of Hell."

8

THE PRINCE OF ROME

Within the walls of Castel Sant'Angelo, Naberus da Roma sat in his candlelit chamber, pondering the four tarot cards that lay face down on the table. The serving girl who had pleasured him after supper stirred naked on the bed, while the largest of his three Neapolitan mastiffs snored at his feet. A fat raven, perched on a brass armillary sphere atop the table, loomed over the hand-painted cards. *"Kraaak,"* it cawed, poking its pointed beak toward the first card.

"Patience, Hermes." Naberus stroked his black beard styled to a point beneath his chin, then poured himself another cup of Falernian wine from an earthenware decanter. "Divination requires lubrication for the mind."

"Mind," the raven repeated.

Naberus took a quaff of wine and wiped his lips with the sleeve of his black cassock. Ever since the siege had begun, Crescentius had demanded to know his future, but each time the cards gave the same answer, and it was not one Crescentius wanted to hear. The tidings might be different if Naberus had access to the ancient shrine where he could talk with the spirits directly. But the shrine lay outside the castle's protective walls, halfway across the city.

Focusing his will on the cartomancy, he whispered the sacred words taught to him an age ago by the Hermetic mystics of Alexandria. He waved a hand over the first card and turned it over, its face revealing a purple-clad emperor on a golden throne. The card portrayed the sixth-century Byzantine emperor Justinian, but Naberus had no doubt whom the image on the card symbolized now. "Otto," he sighed.

"*Otto, Otto!*" the bird screamed.

Each time Naberus had attempted this divination during the siege, the emperor was always the first card, no matter how he shuffled the deck. *Like it or not, Crescentius's future is tied to this boy-king.*

He took a long drink before flipping the next card. It depicted a stone tower with battlements ablaze as lighting struck from above. An ill omen, foretelling a danger or crisis, and trapped within the walls of Castel Sant'Angelo, Naberus feared its meaning now. The fortress was supposed to be impregnable, but it had never encountered a siege like this. Half the lords of Tuscany and Lombardy stood outside the walls, along with an army of Bavarians, Saxons, and Germans larger than any force Naberus ever expected to march on Rome. "Not getting any easier, is it Hermes?"

The raven shook its head.

Naberus turned the next card. The illumination showed a man dangling from a tree by one leg, with his hands bound behind his back —the Hanged Man. *Crescentius's life still hangs in the balance.* "Let me guess what's next," he muttered, knowing the last card would be the Moon, signifying twilight and uncertainty. Crescentius's fate had remained in doubt since the siege began.

"*Tok, tok, tok!*" the raven said.

Naberus flipped the last card and drew a startled breath. In place of the Moon stared a goat-headed abomination with a potbelly and bat-like wings. An inverted pentagram hovered like a halo above its head, and two naked demons sat chained at its taloned feet. It was the most notorious card in the tarot, the image of Baphomet the Devil. "What in the bloody hells ..."

Naberus ran his fingers through his hair. "This is quite the change," he said, struggling to think what this new revelation might mean. To some, the Devil signified occult magic, yet the inverted pentagram held another meaning. It was a symbol of chaos, a disrupting force against the order of things. Had something happened today to change the timeline? Or was there a third meaning in the card? In scripture, the Devil was the adversary, the enemy. "Might a new enemy have come onto the scene?" he asked Hermes. "Someone other than Otto and his papal cousin? I wonder who?"

The bird poked its beak at the new card. *"Who?"*

"That is the question, isn't it?"

He was reaching for the jug of wine when the chamber's door creaked open. In its threshold stood Petrus, the mail-clad captain of Crescentius's so-called Praetorian Guard, named after the soldiers who protected the emperors of ancient Rome. At the creak of the hinges, the servant girl bolted awake. Petrus's gaze darted to her naked breasts before she scrambled to cover them with a blanket. He turned back to Naberus. "Consigliere, the prefect requests your presence on the terrace."

"Does he?" Naberus snapped. Petrus glanced back at the girl as Naberus poured himself another cup of wine, before rising from the table. He stood a full head and a half taller than the brawny guardsman, who, like the rest of the castle's men-at-arms, seemed intimated by Naberus's towering height. No man in Rome stood taller, and while there was a reason for that, it was one Naberus kept secret. For had Petrus known the truth, it might shake the man to his soul.

Naberus followed Petrus into a flagstone-lined passageway illuminated with rushlights. In ancient Rome, this building had been a mausoleum, and Naberus wondered if it would now become Crescentius's tomb—or perhaps all their tombs if Otto made true on his threats.

If only their parlay had gone better with the boy-king just two nights ago . . .

~

59

NABERUS RECALLED THEIR COLLECTIVE APPREHENSION THAT NIGHT AS they departed the castle beneath a white flag, flapping in the cold breeze. Crescentius dressed in a penitent's robes, accompanied by Petrus and eleven more of his Praetorian Guards, all of whom went unarmed. Their party was escorted by the Margrave of Meissen, a Saxon lord with a rugged face and a full beard tinged with gray. His steel-blue eyes held a stern gaze. *This one is battle-hardened,* Naberus thought, *and judging from the appearance of the dozen or so warriors who accompany him, these Germans will be formidable foes.*

The margrave ushered them past the massive siege towers, seven in all, each taller than the castle's curtain wall. Those towers could be filled with men who would drop a gangplank onto the battlements and bring death to the castle's defenders. But the towers were built of timber, which meant they could burn. After witnessing their imposing might from the ground, Naberus determined to have every available cask of oil brought from the cellar and positioned along the battlements. The Germans had catapults and ballistae, too, as well as a battering ram on broad wooden wheels, covered by a gabled roof that made it look like the top of a Russian mead hall. The roof would shield the men from boiling oil, but like the siege towers, it too could be set aflame.

Beyond the siege engines, at the base of the Vatican Hill, stood a sea of tents aglow in the light of campfires and torches, where the smell of cooked meat lingered in the air. Scores of armored men stopped what they were doing to watch the margrave's procession approach the emperor's tent, where a banner of Saint Michael hung beside a scarlet standard adorned with crossed keys, one silver and one gold. *So the pope has joined his cousin for our little parlay,* Naberus realized.

The margrave escorted them into the tent. Bearskins covered the floor and flames flickered from brass braziers, whose crackling coals gave off the scent of Arabian cinnamon. Backed by dozens of warriors dressed in mail, many of whom were Lombard and Tuscan lords, sat the Holy Roman Emperor, Otto the Third, clad in the same purple robes he had worn for his Roman coronation two years ago. He had matured since his last visit, but still was a boy of no more than seventeen, and the more he aged, the less he resembled Otto Rufus, his crude, red-bearded father. Rather, this effeminate child had inherited the graceful looks of his mother, Theophano, the niece of the late Byzantine emperor. Naberus would always remember her wedding day at Saint Peter's Basilica twenty-six years ago. What a lovely flower she had been with her raven hair, her olive skin, and her captivating eyes, like Aphrodite reborn. The boy-king's eyes, however, were far from captivating, but sharp as knives.

To the emperor's left stood a diminutive monk with an aquiline nose and a ginger beard whom Naberus recognized as Otto's counselor, Gerbert of Aurillac. He was a notorious man once dubbed the "Usurper of the See of Reims," a scheming kingmaker who ended Charlemagne's line by putting a Capetian on the French throne. Since then, he had served as a sycophant to three Ottonian emperors, including the whelp by his side. He regarded Crescentius and his party with contemplative eyes, a reminder that Gerbert possessed one of the keenest minds in all of Christendom.

The man at the emperor's right, however, revealed no contemplation in his frost-blue eyes. The handsome young pope looked far more warlike than his boyish cousin, tall and square-jawed with a hard face reminiscent of his great-grandfather, Otto Maximus. Naberus sensed a lust for vengeance in the Saxon's smoldering gaze.

Crescentius stood before them, holding his chin high. Even in these penitent's robes, he appeared far more like a Roman emperor than the boy sitting in the chair. Crescentius drew a deep breath, then knelt. The redness of his clenched jaw betrayed his anger and shame.

"Your Imperial Majesty," Crescentius said, "I implore you—"

"Who?" Otto exclaimed, holding up a hand to silence Crescentius. "Who has allowed this Prince of Rome, who lives as Caesar, making laws and appointing popes, to come into the wretched tent of the Saxons?"

Crescentius swallowed hard. "A man who seeks peace between Romans and Saxons. If you claim Rome as a city you wish to rule, then refrain from shedding Roman blood. Your true enemies are the

Magyars who threaten your northern lands and the Saracens who threaten the south. Fight them, not us, and I will pledge warriors to your cause. I shall even surrender my ancestral stronghold of Castel Sant'Angelo, and make confession to the pope. Then I will return in peace to my home on the Quirinal Hill. On this, I swear."

"Do not listen to him, cousin," the pope said, "for he is a limb of the Devil. His oaths are like the wind, merely a guise for his treachery." He leveled his gaze at Crescentius. "You, sir, are beyond absolution."

Crescentius grimaced and rose to his feet. The margrave's hand moved to the hilt of his sword.

Otto nodded to his cousin, then glared at Crescentius. "Margrave, take this man back to his lofty throne until we have prepared a reception adequate for his honor."

Crescentius stared defiantly at the boy-king, but held his tongue. As he turned to leave, Naberus saw the look in the prefect's eyes. Any hope of a truce had ended.

Only bloodshed would save them now.

~

Unless I can persuade Crescentius to take a different path, Naberus thought as he followed Petrus down the castle's passageway and up a flight of stairs to the broad terrace that overlooked the Vatican Hill.

He took a sip of wine before stepping into the chilled air beneath a crescent moon. Beyond the castle walls, the enemy campfires flickered like a swarm of fireflies. Crescentius stood at the battlement, his face strong and regal like a bust of Julius Caesar. Though this strength could not hide the apprehension in his eyes. A black cloak trimmed with fox fur was thrown over his shoulder revealing a polished mail hauberk. At his side hung his longsword with its gold-plated pommel shaped like a stallion's head.

"So, Naberus," he asked, "have my fortunes changed?"

"No," Naberus replied, choosing not to mention the unexplained development foreshadowed by the Devil card.

"I see." Crescentius glanced toward the besieging army. "How long until they attack? We need time, even if we must repel wave after wave of these German invaders. Time enough for Emperor Basil to send aid."

Naberus sighed. "My lord, Basil the Bulgar-Slayer is busy slaying Bulgars. Our alliance with the Byzantine emperor may have made sense at the time, but then no one expected the German pup to return so quickly. Our Byzantine friends may never come, but there's a better option than waiting—we should flee Rome. We could create a diversion, one that allows us to steal outside the walls. I can arrange for a skiff to take us down the Tiber, beyond the city. Your wife and son are already safe in Spoleto. Surely we could take refuge there."

Crescentius clenched his jaw. "No prefect of my noble house has ever fled Rome in the face of an enemy. We have always defended the city, whether it be from the Saracens or these German chieftains that have plagued us for three generations now. Fleeing would be the coward's move, and I shall not take that path. For the sake of my family name and all of Rome."

"Your late kinsman John had the sense to flee when he ruled Rome after the first Otto arrived with his German army. Yet when the time was right, John returned and reclaimed the city."

Crescentius scoffed. "John the Twelfth was a disgrace, more pope than prefect, and never a true heir to our family's name. For God's sake, he turned the Lateran Palace into a brothel!"

Ah, Naberus thought, *if only you'd truly known the man.* Pope John had always been one of Naberus's favorites. His palace kept the finest wine and the finest whores in all of Italy. But now was not the time to debate the late pope's merits. "The point is that John returned and took back the city. These German emperors never stay long. They always return north to put down some rebellion by the Slavs or an insurrection by a rival Bavarian lord. And when this one's gone, the city again shall be yours."

"No." Crescentius shook his head. "The boy's cousin will remain, and this time, I suspect, the pope will have a legion of Germans and Lombards at his disposal."

"Popes can be poisoned. Or have you forgotten what we did to

John the Fourteenth and poor Boniface, and they weren't even Saxons?"

Crescentius glared back. "I've not forgotten, and I may well murder this Saxon pope. Yet you would have me murder my honor first by fleeing like a dog with its tail between its legs!"

Before Naberus could respond, a female voice sounded from the doorway to the terrace. "The Prince of Rome is no dog."

He turned to see the Lady Theodora sauntering toward them in a damask dress that clung to her perfect breasts and narrow waist. The widowed countess was Crescentius's first cousin and, though thirteen years younger, his mistress. Her hair was so fair it seemed the color of platinum, pulled behind her head into a long braid, and her face shone with an ethereal beauty, with eyes like the sky before a storm. With her slender height, a breath taller than Crescentius's six-foot frame, she looked like an image of Venus incarnate.

"The Prince of Rome is a stallion," she said. "And that stallion fears no man."

"Even stallions fear fire," Naberus replied, "and they should fear the butcher's ax, too."

Theodora shot him a look like a viper. *A beautiful viper with silver-gray eyes.* "Has Naberus da Roma become craven?" she asked.

"There is nothing craven, my lady, about fearing a besieging army ten times larger than our own."

"Our family's fortress is invincible," she said confidently. "We need only wait for the Byzantine emperor to send his fleet, and then this German boy will run back to his frozen homeland."

Naberus grimaced. *She's as stubborn as Crescentius.* "Perhaps we could expect the emperor's aid if John Philagathos were still pope. Putting a Calabrian of Greek descent on Saint Peter's throne was part of the bargain. But our pope has been deposed, and who's to say he's even alive. Without a Byzantine yoke around the Holy See, we should not pin our hopes on Constantinople."

"Basil's fleet will come," Crescentius said. "It *must*, for how could he tolerate this German whelp who deems himself Emperor of the World? We forged our arrangement with Emperor Basil and have time to bid. This fortress has never been taken, and I have five hundred men to defend its walls." As he spoke, his neck became flushed and his nostrils flared. "We shall not turn tail and run. Instead, we will show these Germans what it means to be born of Roman blood."

Crescentius turned toward the battlement overlooking the imperial army camped beyond bowshot. "Even if we have to kill every bloody one of them!"

Naberus drained his wine and tossed the cup over his shoulder, where it shattered on the flagstones. "So cried the Hanged Man," he said under his breath. *And somewhere near, the Devil awaits.*

9

THE FERRYMAN

"Have you lost your wits?" Alais asked that evening after Ciarán and Khalil told her about the dockmaster's plan. She stood, arms crossed, on the ship's stern deck as a breeze wafted through her raven hair. "First, we come here on the word of a demon, and now you're going to seek the aid of a man who's named after the ferryman of Hell?"

"The dockmaster believes Charon can get us inside Castel Sant'Angelo," Ciarán insisted, knowing how anxious she had become since their arrival in Rome.

"How's he going to do that?" she demanded. "You said the castle was surrounded by the emperor's army."

"I've not a notion," Ciarán said. "But right now, he's our only chance."

She gave a huff. "And where will you find this ruffian?"

"At the Basilica of Saint Peter," Khalil replied, leaning against the rail. "In the Leonine City."

Alais looked incredulous. "Truly?"

"He's a quaestor," Ciarán explained.

She blinked. "A what?"

"A pardoner of sins," Khalil said. "It seems your popes employ these men to collect money in exchange for relieving sinners of their penance."

"Charon works for the Church?" Alais said, shaking her head.

Khalil flashed a smile. "Ironic, isn't it."

"Seedy is the word I'd use," she replied.

"Rome is a seedy place," Khalil said. "Remember, it was not I who wished to come here."

Alais glanced away. "Maybe you were right."

Ciarán did not like where this was going. "It doesn't matter now," he said. "We're here, and we know what we have to do. We'll go see the quaestor in the morning." He turned to Alais. "Will you come with us?"

She shook her head. "Évrard has agreed to escort me to the Forum. I want to see the ruins."

Khalil stepped forward and took her hand. "Are you certain that's wise? In your dreams, you sensed danger in those ruins."

"In my dreams," she said, "the danger is in the darkness. I'll be going there in daylight. I don't even know if the place I've seen is real, but I must find out."

Ciarán saw the way she looked at Khalil and felt his stomach harden.

"Then go," Khalil said, "but do not linger there. And tell Évrard to bring Mordechai along. I will feel more at ease if I knew you had someone more than our jovial captain to protect you."

Alais released Khalil's hand. "I promise."

Ciarán glared at Khalil as she retired to the deckhouse. "If you think the ruins may be dangerous, why are you letting her go?"

"A woman is not like a bird to be kept in a cage."

Heat flushed up Ciarán's neck. "So you'd let her walk into harm's way?"

"No," Khalil said, narrowing his gaze. "I just know more about women than what your abbot taught you back at Derry."

Ciarán set his jaw. "If anything happens to her, it's on your hands." He turned and stormed toward the bow, knowing his relationship with Alais would never be the same. He did not speak again with

Khalil that night or with Alais in the morning when he, Khalil, and Josua left for the Leonine City.

The three of them departed Rome through one of the vast gates in the Aurelian Walls and walked up a well-trodden path that cut through a grassy field on the Tiber's banks. Along the way, they passed merchants and their pack animals moving goods between Pope Leo's city and the Roman neighborhood called Trastevere, which stretched west of the Porto di Ripa within the city walls. By the look of the merchants and their companions, the city was home to people from across its once great empire, for among the Romans on the road strode Jews and Franks, Spaniards and Lombards, and even a pair of Moors, judging by their turbans and striped robes. Despite this diversity, more than few of the merchants shot curious looks at Ciarán and his companions, and it was no wonder why.

Dressed in his black Benedictine habit and cowl, Ciarán walked beside Khalil, who wore a linen shirt and an embroidered vest he'd purchased in Barcelona, along with his sword belt and a pair of stripped pantaloons that made him look like a Saracen corsair. Josua, meanwhile, had donned a wide-brimmed hat and a slate-colored tunic with a fine leather purse strapped to his belt. Few Benedictine monks, if any, would associate with a Muslim and a Jew, and together they formed an odd trio that raised more than a few of the merchants' brows.

Ahead, the Leonine Walls loomed forty feet high with crenelated towers spaced every hundred yards and a massive arched gate where the path ended. The white stone archway was flanked by four broad pillars with niches between each pair where Ciarán imagined the statues of Roman emperors once stood. The dockmaster had called it the Porta Saxonum—the Gate of the Saxons—and it was a testament to the magic wielded by Roman architects centuries ago. A half-dozen Saxon guards dressed in cloaks and mail, and armed with spears and swords, waved them inside the tunnel beneath the archway, paying little attention to the travelers who came in and out of the gate.

Through the gateway, Ciarán was met by the smell of refuse, which seemed common to every walled city he had encountered outside of Córdoba. Inside, a city street curved north between close-packed houses and shops with roofs of terra-cotta tile. Merchants hawked their wares along the street, while townsfolk milled about their daily work and a scattering of scrawny cats and dogs, alongside dozens of pigeons and an occasional chicken, picked at the refuse that trickled down the gutter in the street's center. Above the rooftops peeked the battlements of the siege towers, and beyond them rose the massive tower of Castel Sant'Angelo. *"That* is the castle where this Crescentius lives?" Josua asked, wide-eyed.

"Makes you appreciate our problem," Ciarán replied.

Josua nodded. "That is quite a problem."

"You don't say?" Khalil quipped. "If this ferryman works in a church, let's hope he can work miracles."

Soon, the road ended in a broader street that ran east to west. More houses and hostels crammed the sides of this road, and amid them, Ciarán counted no fewer than five cloistered monasteries and convents, each with its own oratory and small garden of olive and fig trees. Yet it was the structure at the end of the road that caught his eye, the largest building in the Leonine City, towering above its surroundings: the Basilica of Saint Peter.

It was the largest church Ciarán had ever laid eyes on, rivaled only by Córdoba's Great Mosque. The edifice was a wonder of stone and brick with a pediment surmounting its entranceway supported by rows of granite columns. More archways and pillars embellished the face of the basilica, which looked wider than a city block, and behind it rose the main church with lofty gabled roofs covered with terra cotta tiles. The face of the church visible above the pediment was adorned with colorful mosaics of saints and apostles against a golden background, with Christ in all His glory beneath the roof's triangular peak. Even from a thousand feet away the mosaics were a miracle to behold, for it seemed the Roman artisanship with colored stones was finer than anything made by an illuminator's quill.

Josua gaped at the massive structure. "What is that?"

"Saint Peter's Basilica," Ciarán explained. "Dónall told me about it. It's the greatest sanctuary in the West, built by Constantine on the very place where Saint Peter was crucified by the Emperor Nero, upside down no less."

"Why upside down?" Josua asked.

"Because Peter believed himself unworthy to die in the same manner as the Savior," Ciarán said.

Khalil nodded. "I suppose that's better than being fed to the lions."

"Never thought of it that way," Ciarán said with a shrug.

The road soon opened into a broad public square. A small palace stood to the north of the square, and another monastery or convent, along with more structures with terra-cotta roofs, dominated the southern side. Ciarán felt a tinge of awe at an object beyond the monastery, flanking the basilica: a spearlike obelisk made of red granite that rose more than eighty feet high. Dónall had spoken of the monument, brought over from ancient Egypt by the Emperor Caligula, but nothing could have prepared Ciarán for what he saw within the square. A city of tents filled the plaza, even cluttering the great stone steps that led to the basilica, like a miniature version of Córdoba's Grand Bazaar.

"It's a bloody marketplace," Ciarán gasped.

"And it looks like your Christianity is for sale," Josua said.

Khalil raised a brow. "Where else would we find our pardoner?"

The aroma of cooked meat mixed with the smell of sweat and the din of a market filled the air. They waded into the square, through crowds of pilgrims and townsfolk gathered around the stalls of moneychangers, cloth merchants, cobblers, and a myriad of vendors.

"Fresh sardines, just plucked from the Tiber!" cried a fishmonger.

"Succulent pears!" called a fruit vendor.

"Prayer beads!" hawked an older woman in a cramped stall.

"*Quantum? Quantum?*" people shouted, haggling with the sellers in Latin.

Josua stopped to admire the wares of a merchant selling both olive oil and holy oil. Meanwhile, Ciarán discovered a plump Benedictine behind a stall waving what looked like a Psalter. "You sell these to anyone?" Ciarán asked incredulously.

"Thanks be to God, brother," the monk said. "They keep our entire abbey well fed. People like to have a holy book from Saint Peter's, even if they can't read 'em."

Ciarán raised an eyebrow and picked up one of the small books. Its binding looked shoddy and its parchment cracked. Flipping it open, he could tell the original contents of the book had been scraped away in favor of a vulgar penmanship with no illuminations. Ciarán shook his head and handed the book back to the monk. "Your scribes should be ashamed."

He walked off before the monk could say another word and found Kahlil at the stall of the old woman hawking prayer beads. "I am looking for a pardoner," Khalil told her. "A quaestor."

She pointed toward the steps climbing to the basilica, then offered Khalil a set of beads, pleading with her hands. "For the Blessed Virgin, my lord."

He reached into his belt pouch and gave the woman two copper coins. "You'll have more use for these than I," he said, handing the beads to Ciarán.

Josua walked up beside them. "What did you buy?"

"Information," Khalil replied.

Ciarán turned back toward the basilica just as a procession of black-clad monks snaked through the crowd. They wore long pointed hoods that enveloped their faces, unlike any cowl Ciarán had seen on a Benedictine monk, or any Cluniac for that matter. Their leader held a wooden cross over his head with an opaque black cloth draped over it like a funeral shroud. *"Dies irae, dies illa,"* they chanted in unison in the tone of a requiem. "The day of wrath shall consume the world in ashes. And when it comes, may no foreigner sit on Saint Peter's throne."

"Who are they?" Ciarán asked the old woman.

"Call themselves the Brotherhood of the Messiah, preparing for the End of Days."

Ciarán glanced back at the monks chanting grimly amid the throng of people gathered outside Saint Peter's. "Why do they say that about the pope?"

"Because they're good Romans," she said with a wicked grin. "They don't want a Saxon pope greeting Christ Almighty when he rides down from Heaven. Can't say I blame 'em."

This is madness, he thought as he left the woman, his gaze still fixed on the black-cowled monks chanting about the end times. As the black procession marched toward the entrance of the plaza, Ciarán, Khalil, and Josua ventured deeper into the market. They passed merchants selling wineskins and others peddling herbs or wooden crosses. And the closer they came to the steps, the more religious the goods became.

"Relics, relics!" called merchants from all sides.

A pockmarked merchant was waving a vial of yellow-white liquid. "Breast milk from the Virgin Mary! A drop on your tongue will cure all ills. Just six denarii!"

Ciarán's jaw fell slack, then someone tugged on his left sleeve. "Forget him, brother," said another merchant in a stained, tawny smock. The man had an emaciated face and a mouth revealing only the stubs of three yellow teeth. "I have here the toes of Saint Valentine, five in all, just three denarii each. Or the glory of all glories"—he held up a tiny canvas pouch—"a piece of the foreskin of our Savior Jesus Christ."

Ciarán yanked his sleeve from the peddler's grasp. "Ignore these charlatans," Khalil said. "And look." He gestured toward one of the larger tents at the foot of the steps with its flap barely open. Over this opening hung a wooden sign carved with the word "Quaestor."

"Let's hope this is the right one," Ciarán said.

Khalil pulled back the tent flap and Ciarán followed him inside. The air reeked of the tallow candles illuminating the tent, which was sparsely furnished with a chair and a small wooden desk cluttered with parchment and inkhorns. On the floor beside it sat an iron-bound strongbox secured with a thick lock. Yet it was the man inside the tent who filled the space. The quaestor stood as broad as an ox and as fat as a hog, draped in a huge black tunic. His bearded jowls obscured any semblance of a neck, and beneath thick brows, a pair of flinty eyes regarded the trio as they entered.

"Ah, brother." The word rolled off his tongue as he gestured toward Ciarán with his meaty hands. "Have you brought me a pair of sinners who wish to purchase an indulgence before the end times? Let me guess the sin: pride, fornication, perpetual drunkenness?" He eyed Khalil and Josua more closely. "Or blasphemy?"

"We don't need an indulgence," Khalil said. "We are looking for a man called Charon."

The quaestor gave a slight chuckle. "What kind of name is that?" He touched his fingers to his ample chest. "I am Ugo Grassus."

"Can you tell us where to find him?" Ciarán asked.

"Find him? Rome is such a big place." A thin smile spread across the quaestor's jowls. "Of course, I suppose, everything can be found for a price."

Josua put a hand on Khalil's arm before he could reach for his belt pouch. "Let's save our coin with this one," Josua snapped. "I'm sure there are other pardoners in this square."

"We have no money to waste," Ciarán added.

"Yet who is so poor that he has not got a penny?" the quaestor asked. "For a morsel of information, perhaps?"

Khalil flashed a shrewd grin. "And why would I pay for something we've already found? 'Who is so poor that he has not got a penny?' Those words were written by the Greek poet Lucian in his *Dialogues of the Dead.* Specifically, the dialogue between Menippus—and Charon."

Ciarán jerked his head back. "You were going to cheat us!"

The quaestor frowned. "Fools and their money deserve to be parted, but your friend here is no fool. My name is Ugo Grassus, yet if I were to be this person you call Charon, where in Rome's underworld might you wish to be ferried?"

"Castel Sant'Angelo," Ciarán told him.

From deep within his belly, Ugo Grassus began to laugh. "This is a joke, no? Castel Sant'Angelo is surrounded by the emperor's army."

"You might know a way inside," Ciarán insisted.

"What do you want inside Castel Sant'Angelo?" Ugo Grassus asked.

"The Prince of Rome," Ciarán replied. "He holds something of value to us."

The quaestor's eyes narrowed. "So you want to steal from Crescentius? To obtain this thing you seek before the Germans take it for themselves? Then you not only need a way inside the castle, but also the location of his vault, the place where a man like him would keep his most precious things." He ran a huge hand across the crown of his bald head. "This access, it will be very expensive."

"How expensive?" Josua demanded.

Ugo Grassus cocked his head toward the roof of his stall. "A hundred solidi for each of you who seeks a way inside."

Khalil eyes flashed wide. "Outrageous!"

"Robbery!" Josua exclaimed.

"Then perhaps you are not very serious about this thing you seek," Ugo Grassus said smugly.

Ciarán glanced at his two friends, his nerves tense. *We need this,* he mouthed to them.

Josua crossed his arms. "Twenty solidi per man, no more."

"Ho-ho," Ugo Grassus chuckled. "One would need more than that just to pay the bribes required for the access you seek. Then there is the matter of a fee, for all men of business deserve a profit, no? Certainly a merchant like you understands this. And then, there is the risk involved. If I were to help you steal this thing you're looking for, I would be crossing men like Crescentius and Naberus da Roma. Some would argue that no amount of money is worth the price of their vengeance."

"We've heard of Crescentius," Khalil said. "But who is this Naberus?"

Ugo Grassus gave a devilish grin. "You are foreigners clearly unfamiliar with Rome, so I will educate you. Naberus da Roma is the consigliere, counselor to the Crescentii. It was Naberus who helped Pope Boniface chase John the Fourteenth from Saint Peter's throne. Some believe it was Naberus who poisoned the deposed pope, and perhaps killed Boniface too after his atrocities angered the mob. The citizens so reviled Boniface that they hung his corpse on the statue of

Constantine outside the Lateran Palace. You see, Naberus and Crescentius know how to read the mood of the people and give them what they want, even if it's blood.

"Some say Naberus is a fortuneteller who can read the future, while a few whisper that he's a necromancer who speaks with the dead. There are even rumors he was a lover of Marozia, the harlot-queen of Rome, and that he murdered her mother's lover, Pope John the Tenth. Yet that was almost seventy years ago, and Naberus da Roma cannot be that old. But he's still a very dangerous man. So you see, to enter Castel Sant'Angelo is to not only enter the house of Crescentius, but also the lair of Naberus, and who wants to earn his enmity? That is a risk no man would take for twenty solidi. The price remains a hundred."

The more the quaestor spoke, the more Ciarán's stomach hardened. At Saint Bastian's, the Dragon's servants had been necromancers, and the rumors about this Naberus da Roma only strengthened his conviction. He pulled Khalil and Josua aside. "Pay the man," Ciarán said under his breath. "He's the only way we'll get inside."

Josua's lips curled. "The man's a thief."

"If he can get us into that vault," Khalil said, placing a hand on Josua's shoulder, "I'll make certain you are repaid."

Josua gave a frustrated sigh, then gestured at Ciarán and Khalil. "Fifty-five solidi per man for these two."

"You're more than halfway to the ferry," Ugo Grassus replied with a voracious look in his eyes. "But Charon never takes less than what he asks. So now let's see how desperate your monkish friend is to get inside that vault."

VENUS AND ROMA

"What is it, milady?" Évrard asked, though Alais barely heard him.

She stared at a vast field in the valley between two hills, certain she had seen this before. Amid the green of the hillside, she noticed the remnants of what had been marble grandstands, and for an instant, she imagined the porphyry obelisks, the giant statues, and the pounding of the horse-drawn chariots as they raced around the track, just like in her dreams. Thousands of people had crammed the grandstands, cheering on the racers with ribbons of white and red. Yet now all she saw were four cows and a flock of sheep grazing under the watch of two shepherds. The obelisks that once stood in the track's center were gone, and the largest structure that remained was a squat tower that may have risen from the grandstands. Her gaze drifted to the green hilltop where those grandstands once climbed. An image flashed in her memory—a stone giant with hollow eyes, its gaping mouth plunging into darkness . . .

She let out a gasp when Évrard put a hand on her shoulder. "Milady?"

Alais shook her head, trying to banish the frightening image from her mind. All that stood atop the hill were grass, trees, and the ruins of a once massive palace. *Still,* she thought, *I will never go up there.*

"Maybe we should go back to the ship?" Évrard suggested.

"No," she insisted. "I want to see the ruins."

"There's almost no one here," observed Mordechai, the strapping young Jew who accompanied them at Khalil' suggestion. He carried a long sheathed dagger and a hunting bow slung over his shoulder, looking every bit as intimidating as Khalil had hoped when Alais and Évrard set off from the Porta di Ripa where *La Margerie* was moored.

"It's the ghosts that keep people away," Évrard said. "Least that's what the dockmaster told me. Evil spirits haunt the old pagan temples."

Mordechai's eyes widened. "And where are we going?"

Évrard winked. "To an old pagan temple, of course."

Mordechai shot Alais a pleading look. "It will be all right," she told him. "We're going in the daylight."

She led them down a road paved with overgrown flagstones on the outskirts of the rubble-strewn pasture that had once been Circus Maximus. At the pasture's end stood a small basilica with a lofty bell tower. "Another church," Évrard remarked. "Must be the eighth one since we crossed the bridge. It's like old Rome crumbled away and churches sprouted in its place like mushrooms."

Alais smiled. "It *is* the pope's city."

"Mordechai," Évrard said, "if we ever add Rome to our trade route, remind me to stock up on relics with all these churches here. A wise man once told me there's good money to be made in relics."

In the distance beyond the basilica, eight pillars towered skyward, topped with the stone remnants of some long-lost structure. A chill washed over Alais. She had seen these pillars before in the darkness of her dreams.

Mordechai gaped as a massive triumphal arch came into view behind the great columns. "These Romans must have been giants . . ."

"Aye, lad," Évrard said. "And no one's built anything like it since."

They reached the entrance to the Forum, where yet another church stood. "Make that number nine," Évrard remarked, "though this one's seen better days." The church's windows were hollowed out and half the structure had collapsed, crushed by rubble from the adjacent hillside. Mordechai gave it a wary look, as if he feared the ruined church was haunted.

Past the church, a trio of towering Corinthian columns rose from a hulking podium. Built of massive blocks of tuff, the podium stood more than twenty feet high, crowned with weeds surrounding the base of the columns. Alais felt small in its presence, imagining how massive the temple must have been in ancient times. Beyond the ruined columns, the road led to a sprawling field where broken pillars and stone blocks jutted from the grass like tombstones in a vast graveyard. Yet amid this desolation grew olive trees, and grape vines clung to trellises.

They approached the remains of a circular building rising from the surrounding ferns. The shard of a broken pillar and five columns jutted from its ornate base, supporting the remains of a roof. Behind it stood the ruins of a massive structure on the side of the Palatine Hill, its arcade filled with shadows. A breeze whistled through the broken columns, and Mordechai jumped as if he had heard the whisper of a ghost. Then a figure darted from behind the ruin into the remains of a street that spanned the center of the ruined Forum.

Alais' heart skipped. It was a girl no older than ten, with a violet ribbon in her dark hair. *Adeline?* The girl ran frantically as if she were being chased. "Adeline!" Alais called, but the girl did not stop. Another name sprang to mind—*"Julia!"*

The girl glanced over her shoulder, her face ashen. Then Évrard grabbed Alais by the arm and jerked her back.

A wolf, larger than a mastiff and as black as soot, tore from the shadows of the ruins.

Alais' heart pounded. The wolf moved five times as fast as the child, bounding toward her down the road.

"No!" Alais screamed.

Beside her, Mordechai drew the string of his hunting bow and let an arrow fly. The shaft sped toward its target and struck hard. With a pained yelp, the black wolf crashed sideways, the arrow jutting from his back. The bowstring snapped again and a second arrow pierced the wolf's neck.

Ten paces from the wolf, the girl kept running, toward a basilica of brown stone and brick that stood near a hulking triumphal arch. She scampered up the basilica's marble steps and disappeared behind the vestibule doors.

Alais pulled away from Évrard's grasp and started after the girl. "Milady!" Évrard called, but she was running as fast as she could. Ahead, the black wolf twitched at the side of the road and snarled, its eyes burning with feral rage until a third arrow thudded into its side.

"Careful, my lady!" Mordechai warned as he aimed another arrow at the beast.

A chill rushed up her neck. For though the life faded from its gaze, the wolf's eyes remained fixed on her. *Just like the man in the black cassock . . .*

"The beast is dead, milady," Évrard said, hurrying down the road as fast as his rotund body would allow. The wolf shuddered, then lay still. "It's dead," he said again, between huffs of breath.

"But the girl . . ." Alais headed for the church. Beyond it stood a colossal amphitheater, larger than anything she had ever seen. *It must be the Coliseum,* she realized, before another alarming thought struck. *The ruined temple, it should be right here.* Yet only the basilica with its gabled roof of terra-cotta tile and a cross-topped bell tower stood between her and the arena. She ran her fingers through her hair, wondering if her dreams had been a mere illusion of a place that never was. But there was still the girl . . .

She strode up the church steps and pulled open one of the vestibule doors. "Julia?" she yelled. Her voice echoed down a yawning nave. Candles burned in sconces along the columns that lined the aisles, stretching to a gilded altar surmounted by a mosaic of the Madonna and Child. Alais searched for the girl, but did not see her. "Julia?" she called again.

"May I help you?" asked a wizened voice in Latin from the shadows of one of the archways. A tall priest emerged with a long nose, a thick gray beard, and a narrow face creased with age. A silver crucifix hung from his neck and a broad-brimmed hat topped his head.

"A girl just ran in here," Alais said, still searching for the child. "Did you see her?"

"A girl?" The old priest wrinkled his brow. "I dare say you're the only girl I've seen today. Do you know this child?"

"No." Alais hesitated. "Maybe, I think her name is Julia."

The priest's eyes flashed with anger. He glared past Alais, pointing a long finger. "No weapons in the house of God!" In the vestibule's threshold stood Mordechai, clutching his hunting bow, with Évrard beside him.

"Forgive him, Father," Alais said. "There was a wolf, my friend killed it."

The priest scratched his beard. "A wolf? Was it black?"

"Yes," Alais replied, following the priest as he strode toward the door. He brushed past Mordechai and peered into the Forum where the black wolf lay dead in the road, arrows protruding from its back.

"Good gracious, that one's been terrorizing the Forum for a month now. Your friend just made many a shepherd quite happy."

"It was chasing the girl," Alais said. "She ran in here to escape it."

"Truly?" The priest looked mystified. "I thought I was the only one here." He gave a slight bow. "My name is Father Michele."

Évrard responded in the best Latin he could muster. "The lady of Selles-sur-Cher, of the House of Poitiers."

"Oh, my," Father Michele replied. "Not many people visit the Basilica of Santa Maria Nova, let alone nobility."

"What about the child?" Alais pressed.

"Oh, yes," the priest said. "If she came in here, the only other way out is through the transept door." He pointed to a transept on the right, where a narrow door was cracked open.

"What's behind there?" she asked.

"This church was constructed on the site of a temple built by the Emperor Hadrian, dedicated to the goddesses Venus and Roma. In fact, part of the temple still stands."

"It does?" she gasped.

"Why yes," Father Michele said. "Back in its day, it was the largest temple in Rome, for Venus was the mother of the Romans, or so they thought, the goddess who gave birth to Aeneas himself and hence the patron goddess of Eternal Rome. Julius Caesar even claimed Venus as his divine ancestor. Would you like to see it?"

"Very much so."

Her anticipation swelled as she followed Father Michele to the transept and out the door, only to find that with each step, the images from her dreams were becoming reality. The basilica indeed backed up to a much older structure. It looked like the nave of a church, though only a portion of the vaulted ceiling still remained, patterned with diamonds in the curvature of its ancient apse. Marble still covered its timeworn walls where arched alcoves once housed precious statues behind an array of porphyry columns broken at the top, the ceiling they once supported now gone. The floor, however, remained in pristine shape, patterned with ovals and squares of porphyry and marble. She gazed in awe, certain she had stood here before. The only things missing were the fireflies and Orionde, dancing gracefully and singing her haunting tune. However, Alais sensed none of the danger she perceived in her dreams, for with the morning sky above there were none of the ominous shadows.

"My dear," Father Michele said, "you look as if you've seen this place before. If I weren't a Christian man, why I might think that Venus had returned to her temple."

Alais smiled at the priest's flattery, then began searching for the girl. She could have run off anywhere, Alais realized, for the temple sat on a hill, and beyond it the rubble-strewn plain of the old Roman Forum led to the massive Coliseum. Her gaze returned to the temple, climbing its ancient walls to the remnants of its apse. The sun rose over the missing rooftop, and its light caught her eyes with a blinding flare. She shook her head, trying to shake the sunlight from her eyes, only to realize the sky had gone dark. An image flashed in her still-returning vision. A woman tall and graceful, with hair like spun silver. A white silken dress clung to the woman's lithe body, though some-thing was wrong. Her eyes were filled with fear. The woman staggered backward, then swooned, crumpling onto the porphyry titles. Alais' head began to spin, her legs gave way.

She blinked twice, only to find herself lying on the cold tiled floor with Évrard, Mordechai, and Father Michele looking down on her.

"Are you all right?" Évrard asked, kneeling beside her.

She felt light-headed. "What happened?"

"You fainted, my dear," Father Michele said.

Évrard helped her sit up. "The woman," she asked, "did you see her?"

"A woman, milady?" Évrard shook his head.

"She was right here . . ."

"My dear, you looked into the sun," Father Michele said. "It's been known to cause people to see strange things. Like a mirage, if you will."

Alais shook her head. "But she seemed so real."

"There's no lady here but you." Father Michele gave her a gentle smile. "Though sometimes people see what they were meant to see."

Alais gave a long sigh. "Or perhaps I'm losing my mind."

CIARÁN WALKED DOWN THE CENTER AISLE OF SAINT PETER'S BASILICA IN sheer awe.

Scores of marble columns lined the cavernous nave, and even more pillars flanked the aisles to each side, where dozens of candles and oil lamps flickered like stars. The nave stretched well more than a hundred yards, and above a bronze-tiled roof loomed a hundred feet high. Pilgrims strolled the aisles, admiring the mosaics of biblical tales that seemed to cover every wall, while others knelt before candlelit shrines spaced along the nave. "Three thousand people could worship here," Ciarán wondered aloud.

"Not since the Great Mosque of Córdoba have I seen its rival," Khalil admitted.

They joined Josua, who was gazing at an elaborate mosaic over a massive archway between the nave and the crossing. At its apex, the mosaic depicted a haloed Christ, like a giant compared to the other figures in the scene. To the Savior's right bowed a bearded man holding two golden keys, an image of Saint Peter at the right hand of the Risen Lord. To the Savior's left bowed a Roman emperor wearing a jeweled crown topped with a cross. His left hand outstretched, the emperor presented a miniature version of the basilica to the glorified Christ, while behind them bowed a communion of saints in resplendent robes.

"Constantine and Saint Peter," Ciarán observed. "Constantine built this basilica. Do you see those pillars?" He pointed to eight pillars surrounding the high altar plated in silver and gold. Each was a wide twisted column of gray marble adorned with spiraling designs, supporting a massive canopy that appeared forged of pure silver. "Dónall once said that Constantine found them in Jerusalem, in the ruins of Solomon's Temple."

Josua walked up to one of the columns, regarding it reverently, while Khalil stood with a hand on his chin studying the mosaic. "What does Constantine have in his other hand?"

Ciarán looked more closely. It was true, in his right hand the emperor was holding a rectangular object. "A book," Ciarán realized. "A Psalter, perhaps, to prove he was a Christian, or maybe it's another gift to the Church."

"Like a legacy," Khalil said, "something one would pass down to an heir."

The poet's words recalled the demon's riddle, but surely Khalil was mistaken. "Saint Peter is not the heir of Constantine," Ciarán insisted. "They lived three hundred years apart."

"True, but perhaps Constantine passed his legacy to someone associated with the Church in his day? I'm just trying to find some meaning to your demon's riddle."

"The demon was speaking of the future. It said Constantine's heir shall fall. Whomever it was speaking of, he's alive today."

Khalil raised a brow "If it was telling the truth at all."

A moment later, bells tolled. "The quaestor told us to return at Nones," Ciarán reminded them. Josua scowled, still bitter about the sum they had paid to engage the quaestor's services. They left the nave and passed through the basilica's lush atrium decorated with flowers and ferns and a large mosaic of Christ walking on water before a boat full of frightened apostles. Through the basilica's bronze gates, they made their way back to the quaestor's candlelit tent.

They found Ugo Grassus standing before his desk with a broad smile. His massive hands propped up two kite-shaped shields, each covered in leather and painted with an image of a black lion. Beside them lay a bundle of dark-gray cloaks, a pair of iron helmets, and two sheathed swords.

Ciarán cocked his head. "What are those?"

"Ah," Ugo Grassus said, "just some things I had to bribe a pair of Saxons to obtain, so you will look the part."

"What do you mean?" Khalil asked.

Ugo Grassus's eyes narrowed. "You didn't think there is some secret passageway into Castel Sant'Angelo, did you? No, every door to the castle is securely barred. And I assume you want to get inside before every last man in the emperor's army."

"No," Ciarán muttered as he began to understand the implication of what the quaestor had planned for them.

"Oh, yes," said Ugo Grassus with a fiendish smile. "If you want to get inside that castle before everything in it is gone, there's only one way to do so—through the covered gangplank of one of those siege towers."

SECRETS IN THE DARK

Naberus da Roma slid his torch into a sconce on the stone wall, its light piercing the darkness that filled the barrel-vaulted chamber in the heart of Castel Sant'Angelo. Ages ago, this chamber contained urns bearing the ashes of Emperor Hadrian and his imperial family before the Visigoths sacked Rome and scattered those ashes to the wind.

The torchlight danced across the yellowish stone of the centuries-old walls as Naberus strode down the narrow stairway that traversed the room, while his raven Hermes balanced on the stair rail. The stairway was more like a ramp, with steps so shallow they allowed the ancient Romans to bring carts to the castle's upper floors. Before he reached the barred double doors at the end of the chamber, he stepped off the ramp onto a short flight of wooden stairs that descended ten feet to the chamber's floor. Barrels of wine, grain, and salted meats filled every alcove of the cramped space, including the archway supporting the stairs. How ironic, Naberus thought, that the tomb of one of Roman's greatest emperors was now nothing more than a wine cellar and a granary.

Naberus made his way around several large casks toward a shallow, arched alcove where two iron-bound chests sat covered in dust.

The chests belonged to him, though much of their contents were but old memories, and nothing inside them was important enough to keep in his personal chamber. He had always been loath to store his possessions in one place, including the vast wealth he had accumulated over the decades, so he had hidden them throughout the city in the ruins of Trajan's Market and the Baths of Diocletian, and in secret vaults on the Capitoline and Palatine Hills. Fortunately, what he needed right now was still here. It sat propped against one of the chests, an old clay amphora, completely sealed, with the stub of a rope protruding from its mouth where a cork should have been. The amphora, which came from his home in Constantinople, did not contain wine, but rather a far more valuable liquid. Naberus lifted it carefully. "Let's pray you've lost none of your potency."

"Pray!" Hermes cawed from the rail.

Naberus looked up at the raven. "Crescentius is stubborn. This may be our only hope."

He carried the amphora up the stairs and the ramp, leaving through the open double doors. With a flutter of wings, the raven followed.

Delicately, Naberus set the amphora against the wall beyond the chamber's threshold. He grabbed his torch, closed the iron-bound doors, and slid the heavy bar into place, knowing that when the invaders came, this door would be one of the few remaining barriers between them and Crescentius. With his free hand, he picked up the amphora, which was so heavy most men would have needed two hands to heft it. But Naberus was unlike most men. Hugging the amphora against his chest, he continued up the ramp through a vaulted passageway, where another stairwell led to the upper chambers.

At the top of the stairs, he found Grimm, one of his Neapolitan mastiffs, waiting for him. The mastiff licked Naberus's fingers as he scratched the fur beneath the dog's jaw. "Come," he said, "they will be waiting for us."

When he emerged on the terrace, Naberus found Petrus and Crescentius gazing over the ramparts at the German army below. Beneath a clouded night sky, scores of campfires glowed amid the sea of tents at the base of the Vatican Hill. The siege towers loomed like timber giants just beyond bowshot of the curtain wall, and between the towers and the tents moved hundreds of men, far more than the castle's defenders.

"Consigliere," Petrus said with a nod, acknowledging Naberus' arrival.

Crescentius eyed the amphora. "What is that?"

"When the Rus attacked Constantinople, they called it lightning from heaven," Naberus explained, "but the Byzantine Greeks call it Greek fire. It burns even on water, and the Greeks used it to immolate the ships of the Rus and the Saracens on the Sea of Marmara. We have but one amphora. It will have to do."

Crescentius furrowed his brow. "How does it work?"

Naberus pointed to the short coil of rope protruding from the top of the amphora. "This is a fuse. If the Germans breach the curtain wall and wheel their battering ram toward the castle's gate, good Petrus here shall light this fuse and then drop the amphora on our attackers."

"And when it lands?" Crescentius asked.

Naberus flashed a wicked smile. "Lighting from heaven. And we'll watch them all burn."

PART II

And the fifth angel blew his trumpet, and I saw a star that had fallen to the earth, and he was given the key to the shaft of the bottomless pit . . .

—Revelation 9:1

THE SIEGE

I n the cabin beneath *La Margerie's* tiller, Ciarán knelt in prayer, wearing only the old breeches Évrard had given him after they left Córdoba. Pale sunlight peeked through the cracked portal and glimmered off the hauberk of polished chain mail that lay beside Caladbolg in its sturdy leather sheath. The armor had been a gift from Orionde, though he had not worn it since Rosefleur, for the mail felt heavy and awkward to one accustomed to the wool habit of a scholarly monk. He used to tell himself that monks were not warriors, but at Rosefleur he came to believe the warrior's spirit lived in every drop of Irish blood, and in desperate times it could be summoned. Today was one of those times, and he prayed his courage would not fail him.

The armor, he reminded himself, once belonged to Maugis d'Aygremont, one of the paladins of Charlemagne who helped preserve the prophecy's secrets for those who would need them at the end of the millennium. Dónall and Remi had given their lives for that prophecy, as had Ciarán's mother and father, Rabbi Isaac and Josua's son Eli, and all of his brothers at Derry who died fighting Adémar of Blois. Ciarán whispered their names as he prayed. *Bran and Murchad, Fintan and Senach, Áed and Ailil, and most of all, Niall.* So many loved and so many lost, yet it was for them that Ciarán knew he must do this. *So that none of them died in vain.*

He finished his prayer with a verse from Saint Columcille: "'Be a bright flame before me, my God. For we have nothing to fear when you are near, O Lord of day and night.'" He made the sign of the cross, then rose to his feet. After a deep breath, he pulled on a linen tunic, followed by the thick wool jacket called a gambeson, and then the armor. The hauberk pressed against his shoulders and hung to his knees. *Maugis must have been a taller man*, he thought, before he realized someone had entered the cabin.

He turned to see Alais and wondered if she had watched him dress.

She shook her head, her eyes pleading. "You know what I think about this foolish plan."

"I have no choice."

"That's not true."

"Yes it is," he said as he picked up Caladbolg.

She stepped toward him and put a hand on his shoulder. "At least try to be safe." She leaned over and kissed him on the cheek.

The touch of her lips sent a warm flush through his face. Yet as much as he enjoyed that feeling, he wanted to remind her that the last time she had kissed him, it had been on his lips. "I will," he said instead.

Ciarán stepped out onto the deck under a gray sky, as a breeze wafted off the Tiber. Khalil waited for him. He had already dressed in the dark cloak and iron helmet Ugo Grassus had given him. With the helm's cheekpieces closed, it hid most of his Persian features, and Ciarán hoped he might pass as a sun-kissed German. Beneath the cloak, he wore a breastplate of boiled leather that they had purchased in the Leonine City. Khalil thought it would look odd to have a swordsman in the front ranks without armor, and had insisted that Josua spare a little more of his coin. Josua had reluctantly agreed and now stood with Évrard on the deck, each one holding a kite-shaped shield bearing the image of a black lion.

Évrard handed Ciarán the other gray cloak. "You still think this is wise, lad?"

"Wise or not, it's the only path we have," Ciarán said as he fastened the cloak.

The captain shrugged as Josua handed Ciarán his helmet. Ciarán found it even more awkward than the hauberk, and heavy, too. When he closed the cheek pieces, his peripheral vision disappeared. "This won't work unless the enemy's coming straight at me."

"But it will keep your skull intact," Josua said. He handed a shield to Ciarán, who clumsily worked his left arm through the leather straps.

Khalil took his own shield from Évrard and turned to Ciarán. "Are you ready?"

"As ready as I'll ever be," Ciarán said with a nod. He followed Khalil to the gangplank, laden with the heavy mail, the suffocating helm, and the awkward shield, which felt like a foreign appendage.

"God be with you, boys," Évrard called out. "Come back in one piece, eh."

Ciarán raised his shield and craned his neck, barely glimpsing Évrard out of the corner of the helmet. "Pray we will."

When they reached the dock, Khalil shot him a stern look. "Listen to me like you never have before. Despite that weapon at your side, you are not a swordsman. You were trained to copy manuscripts, not fight battles. So let me lead, and leave the fighting to me. Focus on your shield and use it to keep yourself alive."

"This is no ordinary sword," Ciarán insisted.

"I know that. But if you light it up like you're wont to do, you'll attract the attention of half the German army. And I'm quite certain the emperor would deem himself a more worthy caretaker for that holy blade than some bastard monk from the edge of the world. Trust me, powerful men are ruthless and never afraid to take what they want. You know as much as I that if we were to lose Enoch's device, all may be lost."

Ciarán had no retort, for Khalil was right. If Enoch's device fell into the wrong hands, all would be lost. And after meeting men like Al-Mansor and William of Aquitaine, Ciarán had no doubt that a lord like them would seize the weapon for himself. "I'll do what you say."

The pair arrived at the Leonine City before Vespers by the same road they had used the day before and entered through the Saxon Gate. The sentries waved them through, much to Ciarán's relief, for neither he nor Khalil knew a lick of the German tongue, and he hoped to avoid the need for any conversation that could ruin their disguise. The day before, Ugo Grassus had assured them he would plan around their lack of fluency, but he also warned them to be careful about speaking Latin. Few of the German foot soldiers could understand it, and it would be unusual to see two Germans speaking it fluently.

A chorus of church bells rang for the holy hour of Vespers, filling the air of the Leonine City with their song. Khalil turned to Ciarán. "It's time to go."

The quaestor had instructed them to meet him in the shadow of the tomb of Romulus, Rome's legendary founder. When Ciarán asked how they were supposed to find this, the quaestor had flashed a fiendish grin. "It is a pyramid, like the ones the pharaohs built eons ago. But smaller, of course." Ciarán and Khalil spotted it after they left the Basilica of Saint Peter, a pyramid of white marble that rose above the terra-cotta rooftops, halfway between the basilica and Castel Sant'Angelo.

They had little trouble finding it again, for the pyramid loomed over the buildings surrounding it. The setting sun cast a broad shadow to the east, and within its shade stood the hulking quaestor, garbed all in black, a bell-shaped cowl hiding most of his face. Beside him stood a tall, burly man clad in the same dark-gray cloak that Ugo Grassus had procured for Ciarán and Khalil. A rusting coat of mail clung to the man's broad chest, and a broadsword hung in a leather scabbard at his side. Clearly one of the Germans, the man had a harsh face with a long scar down the left side, and a high forehead that gave way to a head of fair, short-cropped hair. He looked at them and snickered.

"Even he doesn't take us for Germans," Ciarán whispered to Khalil.

"No, no," Ugo Grassus said as if he overheard the whisper. "You look like good Germans. Heinric, here, means nothing. He is the one who has ensured you a place in one of the siege towers. He's a Saxon, but he knows the Frankish tongue, so you can talk with him."

"Don't you have something for us?" Khalil reminded the quaestor.

"Ah, yes." Ugo Grassus drew a rolled parchment from a pocket in his robes. Ciarán and Khalil huddled around him as he unfurled the parchment, revealing a crudely drawn map of a cross-section of the castle. He pointed to what looked like the entrance. "This is the gate to the inner castle," he told them. "It's the only way in. Once the emperor's men breach the curtain wall, they will open the main gate and bring in their battering ram. You will want to stay near that so that you can be among the first inside. It might have been easier to have simply found you a place with the team operating that ram, but it belongs to group of pious Germans from Breisgau, and let's just say I did not have the same luck convincing them to take in the two of you that I did with Heinric here, who has a healthier appetite for silver."

The burly German shrugged and smiled.

Ugo Grassus pointed to a series of lines on the map that zigzagged up the structure. "This is a passageway that spirals halfway up the castle, then it leads to a ramp and then a stairwell where the Crescentii keep their chambers." He tapped a thick finger on a series of honeycombed shapes near the top of the castle. "That is where the Germans will head, but not you. No, you need to go here." He traced a finger up the ramp to a hollow shape in the dead center of the castle. "There you will find two doors, and Heinric can help you batter them down. Past the second door, the ramp spans a barrel-vaulted chamber; there are stairs that can take you to the chamber's floor. The Germans will head up the ramp, but you will duck onto those stairs and descend into the chamber, the place where Emperor Hadrian's ashes were kept. It is no longer a tomb, but a treasury, and if what you seek has value, you should go there. It is also the last place the Germans will go at first, for they want Crescentius, and he most certainly will make his stand in the upper floors."

Ciarán drew in a deep breath as the quaestor handed him the map. The thought of storming Castel Sant'Angelo was becoming all too real.

Ugo Grassus gestured toward the German. "Heinric will take you from here."

"Come," Heinric said in a surly tone. He led them down a series of alleyways that stank of piss and dung, eventually emerging onto a field between the city and the castle. Scores of tents stood across the field, interspersed with campfires and racks of spears and shields. Mail-clad warriors milled about the encampment, where colorful banners hung before clusters of tents, each standard bearing the heraldry of a lord in the emperor's service. Some bore beasts like lions, hawks, and stallions, while others had diamonds or stripes of crimson, gold, or blue, and beyond this array of colors loomed the siege towers. Three of the monstrous timber structures stood directly beyond the camp, while the tops of several more could be seen peeking over the castle's curtain wall. The towers stood three stories tall, and the only thing more imposing was the castle itself.

Surmounted with battlements, the massive curtain wall surrounded Castel Sant'Angelo, and dozens of archers could be seen moving behind its crenellations. Beyond the curtain wall rose the colossal circular tower, more than a hundred and fifty feet high and two hundred feet broad. Ciarán had never seen anything so fore-boding and seemingly dense, for it looked as if giants had chiseled the citadel out of solid stone. Crenelated ramparts ringed the top of the tower, and over them flew a banner as large as a curach's sail. A giant marble horse adorned the flag, waving defiantly in the breeze.

How can anyone besiege that? Ciarán's stomach churned at the thought.

Heinric's commands were barely more than grunts, but he led them through the camp to an area in front of the center of the three siege towers. Ciarán could now see that the tower had huge wooden wheels attached to timber axles and ladders that climbed three stories where men could wait inside. Great plates of wood covered the tower's sides like a coat of armor, and over them were nailed sheets of water-stained leather.

"Why the skins?" Ciarán asked Heinric.

"Because they burn slower than wood," the German said.

The thought of being trapped inside that tower while it was on fire unnerved Ciarán even more. *Blessed Columcille,* he prayed, *help me be strong.*

"Whose symbol is that?" asked Khalil, looking up at the golden banner that flew atop the siege tower. The banner bore a fierce black lion with a crimson tongue, the same as on their shields.

"The black lion of Meissen," Heinric replied. "We serve Margrave Eckard. Now fall in with these men." He gestured toward threescore of men all wearing the same dark cloaks who were assembling in front of the siege tower. To both sides, similar groups of warriors, some with brown cloaks and others dark blue, gathered in front of the other two towers. Behind that, ranks of archers formed, as well as teams of men who clustered around four siege weapons similar to the catapult Duke William had at Brosse. "Mangonels," Heinric muttered. "The Lombards will use them to help clear the ramparts of the prefect's men."

A line of horsemen cantered behind the ranks of bowmen, each rider bearing a spear and a shield painted with a white horse. "Who are they?" Ciarán asked.

"Tuscans," Heinric said, "but they are just for show. Horses are useless in a siege until we open the main gate." To the left of the Tuscans, a company of rugged-looking spearmen bearing red shields adorned with silver wheels assembled behind a silvery-cloaked rider wearing a bishop's miter. A thick white beard flowed from the rider's age-worn face. "Archbishop Willigis of Mainz," Heinric said, as if anticipating the question.

"He fights?" Ciarán asked.

"He does," Heinric said bluntly.

Soon, the ranks of bowmen and warriors numbered in the thousands. Khalil scratched the chin of his beard. "Are we attacking soon?"

Heinric shook his head. "We assemble like this three or four times a day. The margrave says it's so the Romans get used to it. I am told we will attack after sunset, hoping they are good and drunk behind their walls. But now, all we do is wait."

Captains among the assembled men barked orders to their troops in tongues Ciarán could not understand. Within the ranks, men grumbled to one another, while twilight gave way to the glow of the crescent moon and the glimmer of stars. Around him, some of the Saxons relieved themselves where they stood, adding a scent of urine to the stench of leather, horse hair, and sweat that filled the camp. As time passed, the temperature fell and Ciarán's restlessness grew. His throat felt parched and his stomach empty, though his nerves were no less tense and the weight of the shield and his armor threatened to drag him to the ground. Beside him, Khalil closed his eyes, as if he were asleep while standing. Both men perked up when a chorus of church bells clanged throughout the Leonine City at the holy hour of Compline. *The Night Prayer,* Ciarán thought, *the end of the day.*

Torch-bearing soldiers positioned themselves around each group of the assembled men. In front of Ciarán's group, a warrior rode a black destrier. The horse's muscles rippled under its midnight hide, looking every bit as powerful as the man astride him. Clad in polished mail, the rider was broad shouldered and thick chested, with a rugged face and a full beard flecked with gray. He sat proudly in the saddle with the air of a chieftain.

"Margrave Eckard," Heinric said under his breath.

"Heil Otto, der Römisch-deutscher Kaiser und Herrsher der Welt!" the margrave announced, *"und der vicar Jesu Christi, seine Heiligkeist, Papst Gregory!"*

Around Ciarán and Khalil, every man not on a horse dropped to his knee. "Kneel, you idiots," Heinric growled. Hastily, they knelt, just as three more riders appeared through a broad gap formed by the Tuscan horsemen. Behind them, two more horsemen raised broad banners. The first bore an image of Saint Michael with his flaming sword on a field of gold, while the second was crimson, adorned with a pair of crossed keys, one silver, and one gold. *The emperor and the pope,* Ciarán realized. A chill prickled his flesh.

The emperor rode in the middle on a white charger. Torchlight gleamed off his hauberk and helm, which revealed the clean-shaven face of a man younger than Ciarán. A purple cape draped from his left shoulder, while his right arm raised a lance with a massive iron spearhead edged with glimmering gold. At sight of the lance, many of the Saxons near Ciarán made the sign of the cross.

To the emperor's left rode the pope on a gray stallion. A crimson cloak flowed behind his white cassock and an elaborate, three-tiered crown adorned his head, topped with a gilded cross similar to the larger cross atop his staff. He looked a few years older than Ciarán and as handsome as his imperial cousin—a far cry from the crotchety bishops Ciarán had seen in France. "Who's the third man?" Ciarán asked Heinric, referring to the tonsured rider dressed in a tunic and scapular to the emperor's right.

"The emperor's counselor," Heinric said, "Gerbert of Aurillac."

At the mention of Gerbert's name, Ciarán sucked in a cold breath. Gerbert had been a colleague of Dónall and Ciarán's father at Reims, the first to leave their secret brotherhood. Ciarán still recalled the bitterness in Dónall's voice whenever he mentioned Gerbert of Aurillac, for he was their Judas. The late Pope John had called Gerbert the "Usurper of the See of Reims," but to Ciarán the monk would forever be someone else, someone he never expected to see. Yet now that he had, his Irish blood ran hot. For Gerbert of Aurillac not only had betrayed Dónall and his brethren, but Ciarán's father and mother, too. *And he watched them burn.*

Before he knew it, his hand was wrapped around Caladbolg's hilt.

"What are you doing," Khalil snapped under his breath.

"That man killed my parents."

Khalil's eyes grew wide. "So you'll kill us both?"

Ciarán let go of the hilt and drew a deep breath. *Our cause is greater than this,* he reminded himself. The next thing he knew, the emperor said something in German that brought the men to their feet, bellowing cheers.

The pope urged his horse forward, then addressed the assembled legions in German, raising his cross-tipped staff. He finished his speech in Latin, with a verse from a psalm: "Let our enemies be like chaff before the wind, with the angel of the Lord driving them on. Let their way be dark and slippery, with the angel of the Lord in pursuit.

And let ruin fall upon them unawares.'" The pope thrust up his staff. "For God and for Otto!"

Margrave Eckard raised a fist. *"Für Gott und für Otto!"*

"Für Gott und Otto!" thousands cheered. *"Für Gott und Otto!"*

A half score of archers strode to the tower and began climbing the ladder to the top. "Now we go," Heinric said, urging them forward with half the Saxons. Ciarán looked up. The upper platform was as high as the battlements atop the curtain wall. He watched Heinric go first, his shield slung over his back as he climbed the ladder. Khalil followed him, as did another Saxon. When it was his turn, Ciarán gripped the ladder, his insides quivering as he climbed each rung. When he reached the platform, he found it no more than a cramped timber box where Heinric and Khalil waited. Fifteen more Saxons ascended the ladder. They were packed inside the enclosed structure, man against man, facing a heavy wooden gangplank closed and secured by hemp ropes. "When it opens," Heinric said, "we fight."

As they waited for men to fill the tower's lower platforms, Ciarán tried to calm his nerves, reminding himself this was the third time in his life he had readied for battle. The first time, he had hardly had a moment to think when he and his Irish brothers ambushed Bishop Adémar and his Franks outside the woods of Derry. The Franks had not anticipated the attack, and still it turned into a slaughter. The second was within the hall of Rosefleur. An army of Franks and Nephilim waited outside the gate, but Ciarán and Alais had a vanguard of Orionde and her sisters on barded chargers to clear the way. This time, Ciarán did not know what to expect, but he could sense the fear in the men around him.

Beside Ciarán, a gangly Saxon with a gaunt face and weak chin began to sweat. Ciarán could tell the man was muttering prayers, for he kept saying the word *"Gott"* under his breath. When the tower suddenly lurched forward, the gaunt-faced Saxon began to fidget, his prayers coming faster.

The tower rumbled over the terrain, shaking and even swaying with each advance. Ciarán's heartbeat quickened. "Who's moving it?" he asked.

"Men who will probably die," Heinric said.

Just then, a drumbeat began. The German war drums beat in rhythm while the siege tower rumbled forward. *Boom! Boom! Boom!*

Beyond the tower's timber armor, a horn sounded from within the castle. *Aaaaooooooooo!* More drums answered its call. An arrow thudded into the tower's side, followed by two more. From the battlement atop the tower came the thrum of bowstrings, then a sickening scream from one of the men. Crammed inside the tower, Ciarán heard a hiss, then caught the first whiff of smoke and burning pitch. His heart began to race.

Beside him, the gaunt-faced Saxon started to shake. *"Herr Gott! Herr Gott!"* he repeated as more arrows thudded into the tower and a wisp of smoke snaked through the siding. One man started to cough; others began to fidget. Suddenly, the tower stopped, lurching forward until it slammed hard against something solid, jostling everyone forward. "Shields up!" Heinric yelled.

The gaunt-faced Saxon gagged, then a surge of vomit spilled onto his mail. A smell of urine mixed with the smoke. *Men are pissing themselves,* Ciarán thought, as time stood eerily still. Someone cut the ropes and the gangplank crashed forward. Ciarán crouched behind his shield.

Then to his left came a sickening thud and the warm splatter of blood.

LIGHTNING FROM HEAVEN

Alais was not about to stay on *La Margerie* and pray for their safe return.

Prayers had done nothing when her husband Geoffrey lay dying in his sickbed, nor had they helped when her cousin William sought to marry her off to one of his bannermen just weeks after she became a widow. Back then, only her defiance of William had changed her fate, so she refused to let Évrard and Josua talk her out of it when she demanded they get the rowboat from the cog's hull and take her upriver.

The rowboat sat low in the water, and Alais could smell the water as the glow of the crescent moon danced off the surface of the Tiber. She had traded her slate-colored overdress for the coat of silver mail given to her by the sisters of Orionde. The scales on the close-fitting mail looked like swan feathers forged of some otherworldly steel, bound together by tiny silver rings. The whole coat was no heavier than a woolen smock, and the armor made her feel more secure, even though she planned to stay a safe distance from the battle.

Josua and Évrard rowed the boat through an archway of one of the stone bridges and past a small island where candlelight glowed from the windows of a basilica. In short time, they reached the gap in the Aurelian Walls, flanked by two towers that housed the great chain that could be raised to seal off access from the river. As they passed the towers, they heard the drums, pounding to a steady beat. Alais drew in a breath. *The battle's begun.* Her stomach quivered with each booming beat.

A war horn sounded in the distance as the walls curved to the west and the Leonine City came into the view. Skiffs and rowboats filled the river, along with a few coracles with masts and furled sails, all facing in the direction of Castel Sant'Angelo.

Évrard glanced at Alais. "Milady, you weren't the only one with this idea."

"Get closer," she told him.

They maneuvered around the skiffs and coracles as the castle came into clearer view and the screams of men echoed in the night, mixed with the clamor of battle. Motes of fire streaked from the wall into the massive siege towers that surrounded the fortification, and Alais' eyes grew wide when she realized the tower nearest the river had become an inferno. On the walls, men pushed the tower away with poles, and the whole structure bent backward. Meanwhile, mangonels hurled flaming bales onto the ramparts of the curtain wall, and smoke billowed from within, marring the huge banner that flew from the inner citadel.

With a loud crack, the nearest siege tower collapsed, blasting a shower of sparks into the sky. Alais gasped. *What if they are in that tower . . .* She clutched her hands together and uttered a prayer to Saint Radegonde, the patron saint of Poitiers. *Please let them survive.*

Perhaps prayers were all she had left. And she hoped desperately that, for once, they would be answered.

CIARÁN GLANCED LEFT. THE GAUNT-FACED SAXON FELL BACKWARD, AN arrow protruding from his mouth. An instant later, another arrow slammed into Ciarán's shield. The arrow's tip pierced the willow boards, biting into his mailed sleeve. He found it difficult to breathe as all the pent-up apprehension flooded forth like a tidal wave.

The Saxons surged down the gangplank and their battle cry drowned out the thrum of bowstrings. Ciarán's only choice was to charge with the mass of warriors until wood and steel met in a horrific crash. A sword hammered on Ciarán's shield, and he feared the willow boards would split in two. Through the eyeholes of his helm, he saw Khalil's blade flash. A man screamed, and dead weight fell against Ciarán's shield. He stepped right as the body of one of the castle's defenders fell forward, a bloody gash across his neck.

A mailed warrior took the dead man's place, his blade aimed at Ciarán's head. Ciarán raised his shield just as the steel blade crashed against the willow boards. His heart threatened to pound from his chest, while all around him men yelled and screamed. Khalil lunged in front of Ciarán, his curved blade striking cat-quick into the warrior's side. Ciarán's attacker gasped and collapsed. Ciarán gripped Caladbolg's hilt and slid the sword from its sheath.

"Use your shield!" Khalil yelled as another Roman lunged from his left, hefting a double-bladed ax with both hands. Khalil ducked and caught the ax blade with his shield, then swept his scimitar across his attacker's unarmored thigh. The Roman howled in pain and stumbled forward, just as Khalil's second cut slashed through the flesh between the man's helmet and the collar of his mail.

Smoke billowed from the burning siege towers and blotted out the moon, while atop the curtain wall the air was filled with blood and steel and death. To Ciarán's left, Heinric and the other Saxons traded sword blows with the half-dozen Romans who secured a narrow portion of the curtain wall. Khalil struck at a Roman to their right, but his scimitar glanced off the defender's shield. The Roman lunged with his sword, but Khalil whirled to his left. With a backhanded strike, he sliced his scimitar through the back of the man's neck, followed by a hard kick that sent the man hurtling over the parapet.

To the right of the gangplank, the battlement was free of Romans, though the walkway was narrower than Ciarán would have imagined, barely room enough for two men to move side by side. Thirty paces ahead, another group of Romans engaged the landing party from another siege tower. But the tower was ablaze, and Germans were dying in its flames.

"We won't get past them!" Ciarán cried to Khalil. "Even with your blade."

Khalil glanced the other way, and Ciarán's gaze followed. Heinric and the surviving Saxons hammered sword blows on their attackers, making quick work of the remaining Roman defenders. With a vicious strike, Heinric cut down his much shorter Roman opponent. He waved for Ciarán and Khalil to follow him, but then his head jerked back. An arrow pierced his neck. Heinric clawed at the shaft, then staggered and slumped against the stone parapet.

Ciarán glanced up. "Holy Mother," he muttered, for more than a hundred feet above the curtain wall, archers ringed the battlements atop the inner citadel of Castel Sant'Angelo, picking the attackers off the wall.

"We'll be like fish in a barrel!" Khalil glanced into the courtyard below. "Follow me," he said as he leaped over the side of the parapet.

Ciarán's eyes flew wide until he realized Khalil had landed on the thatched roof of one of the timber structures that filled the castle's narrow courtyard. Next to it, a stable blazed with flames, a victim of one of the flaming hay bales flung from the mangonels to help clear the walls.

"Hurry!" Khalil urged.

An arrow whizzed past Ciarán's ear and clattered onto the stone rampart, providing all the motivation he needed. Sucking in a breath, he leaped.

The thatch broke most of the fall, but pain still shot up his back and shoulder as he collided with the heavy timbers supporting the roof. Khalil shuffled to the roof's edge and dropped to the ground. Ciarán followed and landed feetfirst on the ancient flagstones. Smoke from the burning stable choked the air, but the fire's hellish glow illuminated the area around them. They stood in a cramped alleyway between the curtain wall and the ancient stone siding of the inner citadel. Where the citadel curved, the courtyard widened and a mail-clad Roman looked on in surprise.

He hesitated a moment, then leveled his sword. "Germans!" he shouted in Vulgar Latin. Three more Romans rushed around the corner, swords drawn and oval-shaped shields at the ready, each bearing the marble horse of Crescentius.

"You can't take all four of them," Ciarán told Khalil.

"No, this time I'll need your help."

Ciarán tried to steady his nerves. Shedding blood was forbidden for monks, but Ciarán had already broken that vow in pursuit of the prophecy, and these Romans stood between him and the path to the Key. He gripped Caladbolg's leather hilt and raised the gleaming blade, summoning a cry from his lungs. *"Columcille!"*

The Romans charged, but Khalil moved like the wind, slicing an attacker through the thigh, and slamming the boss of his shield into the face of another. Ciarán parried a sword blow with his own shield, his teeth shuddering at the impact, and struck back with Caladbolg. The blade scythed through the leather covering of the Roman's shield and splintered the willow boards, nearly cleaving the shield in two. The Roman drew back, grimacing, but in a breath another attack came from Ciarán's right. He could not block it with his shield, so he met the sword blow with Caladbolg's blade. Steel clashed, but Calad-bolg continued in the path of its strike, severing the Roman's sword in two. The Roman staggered backward, the stub of the broken blade jutting from the hilt in his hand. Ciarán glanced at Khalil, who stood over the body of his second attacker. In front of Ciarán, the Roman tossed aside his broken sword and fled down the alleyway. The man whose shield Ciarán had destroyed scurried after him, and the two men disappeared in the smoke billowing from the burning stable.

"Not bad," Khalil said.

"Not as good as you," Ciarán replied, huffing for breath.

Khalil shrugged. "Let's make for the gate."

They hugged the curve of the citadel. They stood directly beneath the citadel's battlements, towering more than a hundred and sixty feet above them, and against the citadel's side, they were safe from the

Roman archers targeting the Germans on the curtain wall. Across the cramped courtyard stood the gatehouse in the curtain walls, and around it were warriors whose shields bore a red hawk on a golden field.

"The men from Breisgau!" Ciarán exclaimed.

The Germans assembled in a crescent around the gatehouse, holding up their arrow-ridden shields and forming a wall to defend the men working on the gates. A moment later, Ciarán and Khalil watched as the wall of Germans parted, and through their ranks rumbled a new siege engine on great oak wheels. Its pitched roof scraped the top of the archway, and beneath the roof protruded the trunk of a felled tree, rocking back and forth. The front of the tree trunk was painted red and carved into the crude image of a hawk's head.

"The battering ram," Khalil observed. "The quaestor told us to stay with it."

"How will we be protected?" All Ciarán could see beneath the edge of the roof were the boots of the men pushing the ram. "There's no room under there."

Khalil's eyes narrowed. "We'll stay along the citadel's wall and flank its gate No one should mind two of the margrave's men standing by to watch."

"Right."

They shuffled along the wall as a hail of burning arrows rained down on the battering ram. The shafts thudded into the ram's pitched roof, which, like the towers, had been covered in soaked leather. Smoke hissed from the rooftop, filling the air with the stench of burning pitch.

Ciarán and Khalil made their way to the edge of the archway that housed the citadel's gates. Bronze plates covered the iron-bound gates, encasing them in armor. As the battering ram neared the gate, a blunt-faced German closest to the front yelled something at Ciarán and Khalil, which they could not hear amid the rumbling of the ram and the hammering of arrows against its skin-covered roof. The blunt-faced German gestured for them to move back, which they did several paces. Then the Germans gave a deafening battle cry and the hawk-shaped ram surged forward.

The ram struck the gate like thunder.

The Germans grunted fiercely as they drew back the ram for a second strike. Ciarán's pulse quickened, knowing that with a few more blows, the gate would give way. All they would have to do then was rush inside, find the treasury, and pray the demon was right.

From the highest ramparts atop Castel Sant'Angelo, Naberus da Roma surveyed the siege. Clad in his armor, Crescentius watched grimly by his side as a score of archers strummed their bowstrings. Around them, the reek of pitch and burned timber filled the air and smoke smothered the night sky, nearly swallowing the massive banner of the marble horse that flew atop the citadel.

On the curtain wall below, Crescentius's men had succeeded in felling one of the siege towers, but the Germans had brought seven. Three more of the timber structures billowed black smoke, but whether they would burn completely no longer mattered, for hundreds of Germans and Saxons had spilled from those towers onto the walls and overwhelmed the defenders. The dead littered the ramparts, both Romans and Germans, and while the archers atop the citadel were picking Germans off the walls, most of the besiegers had formed small shield walls, so now the arrows were striking shields instead of flesh. Even worse, the Germans had captured the gatehouse and sent in their battering ram with a head carved like the red hawk of Breisgau. The archers had showered the ram with arrows, but its pitched roof was covered in wet hides, so the arrow shafts burned faster than the siege engine.

His jaw set, Crescentius stared at the battle below. "We will make our stand at the doorway to the urn room. It's narrow enough to defend. Their numbers will not count for so much."

"Not yet," Naberus said. "Petrus and his guards still hold the citadel's gate. The ram has not won. And there's still time to make it go away."

"*Away!*" screeched Hermes atop the parapet.

Naberus hefted the amphora that had rested against the battlement and turned to one of the archers. The barrel-chested Roman had just dipped an arrow dripping with pitch into one of the iron braziers that were spaced along the battlement. "I've need of your flame," Naberus told the archer. The man eyed the amphora warily, but touched his flaming arrow to the amphora's rope fuse. The hemp sizzled, then sparked.

Both the archer and Crescentius stepped back. "Pray it works," Crescentius said.

"Oh, it shall." Naberus raised the amphora above his head and bellowed to the besiegers below. "Your God cannot save you now!"

He hurled the weapon over the battlement. Its fuse spitting flames, the clay vessel plummeted more than one hundred and fifty feet. Naberus held his breath. The amphora struck the battering ram with a sound like a thunderclap and a burst of searing light. Fire followed, billowing outward like the ripples on a lake, blasting shards of timber in every direction. A wave of heat rushed up the castle's wall, bathing Naberus's face. Hermes leaped from the parapet, frantically beating his wings.

Crescentius and Naberus leaned over the battlement and tried to peer through the smoke choking the courtyard. What remained of the battering ram was a raging inferno. Around it, men writhed and screamed as the Greek fire clung to armor and flesh. The blast had even shattered the shield wall guarding the outer gate. Splattered with Greek fire, the attackers and their shields now burned in flames, sending a stench of scorched wood and flesh wafting up the citadel.

The Roman archers looked down at the carnage in awe, while a hearty color returned to Crescentius's face.

"By God, Naberus," Crescentius said with a rare look of joy. "I think you've killed them all."

14

HADRIAN'S TOMB

From above, Ciarán thought he heard the word "God."

He looked up in time to see something falling from the ramparts. *On fire!* Desperately, he grabbed Khalil by his cloak and dove to the ground. He landed on the flagstones just as the air around him exploded. The sound filled Ciarán's ears and pierced his skull, then all around the air became heat and light. A wave of fire rushed overhead as hunks of timber slammed into the citadel's wall and clattered around him. Heat covered his back, and he caught a whiff of burning wool. *My cloak's aflame!* He tore at the simple brooch until it came loose and ripped the burning cloak from his body. Scrambling away, he discovered the battering ram was nothing but a heap of timber engulfed in roaring flames. Men lay in its wreckage, blackened and screaming, though closer to Ciarán, another moaned in pain.

He craned his neck. *Khalil!*

The Persian writhed on the ground while flames licked his cloak and a liquid, burning as bright as a brazier, splattered his right arm. Ciarán clambered forward and threw his own body on the flames, praying his mail would smother the fire. He winced at the searing heat.

"It burns!" Khalil hissed through clenched teeth.

"Fight it!" Ciarán urged. He rolled off Khalil. The flames were gone but his arm was black; smoldering flesh shone from the remains of his sleeve. Khalil clutched his injured limb against his chest.

The flames on the siege engine raged like a Beltane fire, and Ciarán could not see beyond the veil of billowing smoke to determine the fate of the rest of the Germans in the courtyard. *This is lost,* he thought, until he glanced back at the citadel's gates. The bronze plates covering the gates saved it from the fire, but the gates were cracked. Whether the battering ram or the explosion was the cause, Ciarán did not know, yet through the crack he could glimpse the heavy oak bar that sealed the gates, just a head higher than his own. The wood on the bar had started to splinter.

That's the only thing keeping us from the citadel. Ciarán rose to his feet and slid Caladbolg from its scabbard. "To hell with the emperor!" He put the sword's pommel to his lips, summoned his will, and whispered into its gemstone. *"Eoh."* White fire flared within the jewel and surged up the blade. Power pulsed through Ciarán's limbs until the ghostly flames surrounding the steel burst into a halo of light.

Gripping the hilt with both hands, Ciarán roared as he swung the blade into the gap between the gates. Caladbolg cleaved deep into the timber. He wrestled it free and hacked again. More wood splintered, and a crackling white fire spilled into the gash. He hammered the searing oak until the bar cracked and Caladbolg's blade passed clean through. "We're in!" he cried to Khalil, who had abandoned his shield and risen to his feet, grimacing in pain.

With a grunt, Ciarán pushed open the bronzed gates. Hinges creaked as it revealed a barrel-vaulted chamber with a towering alcove in the far wall where a statue of the emperor once stood. But now, torches lined the chamber's walls and the alcove was filled with men. The score of mail-clad Romans stood in close ranks with oval shields and spears. Yet bathed in Caladbolg's light, their faces bore looks of utter fear. Ciarán raised his sword, bellowing a battle cry. *"Columcille!"* The sword's light flared with blinding fury. A few of the Romans dropped their weapons and made the sign of the cross, while others cried out, shielding their eyes. Then, as if seized by a collective terror, the Romans broke ranks and fled through an archway right of the alcove, their boots pounding the flagstones.

Through his painful grimace, a hint of a smile emerged on Khalil's face. "You're right. That's no ordinary sword."

"Aye," Ciarán said. "Now let's find what we came for."

Khalil clutched his ravaged sword arm. "I'll be no use in a fight."

We'll need to treat that soon or he'll lose his arm, Ciarán realized. "Dónall taught me a bit about healing back at Derry. I swear I'll get you well."

Khalil gave him a weary nod before they entered the archway through which the Romans had fled. It was the chamber's only exit and it led to a vaulted tunnel that curved to the left. More torches lit the passageway, which was a curved ramp wide enough for a pair of horses to ride through.

"It's the ramp on the quaestor's map," Khalil observed through pained breaths.

"Right," Ciarán replied.

As they walked up the ramp, searching for any sign of the Romans, Caladbolg's light began to fade. *I have to keep focus to keep the blade aglow,* Ciarán realized, but he was already feeling fatigued. He sheathed the sword and helped Khalil ascend the spiraling passageway. The fleeing Romans were nowhere to be seen, but their distant footfalls still echoed down the tunnel until the slamming of a door cut off the sound.

The torchlit passageway wound its way up the citadel. After what seemed like a full turn, Ciarán spotted the first door, made of stained oak in a two-foot-thick frame. An iron-bound window opened above the door, in the shadows of the vaulted ceiling.

"There's no Heinric to break it down," Khalil said. "So much for the quaestor's plan."

Ciarán thought of the German slumped against the parapet with an arrow through his neck. With Khalil injured, Ciarán was on his own. "Caladbolg just severed the bar on the main gate," Ciarán replied. "I can't see this door standing in its way." He pulled Caladbolg

112

from its scabbard. Focusing his will, he blew gently on its pommel, uttering the Fae word that filled the embedded gemstone with his soul's light. He tried to control the white fire with his thoughts, willing it to dance subtly up the blade. Then he cocked his arm and hammered the sword into the door. The blade sliced through the oak until it hit a wooden bar on the other side. He gave a second strike, and then a third. White fire filled the breach as the sword smashed through the barrier.

Khalil looked on in awe, while Ciarán caught his breath. He pushed the door open, finding it led to another vaulted chamber with a landing illuminated by a lantern hanging from the ceiling. The landing gave way to a ramplike series of shallow stairs that climbed farther up the castle to a pair of iron-bound doors.

"The second doors," Ciarán said. "We're almost there."

They climbed the stairs to the doors. A quick push proved that these too had been barred from the other side. Ciarán grasped Caladbolg with both hands and aimed for the gap between the doors. Fire flared as the blade struck. In three hacks, the doors fell open. Ciarán's anticipation welled, for according to the quaestor, the object of their quest lay just beyond the portal.

He pushed the doors open only to find that the ramplike stairs climbed through a vaulted chamber to another pair of doors. But to each side of the ramp, the chamber plunged ten feet to a room below, where a horde of barrels and casks were visible amid the shadows. To Ciarán's right, another flight of wooden stairs descended to the chamber's depths.

"This looks like a cellar, not a treasury," Khalil said. "The quaestor lied."

Ciarán's spirits sank. Khalil was right, for he could smell the scent of wine and ale mixing with the oak of the barrels. He ran a weary hand across his face. *If only Dónall was here, he'd know what to do . . .*

Ciarán closed his eyes. He remembered the first time Dónall had taught him to summon his soul light, back in the old Roman amphitheater of Poitiers. The light had revealed things unseen to the naked eye, just as Orionde's own light had exposed the demons that invaded Rosefleur. He drew a long breath and prayed it would work as he focused his vision through the glow emanating from Caladbolg's blade.

"What are you doing?" Khalil asked as Ciarán started down the wooden steps.

He ignored the question, trying to maintain his concentration. Through the halo of light, he saw only barrels and motes of dust wafting through the air. Between the barrels and the shadows he had hoped to find the object Saint Beatus had depicted in his writing: a black iron key as long as a man is tall and crooked like a dog's hind leg. Yet there was nothing like that to be found. A bead of sweat ran down his forehead. His hope began to fail, but then he glimpsed something in an alcove in the far wall. The alcove contained a pair of chests, and beneath the lid of one shimmered a faint blue light, flickering like Saint Elmo's fire. Ciarán had seen such light before, and he knew what it meant. *Power, emanating from the magic of an age long past.* "I may have found something," he told Khalil.

The Persian made his way around the barrels to the alcove. "Why would anyone keep something of value in a storeroom?"

"I don't know," Ciarán replied, "but something of power is inside that chest. I can see its glow."

With one clean swipe, Ciarán struck through the chest's padlock. He opened the lid with the tip of his blade. The scent of old parchment and vellum wafted from the chest, which appeared to be filled with parchments, some rolled and sealed with wax, while others were stacked loose sheets. Ciarán picked one up and read it in the light of Caladbolg's blade.

"What is it?" Khalil asked.

"A pledge of sorts involving a debt to one Naberus da Roma."

"He's the one the quaestor mentioned, Crescentius' counselor."

Ciarán shook his head "It can't be. The document's dated 896. That's a hundred years ago."

"Perhaps he had an ancestor of the same name," Khalil said. "How are we going to search all of these for a map? Half the German army will be here soon."

"This can't be right." Ciarán ripped a handful of parchment from the chest and scattered the skins across the alcove. Half buried beneath the remaining parchment was a leather object—a tome—and in Caladbolg's glow, a faint blue light shimmered along the edges of its cover. Ciarán sucked in a breath and pulled the tome free.

The tome's cover was the most opulent he had ever seen. A gilded border studded with glittering jewels framed a dark leather surface into which an elaborate set of symbols had been pressed, each of a different metal or stone, joined to the border with metal cross-strips. The first symbol was a silver ring studded with eight red garnets surrounding a thicker ring with twelve symbols etched into gold. These two rings encircled a disk of black onyx inlaid with silver in the shape of an all-too-familiar image of a septagram, a seven-pointed star. And overlaying the septagram was a final, raised symbol, forged of copper and white gold, which dominated the cover—that of a serpentine dragon coiled around the shaft of an ornate key.

Khalil al-Pârsâ stared wide-eyed at the tome. "I'll be damned, you were right."

ATOP THE CITADEL'S HIGHEST TERRACE, NABERUS CALLED FOR TWO MEN to roll a cauldron of boiling oil to the parapet, while scores of archers strummed their bowstrings and the stench of burning pitch filled the air. Beside him, Crescentius gripped the parapet with both hands, his black cloak draped behind his polished mail as he stared grimly at the carnage below. He slid over as the cauldron arrived on a wheeled frame that two of the men-at-arms positioned over the gateway. From what Naberus could observe through the smoke billowing from the courtyard below, not a German stirred from the wreckage of the battering ram. But when the next wave of attackers approached the gate, a shower of boiling oil would await them.

"My lord!" a voice called from behind. "They've breached the gate!"

Both men turned to see Petrus, huffing for breath, his face ashen.

"Impossible," Crescentius said. "The ram was destroyed."

"I swear it," Petrus replied.

Naberus glanced down. All he saw was the burning wreckage of the siege engine and clusters of Germans near the gatehouse hiding behind arrow-ridden shields. "How?"

"They cleaved straight through the bar," Petrus said, "with a weapon that blazed like fire."

"What in the bloody hells . . ." Naberus peered back down into the courtyard. A score of Germans now inched toward the citadel's gate, before six of them bolted toward the gateway. A triumphant roar erupted from the courtyard.

Crescentius's face flushed red. "Pour the oil!"

Petrus is right, Naberus realized, while two men-at-arms cranked the wheel that tipped the cauldron. Its smoking contents flooded over the parapet, but Naberus didn't even bother to watch the oil land. *If the gate is open, nothing will keep the Germans from storming the castle, no matter how many we kill with arrows or oil. The plan must change . . .*

Naberus whistled for his three mastiffs, who had been scurrying about the terrace, adding their barks to the cacophony of battle. "Anubis, Set, Grimm—to me!"

"Me! Me!" Hermes cawed from the battlement.

The mastiffs darted to their master, just as a frantic Theodora ran onto the terrace. Her platinum hair flowed behind her shoulders; her face looked beautiful even in distress. "What's happening?"

"The enemy's breached the gate," Naberus told her. "Lock yourself in your chambers."

She glanced between him and Crescentius, her jaw slack. "Where are you going?"

"They'll spare your head," Naberus said, "but they'll most certainly take mine. I'm leaving to die another day."

She gasped as he strode past her, his mastiffs padding beside him. "You can't." Fear welled her eyes. "We can fight them."

"But not win," Naberus snapped.

"Naberus, stop!" Crescentius bellowed. "I command it!"

This had been expected. Naberus turned and met Crescentius's gaze. "All my life I've only listened to one man's commands. My own."

Crescentius's eyes flashed wide. "Petrus, seize him!"

Petrus stepped forward, only to meet the bared teeth of three Neapolitan mastiffs. Anubis growled, Grimm and Set started barking fiercely. What color remained drained from Petrus's face.

A sword slid from its scabbard. Naberus spun as one of the Praetorian guardsmen raised the blade, but Naberus struck fast. He caught the man's sword arm in his long-fingered grasp; then, with a surge of rage, twisted the arm until the bone snapped. As the man cried out in pain, another guardsman lunged, but so did Grimm. The mastiff barreled into the man and ripped his teeth clean through the man's neck.

Theodora watched in horror.

Naberus gave the countess one last glance before retrieving the dying man's sword. Without another word, he turned his back on Crescentius and the rest of his stunned guardsmen and stormed into the citadel.

As he strode down the passageway, Naberus knew what he had to do, for he had contemplated this scenario many times since the siege began. He would hide in the shadows of the urn room while the battle commenced in the upper floors, and then, in the chaos of that fight, he would find his way to the gate.

Even if he had to shed the blood of every man who stepped in his way.

EIGHTY FEET BELOW THE TERRACE, WITHIN THE BARREL-VAULTED chamber that once held the urns with the ashes of Emperor Hadrian and his family, Ciarán stared at the gold and silver hieroglyph on the tome. Khalil and Alais had doubted him, even questioned whether the journey to Rome was the right course of action, but this tome proved him right. Why the demon had revealed this secret no longer mattered. Ciarán had expected a map showing the path to the Key, but somewhere that map must exist within this tome, for there was no other way to interpret the image on the book's cover.

"Open it," Khalil said, still grimacing with the pain of his burned arm.

Ciarán moved to sheathe his blade, but stopped when he realized it was their only light source.

"It's the least I can do." Khalil picked up the tome with his good hand, but winced as Ciarán unlatched the twin silver latches that clasped the book shut. The scent of centuries-old vellum rose from the pages, which contained the most graceful Latin script Ciarán had ever beheld, as if an angel itself had penned the words. Illuminations as beautiful as the mosaics in Saint Peter's framed the pages, their margins adorned with images of Greek or Roman gods and mythological beasts—hydras and harpies, satyrs and Minotaurs, and serpent-haired gorgons that reminded Ciarán of the Furies. The artwork and penmanship were more elaborate and beautiful than anything Ciarán had ever seen in the books Merchant mac Fadden brought over from the continent. *Whoever created this was a true master.*

Ciarán flipped back to the title page. Scrollwork of blue and gold framed the vellum sheet, which contained an elaborately illuminated title:

THE BOOK OF GIANTS

Khalil gave Ciarán a quizzical look.

"I've never heard of it," Ciarán said. "Obscure texts were Brother Remi's specialty."

Khalil glanced back at the wooden stairs that led up to the ramp. "We'll have time to study it later."

Ciarán nodded. With Caladbolg still aglow, he led the way back up to the ramp. Khalil followed, then froze as the bar slid behind the doors atop the ramp. A chill rushed up Ciarán's spine.

The doors cracked opened; a seam of torchlight filled the gap. Three dark shapes emerged next, each as large as a wild boar, followed by a towering figure clad in dark robes. The man held the torch in one hand and a sword in the other. Piercing eyes glared from a stern face framed by dark, pointed beard.

Torchlight gleamed off the tome in Khalil's arms.

"That doesn't belong to you," the intruder said.

As tall and imposing as the intruder looked, Ciarán kept his eyes on the three beasts. *War hounds.* At Derry he had witnessed how deadly such dogs could be, yet these mastiffs did not bark or growl. They just stared at the glow from Caladbolg's blade. The intruder's eyes too were fixed on the sword, and Ciarán sensed he held the advantage. "Stand back," he told the intruder.

"Whoever you are," the intruder said, "you play a dangerous game. There are four of us and two of you. My dogs will tear you limb from limb."

"Your hounds fear this blade, and you should, too." Ciarán focused his will and raised the sword. From its pommel, the gemstone flared and light blazed like a sunburst from its blade.

The mastiffs recoiled with a chorus of whimpers; the intruder shielded his eyes. "Who are you?" he asked, grimacing in the blinding light.

"No one that matters," Ciarán said. "And you'd best leave. There are a hundred Germans heading up this ramp."

The intruder hesitated as if he was trying to peer through the glare and measure his opponents. Then he darted out the doorway, his three mastiffs following.

"Go," Khalil urged.

Ciarán headed through the lower doors and hurried down the stairlike ramp to the second door that opened to the spiral passageway. As they neared the doorway, the drumming of boots echoed up the tunnel. *Here they come,* Ciarán knew. Scores of men by the sound of it.

Khalil glanced at Caladbolg, still dimly aglow in Ciarán's hand. "You should sheathe that. Remember what I told you about the emperor and powerful men."

Ciarán nodded and slid the sword into its scabbard. Down the spiral ramp, men emerged marching four wide, shoulder to shoulder, shield against shield, each bearing the symbol of a red hawk. *The men of Breisgau.* Spearmen manned the front ranks, while swordsmen followed in rows six deep. Their broad-shouldered captain leveled a longsword at Ciarán and Khalil, bellowing at them in German. *"Kapitulation oder sterben!"*

They can't tell if we serve Crescentius or the emperor, Ciarán suddenly realized, for he and Khalil had cast away the shields that marked them as Saxons.

The captain's face reddened. *"Kapitulation oder sterben!"* He raised his sword, and in five paces he would be close enough to use it.

Ciarán summoned the only German words he could think of. *"Für Gott und Otto!"*

Beside him, Khalil muttered the same phrase. *"Für Gott und Otto!"*

The captain stomped a boot, then berated them in German, gesturing for them to fall behind his men.

Ciarán nodded sheepishly and made his way along the wall, where the outer ranks of Germans let him pass. *"Für Gott und Otto,"* he said politely, but a thick-bearded warrior just glared at him.

"Hund stinkit idiot," the warrior said as they slunk past.

Ciarán breathed a relieved sigh when they were behind the Germans, who continued their march. From the spiral ramp came the sound of more men, but behind the German front line, Ciarán felt certain no one would mistake them for Romans.

As they followed down the curved ramp, a roar erupted behind them. Fierce barking mixed with the cries of men. *"Krieg-hunde! Krieg-hunde!"*

Khalil's gaze darted between the sound and Ciarán. *"Hunde,"* Ciarán said. "Hounds—run!"

They bolted down the ramp only to run into another formation of Germans, all bearing kite-shaped shields with the black lion of Meissen. The margrave himself led the men, his mustard cloak flowing behind his polished hauberk. *"Was ist es?"* the margrave shouted.

Ciarán repeated the German's cries. *"Krieg-hunde!"*

The margrave stopped in his tracks, as several Germans cocked their heads and lowered their shields. Ciarán pushed past the first man in his way. Barks and growls echoed down the passageway, and the cries of startled Germans rose to meet them. Behind him, the ranks surged backward as the first mastiff charged into their front line. An alarmed warrior nearly knocked Ciarán to the ground, but in a heartbeat he was free of the formation and tearing down the ramp.

"The dogs broke the ranks!" Khalil cried.

Ciarán craned his neck, only to see half the formation fall into chaos as a second black beast, snarling like a hellhound, fought its way through.

"Move!" Khalil shouted.

Ciarán wanted to glance back, but knew it would only slow them down. Ahead, a score of warriors stormed up the ramp. A heavyset German with a straw-colored beard called up to them. *"Was passiert?"*

"Krieg-hunde!" Ciarán cried as he rushed past the man, praying that the sheer number of invaders might slow the dogs down.

"The gate's just ahead!" Khalil yelled.

They bolted into the vestibule, where dozens of warriors were assembling under the command of their lords, turning heads as they sprinted by. As Ciarán crossed through the open gateway, a cacophony of barks exploded from the chamber. In the courtyard ahead, the smoldering wreckage of the battering ram cast off a haze of smoke. Ciarán darted through the smoky veil and headed for the open gateway in the curtain wall. He glanced to make sure Khalil was by his side, then sprinted through the gateway as startled cries erupted from the courtyard.

Ahead, an impassable wall of horsemen and spearmen clogged the Aelian Bridge. Ciarán glanced right, where the riverbank descended to the Tiber. Dozens of boats and skiffs crowded the black waters.

"They're coming!" Khalil cried. Ciarán turned his head as one of the mastiffs hurtled into the gateway. Blood soaked its fur in places, but spittle flew from its jaws.

From the banks someone started yelling. "Over here!"

Ciarán peered ahead, his heart racing. A lantern flashed from a rowboat. He recognized Évrard at once. Alais and Josua were with him, calling his name. Ciarán plunged into the river. Khalil splashed beside him, holding the tome high with his good hand to keep it from getting wet. They moved as fast as they could through the deepening river until they waded waist deep. Josua pulled Ciarán into the boat, while Alais reached out to Khalil. "Take this," he said, handing her the tome.

"Thank God," Alais said once she and Josua pulled Khalil on board. She kissed Khalil's forehead and then Ciarán's. "You foolish men, thank God."

Safe on the boat, Ciarán closed his eyes and drank in the night air. *Thank God, indeed.*

CRESCENTIUS TYRANNUS

Theodora slammed the door to her chambers and turned the key. Through the thick oak came the pounding of boots and the cries of soldiers. She pulled a cloak off a peg on the wall, wrapped it about her, and shuddered. *This can't be happening.*

She stood alone in her chamber, aglow in the light of beeswax candles lit before the siege began. Moments before, on the citadel's terrace, Crescentius had given her one last look that betrayed his thoughts. She had never seen her lover like this. Though fierce and strong, he looked alarmed and stunned by Naberus's betrayal. The consigliere had murdered one of Crescentius's Praetorians and fled before the fight even began. She clutched the cloak's wool in her fists. *He should die for his betrayal!*

Outside the door, the din of battle roared like a thunderstorm. She scrambled for a chest at the foot of her canopied bed, opened the lid, and drew forth a dagger. Her heart pounded in her chest. *The dagger would sting at first, but then . . .*

She brought the dagger to her wrist, then hesitated. The roar of battle was fading. *Might Crescentius have won?* The answer came with the sound of a fist pounding so hard the door quaked in its frame.

She clambered to the corner of the room. The next blow on the door was not from a fist, but an ax. Wood splintered with each hack.

Her hand shook as she returned the dagger close to her wrist. Then terror flashed to rage. She cared not what the blade would do to her flesh, only how she would drive it into the heart of the first German through that door.

With a final hack, the door exploded inward. The man who stood in its threshold wore a coat of bloodstained mail, with a thick russet beard splattered with gore. His eyes widened at the sight of her, then settled into a lecherous gaze. He stepped into the chamber, with the ax in his left hand and a longsword hanging at his side. A taller German followed him, an eager grin spreading across his boyish face.

"Get back!" she hissed. "I'm a countess—you'll hang if you lay hands on me!"

The bearded German grunted and let his ax thud onto the flagstones. He began unhooking his belt.

As he fumbled with the buckle, Theodora lunged, knife raised, her eyes fixed on the pale flesh of his neck. But before the dagger struck, the boyish German sprang and grabbed her arm, wrenching it back. His fingernails bit into her wrist as the dagger tumbled from her grasp. The boyish German threw her onto the bed, his eyes burning with lust. With a violent yank, he tore off the skirt of her damask dress.

The bearded German hiked up his mail. His breeches slipped to his knees as a voice boomed behind him.

"*Stopp!*" A gloved hand grabbed the bearded German's shoulder and flung him backward.

Her attacker landed on his arse. The man who stood in his place bellowed orders to the boyish warrior, who backed sheepishly toward the door. The commander, tall and bearded, had the look of a battle-hardened warlord. His torso was broad and muscular, draped in a hauberk of blood-flecked mail with a mustard cloak clasped by a lion-shaped brooch inlaid in jet. He regarded her with ice-blue eyes, but in them she sensed a hint of compassion.

"You are the Countess Theodora?" he asked in Latin as her bearded attacker pulled up his breeches and scurried from her chamber.

She nodded her answer, tasting the salt of a tear on the corner of her mouth. She hated that she shed tears in the face of Rome's invaders, and part of her wanted to spit in the man's face and shower him with Latin curses. Yet he had saved her.

He held out a hand. "I am Margrave Eckard of Meissen, no harm will come to you now."

She did not take his hand, but stood on her own, using her cloak to cover her rent dress. "Does Crescentius live?"

"He does."

Theodora sighed with relief.

"But he will be judged for his crimes," the margrave said.

A feeling of dread smothered any sense of hope. "What of me?" she asked.

"That will be for the emperor to decide. Until then, you will stay here. I'll post guards at your door."

She glared at him. "Men who wish to rape me?"

"No, men loyal to me. Not these Bavarian curs." He glanced down and picked up the ax, followed by her dagger. "I'll send food and drink."

He left and wedged the broken door shut.

As she sat on the bed, she realized she had become a prisoner in her ancestral home. Castel Sant'Angelo was once the abode of the great-grandmother after whom she was named, the Senatrix Theodora, an indomitable woman who ruled Rome in her husband's stead and even took the pope as her lover. When she died, her daughters Marozia and Theodora seized the reins of power, installing popes and deposing others, and even birthing one, John the Eleventh, if the rumors about Marozia and Pope Sergius the Third were to be believed. In all, their descendants included four popes, two counts, one duke, and the men who for nearly a century had been called the Princes of Rome. All her life, Theodora aspired to the greatness of her ancestors. Never in her imagination had she thought she would be at the mercy of these German barbarians.

She faded off to sleep, her mind numb with these thoughts. However long she slept, she did not know, but she woke to a loud knock at the door. Sunlight spilled through the chamber's windows.

The door opened and a blunt-faced German soldier stepped into her chamber. "The emperor summons you."

He allowed her to put on a damask dress embroidered with golden thread and offered her a breakfast of bread and watered wine. When she was finished, she followed her jailer down a passageway. *He's taking me to the terrace.* With each step, her insides quivered. Through the archway at the end of the passage, men filled the terrace, bathed in morning light. Most were lords and warriors dressed in cloaks and mail, though some were priests, and still others were monks in black robes with drawn cowls. An array of banners clapped in the breeze, but one bearing the image of Saint Michael dominated them all.

The men in the back parted for her jailer, and Theodora gasped when she saw what awaited them at the far end of the terrace. Twelve of Crescentius's best men knelt in two rows, their hands bound in chains behind their backs, and at their head knelt Crescentius. Blood-stains marred his white tunic, which was all he wore save his black breeches and leather boots. Like the others, chains bound his hands, but he held his head high in the face of his captors. Otto stood before her lover. The emperor's mail was so polished it seemed clear he took no part in the siege. Yet despite his armor and his golden crown, he looked like a child compared to Crescentius. To the emperor's left stood Margrave Eckard and a half-dozen other barbarian lords, while to his right stood a handsome archbishop and the young Saxon pope. Along the battlements, a murder of crows watched the spectacle, which brought a rush of bile to her throat, for she had no doubt what the crows portended. Her jailer grabbed her in a vise-like grip. "His Majesty and His Holiness want you to see this."

The archbishop stepped forward. Theodora recognized him as Heribert of Cologne, the emperor's chancellor. Heribert unfurled a scroll and cleared his throat in a manner designed to draw attention. When the crowd grew quiet, he read from the scroll in a commanding voice. "With the advice and consent of these noble lords of Italy and

Germany, and that of His Holiness, Pope Gregory, and by the authority of almighty God and that granted by Him to Otto, King of Germany and Italy, Servant of Jesus Christ and His Apostles, Consul of the Roman Senate and People, and Emperor of the World, we find you, Crescentius Tyrannus, guilty of the crimes of treason, perjury, and murder, and of mortal sins against God and men. For these crimes, you are condemned to death."

Theodora fought to hold back tears as a hulking German stepped forward dressed in boiled black leather. The executioner had a chest as wide as a barrel and a face as ugly as an ogre, with an unruly beard and hungry eyes. From a scabbard on his back, he drew a long, double-edged sword.

Theodora gave a faint gasp when Crescentius spoke, his voice still strong and noble.

"Your Holiness," he said, addressing the Saxon pope, "let me repent the wrongs I've committed against you, so I may receive absolution before I enter the next life."

The pope's expression turned to stone. "John Crescentius," he said coldly, "you are anathema to God, unworthy of absolution. Your fate lies in the Lake of Fire, with Judas Iscariot and the other traitors."

Crescentius's voice cracked. "Please—"

"Enough!" the emperor yelled. "This is done!"

The pope nodded to the executioner. Theodora's heart jumped as he raised his sword with both hands. With a roar, the executioner swung his blade. Steel bit into flesh and her lover's head thumped onto the flagstones. Theodora's hands flew to her mouth to stifle a scream and an explosion of nausea. The only thing that kept her standing was the grip of her jailer, who forced her to watch the execution.

A cheer erupted from the crowd. Theodora covered her ears. The executioner had picked up her lover's head and was holding it over the battlements. From below came another cheer, loud and raucous, as if half of Rome had gathered to celebrate this murder.

"Remove this so-called Prince of Rome from my sight," the emperor said.

The roar of the crowd punctuated his words, and Theodora gasped when three Germans lifted her lover's lifeless body. They carried it to the end of the terrace and hurled it over the parapet. This time she could not hold back her screams. From the courtyard below rose a bloodthirsty cheer.

Her jailer stood laughing while tears streamed down her cheeks. Only one man beside her jailer appeared to notice, for across the terrace, Pope Gregory watched her like wolf eying its prey. Not a glimmer of mercy shone in his blue eyes.

Theodora sucked in a breath and blinked away her tears. Her life lay in ruins, yet inside her something began to kindle. The pride and rage of her pure Roman blood. She clenched her jaw and made a silent vow. She would teach them the price of crossing a descendant of Senatrix Theodora.

And she swore that before she drew her last breath, the Saxon pope must die.

～

AT SUNSET, GREGORY AND RUMEUS STOOD ATOP THE VATICAN HILL overlooking Rome, where beyond the Leonine City, Castel Sant'Angelo flew the golden banner of Otto the Third.

More than a hundred Saxons and Lombards surrounded the pope and his archdeacon on the grassy hilltop, where a ring of thirteen gallows loomed like Celtic standing stones. Scores of curious Romans had hiked up the hill to join the men-at-arms and gaze at the spectacle. From the gallows, twelve of Crescentius's so-called Praetorians hung by their necks, and the crows and ravens had already started feasting on their flesh. The corpse on the thirteenth scaffold, however, hung from its bare feet, bloodied and headless.

After Crescentius's body had been thrown down from the citadel's terrace, a mob of Germans and Romans had slung it on a cow skin and pulled it by horseback to the place it now hung, arms dangling from his shoulders, the stump of his neck coated black with dried blood. A crow perched on the crossbeam and picked at Crescentius's big toe, while broad-winged vultures circled above, waiting to dine on whatever the crows left behind.

The corpse's state did not trouble the pope. Before he took the name Gregory, when he was known as Bruno of Carinthia, the great-grandson of Otto Maximus, he had grown accustomed to witnessing the dead and dying. He had accompanied his cousin on campaigns against the Slavs on Germany's eastern frontier and administered last rites to many a dying warrior. While he took no joy in death, he felt a perverse satisfaction at the present condition of the villain who had chased him from Saint Peter's throne. Victory had come swifter than Gregory could have imagined, resolving a years-worth of trouble in a single night of battle. Though John Philagathos, wherever he was hiding, remained a problem. He, and the woman who had screamed when his cousin's men threw Crescentius over the battlements.

"He should not have freed her," Gregory said.

Rumeus let go of the gold crucifix around his neck, which he had been clutching since they arrived at the gallows. "Who, Countess Theodora?"

"Who else? I saw the look in her eyes at the execution. I fear she loved him as more than kin."

"Your cousin found she committed no crime," Rumeus said. "She had been resident in Castel Sant'Angelo since her late husband's death, and one cannot fault the lady for merely being present during your cousin's siege. I even heard that Margrave Eckard saved her from violation at the hands of two Bavarians. She's a victim, not a criminal. Watching her cousin's execution was punishment enough for whatever sins of which she is guilty."

Gregory shook his head. "Rumeus, do not be naïve. She's descended from a line of cunning harlots who for a half-century murdered popes and debauched all of Rome. And if she's followed in their ways, and took Crescentius as her lover, who knows what she's capable of?"

"With all respect, Your Holiness, what would you have done? Imprison her for mere suspicion of incest? Or perhaps execute them all—her and all the living descendants of Senatrix Theodora who might follow the ways of their ancestors? If I may be so bold as to give advice, it might aid your cause with the Romans if you displayed some mercy. Your namesake, Gregory the Great, was beloved in Rome precisely because he was merciful."

"Gregory the Great lived in a different time. Unlike him, I must scour away the filth that for too long has stained Saint Peter's throne. When that's done, then I'll rule as Gregory did, but you of all people Rumeus, know what they would have done to me had I not fled Rome. To show the Crescentii mercy is to show them weakness."

Rumeus glanced at Crescentius's dangling corpse. "No one could gaze upon this hill and suspect you or your cousin of weakness."

"Good," Gregory said with the hint of a smile. "Yet still, I want your spies to keep an eye on the countess. If she is found cavorting with any of the more dangerous remnants of her family, you shall have her arrested. We can determine the charges after the fact."

Rumeus nodded, a frown on his face. "As you wish."

THE OBELISK

lais rested against the bulkhead of *La Margerie's* cramped cabin, keeping watch on Khalil.

The poet slept soundly. A lock of hair fell over his handsome face, and a linen bandage covered his burned right arm. Back in Ireland, Brother Dónall had taught Ciarán how to heal burns using herbs, so after the battle he had Josua procure some butter and marigold petals, which Ciarán used to make a salve for Khalil's wound. Alais was grateful that Ciarán proved to be a good student of Dónall's teachings, though this was hardly surprising given the monk's keen mind and scholarly bent. Part scholar himself, Khalil had taken great interest in Ciarán's concoction, although once his arm was bandaged, a skin of Évrard's strong Spanish wine helped the poet drift off to sleep.

Ciarán left her with Khalil and went off to study the book he had claimed from Castel Sant'Angelo. Alais did not know what she'd expected the map to the Key would look like, but she never imagined it would be a gem-studded tome. The ominous image on the cover of a dragon coiled around a key that looked like one she would use to lock a door gave her hope they had found what they were seeking, but the key appeared nothing like the Key that Saint Beatus depicted in the book they'd discovered in Limoges. Beatus's Key was black and bent and as tall as man, looking more like a farmer's scythe, except for the L-shaped head and three prominent teeth where the blade should have been. How that instrument could be the same as the key depicted on the tome's cover, she did not know, yet she felt certain Ciarán would figure it out. He always did. She glanced down at Khalil and wondered how she had ended up between such brilliant, yet different, men.

She had not slept since setting out on the Tiber the night before, and judging from the fading light seeping through the cracked-open hatch, almost an entire day had passed. Her eyelids grew heavy and her body began to surrender to the weariness.

The next she knew, she was standing barefoot atop the Palatine Hill . . .

The dream played out the way it always did with the lavender butterfly and the girl who looked like Adeline but called herself Julia. The chariots raced along the track ringed with the wrong-colored banners, until Alais felt the sensation of being watched.

"Run!" Julia screamed. Beneath a marble archway lurked the man in the black cassock who reminded her of Adémar of Blois. Alais tensed.

"We can hide in Father's temple!" her sister cried. Alais tore off after her.

The ruined temple came into view, just thirty paces away. Julia disappeared beneath the shadows of a sunken stairwell. The man in black huffed behind Alais, and she could sense his reaching hands. She sprinted toward the temple, her heartbeat racing, and scurried down the steps. Old stones crumbled, and Alais pitched forward. She gasped as she plunged through the mouth of the stone giant, gaping like a wild demon. She plummeted down the shaft.

And this time she hit the ground.

She lay, barely breathing, fearing her bones had been crushed. Yet she felt no pain. As her eyes grew accustomed to the darkness, she found herself in an ash-gray wasteland. In the distance towered curved bronze cliffs, like the sides of a gigantic cauldron, and around her the cracked ground glowed faintly with moonlight. *But there is no moon,* she realized, *and no stars in the sky.*

Her breathing steadied, though she gasped again when a bright flame streaked past her vision. The streaking flame held the shape of a bird, as majestic as an eagle, yet with feathers that burned like fire. She could feel its heat against her body. She picked herself up off the ground. The bird watched her with thoughtful black eyes, then it beat its wings harder, throwing off flames as it lofted into the night sky. As she watched, the bird circled back. *It wants me to follow it . . .*

The firebird seemed the only sign of life in the ash-gray wasteland. She followed it to the base of a series of jagged hills and began to climb. The firebird circled for a time, then glided forward, beckoning her onward.

When she reached the hillcrest, she saw another valley stretching to a wall of cliffs, bronze like the others that ringed the valley. Yet unlike the one she had just traversed, this valley was not devoid of life, for in the distance marched an army. Some of the soldiers appeared to be men, but others were larger, with spears as tall as a boat's mast. Icy fear coursed through her veins as she recalled the giants on the battle-field outside Rosefleur. The familiarity of the two scenes was undeni-able, and in the distance, before the towering cliffs, stood a dark spire similar in shape to the tower of Rosefleur.

To her horror, the firebird soared toward the plain, as if leading her to the monstrous army below, but then it banked sharply right, away from the men. She climbed down the hill and scrambled toward the cliffs, all the while fearing the bird might draw the army toward her like a beacon in the sky. Yet the soldiers never moved any closer, as if they somehow could not see the firebird or gave it no mind.

The sheer cliffs climbed hundreds of feet into the midnight sky. In the light of the firebird's flames, the face of the cliffs shone a fiery bronze, and when she reached the cliffs and could touch them, the wall was smooth and cold, more like metal than rock. She followed the bird's lead, skulking in the shadows beneath the cliffs. The path kept her a half league from the soldiers, who stood as tall as leaf-bare trees across the unnaturally moonlit plain. In time, the distant spire came more clearly into view, and Alais realized it was not a tower at all, but a titanic pillar of glassy black stone. Shaped more like an obelisk than a column, it looked nearly as tall as Rosefleur had been, standing atop a hillock of dark-gray stones. Despite its height, the obelisk was dwarfed by the bronze cliffs behind it, giving it the appearance of a solitary gravestone.

The firebird banked left and glided toward the obelisk. Alais hesitated. Something about the ominous pillar sent a chill down her limbs. Yet she knew that if she did not move, the bird would be too far away. *It's my only guide, I have to follow it.*

She crossed the broken plain and headed for the obelisk. As it came closer into view, she noticed spidery runes crawling up its shaft to its pointed crown, but it was the stones on the hillock that made her suck in a breath. For what looked like boulders of dark-gray stone were actually thousands of mammoth skulls, piled atop one another in the shape of a hill. Curved tusks and daggerlike teeth jutted from the jaws of the nightmarish skulls, making them look like the heads of tarasques and manticores and every other imaginable beast of legend.

A faint moaning wafted from the hill of skulls. The sound made her stop, but the firebird was now circling the obelisk, with each pass drawing closer to the ground. She stepped forward. The moaning rose into a ghastly wail, as if hundreds of men and women were trapped beneath the skulls. Her hands flew to her ears, for in the wailing was a message that froze her blood.

Save us . . .

As if drawn to those words, the firebird glided to the base of the hillock and perched on the skull of a beast larger than an aurochs. The bird cocked its head, regarding her with eyes as black and glossy as the obelisk behind it. Then light flashed and the bird exploded into a ball of fire.

Alais glanced down at her outstretched arms. Crackling with flames, her limbs were on fire.

~

SHE BOLTED AWAKE. BESIDE HER, KHALIL SLEPT SOUNDLY. *THESE DREAMS are becoming too real,* she thought, rubbing her temples. *This cannot go on.*

She staggered to her feet and walked outside, knowing she had to talk to someone about her dreams, and she had a feeling who that someone should be. On deck, several of the crewmen napped in the afternoon sun, while Ciarán sat against the bulkhead studying the ornate book he had taken from Castel Sant'Angelo. He did not look up as she emerged from the cabin. She spotted Mordechai working on the rigging attached to the bowsprit, and strode toward him. "Mordechai," she asked, "would you be so kind as to escort me back to the ruins?"

He nodded yes, but asked why.

"Because I need to go back to the church of Santa Maria Nova. I want to talk with Father Michele."

MORDECHAI ACCOMPANIED HER TO THE RUINS, WITH HIS HUNTING BOW and quiver slung over his shoulder in case they encountered another wolf. Much to Alais' relief, the journey was uneventful, and she felt anticipation well within her as she spotted the basilica, one of the few healthy-looking structures standing in the ruins of the ancient Forum. They climbed the steps and Mordechai placed his bow and quiver outside the double doors, trying to avoid the old priest's ire this time around.

She pushed open the doors to the dimly lit nave. A hint of incense lingered in the air. "Father?" she called out.

No one answered. "Father Michele?"

Deep within the church, hinges creaked, followed by the patter of sandals on the marble floor. The tall old priest emerged from the shadows of the chancel. "Who's there?"

Alais clasped her hand to her chest. "Father!"

"Lady Alais?"

"Yes, Father, it's me. I would like to speak with you if you have time."

"Always, for a lady," he said with a wink.

She turned to Mordechai. "Do you mind waiting outside? I won't be long."

Mordechai gave a dutiful nod as Father Michele beckoned her to a stone bench next to a side chapel illuminated with candles. He took her hand. "Now tell me, child, what is it you wish to talk about?"

"About dreams," she said, shaking her head, "or maybe they're visions. They're plaguing my mind."

Father Michele furrowed his thick brows. "Tell me about them."

She told him about the images of Rome and the girl Julia, the same one she saw in the Forum two days before. She mentioned the ruined temple and the archway shaped like a gaping mouth, and finally the wasteland as gray as ash and the firebird lighting up the sky. "The bird led me to this awful place," she said. "There was a pillar and a hill made of skulls. And I swear, Father, there were people trapped beneath that hill. I could hear them."

"They spoke to you?"

A chill crawled down her limbs as she remembered their ghostly words. *Save us.* "They wanted me to help them."

Father Michele ran a long-fingered hand across his face and glanced briefly at the ceiling. "These sound like nightmares, not dreams."

"But what about the girl? I keep dreaming I'm in Rome, not France. And that ruined track, the one you pass to get here from the wharf, in my dreams it's filled with grandstands and people and chariots. The girl is my sister, I swear it, but her name is Julia. It feels so real, as if I'm living another life."

The old priest gave a faint chuckle. "You speak of reincarnation. Though the Church refutes any notion of it. When the body dies, the soul is judged, then off to the afterlife, Heaven or Hell, whichever it may be. Of course, there are some who point to the Book of Matthew and read it to say that John the Baptist was the prophet Elijah, reincarnate. And others look to the passage in the Book of

Jeremiah that says God knew the prophet before he was born, suggesting some past life. Those views, however, are highly unorthodox."

He placed a hand on her shoulder. "Sometimes, my dear, dreams are just dreams. I suspect a well-educated lady like yourself learned tales of the old Roman Empire and chariot races, and the many Julias of that age. The daughters of Caesar often took the name. Perhaps being in Rome has awakened memories of those tales, nudging them to life in your dreams."

"But it seems so real, Father. And even if you're right, I've never heard tales of this wasteland I dreamed of."

"Are you sure? Perhaps in church on the Sabbath. The second letter of Saint Peter speaks of a place called Tartarus, which to the Romans of his day was a gray, barren wasteland, the prison of the Titans. Though Saint Peter uses the term in reference to the fallen angels."

Alais blinked as a torrent of thoughts flooded her mind. *The fallen angels . . . the Watchers of Enoch's book, imprisoned in the bottomless pit.* The whispering voice from her dreams took on a terrifying new meaning. *Save us . . .*

Father Michele was tapping her hand. "My dear, are you all right? You went pale, like you've seen a ghost."

She stood up and shook her head. "I'm fine. You've been most kind." Though as she bid the priest farewell, her mind was churning. Isaac had dreams like these before Rosefleur, but his foreshadowed the future, and hers were of the past—all of them, save for her dream of the woman dancing in the Temple of Venus and Roma, whose ruins stood beyond the walls of this basilica. Alais recalled the shadows surrounding the woman, certain there was danger in the darkness, reminding her that danger still awaited them in Rome. She prayed Ciarán had found what he came for, so they could leave this place. The sooner the better.

Halfway down the nave, the priest called out behind her. "Red wine," he said.

She looked back. "What?"

"Red wine. Have some before you go to bed, it will help you sleep. I have a cup or two each night. It works wonders."

Alais could not help but smile. "I'll try that."

She and Mordechai arrived back at the cog in the fading light of dusk. Upon climbing the gangplank, Alais found Khalil on his feet alongside Josua and Évrard, huddling over something on the deck.

"You're not supposed to be up and about," she told Khalil with a smile.

Khalil shot her grim look and made room for her to see. Ciarán lay on the deck unmoving, his skin ashen. At his side lay the ornate book with the dragon coiled around a key.

Alais gasped. "What happened?"

Évrard turned to her, wide-eyed and shaking. "Don't know, milady. One moment he was just reading that book, then I heard a scream and watched him slump to the deck like a dead man."

THE BOOK OF GIANTS

Alais dropped to a knee and touched Ciarán's face. His flesh was cold, but he moaned faintly. "Ciarán, can you hear me?" His eyelids flickered.

"Can you speak?"

Ciarán grimaced. "I know . . ."

She grasped his hand. His eyelids looked heavy, threatening to close. "What?"

"How . . ." he said between heavy breaths. "How I found the book."

Alais shook her head. "Can you sit?"

He nodded weakly, then groaned when she and Josua helped him sit up.

"I know how you found the book," Khalil said. "In the light of Enoch's device, the book glowed. I saw it with my own eyes."

"But I've discovered why it glowed," Ciarán replied with a delirious smile. "To cast off such light, there had to be some power within the book, some enchantment. I learned what it was . . . the hard way."

"What do you mean?" Alais asked.

Ciarán closed his eyes and took a deep breath. "There's some type of ward on the cover, like the one Dónall put on the talismans that protected us from the demons back in Córdoba. When I triggered this one, it felt like the life was being sucked from my limbs."

"But how?" Josua said. "You've been reading it all day."

Ciarán swallowed hard. "The ward isn't on the pages, it's on the cover. I think there's something hidden beneath the symbols."

Évrard reached for his dagger. "Then we'll cut the damn cover open."

"No," Ciarán replied, his voice still weak. "The ward's still there. If you tried, it could kill you."

Alais had had enough of these questions. "Come inside," she insisted. "Let's get you some food and drink. Then you can tell us about it."

She watched with concern as Ciarán retrieved the book. With Josua's aid, Ciarán lumbered inside the cabin, and Alais and Khalil followed them. Josua lit an oil lamp, and Évrard returned with a bowl of stew made of clams and cockles, while Mordechai brought a wine-skin and an armful of cups. The wine helped ease Alais' mind as Ciarán drank from his bowl until the color began returning to his face.

When he had finished the broth, Ciarán began digging out clams with his fingers and stuffing them into his mouth.

"You're looking a bit better," Alais said.

Ciarán answered her between gulps of wine. "I'm feeling . . . better."

"When you are ready," Khalil said, "tell us what you learned."

Ciarán drained his cup. "Back in Solignac, the demon told us the Prince of Rome holds the path to the key. I feel certain now the demon was speaking of this tome." The garnets on the cover of the tome glittered red in the lamplight, reflecting off the tiny scales of the dragon coiled around the white-gold key. "I started with the text, hoping it might tell us where the Key to the Abyss is hidden."

"Does it?" Josua asked.

"Unfortunately, no. This book tells the same story as the Book of Enoch, but from a different point of view."

Khalil's eyes narrowed. "Whose?"

"The Nephilim's." Ciarán let that word sink in. "Like the sixth chapter of Genesis, it tells how the Watchers—angels from Heaven— descended to earth, drawn to the beauty of mortal women. The leader of the Watchers, named Samyaza, orchestrates this act in defiance of God. The Watchers take wives from the daughters of men and sire their offspring, the Nephilim. The Watchers also teach men the 'sacred mysteries,' what I believe Dónall used to call the sorcery of scripture."

"The same sorcery that put this ward on the tome?" Alais asked.

Ciarán nodded. "Aye. Dónall and I experienced a similar dark magic at the priory of Saint Bastian's."

"I witnessed it, too, Khalil said grimly, "at the death pit outside Rosefleur."

"But the book says nothing about this Key to the Abyss?" Josua pressed.

"Not the Key, but it does speak of the Abyss, though the book calls it *Dudael*, the place where the Watchers are imprisoned."

As she listened, a chill washed across Alais' skin. *Father Michele called it Tartarus.* She recalled the image of that ash-gray wasteland and the haunting plea from beneath those gargantuan skulls. *Save us.* Alais tried to purge those words from her mind and focus on Ciarán's tale.

"Enoch," Ciarán went on, "tries to warn the Watchers against spreading their evil. Yet they ignore him. Their leader is Samyaza's son, Ogias, a giant of unmatched strength who boasts that he shall rule for all eternity and bring further ruin upon the race of men. But the lamentations of men reach to Heaven, to the ears of God, and that's when the book first mentions a prophecy. Ogias receives the prophecy through a dream, where he sees symbols etched on a great stone. The symbols were the names of all the giants, but when the tablet is thrown into water, all the names wash away. A second dream comes to Mahway, another leader of the Nephilim, who foresees a garden with two hundred trees that become torn from the ground. Mahway then takes up wings of some sort and flies to find Enoch, whom Mahway implores to interpret the dreams. Enoch does, and inscribes the interpretation on two stone tablets.

"Mahway brings the tablets to Samyaza and the giants. The writings warn that the Watchers have misused their power. For that, they shall face eternal damnation, while the Nephilim shall perish in a great cataclysm. The prophecy causes a schism among the giants. Ogias urges them to be defiant, while Mahway and his father believe they must find a way to survive the coming doom."

"I take it Mahway's plan works," Khalil observed, "as the Nephilim we encountered at Rosefleur would seem to prove."

"It would seem so," Ciarán said, "though the book doesn't say either way. Rather, God sends His archangels—Michael, Gabriel, Uriel, and Raphael—to enact justice. The Watchers try to hide among the humans, but the archangels discover them, and a fiery battle ensues. Many giants are killed and Mahway is entombed within the earth."

"Yet some did survive." Alais would never forget the gigantic Nephilim who besieged Rosefleur and slew Orionde.

"The book talks about Mahway's sons, though it doesn't say what happened to them. Instead, it tells how the archangels imprison the Watchers in Dudael, while the giants retreat to their cities to await the cataclysm God shall bring upon the world."

Josua raised a brow. "The Great Flood?"

"Aye," Ciarán said, "but the book ends before the Flood. In a final battle, Ogias vows revenge and summons the Leviathan from the depths of the sea. The book portrays Ogias as a warrior, as brave and mighty as any demigod of Greek mythology. He tames the Leviathan and rides him like a stallion, and together they engage the archangel Raphael in an epic battle. In the end, the book says all three vanish beneath the waves."

Alais ran her fingers through her hair. "That's all?"

Ciarán nodded again. "In the end, Ogias is a messianic figure to the Nephilim, the only one mighty enough to stand against an archangel. That's why I believe the Nephilim wrote this book. I think the ending is intended to inspire hope among the enemies of God."

Khalil looked perplexed. "Why would Crescentius keep this book? His family has been connected to the papacy for a hundred years. His own uncle was pope, and he placed more than one pontiff on your Saint Peter's throne. Those are hardly the acts of an enemy of God."

"It may not be the text he's interested in, but the book's cover," Ciarán said. "Look at the symbols. Those in the second ring are astrological, just like the hieroglyph in the Book of Maugis, though they're not signs of the Zodiac. But these are." He pointed to one of the garnets. "A symbol of the Zodiac is etched on the surface of each one."

"But there are only eight," Khalil observed.

"Aye, four of the symbols are missing. Sagittarius, Pisces, Gemini, and Libra. I can't explain why, but the star in the center is a heptagram just like the one in Maugis' hieroglyph. Which reminded me of something I've been thinking about lately. The prophecy does not say who prevails, it just tells of the battle between the Dragon and mankind at each millennium. So the prophecy has as much meaning to the enemies of God as it does to those who fight on His side. I suspect all these symbols somehow relate to the prophecy, and as for the symbol in the center—that key—its meaning seems unmistakable."

"Look." Ciarán turned the book on its side. "The front cover is a bit thicker than the back, which is why I think there's something inside it." He flipped the book back over. "Now watch." Ciarán pointed at the left edge of the outer silver ring in the covers' center. There was a tiny groove between it and the cover's boiled leather. He moved the outer ring a quarter turn. "The rings turn, both the silver one with the garnets and the inner ring with the other astrological symbols. When I moved the outer ring in a full revolution, that's when I triggered the ward."

Khalil shook his head, his eyes bright with wonder. "So this is some type of trap? And you think the only way to disarm it is to arrange these gemstones and the symbols into a certain pattern?"

Ciarán answered with a grimace. "That's exactly what I think."

"With Maugis' hieroglyph," Khalil said, "we could only understand it because I knew the cipher of Fierabras. How are you going to decipher this one?"

"I can't," Ciarán said. "But I can think of one person who could help us."

"Who?" Alais asked.

Ciarán curled his lips. "Gerbert of Aurillac, the man who killed my parents."

THE SHRINE OF ORCUS

The sprawling ruins of the Domus Augustana loomed over the rubble-strewn gardens of the Palatine Hill, bathed in the light of a crescent moon. In their ravaged state, the moss-covered ruins looked more like the remnants of a hulking fortress than the lavish imperial palace built by Emperor Domitian, surrounded by the silence of a necropolis.

Naberus gripped a blazing torch and strode through the remnant of cypress-lined gardens where emperors and their consorts gallivanted centuries ago. Overhead, Hermes glided in the cool night air, and beside Naberus pattered his mastiffs Set and Grimm. Their brother Anubis had given his life during the escape from Castel Sant'Angelo, and but for the dog's sacrifice and a coat of mail Naberus stole from the armory before his flight, he might have lost his head with Crescentius a night ago. Still, his ribs ached with every step where a German sword had hammered his mail during the escape, and the cut along his left arm still stung from a Saxon's blade before Naberus had impaled the man with the sword he stole from the dying Praetorian.

Out of the corner of his eye, something flitted in the shadows of the ruined palace. Thieves were known to haunt the Palatine, and

Naberus wondered if one of them was measuring him as a mark. Yet with two battle-scarred mastiffs by his side, the thief would reconsider unless he was a bloody fool, in which case Naberus's hounds would eat well tonight.

But there were more than thieves to consider this evening. The siege had deprived Naberus of the ancient shrine that aided his divinations, and too many odd things had happened since then. First, there was the emergence of the Devil card. It had not changed Crescentius's fate—the Hanged Man foretold as much—and now Crescentius hung headless from the gallows on the Vatican Hill. But the Devil hinted of magic and a great disruption, a new force that would alter the future. Then there were the two strangers in the Chamber of the Urns and the weapon one held. The ghostly flames on its blade were not of this world, and when they flared, Naberus had never beheld such power. Not from the Hermetic mystics he apprenticed with in Alexandria, nor from the necromancers who tutored him in Aksum. There was a radiance in that light, both awesome and terrifying.

Strangest of all, it appeared the two men with this weapon had come for his grandfather's codex. *Why that of all things?* Naberus could not even remember why he had brought that chest of old documents to the citadel instead of storing it in the half-dozen other sanctuaries across the city where he'd stashed his belongings over the years. Since his escape, however, the codex, even more than the enchanted weapon, nagged at his mind. *Could there be a connection between the two?*

Although it seemed ages ago, he still recalled the night he left his ancestral home in Constantinople—the night he stole the codex. He was only twenty-two then, with his few belongings in a burlap sack, an old pair of boots on his feet, and a gray cloak that once belonged to his father clasped with a silver brooch. His beard was closely trimmed and his hair was short and shaven. *I still wore a monk's tonsure back then . . . though I had burned my robes.*

He tiptoed across the floor of his family's hall, hoping the boards would not creak and wake his grandfather. Bone thin, the ancient man slumped over a trestle table near the stone hearth aglow with embers. A wine goblet sat on the table amid a clutter of scrolls and books. Grandfather treasured his books, and they seemed to follow him to whichever room he chose to rest his decrepit limbs.

Naberus traversed half the hall before a hoary voice called out, "Where are you going boy?"

His grandfather raised his head, bathed in the hearth's hellish glow. Three centuries of time cut deep creases down his face, his skin as hard as leather. His one good eye fixed on Naberus like a huntsman's stare, while the other lolled dead and milky beneath the white ruff of his brow.

"Someplace other than here," Naberus replied, "or else the elders will have my head."

"The elders are fools."

"Then they're unhappy fools. Apparently murdering the Prior of Stoudios did not sit well with them. They fear an inquiry by the emperor's men."

"You should not have done that," his grandfather rasped, pointing at him with a crooked finger.

Oh, but it felt so good, Naberus wanted to say. *That old man needed killing.* "It was a rash decision," he admitted instead.

"As was your decision to join that monastery. It was a mockery for one of our kind."

"I wanted to understand them . . . and their faith."

The sliver of a grin spread across his grandfather's nearly toothless mouth. "And what did you learn, boy?"

"That we are damned, dear grandfather, destined to the Lake of Fire for the sins of our ancestors, both Watcher and Nephilim."

"Is that what the priests taught you?"

"Indeed. So over the prior's corpse, I made a vow. To live life with abandon. For if my future is fire and darkness, I shall taste every drop of pleasure in this world. And may the sweet memories of my debauchery comfort me through the afterlife."

"Then you shall waste your life," his grandfather snarled.

As you wasted yours with your books? Naberus thought as venom rose in his throat. "One man's waste is another man's treasure."

"Don't be glib with me, boy!" His grandfather's good eye smoldered with sudden rage. "Your vow should be to follow in my stead. My spirit shall soon be free of this ancient shell and my own torment shall begin, and the race of Magog shall have one fewer warlock to uphold our ancestors' sacred purpose. Unless you take up our cause."

Naberus sighed. His grandfather's persistence on this point had grown tiresome over the years. "There's a reason there are no more warlocks, grandfather. Because their goals proved to be folly two thousand years ago."

"Then you are truly damned," his grandfather growled. "You and the elders and all the fools who believe this heresy!"

Who is the fool? Naberus wondered. *The many who accept their existence for what it is, or the dying few who cling to ancient fables?*

Save for the few remaining warlocks, the race of Magog had abandoned any hope of prophecies and salvation thousands of years ago, choosing instead to weave themselves into the world of men like a thread through a woolen blanket. His ancestors diluted their Nephilim blood, mixing their seed every three generations with that of human women. It cost them much of their once tremendous height and longevity, but made them indistinguishable from their human cousins, allowing them to live richly among the cities of men. It also saved them from the darkness of the Otherworld, where the race of Gog wallowed in purgatory, clinging to the same old fables the warlocks believed, praying that someday they would bring vengeance to the world of men. It was better to live life in riches than linger in purgatory, Naberus firmly believed. And for the lifetime ahead, he intended to drink the nectar of this world until he consumed every last drop.

"Damned or not," Naberus told his grandfather, "I'll be headless if I don't leave the city soon."

The anger in his grandfather's brow melted away. "I could talk to the elders and tell them I need an apprentice to complete my work."

"They don't believe in your work, so what good would that do?"

His grandfather hefted a codex from the table, clutching it in his gnarled hands. It was the one covered in black leather, adorned with gold and jewels, with the silver image of a serpentine key in its center.

"This book tells the story of our kind," his grandfather said. "It is a testament to the work that must be done, to our destiny as a race. And locked within its binding are the sacred words of our ancestors back in the age they dwelt in Rome. The elders must hear these sacred words. I shall take this message to them, and for once, they shall listen!"

Naberus shrugged, realizing how pathetic the old man looked. "The elders don't respond well to threats. And, alas, I must be going."

His grandfather slammed the codex onto the table. "If you leave, I shall find another. You'll forfeit your birthright, and accursed shall you be!"

To hell with you and your curses. Naberus gave the old man a parting glance. "Good-bye, grandfather."

He left the hall, but lingered in the darkness, waiting. The image of the codex stuck in his mind. *The gold and jewels could fetch a small fortune when he reached Alexandria,* he remembered thinking back then. So when he heard his grandfather's snores, he sneaked back into the hall and lifted the book from the table.

That was twelve decades ago. With his guile and cunning, silver and gold came so easily in Alexandria and elsewhere, he never needed to sell the codex, so he kept it on his travels to Egypt and Aksum, where he learned the forbidden mysteries of this world, and on his journeys to Gaul and Al-Andalus, where he sampled all the delights those lands had to offer. The codex remained among his growing possessions when he found a new life in Rome and became counselor to the powerful counts of Tusculum, whose descendants would become the dukes of Spoleto and the self-styled consuls and prefects of Rome. The codex sat buried in its chest while he used his subtle arts to shape the destiny of Rome's ruling families, amassing his own fortune along the way and enjoying the pleasures of some of Rome's most scandalous and influential women, including the Senatrix Theodora and her cunning daughter, Marozia. Sometime in the last century, Naberus had read the codex's contents and even unlocked the verse his grandfather spoke of, but it was just a cryptic riddle about an ancient fable, hardly worth his time or thought. He couldn't remember the last time he'd read those words, yet now the codex was gone. *Why?*

He prayed Orcus would have the answer.

The spirit, with whom he had communed since arriving in Rome, dwelt in an old Etruscan shrine buried beneath the ruins of the Temple of Apollo on the Palatine Hill. After crossing through a grove of cypresses and the remains of yet another imperial garden, the ruined temple came into view, just before the hill sloped downward towards the remains of Circus Maximus. Moonlight illuminated the temple's foundation of mortared gray stone now covered with moss and vines, next to a pile of bricks that once had been a wall. That and a few broken columns with their capitals strewn about the grass were all that remained of Caesar Augustus's once glorious temple to his patron god.

The cult of Apollo, which flourished during Augustus's reign, built their temples over the shrines of older gods, and Augustus built his personal temple over a shrine to Etruscan god Orcus. Though long ago, Naberus had discovered Orcus was no god. He was a demon, one of the spirits of the ancient Nephilim condemned to haunt the Otherworld until the End of Days, when a worse fate would befall them all. The spirit's existence confirmed everything the sadistic prior had told Naberus back in Constantinople. *We are all damned—but only when we die.* In this life, mastery over demons brought certain power, and for nearly a hundred years this spirit had fueled Naberus' divinations, keeping him a step ahead of his enemies.

As Naberus approached the ruined temple, Set and Grimm dug their paws into the grass, the hair on their necks standing straight. Grimm let out a low growl. Hermes perched on a nearby cypress but would come no closer. The beasts could sense the presence of the spirit beneath those ancient stones, and they feared it.

Naberus walked alone into the ruin. He stopped at a huge flagstone rimmed by ragged grass, bent down, and worked his fingers under the stone's edge. It would have taken two mortal men to lift the stone, but he did so with one hand. The stone grated against its fellow flagstones as Naberus slid it aside to reveal an ancient stairwell that plunged into darkness. Many of the steps were crumbling, so Naberus was careful in his descent. Eighty feet beneath the foundation, his torchlight illuminated a portal ahead, the entrance to the ancient shrine. The archway looked like a gaping mouth with two fangs surrounded by a bestial head, a depiction of Orcus roaring in the dark. Naberus passed through the creature's mouth and felt a faint sizzle in the air, like the whisper of breath.

His skin prickled as he set his torch in an ancient sconce on the wall. The shrine was a cave, barely wide enough for three men to stand side by side, ending in an alcove of mortared stone. Dark stains marred the flagstones at the alcove's base, and a black mold speckled the stones within it.

He slid a dagger from a sheath on his belt and knelt before the alcove. Stretching the long fingers of his left hand, he exposed his palm and readied his mind. After a deep breath, he laid the blade to his palm and sliced it across his flesh. A sting of pain preceded a gush of blood, which he let drip onto the flagstones as he whispered an ancient Nephilim verse:

> *I call upon you, spirit of the ancient world,*
> *Soul of god and man,*
> *Mighty Orcus, serve me now,*
> *For there are answers to be had.*

His blood on the flagstones began to hiss and steam, rising into a billowing red vapor that filled the alcove. Naberus could sense a presence in the mist. The hairs of his arms stood on end and a chill crawled up his skin.

"Orcus?"

From the mist answered a voice like the howl of wind through the trees. *"There is no Orcus. Only me."*

His hands began to tremble. "Who . . . are you?"

The voice told him.

And Naberus's veins filled with ice.

GERBERT OF AURILLAC

"Gerbert of Aurillac is a no-good traitor," Évrard said as he rowed his companions across the Tiber in the damp morning air. "Are you sure you want to do this lad?"

"We've no other choice," Ciarán said, sitting in the rowboat and clutching the tome wrapped in sackcloth. He wore his Benedictine habit while Alais huddled beside him, her russet cloak pulled over her shoulders. Khalil crouched behind Évrard, the hood of his dark cloak shrouding his head. Across the river, the sun rose over the Aventine Hill dotted with marble palaces and towering mansions from a more glorious age. Somewhere among them stood the emperor's fortress where they would find Gerbert of Aurillac.

Évrard grimaced as he tugged the oars. "Of course there's a choice, there always is. And probably a better one than seeking counsel from a man who bloody well can't be trusted. He turned on his own king to put a Capetian on the throne, all the while working as a spy for the German queen so the King of France would pay homage to the Holy Roman Emperor. And he damn well stole the See of Reims. Only gave it up after good Pope John excommunicated him. He's a bloody Judas, and you of all people should know that. For Christ's sake, he betrayed

Brother Dónall and handed your own parents over to an archbishop's inquisition!"

The words stung Ciarán. Dónall had sworn Gerbert had been there with Archbishop Adalbero on the day his mother and father died, burned as a witch and a sorcerer because of the same Fae knowledge that Gerbert secretly possessed. The same knowledge that Dónall and nine more of their brothers at the Cathedral School of Reims discovered when they found the Book of Maugis d'Aygremont, and most of them too died as heretics. Ciarán fought to suppress his hatred for the man. *I have to,* he told himself. *Our cause depends on it.*

"Ever since Rosefleur," Ciarán replied, "it's as if we've been in a labyrinth, with no clear notion of where to go, or even where this journey's supposed to end. But every time I think we've hit a dead end, a path appears—but only one path, never two. Even after we discovered Saint Beatus's depiction of the Key in Limoges, we had not a clue where to find it until we learned of the demon at Solignac. The demon's words led us in a single direction, to the Prince of Rome, and in the prince's castle, we found only one path—this book. Something's hidden inside it, but we can't unlock it without killing ourselves. As much as Dónall disliked the man, he claimed Gerbert of Aurillac possessed the keenest mind in Christendom. Gerbert also knows the secrets of Maugis d'Aygremont and about the power of the Fae, the very power that likely created the ward on this tome. No one else in Rome, or anywhere else I can think of, has such knowledge." Ciarán sighed. "He's our only hope."

"I don't doubt Ciarán on this one," Khalil added. "If this Gerbert knows the things Brother Dónall knew, I can think of no one better who can help us."

"Nor can I," Alais said. "But don't fret, Évrard, we know not to trust the man. We'll be careful about what we tell him."

Évrard curled his lips. "As you wish, milady."

When they reached the east bank, he got out and pulled the rowboat onto the muddy riverbank where a group of fishermen emptied eelpots and crab traps filled with the morning's catch. "When you're done, just wave over to *La Margerie,*" Évrard told them after they disembarked. "I'll have someone keep a lookout, and we'll come get you."

Ciarán nodded, then looked ahead. Olive trees framed a field where two ancient temples stood. One was circular and surrounded by ten-foot columns in a concentric ring, while the other was rectangular with a gabled roof. An assortment of peddlers hawked wares from the column-lined portico of the second temple, while a gaggle of beggars lounged within the circular colonnade of the first one. Between them, herdsmen watched their cattle graze on the patchy grass, while nearby a pair of pigs wallowed in a slick of mud. Across the field stood another church, the one with the lofty bell tower that they could see from across the river.

The air stank of dung as Ciarán, Alais, and Khalil made their way across the cattle field. "We should heed Évrard's warning," Khalil said, wrinkling his nose. "I would not mention Enoch's device. Remember what I told you about powerful men."

"Right," Ciarán replied with a nod. He had left the weapon back on the cog for that very reason. Khalil too traveled unarmed, certain the German soldiers would not welcome a Muslim with a blade.

They headed toward a plaza lined with packed houses where a hulking triumphal arch of ancient gray stone stood in the plaza's center. Vines hung from the top of the square-shaped archway, while goats nibbled grass at its base. The surrounding plaza teemed with merchants selling bread and salted fish, as well as shopkeepers and their mules pulling carts of melons and half-rotted vegetables. Hens pecked seeds from between the remains of ancient flagstones, while stray dogs hunted for scraps.

Beyond the plaza loomed another church and the first of several mansions with high walls of marble and stone. Terra-cotta tiles covered the gabled roofs of these elegant structures, and some featured square towers flying the bright banners of the noble Romans who lived there. To the east, the top of a pyramid faced in white marble rose over rooftops of clay and thatch, reminding Ciarán of Romulus's tomb. He wondered which ancient Roman this one belonged to.

Khalil pointed with his good hand toward a fortresslike palace with a crenelated tower flying the banner of Saint Michael. "That's the emperor's." The fortress's walls stood a good thirty feet high, and in the shadow of an arched gatehouse stood two sentries, both bearded and burly Saxons. Their kite-shaped shields, propped up against the wall, bore the familiar image of the black lion of Meissen.

Ciarán took the lead up a path of ancient flagstones and bowed slightly at the first guardsman. "Peace be with you," Ciarán said in Latin. "I come bearing a message for Gerbert of Aurillac."

The guardsman furrowed his brow, as if he was trying to understand all the words, then grunted something in German and disappeared through the open gateway. The second guardsman cast a suspicious glance at Khalil before his leering gaze settled on Alais. She glanced away, but Ciarán wondered if the man would ever blink.

After a wait, the first guardsman returned, accompanied by a spear-thin priest with a weak chin and bulbous eyes. His face held a pinched expressed. "I'm told you bear a message for His Excellency, the archbishop?"

Ciarán's eyes narrowed. "Archbishop? No. My message is for Gerbert of Aurillac, the emperor's counselor."

"His imperial majesty has appointed Gerbert of Aurillac Archbishop of Ravenna, so your message should be addressed to His Excellency," the priest said, holding out a hand. "Give it to me."

"I'm to deliver it in person."

The priest crossed his arms. "The archbishop is a very important man. He has no time to speak with a foreign monk."

"The archbishop was once a monk."

The priest's face reddened. "So were half the clerics in Christendom."

Ciarán clenched his jaw. "My name is Brother Ciarán, and I've come all the way from the monastery of Derry in Ireland. Tell His Excellency that I bear tidings from Brother Dónall mac Taidg, and let His Excellency decide if he wants the message."

"We shall see about that," the priest huffed. He spun around and stormed through the gateway.

Khalil whispered over Ciarán's shoulder. "If this fails, we'll need a new plan."

"Aye," Ciarán said.

"Do you have one?"

Ciarán gave a long sigh. "Not a one."

They waited. By the time the bells tolled for Terce, Ciarán was slouched against the fortress' wall with his chin in his hands. Beside him, Khalil closed his eyes, resting, while Alais laid her head on the Persian's shoulder. The two Saxon guardsmen had all but forgotten them, chatting and laughing about something in their foreign tongue. The sun neared midday, and Ciarán dreaded the bell for Sext. He felt certain that if they were forced to wait that long, Gerbert had refused to see them. These thoughts grew worse as the day went on, yet they vanished when the priest emerged from the gateway.

Ciarán jumped to his feet.

The priest's expression was even more pinched than before. "His Excellency will see you," he said sourly.

Ciarán drew a deep breath. *Thank the Blessed Virgin.* He brushed the grass from his habit while Khalil and Alais stood, and the three followed the priest into the courtyard filled with a stable, a smithy, and a statue of some proud Roman statesman from ages past. The priest led them through bronzed doors into a pillared hall with a high ceiling and mosaics adorning the walls. Ciarán recognized one of the Battle of Troy, while others depicted scenes from Ovid's *Metamorphoses*, featuring centaurs, nymphs, and a lust-filled Apollo chasing after fair Daphne. From there, the priest took them down several more-modest passageways and up a flight of stairs to a chamber with a fine wooden door carved with reliefs of grapevines.

An imposing Lombard dressed in mail and a sage cloak stood sentry at the door. His clean-shaven jaw framed a suspicious frown, and his grim blue eyes watched Ciarán and his companions as they followed the priest.

The priest rapped twice on the door and then opened it, revealing a chamber that looked more like a Moorish library than a Roman solar. From floor to ceiling, mahogany shelves held scores of leather-bound tomes and neatly stacked scrolls, while fine Spanish rugs covered the floor where a carved desk stood, topped by quills, inkwells, and a stack of open books. In one wall, double doors opened to a terrace, where a slight man dressed in a scarlet cassock leaned over a curious-looking pedestal, atop which sat a bronze disk the size of a shield with a jutting fin in its center.

"Niccolo," said the man whom Ciarán recognized as Gerbert of Aurillac, "take a note. When we get to Ravenna, make sure to find a suitable courtyard for my sundial and record its readings, every hour on the hour, with the water clock. We may synchronize that device yet."

Gerbert gestured toward a contraption on the far wall, which Ciarán thought must have been the device to which Gerbert referred. It stood as tall as a bookshelf and supported a large copper funnel and a tube that ran into a well of some type, from which an iron rod rose, affixed to a copper wheel etched with symbols. With a ticking sound, the wheel moved slightly, ringing a small chime attached to its wooden frame.

"Ah," Gerbert said as a smile spread between his ginger beard and mustache, "it's Sext." An instant later, a chorus of church bells rang through the city.

Ciarán stood amazed at the workings of the water clock, which stood beside an array of other strange devices on a nearby table, including a sphere that appeared as if it could spin on its axis, a metal semicircle affixed with seven bronze tubes of varying sizes, and a brass bust of a human head with a hinged jaw and eyes that glittered like jewels.

"Of course, Your Excellency," the priest said. "In the meantime, this is Brother Ciarán, the messenger from Hibernia."

Gerbert's eyes narrowed at the sight of the three visitors. "Father Niccolo tells me you bear a message from my old acquaintance, Dónall mac Taidg."

"Aye, Your Excellency," Ciarán answered.

"You travel in curious company for a Hibernian monk, Brother Ciarán."

"We've been on a rather long journey," Ciarán explained, "through France and Moorish Spain." He gestured to Alais. "This is the Lady Alais of Selles-sur-Cher, and Khalil al-Pârsâ of Córdoba."

"Khalil al-Pârsâ?" Gerbert asked with a raised brow. "The poet?"

Khalil stepped forward and bowed. "One and the same, Your Excellency."

Gerbert's eyes brightened. "I have copies of some of your poems in one of my books, right near my own work on the abacus. I've even dabbled in poetry myself."

"Your library is most impressive," Khalil said.

"Ah, yes," Gerbert said with a smile. "It took a lifetime to assemble, you know, but it contains works from all the great thinkers: Boethius, Pliny, Pythagoras, Macrobius, Plato, Aristotle, and Cicero, of course."

As Gerbert recited the names, Ciarán listened in awe. *Dónall only dreamed of a collection like that.*

Gerbert turned to Alais. "And you, my lady, are cousin to the Duke of Aquitaine, if my recollection of the House of Poitiers is correct. You wed Lord Geoffrey of Selles-sur-Cher."

"Lord Geoffrey was my late husband," Alais acknowledged.

Gerbert frowned. "I am sorry to hear of his passing. Though I must ask, how on earth did you three come to travel together?"

"We were all friends of Dónall's," Ciarán said.

Gerbert's eyes narrowed once more. "Were?"

"Dónall mac Taidg is dead," Ciarán admitted. "And so is Brother Remi of Paris."

Gerbert's expression hardened. "I was told your message was *from* Dónall mac Taidg, and now you tell me he's dead. I do not like subterfuge, Brother Ciarán."

A swell of concern washed through Ciarán's gut. "I beg your pardon, Your Excellency, but they died chasing a prophecy, one I believe you know the meaning of. We've found something that pertains to that prophecy, and we need your help understanding it."

"Dónall never believed in that prophecy," Gerbert said with a bitter smile.

"Aye," Ciarán replied. "Not at first, but he came to. He found proof."

"I can't imagine what he found," Gerbert replied, "but that thing he chased was but a phantom conjured by Brother Remi and his deluded friends from the cryptic words of the madman who wrote them two hundred years ago. You would be wise to remember that, Brother Ciarán. Contrary to some in our Church, I do not believe the end times are upon us, and I believe Saint Augustine said it best. The thousand years before the End of Days is not an exact time, but rather a *metaphora*—a way of referring to the entire fullness of time. So it's as likely to be ten thousand years as it is a millennium. And remember Augustine's admonition: To guess the mind of God is folly, and to try to predict when the end shall come is blasphemy."

Ciarán swallowed hard. *Remi believed Saint Augustine led a conspiracy to conceal the truth.* He glanced at Alais and could see the concern in her eyes. "I don't seek to change your mind," he insisted, "but to show you this." He pulled the sackcloth off Crescentius's tome, revealing the ornate cover.

Gerbert touched his throat. "What's this?" he asked, unable to take his eyes off it. "Those symbols … and that image . . . is that a dragon coiled around a key?"

"Aye," Ciarán answered. "This tome was hidden in Rome, and the key, we believe, is a symbol for the Key to the Abyss. We think this tome holds the secret to finding it."

Gerbert's eyes widened. "The key from Revelation?"

Ciarán nodded. "The one."

"Brother Ciarán, if this is why you've come here under false pretenses, then you're wasting your time. You will never find this Key."

"Why not?" Ciarán pressed.

Gerbert chuckled. "Because it doesn't exist."

SACRED GEOMETRY

C iarán stared at Gerbert in disbelief. "That can't be right. The Key to the Abyss is written of in scripture."

"In Revelation," Gerbert said, "which we've already discussed is a *metaphora*. Now, you'd best be moving along, Brother Ciarán." He waved toward the door. "I'm terribly busy with my move to Ravenna."

The priest, Niccolo, nudged Ciarán toward the door, but he shook off the priest's grasp. "Whether you believe it's a *metaphora* or a myth, Dónall mac Taidg always said there's truth buried in those myths, and that truth is what I'm seeking."

Gerbert rolled his eyes. "Even if you want to believe in the truth of this Key, it still does not exist. Not in this world, at least."

"How can you know?" Ciarán insisted.

"Because according to the Book of Revelation, it was given to one of the angels."

"An angel?" Alais asked.

"Indeed, my lady." The archbishop walked to one of the floor-to-ceiling bookshelves, picked out a tome, and began flipping through the pages. "In the ninth chapter of the Book of Revelation," he said, his finger pressed on a verse, "John of Patmos wrote, 'When the fifth angel blew his trumpet, I saw a star that had fallen from Heaven to earth, and he was given the key to the shaft of the bottomless pit.'"

"It says a star," Ciarán said, "not an angel."

Gerbert peered up from the page. "Didn't Brother Remi teach you anything about the stars in scripture?"

"Not in scripture," Ciarán admitted.

"In the Book of Job," Gerbert explained, "the stars are equated with the sons of God, and in the Book of Isiah, Lucifer is called the Morning Star. Later in Revelation, it says the Dragon swept his tail, and a third of the stars of Heaven fell to the earth, a clear reference to angels who followed him."

"If the Key was given to a star that had fallen to the earth," Khalil reasoned, "then it was given to a fallen angel. Yet they were the ones imprisoned in the Abyss."

Khalil's words struck Ciarán like an epiphany. "Not all were imprisoned. We know some were granted clemency, even if they were destined to dwell in the purgatory of the Otherworld. The Key must have been given to one of the Fae."

"The Fae?" Gerbert scoffed, setting the book aside. "To a creature of myth? You may as well go back to your distant homeland and search for leprechauns."

"You know they exist," Ciarán insisted. "In the Book of Maugis d'Aygremont, you saw evidence."

Gerbert pursed his lips. "Niccolo, leave us."

Niccolo gave a nod, and Gerbert waited, stone-faced, until the priest closed the door behind him.

"The evidence I saw," Gerbert said with an edge to his voice, "was of an ancient language and a power too dangerous to wield, one that poisons the minds of men. From where that power truly comes, I do not know. But to toy with it is like playing with lightning. Have you ever seen how a tree struck by lightning burns?"

Ciarán wanted to tell Gerbert he was being a fool. The Fae were real, and demons too, but Ciarán remembered his friends' warnings about the man standing before him, so he held his tongue. "There's a reference to the Fae in the Book of Enoch," he said instead.

"The Book of Enoch has been lost for more than a thousand years," Gerbert insisted. "I doubt you've read it."

"There was a copy in Charlemagne's library," Ciarán explained, "but it was lost when his grandsons divided his empire in three. Brother Remi discovered the copy had been hidden in Selles-sur-Cher, which we found before it was stolen from us. But we uncovered another copy in the Great Library of Córdoba."

Gerbert' blinked twice. "Do you *have* the Book of Enoch?"

"Unfortunately," Khalil interjected, "it was destroyed, by agents of Al-Mansor."

"The hajib of the Córdoba?" Gerbert asked incredulously. "I'm beginning to understand how the three of you came together."

Ciarán held up the ornate tome. "This book is a twin of sorts to the Book of Enoch, though it was written from the perspective of the Nephilim, and perhaps by the Nephilim themselves."

"That is the Book of Giants?" Gerbert stared wide-eyed. "That book's but a legend . . ."

"Not anymore." Ciarán opened the tome to reveal its illuminated title and handed it to Gerbert.

"Astonishing . . ." Gerbert's hand shook as he turned the vellum pages. "The illuminations are magnificent." After several moments, he looked up. "This book contains a reference to the Key to the Abyss?"

"Not the text," Ciarán replied. "I think that answer lies in the symbols on the cover. But we can't decipher them. That's why we need your help."

Gerbert cocked a brow and examined the cover. "It looks like some form of sacred geometry."

"What is sacred geometry?" Alais asked.

Gerbert made a twirling gesture with his hand. "Patterns and designs that when placed in the proper order represent the spiritual connection between man and the divine. See, there's a heptagram, and these symbols . . ." He glanced up. "By Jove, I've seen those before."

"In the Book of Maugis d'Aygremont," Ciarán said with a nod. "We believe there's a connection. Except in this book, the rings containing the symbols can move and be realigned. I'll show you." Ciarán took the book from Gerbert and turned the golden ring with the astrological symbols ever so slightly.

Gerbert blinked. "You think there is some pattern to be found? Whatever for?"

"We think something is hidden inside the cover."

"And the combination can somehow unlock it?"

"Aye," Ciarán said.

"Astonishing," Gerbert said, before holding up a hand, as if to stop them for interrupting his thoughts. He turned toward the table of contraptions and grabbed a board the size of a small shield. Lines in the shape of boxes and arches were painted across the board, along with a grid of Roman and Arabic numerals.

Khalil leaned toward Ciarán and said under his breath, "An abacus."

"Eight symbols on the outer ring," Gerbert muttered to himself. "Twelve more in the inner ring, seven points on the star . . ." He started moving his fingers in the strangest of fashions, gesturing almost randomly to points along the painted board. "There are six hundred and seventy-two possible combinations." He shook his head. "This will take much time. We would have to manipulate each combination until finding the one that works. Alas, I leave soon for Ravenna and have much to do before then. If you leave the book with me, I could study it in my spare time. You could meet me in Ravenna after Midsummer. By then, I might have results."

Ciarán drew in a long breath. "We don't have that kind of time, and there is no way you could attempt every combination. It would kill you."

"Kill?" Gerbert said with a pinched expression. "Exhaust, perhaps—"

"No," Ciarán insisted, "literally kill. There's some type of ward on the book, more of this power you're aware of. It sends out a shock, strong enough to draw the life from your limbs, and I'm certain that after two or three wrong combinations, the torture would kill a man."

"A curse?" Gerbert said, narrowing his gaze. "What sorcery are you involved with, Brother Ciarán?"

"None, I swear," Ciarán replied. "It was the maker of this book, I believe, who had dark designs, and this book holds the secret to fulfilling those. With it, we can stop them, but the only way to do so and avoid the curse is to align the symbols in the proper order—on the first try."

Gerbert sighed. "This sounds like a dangerous game you are playing, Brother Ciarán, and I pray you are aware of the consequences. You suggest deducing the correct combination from the meaning of the symbols themselves?"

"The symbols are astrological," Ciarán said.

"The ones on the outer ring are of the Zodiac," Gerbert noted. "But four are missing, which is curious. The symbols on the inner ring include four of the Five Wanderers, as well as the sun and the moon. Yet there are six more . . ."

"The Five Wanderers?" Khalil asked.

"The *asteres planetai*—Mars, Jupiter, Venus, Mercury, and Saturn." Gerbert gestured toward the bronze globe among the other strange devices on the table. "They are among the stars at night and wander around our own orb, as demonstrated by this spherical astrolabe. Yet on this cover, Saturn is missing."

Ciarán peered at the device Gerbert called an astrolabe and noticed the outer ring bore the symbols of the Zodiac, while the so-called Five Wanderers were on separate rings that comprised the globe. "In the night sky," Ciarán pointed out, "there are hundreds of stars, and this globe shows the five you speak of within the constellations of the Zodiac. From the Book of Maugis, we know the prophecy is etched in the heavens, hidden in the meaning of the Zodiac's symbols. Perhaps that is where you should start."

"Enough of this prophecy!" Gerbert snapped. "It's a delusion, born of the poisoned mind of Maugis d'Aygremont, and this power you speak of is even more dangerous. Every one of my brothers at Reims who pursued these things ended up dead. And I warn you once more, Brother Ciarán, seven of those brothers paid for their sins by burning at the stake."

Heat rushed up Ciarán's neck. "Like Thomas of Metz and Martha of Kildare?"

Gerbert's eyes widened at the mention of their names. "Thomas of Metz became so obsessed by this delusion it fouled his thoughts, and even turned him to darker arts. The truth of this was sworn to me by one of his own brethren who discovered these crimes."

"One of his own brethren . . ." The possibility hit Ciarán like a thunderbolt. "Lucien of Saint-Denis. He was your confessor?"

Gerbert stepped back.

Ciarán's voice rose in anger. "Everything he told you was a lie. It was Lucien of Saint-Denis who killed Dónall mac Taidg and Brother Remi, and who murdered Canon Martinus when you were at Reims. Lucien of Saint-Denis was a servant of the Devil, and through you, he sent two innocent people to their deaths!"

"Thomas of Metz was not innocent!"

"Thomas of Metz was my father, and Martha of Kildare was my mother, and you watched them burn!"

Gerbert's jaw fell slack. Then he yelled, "Get out!" He thrust a finger toward to the door. "Niccolo! Ewin! Guards!"

The door burst open and the priest rushed in, followed by the mail-clad Lombard, a look of alarm in his cold blue eyes. The brawny Lombard snarled as he wrapped his hand around his sword hilt.

Then, with the scrape of steel, he drew his steel blade.

THE BROTHERHOOD OF THE MESSIAH

A t sunset, Theodora strode into the ruins of Trajan's Market. A dark cloak flowed over her shoulders, its hood covering her platinum hair. Her slender hand clutched the hilt of a dagger sheathed in the sash around her waist.

The merchants had closed up their stalls, leaving only a lone shepherd and his sheep grazing on the grass between the ancient flagstones and broken columns. Ahead loomed the five-story structure of reddish stone with its arcades and rooftops of terra-cotta tiles. The market was once the jewel of Emperor Trajan's Forum, yet now debris littered its terraces, mortar crumbled from the walls, and its once magnificent archways stood dark and desolate. Theodora ducked into one of the archways, her muscles tense. Charon had told her that Naberus used this place as a hideaway, though she worried that thieves and robbers lurked here too.

She found the passageway torchlit and followed Charon's directions until it dead-ended in a black-stained door. She rapped on it. Through the thick wood, a man spoke a phrase: "The thousand years are ending, the Savior soon returns."

Theodora responded with the words Charon taught her. "When he comes, may no foreigner sit on Saint Peter's throne."

A bolt slid and the door opened. A handsome young monk stood in its threshold while Gregorian chants echoed from the chambers beyond. "Sister," the monk said, "which brother are you here to see?"

"Naberus," she said icily.

The monk's eyes narrowed. "As you wish." He led her down another passageway. In an adjacent room, Theodora glimpsed a half-dozen men seated around a table, uncowled in their black robes, playing dice and quaffing ale. The men laughed and swore, reminding her of another thing Charon had told her. *Not all the brothers are monks. Most are bravos and rogues who despise our German invaders.*

One of the more roguish-looking gamblers leered at her as she walked by, licking the ale from his lips. Theodora glanced away, her fingers tightening around her dagger's hilt.

The monk led her past a second chamber that had been converted into an oratory, the source of the Gregorian chants. Wreathed in candlelight, a score of monks sang from the choir, and Theodora found their chanting as beautiful and haunting as the gamblers' talk was lewd and lecherous.

Past the oratory, another oak door was cracked open. The monk gestured toward it. "You'll find him there."

Theodora answered with a nod, her heart pounding in her chest. *I'll plunge my knife into his throat.* She waited until the monk walked away, and then slid her dagger from its sheath. Clutching the hilt, she drew a deep breath and stepped into the chamber.

Five feet before her, two mastiffs looked up, their massive bodies sprawled upon the floor. Behind them, hunched over a table with two tallow candles, Naberus raised his head. A strand of his unkempt hair fell across his face, and red wine stained his lips. "Have you come to kill me?"

"I should," she said coldly. "You abandoned Crescentius, and then they murdered him!"

Naberus's gaze bored into her. "They would have murdered me, as well. Then all would be lost."

A tear tinged her left eye. "All is lost."

"Only Crescentius's cause," Naberus insisted. "Like old Saint Paul,

I've received a *higher* calling." He stepped out from behind the table, rising to his full height, never taking his eyes off her.

Her hand gripping the dagger began to shake.

As if sensing her hesitation, he lunged, grasping her arm. The dagger tumbled to the floor. He wrenched her toward him, his lips but inches from hers.

"You've not come to kill me," he said. The scent of wine lingered in his breath; his grip tightened around her wrist. "If so, you would have already tried, and Grimm and Set would have taken your life."

Theodora stifled a scream.

"No," Naberus said. This time his lips touched the corner of her mouth. "You've come here because you have nowhere else to go. You can't flee to Crescentius's son, for he's with his mother Stephania and she would not tolerate your presence. And still, you want something in Rome, don't you?"

Theodora swallowed hard. "I want revenge."

"Against the emperor or the pope?"

"Both," she replied, her voice but a whisper.

Naberus pulled off her cowl and drank in the scent of her hair. "You seek the Brotherhood of the Messiah as allies. You want me to bring them to your cause."

She tried to steel her nerves, but her body still trembled. "They were always loyal to Crescentius."

"Indeed they were. But I have a more immediate use for them, at least those without scruples. Two interlopers have entered the city, and I must retrieve something they stole before I leave here."

"Leave Rome?" Theodora shook her head. Naberus had lived here forever; the thought of him leaving seemed unimaginable. "To go where?"

He released his grip, as if her question turned his thoughts to something far greater than she. His long fingers gestured to four Tarot cards lying face up on the table. "I have a journey ahead, one that will end in sacrifice."

Theodora felt a chill as he spoke those words. "Will you still help me?"

"Perhaps." He took her hands. "For a price, I could bend the brotherhood to your cause. They would become your sword of vengeance, for the thousand years are ending . . ."

Her voice quivered. "And when they do, no foreigner shall sit on Saint Peter's throne."

Naberus flashed her a ravenous smile. "So true." His arm wrapped around the small of her back as he pressed his lips to her cheek. "Now, my dear, let's talk—what price are you willing to pay for your vengeance?"

22

DII CONSENTES

That evening, Ciarán sat slumped against *La Margerie's* mast, staring at Crescentius's tome and pondering how futile their efforts had become.

Moonlight glinted off the gold and silver symbols on the tome's cover, but they were no closer to solving its puzzle than when they had set out to find Gerbert. The only glimmer of hope was that they avoided arrest at the emperor's fortress. Instead, the new archbishop had been content to have his Lombard guardsman forcefully usher Ciarán and his companions out the gate and warn them never to return. Their attempt to secure Gerbert's aid had failed, and Ciarán knew his Irish temper was to blame.

Khalil and Alais walked up beside him, deck planks creaking with their approach. She handed him a cup of Roman wine that Josua had procured earlier that afternoon. "You're too hard on yourself," she said. "The man did help cause your parents' deaths."

Ciarán took the cup she offered. "He was the only one who could help us. If Gerbert was right about the stars in scripture, all we learned is that the Key to the Abyss was given to one of the Fae." He gestured at the cover of the tome. "But we're no closer to understanding these symbols. Without Dónall and Isaac and everything they knew, we're like a ship in the fog, and I fear we're lost."

He drank a deep quaff of wine, while Khalil knelt down beside him. "There's still another way," the Persian said.

Ciarán tipped his head to the star-glazed sky. "What?"

"We could do what I recommended back in Solignac—go to Constantinople or Baghdad. There are scholars there who can decipher the meaning of these symbols. And I refuse to believe the magi of the last millennium would not have left some guidance or wisdom for the next time the wheel of prophecy came full circle. There are answers out there, but we are searching in the wrong places."

Ciarán sighed. "How can you be so sure those answers don't lie in Rome?"

"How can we be sure of anything?" Alais asked. "Save the fact that I have been feeling more and more certain there is something dark in this city."

"Those are just dreams," Ciarán insisted.

"They're more than that," she said. "I don't know how or why, but I swear I have seen this place you called *Dudael.* It's a gray wasteland surrounded by bronze cliffs. I saw giants there, legions of them, and an immense pillar rising from a hill of skulls. And I heard voices, people trapped beneath the hill. I do not doubt these are the ones you called the Watchers, desperate for their release, and I cannot help but believe their freedom is somehow linked to the Key."

Ciarán listened to her, wide-eyed. *Isaac had dreams like these.*

"But I also feel the darkness of that place is somehow connected to this city," she continued. "There's a danger here, and I'll rest better once we're gone. Maybe Khalil's plan would be best."

Ciarán did not know what to say. The demon's words had led them to Rome and he was certain the symbols on Crescentius's tome held some answer to the Key's location. From the demon, he also knew the enemy was searching for the Key too. *The enemy has servants that hide in the shadows,* Remi had warned, *and not just men.* Yet Remi was dead and his warnings were but memories now. Ciarán held his head in his hands. "I don't know what to do."

He glanced up as Évrard came stomping across the deck. In his thick fingers he held a folded piece of parchment and what looked like a small leather book. "Some scrawny priest brought these for you," he said, handing them to Ciarán.

Ciarán stood up. "It's a letter," he said, noting the wax seal pressed with the symbol of a cross. He glanced at his friends and then strode toward the deckhouse.

"Where are you going?" Khalil called back.

"To find a bloody candle so I can read it." He threw open the door. In the deckhouse, a candle still burned on a small table. After breaking the seal, he unfolded the letter. Words flowed across the parchment, penned in Carolingian script, with an elaborate cross-shaped signature at the bottom.

To Brother Ciarán, from Gerbert, Archbishop of Ravenna, with grace.

I am not certain I should be aiding you, but suffice it to say your accusation about Lucien of Saint-Denis has left me deeply troubled.

I have been ruminating on the symbols etched on your book's cover, and had a thought. Symbols often have dual meanings, and in the case of the twelve symbols on the golden ring, I believe that to be the case. While the symbols may be astrological, they are also glyphs of the Dii Consentes, the twelve major gods of ancient Rome: Juno, Vesta, Minerva, Ceres, Diana, Venus, Mars, Mercury, Jupiter, Neptune, Vulcan, and Apollo. How they fit with the heptagram and the eight signs of the Zodiac, I do not know. However, if I were you, I would begin my search for answers at the Church of Santa Maria Rotunda.

T

GER BER

VS

P.S., this journal was discovered by your father when we were at Reims. By right it belonged to him, and you should have it now.

Ciarán shook his head slowly, still comprehending what he had just read. *I am not certain I should be aiding you . . .* Had Gerbert come to realize Lucien may have been the real traitor at Reims?

"What is it?" Khalil asked.

"It's from Gerbert of Aurillac."

Khalil looked confused. "What on earth does it say?"

Ciarán read them the letter. "I don't know what happened to change his mind."

Alais gestured to the thin, leather-bound book beneath the letter. "What about the journal?"

Ciarán had almost forgotten about the journal in his hands. The leather cover was unadorned and creased with age, and the vellum pages were dry and yellowed. He set down the letter and opened the journal. Inside, was a brilliantly illuminated page with words that made Ciarán's jaw fall slack.

Turpin, by the Grace of God
Archbishop of Reims, and Constant
Companion of the Emperor Charlemagne, to Maugis,
Noble Lord of Aygremont. Blessings in Christ.

Ciarán shook his head. "This must be Turpin's journal. Dónall told me about it on our voyage to France. He said my father discovered it at the Cathedral School of Reims. It's what led them to the Book of Maugis d'Aygremont. Why would Gerbert let this go?"

"Perhaps," Kahlil said, raising a brow, "there's more to the arch-bishop than we witnessed today."

Ciarán gave a faint nod. He could hardly believe their reversal of fortune. For whatever had caused Gerbert's change of heart, the arch-bishop had unveiled a new path. One that lay within Rome, and in a church no less. Tomorrow, he vowed, they would find this church of Santa Maria Rotunda, and hopefully some answers.

23

THROUGH THE OCULUS

"The Church of Santa Maria Rotunda? I know of it," the dockmaster said. "One of the oldest churches in the city. Go across the river, over the Capitoline Hill, northwest of the Forum. Has a big round dome, you can't miss it."

Ciarán thanked the man, then joined Khalil and Alais in the rowboat where Évrard manned the oars. The day, Ciarán realized, was beginning the same as yesterday, and they were even dressed as they were a day before, bearing Crescentius's tome wrapped in sackcloth, while both Caladbolg and Khalil's scimitar remained safely on the cog. Weapons were forbidden in churches, and the last thing Ciarán wanted to do was earn the wrath of some parish priest.

When they reached the Tiber's far bank, Ciarán, Alais, and Khalil bid Évrard farewell. They followed the dockmaster's directions down narrow streets with cramped houses and storefronts along the river. Eventually, they came to a road Alais recognized from the times she visited the Forum. They passed the field that used to be Circus Maximus, where cows and sheep grazed on the dew-slick grass. To the west rose the Capitoline Hill, crowned with the ruins of ancient temples and the bell towers of Christian churches, while a bustling marketplace ran down one slope. They asked directions to the church from a grain merchant at the base of the hill. He directed them through a labyrinth of narrow streets between houses packed wall to wall, with rooftops so high that the streets looked like shadowy tunnels where only slivers of sunlight threatened to peek.

Through an archway between two houses so tall they leaned into the street, the trio emerged into a plaza dominated by a massive domed structure that had to be the Church of Santa Maria Rotunda. Most of the building was round, but a rectangular portico stood at its entrance with more than a dozen granite columns supporting a triangular pediment. Across the pediment's face were words inscribed in Latin: *"M. Agrippa L.R. Cost Tertium Fecit." Marcus Agrippa, son of Lucius, three-time consul, made this.*

"I'll be damned." Khalil's lips parted into a smile. "That's the Pantheon, the ancient Roman temple whose name means 'all the gods.'"

Ciarán cocked his head. "The popes must have turned it into a church."

"Of course," Alais said. "Gerbert sent us to the temple of the twelve Roman gods. The *Dii Consentes.*"

Ciarán led the way, striding up the ancient marble steps into the shadows of the colonnaded portico. A solitary monk stood beside one of the granite columns, fingering prayer beads strung with a cross. He glanced up briefly, his face hidden beneath his black cowl.

The temple's imposing bronze doors opened into an expansive circular chamber. Though it was dimly lit, Ciarán stared in wonder. Alternating squares and circles of red porphyry and yellow marble covered the floor, over which loomed the dome. Rings of coffers arched up the curved ceiling, one hundred and fifty feet high. In the center of the dome was a circular opening, or oculus, through which a shaft of sunlight illuminated the temple, offering the only light save for the candles burning at shrines spaced around the rotunda's walls and on an altar at the far end. Flanked by Corinthian columns, the altar stood in a deep niche beneath an apse covered in golden mosaics. Six more deep niches, each bordered by a pair of columns, were set around the curved walls, containing the shrines, where tiny candles glowed in the niches' shadows. Eight smaller, and even darker, alcoves filled the spaces between the niches, each a man's height above the floor, framed by pillars supporting triangular or arched pediments above the hollows where statues of gods or men once stood.

The church looks like it was made by angels, not men, Ciarán thought.

A peaceful silence filled the rotunda. At the altar, two priests glanced at the trio as they entered. One priest was portly and swarthy; the other tall with a thick gray beard. Other than the priests, only a scattering of lay folk lingered in the church, praying at the shrines within the deep niches.

"Now what do we do?" Alais whispered.

"Figure this out." Ciarán unwrapped the tome from the sackcloth and realized the rings on the tome's cover mirrored the chamber's shape. He stepped toward one of the deep niches, where the shaft of sunlight beaming through the oculus formed a perfect circle over one of the shrines.

He began studying the walls. Like the floors, they were covered with patterns of marble and porphyry in shapes of circles and squares, perhaps elements of the sacred geometry Gerbert spoke of. Ciarán searched for any other symbols, wondering if they might match those ringed on the cover of Crescentius's tome. Yet amid the spectacular architecture, he found none.

"I think we should imagine this place as it was before the Christians came," Khalil suggested. "I suspect at one time these niches contained statues of the Roman gods. For where else here would they be honored?"

"Not a bad thought," Ciarán replied. He counted the niches. "There are only seven, but the inner ring shows twelve symbols for twelve gods."

Khalil stroked the chin of his beard. "Perhaps five of them were less prominent."

Alais pointed to the heptagram in the cover's center. "There are seven niches and the star has seven points."

Ciarán thought about that. "What if we have to align seven of these symbols with the points on the star? But to choose the right seven, we'd need to know which god stood in each niche."

"I know someone we can ask." Alais smoothed the skirt of her slate dress and walked toward the altar.

Ciarán blinked. "She knows one of the priests?"

"I think our Alais is full of surprises," Khalil said.

At the altar, Alais tapped the arm of the taller priest, who appeared surprised at the interruption. But his age-worn face lit up upon seeing her. "Lady Alais!"

Curiosity drew Ciarán and Khalil across the chamber. She turned and introduced them. "Father Michele, these are two of my traveling companions: Khalil al-Pârsâ, a poet from Córdoba, and Brother Ciarán, a scholar from the Irish monastery of Derry."

The gray-bearded priest, who must have seen sixty winters or more, raised a brow at the sight of Khalil, but greeted them both with a smile.

"I will leave you to talk," the swarthy priest told Father Michele before wandering off to the nearest shrine.

"My apologies," Alais told the old priest. "I did not mean to interrupt your conversation."

"No need to apologize," Father Michele said. "Canon Ubertus and I were just talking Church politics, the fuss over this antipope, John the Greek, and what Pope Gregory intends to do about him. Nothing more than gossip, and I always have time for one of the flock."

Alais smiled warmly. "I met Father Michele at a church in the Forum," she told Ciarán and Khalil. "I mentioned our curiosity about this place."

"The Lady Alais appears to have a keen interest in the old Roman temples," Father Michele said. "From her studies of antiquity back in Poitiers, no doubt. A woman with her education is a rare gift."

Ciarán gave her a subtle nod. *Well done, my lady.*

She answered with a playful shrug, before turning her attention back to the old priest. "We have a theory that these niches around the rotunda once contained statues of the old Roman gods."

"That would be correct," Father Michele replied with a proud smile. "Statues of the gods stood in the magnificent niches, while those of emperors and demigods were in the raised alcoves."

"Do you know which gods stood in which niches?" she asked.

"Oh Lord, no. When Pope Boniface the Fourth converted this temple into a church nearly four hundred years ago, he rid it of pagan adornments and replaced those old statues with shrines to Rome's blessed saints. Why, look there." Father Michele gestured toward the deep niche Ciarán had been studying. "The sun is shining on the shrine to Saint Longinus. But just you wait—by Sext the light will fall upon the shrine of blessed Saint Agatha."

Ciarán clenched his jaw. *The priest can't tell us.*

Khalil glanced at the oculus. "The light, it moves from niche to niche?"

"With the movement of the sun," Father Michele replied. "This is a fascinating place, like no other built in ancient Rome. Some believe the whole temple is a giant sundial. Did you know that at midday on the vernal equinox, the sun illuminates the temple's entrance? It's as if the building itself marks the passage of time."

Just then, a dark shadow emerged in the circle of light above Saint Longinus's shrine. Father Michele glanced up and furrowed his brow. At the edge of the oculus perched a large black raven.

"That's odd," the priest said. "I've never seen a raven do that before. It's like he's watching all the people in the church. And speaking of, I really must get back to my own basilica. You never know who might be looking for me."

After Father Michele bid them farewell, Ciarán glanced up at the bird, who seemed to be staring straight at him. *Strange,* he thought, before turning back to the problem at hand. Something the old priest had said reminded him of his Celtic heritage—an ancient monument in Ireland called Brú na Bóinne that marked the passing of Yule when the rising sun illuminated its inner chamber. He wondered if there could be a connection. *Yule and the vernal equinox are all part of the Wheel of the Year,* he recalled. His gaze fell on the cover of Crescentius's tome, where garnets studded the silver ring encircling the inner ring that featured the symbols of the gods. "There are eight jewels on the outer ring," he said, thinking aloud, "each one bearing a symbol."

Khalil shrugged. "So?"

"So," Ciarán said, "what if this building is truly like a sundial? If it marks the vernal equinox, then as the days go on, it would mark all the festivals in the Wheel of the Year."

Khalil cocked a brow. "What wheel?"

"Since ancient times," Ciarán explained, "the Celts, and I suppose most European pagans, observed eight great festivals, each one a point on the Wheel of the Year. There are the equinoxes—Ostaria and Mabon—and the solstices—Midsummer and Yule—and four more festivals in between: Lughnasadh, Beltane, Imbolc, and Samhain."

"The outer ring might have eight gemstones," Khalil said, "but they are marked with symbols of the Zodiac, not pagan runes."

Ciarán shook his head. "I don't think that matters. Remember what Gerbert said about dual meaning? The symbols of the Zodiac not only represent constellations, but also points in time."

"So there's a symbol for each festival?" Alais asked.

"Aye," Ciarán replied. "I'm certain of it. On the vernal equinox, the sun enters Aries, one of the symbols on the gemstones. Next comes Beltane, which occurs when the sun is in Taurus, followed by Midsummer when the sun enters Cancer. Both of those symbols are on the outer ring, and they're in the correct order. Lughnasadh follows Midsummer during the time marked by Leo, and then comes Mabon, the autumnal equinox, when the sun leaves Virgo. The dark night of Samhain happens in October, the month marked by Scorpio, and then comes Yule, when the sun enters Capricorn. Last is Imbolc in February, the time marked by Aquarius. Each of these eight symbols is etched on one of the garnets on the outer ring."

"If you're correct," Khalil said, "whoever created this puzzle had been to this place. If the seven points on the heptagram coincide with the seven niches around the rotunda, it would fit perfectly."

As Khalil spoke, Ciarán traced lines in the air to indicate that of the seven-sided star. It was not difficult to imagine the heptagram painted across the rotunda's floor.

Khalil pointed to the tome's cover, in the space opposite the apex of the seven-pointed star, between its two lowest points. "The chamber's entrance would be here."

"According to Father Michele," Ciarán reasoned, "the entrance marks the vernal equinox. What if we position the symbol for Aries there?" He drew in a breath and carefully spun the outer ring until the garnet etched with the astrological symbol of Aries was directly between the star's two lowest points. For an instant, he feared a jolt a searing pain, but it never came. "The ward wasn't triggered," he said with a breath.

"Yet nothing happened," Khalil observed. "We must have to align the correct symbol of each god whose statue once stood in those niches."

Concern spread across Alais' face. "Father Michele couldn't tell us which gods go where."

"Then let's deduce it from what we know of mythology," Khalil replied.

Ciarán ran his fingers through his hair. "When you enter the temple, what's the first niche that you'd see?"

"The one with the altar," Alais replied.

"Right," Ciarán said with a nod, "the one that corresponds to the apex of the star. It's the niche most prominently situated in the rotunda."

Khalil gave a nod. "The place where the most prominent of the gods would stand."

"I can only think of one ancient god who would fit that role," Ciarán said. "Jupiter, the king of the Roman gods." He sucked in another breath and placed a finger on the golden inner ring. The metal felt cool to his touch. Khalil and Alais huddled around him as he turned the wheel to position the symbol for Jupiter at the star's apex.

Pain struck like lightning.

It surged through his limbs, an icy, searing sensation that threatened to turn his bones to jelly. Ciarán grimaced, doing everything in his power to avoid screaming. His knees buckled and he slumped to the floor, feeling his life bleeding away.

Alais dropped to a knee. "What happened?" she asked urgently, wrapping an arm around his shoulders.

Pain wracked Ciarán's whole body. He doubted he had the strength to stand.

Khalil hunched over him. "You triggered the ward."

Gritting his teeth, Ciarán nodded. He feared all might be lost, for he knew he could not survive a third strike from the ward. Alais and Khalil helped Ciarán to his feet as Khalil supported his weight with the strength of his good arm.

"Let's get him back to the cog," Khalil said.

"Wait!" Alais looked as if she just had an epiphany. "There was no god in that niche—but a goddess."

"How do you know?" Khalil asked.

"At the temple in the Forum, Father Michele told me that Venus was the mother of Aeneas and the patron goddess of Eternal Rome." She reached for the tome. "Let me try."

Ciarán shook his head, mouthing the word *no,* but he was too weak to stop her from taking the tome.

"Alais," Khalil said, "it's too dangerous."

"Do you want to learn what's inside this or not?" She placed a slender finger on the inner ring and rotated the wheel until the symbol for Venus was at the star's apex. The ring made an audible click, and the entire circle of metal rings protruded slightly from the leather cover.

Ciarán's eyes widened as she slid her finger beneath the metal disk and lifted it from the tome. Alais turned it over. Etched into the smooth metal were words arranged in a spiraling pattern.

"It's in Greek," she said. "I can't read it."

"Allow me." Khalil took the metal disk. He narrowed his gaze, turning the disk as he read the words aloud.

As the sun sets on a thousand years, seek the Giant's Ring,
On the Solstice, at the Altar Stone, with blood the Spirit brings,
The answer to the mystery forged when Atu sank into the sea,
The way to our salvation, the revelation of the Key.

Alais sighed. "A riddle."

Ciarán shut his eyes and tried to summon enough strength to speak. "Remember what the demon said . . ." His voice strained to utter the words. "The riddle must reveal the path to the Key."

Khalil looked up from the disk. "I have never heard of a Giant's Ring, but I recognize the other word, Atu. It is from Sumerian mythology, another name for the lost island of Atlantis, where the goddess Inanna stole the Mes, a tablet of sacred knowledge."

"Sacred knowledge," Ciarán said but the sound came out like a cough. "Mysteries."

"One forged when Atlantis sank into the sea," Alais offered.

Khalil nodded slowly. "And this one would concern the location of the Key."

Alais glanced over her shoulder to where a group of black-robed Benedictines stood near one of the shrines. "Those monks are watching us. We should leave before we encounter a problem with the Church. I doubt they'll look kindly on this tome."

"That may be wise." Khalil looked to Ciarán. "Can you walk?"

Ciarán tried, but winced at the first step. "Need help."

Khalil handed the disk to Alais, who set it back into the empty circle in the tome's cover. He wrapped his good arm around Ciarán and helped him toward the entranceway. Pressing the tome to her chest, Alais walked beside them, glancing back frequently. "The monks are following us," she whispered.

Ciarán tried to look back, but the sharp pain in his neck and shoulders made him think twice about it.

Alais led the way from the rotunda into the shadowy portico and its forest of granite columns. Three paces in, she abruptly stopped. From the shadows between the columns emerged a dozen more cowled monks, but these held cudgels clutched in their fists.

Ciarán's blood ran cold. One of the black-robed men stood a head taller than the rest. A pointed beard jutting from his cowl and his familiar face simmered with subtle rage. *The intruder from Castel Sant'Angelo . . .*

Alais gasped as the tall Roman ripped the tome from her grasp.

"That belongs to me," he said.

Cudgels flashed. To Ciarán's right, Khalil cried out in pain. Then something hard cracked against Ciarán's skull. His head whipped back and his vision exploded in a thousand bursts of light. Another cudgel smashed into his gut; the breath rushed from his lungs.

Ciarán's legs gave way. The last thing he felt was the cold, hard granite before his whole world went black.

24

THE GIANT'S RING

Alais gaped at the tall man who tore the tome from her grasp. With his simmering gaze and pointed beard, it was as if she was staring at the black-clad man from her dreams.

The man turned his back just as other monks hammered their cudgels down on Ciarán and Khalil. Alais screamed as the blows fell. From between two columns rushed a monk with a pockmarked face, his eyes burning with madness. He threw a forearm hard into her chest. The blow knocked the breath from her lungs and sent her tumbling off the portico. She feared her head would strike the marble, but she managed to catch herself from careening down the steps.

In the portico, all she could see amid the granite columns were men in black robes, then a voice cried out behind her.

"In the name of Christ, stop!"

Father Michele stormed across the plaza, along with a half-dozen warriors clad in chain mail with shields bearing the symbol of a black lion.

"Help us!" Alais cried.

When the warriors saw the mass of cowled men, they broke into a sprint. The largest of them, an older, bearded warrior with the stature of a lord and the face of a battle-hardened veteran, ripped a longsword from his scabbard. "Halt in the name of the emperor!" he bellowed, bounding up the stairs.

"Think of your souls!" Father Michele yelled.

The pockmarked monk drew a dagger from a sheath at his belt. With a cry, he raised the blade and lunged toward Alais.

Her eyes fixed on the blade, Alais scrambled backward. Through her line of sight, a second blade flashed. It struck the monk straight through his neck. Blood streamed as the monk's head left his body and thudded lifelessly down the steps.

Breathless, she glanced between the veteran warrior clutching his bloodied sword and the portico, where the black-robed men were fleeing like hares from a pack of hunting dogs.

The warrior offered her a hand, but instead of taking it, she clambered up the steps. In the portico's shadows, Khalil knelt over Ciarán, who lay unmoving on the marble floor. The poet clutched his already wounded arm, while blood stained his cheek.

"Is he alive?" she asked, rushing to Ciarán's side.

Kahlil shook his head "I don't know."

The veteran warrior knelt beside them and touched his fingers to Ciarán's neck. "He lives."

Alais sighed with relief.

Father Michele knelt beside them and made the sign of the cross. "I'll pray he heals, my lady."

She nodded and turned to Khalil. "Are you all right?"

"Bruised but that's all." He put a hand on Ciarán. "We must get him back to the cog."

"My men gave chase," the veteran warrior said. "I must join them."

Father Michele patted the man's shoulder. "Margrave, you've done enough today. I'll get them home."

The margrave stood and bowed to Alais. "My lady."

"Thank you," she said.

As the margrave hurried to join his men, Khalil looked to the wizened priest. "How did you know to save us?"

"As I left," Father Michele replied, "I saw those black-robed fellows skulking toward the church. I've seen their kind before, more brigand than monk. It just so happened I spied the margrave and his patrol of Saxons down a street from the piazza, so I summoned their aid."

"For that, I am grateful," Khalil said.

"As am I," Alais added, before kissing the old priest on his hand.

Father Michele beamed at her. "You make an old man blush, my lady. Now let's move with Godspeed and get your friend home."

CIARÁN WOKE TO THE PEAL OF BELLS, HIS HEAD POUNDING WITH EACH clang. Faint sunlight seeped into *La Margerie's* cabin. *It's daytime,* he realized. The last thing he remembered was being beaten by men dressed as monks.

Still wearing his Benedictine habit, he stretched his aching limbs. He felt strength in his muscles and figured the damage inflicted by the ward must be waning. He stood with a grimace and opened the cabin door to the deck. A platinum sky loomed over Rome and a ghostly fog wafted above the Tiber, while across the river, a low-hanging cloud shrouded the Aventine Hill. Alais stood at the rail in her slate-colored dress, her raven hair tied back, gazing at the city.

"The bells," Ciarán asked her, "were they for Terce?"

She turned around, her eyes wide. "You're awake!"

"And no worse for the wear, it seems, but hungry as a bear. What happened to us?"

"You don't remember the attack?"

Ciarán shook his head. "There were men dressed as monks, I was struck in the head . . ."

"They stole the tome," she said, triggering Ciarán's memory of the intruder from Castel Sant'Angelo ripping the book from her grasp.

"I thought they were going to beat you to death," she continued, "but then Father Michele arrived with a patrol of Saxons and chased our attackers away. Father Michele said they're part of a group bent on overthrowing Pope Gregory before the millennium. They want a Roman on Saint Peter's throne when Christ returns at the End of Days."

186

Ciarán rubbed a tender lump on the side of his head. "Why would they want Crescentius's tome?"

"The man who stole it said it belonged to him. Other than that, I don't know. Khalil and Josua left this morning in the hope of finding an answer to that question."

"They went without me?"

She placed a hand on his shoulder. "You've been asleep for nearly two days."

Ciarán blinked. "What?"

"We couldn't wake you, and didn't know, frankly, when you might wake again. We feared what that ward might have done to you."

Ciarán shook his head. "Where did they go?"

Alais crossed her arms. "To see the ferryman."

"The quaestor? Whatever for?"

"Khalil believes he'll know how to find the man who stole the tome. He wants to reclaim the book and determine what this man is up to."

"But we discovered the book's secret. I still remember the words."

"Khalil wrote them down," she said. "And I think I've solved part of the riddle, about the Giant's Ring."

Ciarán's eyes widened. "How?"

"Your gift from Gerbert; the answer was in Turpin's journal. I've been watching you for two days, so I had plenty of time to read it."

Ciarán shook his head again. Alais never ceased to amaze him. "What did it say?"

She clasped her hands together as she spoke. "Do you remember when you asked Brother Dónall if the Book of Maugis d'Aygremont had any connection to Britain, and he told you that Turpin's journal contained an account of such a journey?"

Ciarán nodded, recalling the moment outside Córdoba where he and Khalil had solved the riddle in Maugis' book that led them to Enoch's device.

"Well," she said, "I found that account in Turpin's journal. He journeyed to Britain along with the paladins Roland and Maugis, and the warrior Bradamante, to seek the tomb of a druid named Merlin. They go to an island named Glastonbury, where they find the entrance to a place called Avalon, near an abbey on the island. From Turpin's description, fog surrounds the entrance, so my guess it lies in the Otherworld, like Rosefleur. There, the paladins encounter a woman called the Lady of the Lake. If I'm guessing, she may be one of the Fae. She takes them to Merlin's tomb, where they speak with his ghost and retrieve a sword, which Turpin calls Flamberge, but we all know now how many names it's had. Caladbolg is just one of them."

Ciarán listened intently, realizing how everything seemed connected: the paladins, the prophecy, and Enoch's device. "Does she also give them this Giant's Ring?"

Alais smiled. "No, but Turpin wrote about it. The ring's not like one you'd wear on your finger. Rather, it's a place—an ancient ring of standing stones not two days from Avalon that, according to Turpin, the Britons believe was built by giants. But the Saxons who conquered the island call it by another name—Stonehenge."

Ciarán ran his fingers through his hair, overwhelmed by what she'd told him. "A temple . . . built by giants. One that must have an altar, just like the riddle said . . . *Sweet Jesus!*"

Alais cocked her head. "What?"

"If it's a ring of standing stones, it might be like the old monuments in Ireland, like Brú na Bóinne, where the rising sun marks the passing of Yule, just like the Pantheon marks the vernal equinox. The riddle suddenly makes sense. 'Seek the Giant's Ring, on the solstice . . .' Whatever mystery is to be revealed about the Key, my guess is it'll happen when the sun marks the solstice within the ring of stones." He glanced hurriedly around. "Where's Évrard?"

Alais stared at him wide-eyed. "With the dockmaster, I think."

Ciarán rushed to the rail overlooking the wharf. Beside a stack of barrels, Évrard stood negotiating with the haggard dockmaster. "Évrard!" Ciarán called.

The rotund captain looked up, his eyes bright. "Ah, Brother Ciarán, you're awake!"

"I have need of you."

Évrard shrugged and muttered something to the dockmaster, who spat and shook his head. The captain made his way up the gangplank. "How fast can we set sail?" Ciarán asked, his mind racing.

Évrard scratched the stubble on his jaw. "A day, maybe two. What's your hurry?"

"What day is it?"

"The twelfth of May," Évrard replied with a cocked brow.

"Is there any way we could sail to England by Midsummer? It can't be farther than going to Paris by way of the Seine."

Évrard shrugged. "I don't know," he said warily. "Why are you asking?"

"It may be the only chance we have of locating the Key to the Abyss before Midwinter, nearly three-quarters of a year from now. A bit too close to the millennium."

Évrard sauntered toward the cabin. "Let me look at my charts."

Ciarán and Alais followed him inside. From a chest on the floor, Évrard removed his charts and unfurled them across the small table. The maps showed all the lands of Western Europe, embellished with brilliant illuminations of tentacled sea monsters, giant toothy fish, and spewing whales. Évrard pointed a thick finger at a number of ports, muttering his thoughts. "Marseille in six days with good wind . . . another five to Barcelona . . . eight to Malaqha if we don't catch bad weather through the strait . . . eight more to al-Ushbūna if we're lucky . . ." He shook his head. "We'd not even be to Brest by then, and that's if the wind's in our sail."

"But that's if we sail along the coast?" Ciarán asked, praying that was the case. "What if we sailed through the strait between Corsica and Sardinia en route to Spain, and then, at Galicia, crossed the Basque Sea to Brittany?"

Évrard raised a brow. "That would be crossing open seas, a perilous path even with fine weather."

"Yet imagine the peril we'll all be in if the enemy's servants find the Key? It's worth the risk."

Grumbling, Évrard traced the path Ciarán described. "With some luck, maybe we could make it."

Ciarán smiled. "We Irish are known to have a bit of luck."

Across the table, Alais beamed. "Would you do it, Évrard?"

The old captain ran a hand through his brine-slick hair and looked at her sheepishly. "I could never say no to you, milady."

"Then that settles it," Ciarán said with wink to Alais. "To England we go."

∾

WITHIN THE HOUR, ÉVRARD CALLED ALL HANDS ON DECK. THOUGH STILL weak in his limbs, Ciarán helped the crew lower barrels of salted cod and casks of wine, ale, and water down into the hold as gulls screamed over *La Margerie*. Évrard studied his charts, working on the route across the Mediterranean through the strait of Corsica, while Mordechai readied the rigging and the sail.

By Nones, Ciarán's habit was soaked with sweat. Taking a break, he slumped down against the bulkhead to the cabin and felt himself drifting off to sleep before the sounds of boots stomping up the gang-plank jolted him awake. Josua and Khalil emerged on deck. "You're alive," the Persian said with a smile.

"I didn't want to miss all the fun," Ciarán quipped. "What did you learn?"

"That the quaestor is still a cheat," Josua said bitterly.

"His information came with a price higher than our friend had hoped," Khalil explained, "but I convinced him to pay it nonetheless. The man who stole the tome appears to have been Crescentius's counselor, Naberus da Roma. He left Rome this morning on the ship of a man called the Varangian."

Ciarán ran a hand across his face and groaned.

"What?" Khalil asked. "We are rid of this man, though I fear we will never retrieve the tome. But we've already unlocked its secret."

"You don't understand," Ciarán replied. "He's sailing for England."

Khalil's eyes narrowed. "Why on earth would he go there?"

"Because that's where he'll find the Giant's Ring. While you were gone, Alais discovered a reference to it in Turpin's journal. It's an ancient ring of standing stones, the place where the mystery of the

Key will be revealed when the sun rises on the summer solstice. That's what the riddle means, and my guess is that's why he stole the book."

Khalil shook his head. "How would Crescentius's counselor know about the prophecy, and why would he want the Key to the Abyss?"

"I don't know," Ciarán replied, "but now he's a day ahead of us."

"Ah," Khalil said, "that's why the crew is working so hard."

Ciarán nodded with a sigh.

"Then I have even darker tidings," Josua said. "The quaestor told us this Varangian sails a drekar, a longship like those the Norsemen use. Such a ship has a square sail, but also thirty pairs of oars, so she can move fast even when the wind is still. Our cog will be hard pressed to keep within two days of her."

Ciarán rose gingerly to his feet. "Then let's pray for fair winds and following seas." He turned to Khalil. "Before we leave, may I borrow your quill and some parchment? I need to write a letter."

Khalil furrowed his brow. "To whom?"

"Gerbert of Aurillac."

"Whatever for?"

Ciarán sucked in a breath. "I'm going to tell him everything we know."

THE VARANGIAN

The longship glided past the hulking ruins of Ostia where the Tiber emptied into the Tyrrhenian Sea. The ship's name was *Reaver* and she was a sleek and imposing craft, oak hulled and a hundred feet long with thirty benches for sixty oarsmen. Her massive square sail, filled with wind, bore the image of a black eagle, a predatory symbol for a predatory vessel.

Naberus stood on the swan-shaped prow with the wind in his face. Beside the craft glided Hermes, while Set and Grimm lounged on the deck in front of the rows of benches where the Varangian's motley crew took rest from their oars. Like their captain, many of these men were Rus from Kiev and Constantinople, yet they were joined by Romans and Greeks, Arabs from Sicily, and dark-skinned Nubians from Egypt and Makuria. All were lawless and violent men driven by greed and a lust for adventure, much like the Varangian, who approached Naberus once *Reaver* left Ostia in its wake.

The Varangian was an imposing man, nearly as tall as Naberus, but twice as broad. A vest of boiled leather covered his barrel chest, and golden bands adorned his muscled arms, though it was the captain's face, more than his size, that disturbed most men. His shaven head was tattooed with images of serpents, and his gaze lacked even a hint of compassion. A jagged scar stretched from his forehead to his cheek across weather-burned skin, marring what once might have been handsome face, while an unkempt beard, streaked with gray, only added to his savage appearance. Rumors held he was named Oleg and had served as a member of the Varangian Guard, the elite band of Rus and Norsemen who protected the Byzantine Emperor. Some believed he had fled Constantinople after sleeping with the notorious empress Theodora, earning the wrath of her murderous husband, Emperor John the First. Others believed the Varangian had killed a servant girl beloved by the empress and was marked for death. In Rome, the Varangian posed as a merchant, but worked as a pirate in the Tyrrhenian and Ionian Seas, and even the Adriatic, where he had earned a price on his head from the Doge of Venice. Crescentius had tolerated the Varangian's presence in Rome because he helped the prefect collect old debts from seafaring merchants and sent forceful messages to the Duke of Naples and the pirates of Sardinia, whenever such messages were needed. But Crescentius's execution had cost the Varangian his protector in Rome, so it did not take Naberus long to convince him and his crew to leave the city. To encourage them to sail halfway across the world to England, however, required the persuasion of gold. A small fortune in gold.

Yet what worth is gold in a time like this? Naberus reminded himself. *Not after my epiphany . . .*

The Varangian smiled, revealing a mouth half filled with golden teeth. "Is she fast enough for you, consigliere?"

"She had best be," Naberus replied. "We must arrive before Midsummer."

"We will reach this northern island by then," the Varangian assured. "Though it would not hurt if you told me what is so important about that place."

Naberus's eyes narrowed. "I paid not only for your ship's speed, but for your discretion."

The Varangian replied with a surly frown. Naberus knew he could not say more, for the Giant's Ring and the purpose it served was beyond most men's comprehension, its secrets lost to the passage of time long before the Celts ever set foot on Albion's shores. Even Naberus might not have believed the monument's secrets until that terrifying moment in Orcus's shrine when the voice reached him from beyond. The voice with power over the spirits, the voice of salvation. In that moment, when his blood ran cold, Naberus realized his grandfather had been right.

It was my birthright, and I was a fool for denying it so long.

The Varangian scratched his head. "Perhaps you will be more candid when we get closer to our destination. My men become restless when they don't know the purpose of a voyage."

"Your men will get rich from this voyage," Naberus snapped, "whether they know its purpose or not." He held out his arm for Hermes to land on. The raven fluttered to his outstretched limb and then scrabbled to perch on his shoulder.

The Varangian gave the raven a wary look. "My men could get rich raiding in these seas. Give me something to whet their appetite."

Naberus scraped his fingers through his beard, thinking for a moment. "How about a race?"

"Race!" Hermes screeched.

"A what?"

"A race of two ships, for we'll be pursued on this voyage." The voice from beyond had assured Naberus as much. He had considered trying to dispatch the interlopers while they were still in Rome, but the voice had commanded otherwise. *Pay them no heed, it said. They shall come to you.*

The Varangian furrowed his brow. "Who?"

"A Moor and a Celt who carries a rather big sword, but there are likely others with them too. They seek the same thing I do, and when they find us, I will leave them to you and your men."

The Varangian glanced toward the mast, where twin racks held a wicked array of bows, spears, axes, and swords. "My men also have an appetite for slaughter," he said with a cruel grin. "If these pursuers find us, then slaughter is what they'll get."

Naberus gave him a satisfied nod. "Then the Lord's will shall be done."

THE RACE

B y the time *La Margerie* reached the palm-lined port of Barcelona, after a day at sea battling wind and rain that swamped the cog's deck and soaked its square sail, Ciarán learned his fear about Naberus da Roma had come true.

Évrard delivered the ill tidings after speaking with the dockmaster, a gangly man with a bristly gray beard and skin baked brown by the sun. A day before, a longship named *Reaver* had arrived from Rome, proof that Naberus and this Varangian had sailed through the strait between Corsica and Sardinia. "Can't come as a surprise, lad," Évrard told the Irish monk. "If they're hell-bent on reaching England by Midsummer, you'd already charted the only course that'll allow 'em to make it."

"Will anything slow them?" Ciarán asked.

"Only God's foul weather," Évrard replied, "but that'll slow us, too. And they have oars."

"What if they take the brunt of a storm and we skirt along its edge?"

Évrard ran a hand through his brine-slicked hair. "Perhaps, but if you're going to go praying for bad weather, best not let the crew hear you. I'd rather not hear ya, either."

So Ciarán prayed silently for God's foul weather. A squall that might blow the longship off course or a thunderstorm that would drive it to shore—anything to slow their adversary in the race for the Key.

But God did not listen.

Much to Ciarán's chagrin, their voyage down the eastern coast of Al-Andalus was met with fair winds and bright skies, vast swaths of blue over the turquoise water of the Mediterranean Sea. Still, he kept watch for any sign of the longship, passing time by serving as an eighth member of *La Margerie's* crew. He traded his Benedictine habit for a simple linen tunic and a pair of breeches, working in the hot sun to trim the sail, secure the rigging, and even man the tiller at times. As the days passed, his hair grew over his tonsure and wisps of a beard covered his jaw, while his hands, used to holding vellum pages and goose quill pens, became rough and callused. Mordechai even joked that Ciarán had become the best fisherman among them. "Irish luck," Ciarán quipped, but he knew luck had failed him, for two weeks into the voyage they were no closer to catching the *Reaver.*

The daily labor, however, kept Ciarán from dwelling on his worst fear: *What if Naberus da Roma arrives first and finds the Key?* Whether he might use it to unleash the terror of the Apocalypse Ciarán did not know, for he could only imagine what purpose drove the Roman. But Brother Remi's frequent warning nagged at his mind. *The enemy has servants that hide in the shadows ... and not just men.* As mad as Remi once seemed, Ciarán was beginning to believe he had been the sanest of them all. The only one to appreciate the truth.

At times, Ciarán wondered if Gerbert of Aurillac had come around to this same truth. In the letter he sent, Ciarán spared no detail. He described Lucien's treachery and his alliance with Adémar of Blois. Ciarán explained how he and Dónall had found clues about Enoch's device in the Book of Maugis d'Aygremont, and how it had come from ancient Atlantis to Abraham and later King Solomon, before it passed into the hands of the Babylonians and the Magi of Persia. Ciarán described the magi's journey and how the device had gotten to England through Joseph of Arimathea, and ultimately to France and

Rosefleur through Maugis and the paladins of Charlemagne. He told of the battle at Rosefleur and of Orionde the Fae, and the Nephilim prince and the demons who served him. And he wrote about the Key to the Abyss and the riddle about the Giant's Ring. For as much as Ciarán hated the archbishop of Ravenna, if their journey to England were to fail, Gerbert might be the only one left with enough knowledge to prevent the End of Days.

During the long hours at sea, Ciarán's companions passed their time in different ways. Khalil's right arm had healed to the point where he could once again grip the hilt of his scimitar. He began teaching Mordechai, who was ever curious about the curved blade, how to wield it, and spent an hour each morning fencing with the strapping Jew using belaying pins instead of swords. In the afternoons, Khalil taught Persian and Arabic to Alais, who had a strange affinity for foreign tongues. She asked for the lessons because she wanted to read Kahlil's poems, and Ciarán could only wonder what mellifluous verses the Persian was whispering into her ears. The thought of this churned Ciarán's stomach, but gave him even more reason to focus on the art of sailing and keeping lookout, throwing all his energy into the race. The journey was all that mattered now.

In the early days of their voyage, he studied Turpin's journal. The thin leather book was filled with tales of the archbishop, his fellow paladins, and the emperor Charlemagne, but they did nothing to ease Ciarán's thoughts. For it became clear that Turpin, Maugis, and the other paladins knew the secrets of the prophecy and were determined to protect them for the time when those secrets would be needed. Yet somehow, the men who followed in their stead and were supposed to pass on those secrets had failed or abandoned the cause. It was only by sheer luck, and the curiosity of men like his father and Dónall, that those secrets were rediscovered in a hidden chamber in the Cathedral School of Reims. That is what they died for. His father and mother and Dónall, and Isaac and Eli and Niall. And his brothers, Bran and Murchad, Fintan and Áed and Ailil. Their deaths, Ciarán promised himself, would not be in vain. Although with each passing day at sea, Ciarán feared that promise would be broken.

On the last day of May, Anno Domini 998, they reached the Moorish port of Malaqha, where they learned the *Reaver* had left the port two days before. "How are we slipping so bloody far behind?" Ciarán snapped upon hearing the news.

"Because this cog is built for hauling cargo," Josua said. "That long-ship is built for speed."

Ciarán cursed under his breath and went back to helping the crew load barrels of fresh supplies on board the cog. The next day, the Pillars of Hercules came into view: Jebel Tariq on the European side and Jebel Musa on the African side, to use Khalil's terms for the two peaks that rose at the horizon into the clear blue sky. Past the pillars, *La Margerie* would enter the Atlantic, where perhaps God's foul weather awaited to slow the longship ahead of them. At least that was what Ciarán prayed for to the Lord above and to every saint he could think of. To Saint Brendan the Navigator and Saint Elmo, the patron of sailors, and to his own patron, Saint Columcille, and the great Irish saints Patrick and Brigid. And to the Blessed Virgin and the apostles Peter and Paul, and even to Alais' patron, Saint Radegonde, whose legend had played a role in their discovery of Enoch's device.

"Do you really think that will help?" asked Mordechai, who must have overheard Ciarán whispering his prayers as he stood in the sterncastle manning the tiller. But Ciarán could hardly think about Mordechai's question. Instead, he was focused on the sail. Hanging from the yard, the twenty-foot-wide sail of square-shaped cloth had gone slack.

Whatever hope Ciarán had left faded away. For at the Pillars of Hercules, the wind had died and the sea was as smooth as glass.

La Margerie sat still in the clear blue waters. As time passed, the sun drifted further to the west, and with each hour, the tightness in Ciarán's chest grew worse. *We'll never catch them now.*

He sat on the ladder to the sterncastle, holding his head in his hands, as boots clomped down the deck planks. He looked up at

Évrard's round stomach. The captain's lank hair fell over his broad forehead. "Give it up for the day, lad," Évrard said. "But if you're gonna pray, why don't you pray that we have enough drift to get us to Gibraltar so we aren't stuck out at sea tonight?"

Ciarán stood up. "No one's listening to my bloody prayers." He stormed away and headed for the bow, staring at the still waters to the horizon where the sun stained the sea a violet red.

"You can't lose faith," a woman's voice said from behind.

He turned to face Alais. Compassion filled her storm-gray eyes. "You are the champion of the prophecy, the one who answered the call," she told him. "Orionde said so."

"What good is that if I've no idea what to do?" he said. "Dónall might have known . . ."

"But he's passed on."

Ciarán gave a futile laugh and threw back his head. "That's why we've lost. He would have spoken some Fae words and just summoned the wind, I suppose, waving that leaf-shaped sword of his, and we'd be speeding our way to Stonehenge. Instead, we're sitting dead in the water. *He* should have been the bloody champion. I can't do it."

She put her hands on his shoulders; her face was just inches from his. "But he didn't find Enoch's device," she said. "You were the one who recognized the sequence. Who figured out the device had taken different forms in different ages, from staff to stone to cup to sword. And it was you who solved Maugis' riddle and discovered the device was at Rosefleur. You took it from the sanctum sanctorum and got us out of that tower before it fell. And it was you, not he, who killed Adémar of Blois."

Ciarán shook his head as if trying to clear a fog from his mind. He had almost forgotten about the sequence, the different manifestations of the device over time. His memory flashed to a wheel cross drawn in the snow many months ago in the ruined amphitheater of Poitiers. At each point of the cross, Dónall had sketched an object.

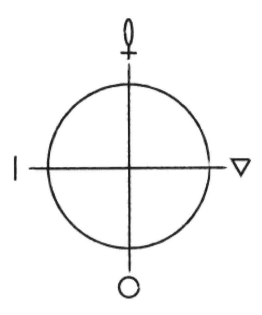

The circle represents our world, Dónall had explained. *Earth, fire, air, and water. Each element is associated with an object to focus the power. Maugis had an apothegm for it. Stone cuts earth, staff kindles fire. Sword parts air, cup binds water. Spirit incites the power.*

"What?" Alais asked.

"The four objects, like the Four Hallows of Ireland. Dónall said they help focus the Fae power, to manipulate the elements. A sword is the symbol for air."

Her eyes grew wide with understanding. "Caladbolg."

He nodded eagerly. "Let's pray it works."

Ciarán rushed to the cabin and retrieved the sword. Alais was waiting on deck when he returned with the blade sheathed in its leather scabbard. "There's only one problem," he said. "I only know one Fae word."

"Maybe that will be enough."

Ciarán could only hope. The only Fae word Dónall had taught him before he died was the word to infuse a gemstone with the light of one's soul. The light resided in the spirit of every living man and woman, and coupled with the words of the Fae it could ignite the power for even mortals to wield. Dónall believed those words, preserved in the Book of Maugis d'Aygremont, were part of the language of creation, brought to earth by angels in the age before the Great Flood, when, as Genesis said, the sons of God went into the daughters of men.

Wrapping his hand around the sword's massive, cross-shaped hilt, he unsheathed the blade. The gemstone in its pommel looked as gray as the surrounding steel, but Ciarán knew it would not stay that way for long. He closed his eyes and tried to clear his mind. Then he took a deep breath and whispered into the gem. *"Eoh."*

White light burst from the stone and rushed down the blade like hungry flames. The crewmen watching this spectacle backed away. The Christians among them made the sign of the cross, while Mordechai stared slack-jawed at the sword.

"It's all right," Ciarán assured them. With the exception of Mordechai, the rest of the crew had seen Dónall invoke the power against the storm-bringing furies who had pursued them to Córdoba, yet despite that experience, there was something about the light from Caladbolg's blade that struck awe or fear in the hearts of men.

"He's right, lads," Évrard told his crew, gazing wide-eyed at Ciarán and the sword.

Ciarán felt the sword's power surging through his limbs, yet he struggled to think what to do next. He held the same device that King Arcanus had wielded in mighty Atlantis and King Solomon used to conquer demons. It was the device the magi had employed to fulfill this same prophetic journey a millennium ago. *If only they had left some lessons on how to make it work,* Ciarán lamented. He closed his eyes and tried to remember how Dónall would summon the wind with his leaf-shaped blade, waving it in the air in flowing arcs.

When he opened his eyes, every soul on *La Margerie* was staring at him with anxious looks. He swung the sword in a wide arc, then cut circles in the air. Light from the blade shimmered in its wake, though it made no impact on the cog's flaccid sail. *All I'm doing is wearing out my arm.* Yet he persevered, waving the sword through the air until sweat dripped from his forehead and soaked through his tunic. He dropped to a knee, heaving for breath and bearing his weight on the sword, whose tip stuck into the wooden deck. The light faded from the blade. Grimacing, he looked into the sword's pommel where the coin-sized jewel still flickered with white fire.

"God in Heaven," he muttered through his clenched jaw, "all I'm asking for is some bloody wind."

In front of him, Alais gasped. Khalil looked on in disbelief. "Whatever you just said," he told Ciarán, "the words came out in a foreign tongue."

"Just like the words Dónall used," Alais said.

Ciarán shook his head. "They didn't."

"Yes," Khalil said, nodding slowly, "they did."

Ciarán glanced down at the gemstone in the sword's pommel. The light within it blazed, seeping through his eyes into his skull. He felt a subtle tingle in his head that he had not noticed moments before, trickling down his veins into his throat and lungs. He stood to his full height and pressed the cross-shaped hilt to his lips. "God in Heaven," he prayed, feeling the light's warmth envelop his vocal chords, "bring me wind." He swung the blade in a sweeping arc. Air rushed in the sword's path. Sailcloth clapped. Ciarán could sense the air around him as if it was moving with his limbs and bending to his will. One more time he prayed, and this time he heard the words flowing from the warmth in his throat. Neither Latin nor Irish, but alien sounds in an immortal tongue, yet their meaning was clear.

Bring me wind.

He leveled the blade toward the sail. Its rigging snapped taut. The wind surged at his back, into the sailcloth, propelling the cog forward. With each breath, the cog gained speed. The crew stood in awe as sea spray blasted over the bow.

"God's bones," Évrard muttered, a smile stretching across his face.

Ciarán kept his focus on the wind as a sense of triumph surged through his chest. "Évrard," he said, "let's see how fast she can go."

THE FALSE POPE

Pope Gregory waited on Saint Peter's throne. Pearls and gemstones adorned the high-backed marble chair, which sat on a dais at the end of the *Triclinium*, the great hall of the Lateran Palace, within an apse featuring an elaborate golden mosaic of Christ and His Apostles. Since the days of Constantine, the palace had been the seat of the Holy See, and today it would be the place where Gregory delivered his judgment.

Beside the pope, on a finely carved oak chair, sat his cousin Otto. The young emperor slouched in his seat, pale and sullen as if he were the one awaiting judgment. Gregory glanced between his cousin and the mosaics of Charlemagne that graced the walls of the massive hall. One portrayed Charlemagne accepting a gift from the Holy Savior, the Labarum of Constantine, a crimson banner surmounted with a golden Chi-Rho. Another showed Saint Peter with Pope Leo the Third kneeling to his right, and Charlemagne to his left, both receiving the saint's blessing. In each, the emperor, with his full beard, strong nose, and piercing eyes, reminded Gregory of the images of his great-grandfather, Otto Maximus, a warrior born and bred whose mere name would strike fear in the hearts of his enemies. Yet sitting on the dais, Gregory's cousin looked more like his gentle Byzantine mother than their fierce German forefather.

To Gregory's right stood Rumeus before an audience that filled the *Triclinium,* save for a clear pathway down its center. On each side of that pathway, throngs of black-robed canons and monks, along with every bishop and abbot in Rome, waited and whispered, casting a murmur throughout the hall. Gregory gazed impatiently down the pathway, where light from oil lamps reflected off the floor of polished white marble and red porphyry. At the far end, two scarlet-clad Lombards stood like statues to each side of a pair of towering bronze doors.

A rap on the doors quieted the murmurs, while Otto jumped at the sound as if it were a thunderclap. One of the guardsmen cracked open a door, then announced: "'Tis Count Berthold of Breisgau, Your Holiness. He has the prisoner."

"Send him in," Gregory commanded.

The guardsmen pulled open the heavy doors and a thickset German clad in a mustard cape and shining mail strode inside, his footfalls echoing through the hall. Count Berthold walked with an air of a conquering hero, a smug look on his bearded and blunt face. "Your Holiness and Your Majesty, I bring you the antipope, John the Greek!"

Into the hall stepped two of Berthold's men-at-arms, holding the prisoner. Otto gasped. Gregory swallowed hard at the sight of the creature who stood before him. For the soldiers held up a wraithlike figure, barefoot and shackled and dressed in a stained brown tunic. The prisoner's eyes had been gouged out, and where his nose should have been, only a red stump remained. His ears, or what was left of them, were but wisps of mutilated flesh, like the horns of a demon in some apocalyptic illumination.

Rumeus shot Gregory a horrified glance. "Holy Mother of mercy."

The prisoner's head swayed from side to side before he let out a loud and sickly moan. Gasps hissed from the priests and monks.

"Silence!" Gregory slammed the butt of the *ferula* onto the marble floor. The sound cracked through the hall, quieting the prisoner and the crowd. The prisoner's mouth hung open, his tongue clearly gone.

"Why was this done?" Otto asked, his face ashen.

Gregory clenched his jaw. "Before Count Berthold embarked on this mission, I read him the words of the prophet Ezekiel. 'I will turn my wrath against you so that they may deal with you in fury. They shall cut off your nose and your ears and, in the end, they will kill you with the sword.' At least Berthold did not take the complete verse to heart."

"He is my godfather . . ." Otto said faintly.

"Cousin, that man is a traitor. He confessed to Count Berthold. He conspired with Crescentius to place the Holy Church under the authority of the patriarch of Constantinople. No more treacherous villain has ever sat upon Saint Peter's throne."

Otto shrank in his chair, unable to look at John the Greek.

Gregory glanced at Rumeus, who made the sign of the cross. "Christ have mercy," the archdeacon muttered, loud enough for Gregory to hear.

Gregory stiffened his jaw. "Count Berthold, you shall be rewarded for your service."

The German count grinned as Gregory glared at the shattered figure before him. "John Philagathos!" he announced. The prisoner turned his head toward the sound of Gregory's voice. "You have sinned against God and the Holy See. You are anathema, condemned to the Lake of Fire to share the fate of Judas Iscariot! Let all who look upon your monstrous visage know the sins you've committed and the price you have paid."

The prisoner let out a yawning moan, before convulsing in hacks and sobs. Gregory looked away.

"May God forgive us," Otto said.

Gregory grimaced. "What do you think your grandfather would have done if someone had stolen his throne?"

"He would give him a swift death."

"I don't want his death, I want him to live. To be an example for these Romans who would seek to challenge my authority and that of the Church."

Otto stared at his mutilated godfather. "What will you do with him?"

"After he's defrocked, I'll imprison him in Castel Sant'Angelo."

"To let him rot?" Otto asked aghast.

"Yes," Gregory snapped, as his anger swelled. "Because that is *exactly* what they would have done to me."

STORM BRINGER

At al-Ushbūna, a Moorish port on the Atlantic where prayer towers soared over the stout city walls, Ciarán learned they had regained a day on the *Reaver*. And with the winds in her sail, the cog might even pass the longship before she reached Brittany.

Each day, he used Enoch's device to summon the wind and propel the cog toward their destination. Évrard swore she could reach eight knots during these spells, though Ciarán could only sustain the winds for a few hours before fatigue claimed him. This exhaustion seemed to be the price for wielding this power, as if the energy of his soul light fueled the winds until that energy was spent. Fortunately, sleep and food replenished it, but Ciarán had to spend long hours asleep in the cabin or he would lack even the strength to cross the deck by midday.

By the time *La Margerie* reached the Basque Sea, Ciarán had sensed the apprehension in Évrard and his crew. Sailors preferred to keep land in sight, for they always knew the direction of their travel and could moor their vessel if a storm approached. Crossing the open seas, however, required navigation by the sun and stars, but when obscured by clouds, a ship might stray off course into peril. Even worse, a gale or storm could ravage a ship on the open water where there was no way to escape the storm's wrath. Yet crossing the Basque Sea was the only way they would reach England by Midsummer and their only hope of catching the *Reaver*.

The first sign of trouble came a day into their crossing when Mordechai spotted a line of black clouds on the western horizon. By noontime, an angry wind had borne the clouds eastward, roiling the sea. Swells crashed over *La Margerie's* hull, rocking the cog so violently that Ciarán had to grab hold of the rigging to keep his feet.

"You've found God's foul weather now, lad," Évrard said as spray blasted over the cog's starboard side.

"I prayed it would come from the north," Ciarán replied, still glancing at the brewing storm. "To hinder the *Reaver*."

"Well, you fouled that one up to a fare-thee-well." Raindrops beaded down Évrard's forehead. "But maybe you could use that device of yours to get us away from this storm."

Ciarán nodded and did as he was told. Yet even with the power of Enoch's device, he struggled to wrestle the storm's winds, and feared for a moment that the competing gales might rip the cog's sail from its yard. In time, however, his will prevailed and the winds carried the cog northeast through the driving rain of the storm's outermost bands until the dark clouds faded beneath the southern horizon.

By the time exhaustion claimed him, he was so soaked with rain and seawater that he nearly slipped from Khalil's grasp when his friend and Mordechai helped him to the cabin. As soon as he hit the straw pallet, Ciarán fell into a deep slumber. He did not know how long he slept, but he woke abruptly to a man yelling.

"A sail, a sail!"

The voice was Mordechai's. "A sail to the north!"

Ciarán bolted to his feet. Someone had removed his rain-soaked tunic, and he didn't bother to find it. He threw his baldric over his shoulder, feeling Caladbolg's weight hanging at his side, and rushed onto the deck. Gray clouds filled the sky and a favorable wind bowed the sail, but everyone on board crowded around the bow, staring to the north. Ciarán leaned over the cog's starboard side. He had to squint before he spotted it, yet just as Mordechai said, a ship sailed at the edge of the horizon.

"Is it a longship?" he asked Josua, who stood just beyond the mast.

Josua shook his head. "She's too far away to tell, and the wind's in her sail."

"Let's try to remedy that." Ciarán slid Caladbolg from its sheath. His limbs were still weak, proof that Mordechai's call had awakened him before he could replenish his strength, though he believed he had enough left to close the gap between the two vessels.

"Be careful," Alais told him. "You've not slept long."

"Aye." Ciarán stepped behind the mast and looked up into the sail. Clearing his thoughts, he took a deep breath and whispered into the gemstone in the sword's pommel. *"Eoh."* When the light flared within the gem, Ciarán drank it in, allowing its warmth to coat his throat and lungs. As he uttered the now familiar verse that summoned the winds, a growing breeze coursed across his back. He pointed the blade toward the mast and willed the rushing air into the sail.

La Margerie sped forward, whipping spray across her bow. After an hour of full wind, Évrard steadied the tiller, his hair slick with brine. "She's but a knot away, lad."

"And she's a longship!" Mordechai hollered from his lookout point at the masthead.

"We'll pass her on the larboard side," Évrard said. "But lad, take care not to get too close."

The cog pitched left when Évrard pulled on the tiller. Between the mast and the crew crowding the bow, Ciarán could not see the long-ship. Mordechai served as his only guide.

"She's dropped oars!" he yelled.

As water sprayed across the deck, Ciarán focused on the wind, praying it would defeat the speed *Reaver* would gain from its oars.

"Keep it up lad," Évrard called from the stern. "We're closing on her!"

Ciarán's heart pounded. He fought to calm his nerves and keep his thoughts on the wind.

"She's turning," Mordechai cried. "Larboard!"

"God's bones," Évrard cursed. "They're trying to cut us off!"

Those words broke Ciarán's concentration. As he leaned over the starboard gunwale, the wind died to a zephyr. Two hundred yards away, the sleek-hulled longship, its oars churning the sea, maneuvered across *La Margerie's* bow. Bronze-skinned men crowded the *Reaver's* deck.

Khalil hurried to Ciarán's side. The Persian pointed toward the longship's prow, where the silhouette of a man stood a head above the rest. "That must be Crescentius's counselor."

Across the span of sea, the *Reaver's* crew drew in its oars. Ciarán shook his head. "What are they doing?"

The answer whizzed by his ear as an arrow pierced the sail and thudded into the bulkhead behind him. A scream followed, and Ciarán turned toward the sound.

He watched in horror as Alais collapsed to the deck.

~

"SHOWER THEM WITH ARROWS!" THE VARANGIAN BELLOWED FROM *Reaver's* stern. Half his crew leaned over the larboard gunwale, their bowstrings snapping as they fired upon the cog.

Naberus watched from behind the line of bowmen. *They shall come to you,* the voice in the shrine had promised, and now that promise had come true.

Across the rolling waters, painted gray beneath the cloud-laden sky, the cog's crew hid behind her gunwales. Arrows jutted from her hull. "You're wasting your shafts, Varangian," Naberus observed. "Your men haven't hit a soul."

"They hit two when they opened fire," the scar-faced Rus replied. "Besides, you promised my men a slaughter, and when we're done, that cog's cargo will bring a rich reward."

Naberus's thoughts flashed back to Hadrian's tomb and the sword blazing with supernatural light. The voice had warned him of the true nature of that device, and now that he knew what it was, the thought of boarding that vessel gave him pause. "Have your men light their arrows on fire," he told the Varangian.

"Burned cargo is worthless!"

"I'll compensate your loss when we return to Rome," Naberus snapped.

The Varangian ran a thick-fingered hand through his tangled black beard, thinking for a moment. "Five hundred pounds of silver."

Naberus furrowed his thick brows. "That's preposterous!"

"Preposterous!" Hermes echoed from his perch on the rigging.

"That's my price, consigliere. Otherwise, we board her and seize her spoils."

Naberus grimaced. *The cause is worth the price.* He glared at the fierce-looking pirate. "You win, Varangian. Now rain fire and make her burn."

∾

CIARÁN RUSHED TO THE BOW WHERE ALAIS HAD FALLEN BACK INTO Khalil's arms, blood soaking her shoulder.

She stared at the wound, her face as pale as ash.

"The arrow only grazed you," Khalil said, and he was right. The shaft had flown into the sterncastle, but a finger-long gash marred her shoulder, pooling with blood.

Ciarán exhaled, having feared it struck her chest. "Get her in the cabin!"

Khalil pulled her back as Ciarán shielded her with his body. Another arrow sped past his ear, while more thudded into the hull. But Ciarán stayed on his feet until Khalil got her into the cabin. As soon as the hatch closed, he dropped to the deck. Arrows protruded from the bulkhead, where Mordechai leaned, grimacing, as a shaft pierced his right arm.

"I'll live," Mordechai huffed through gritted teeth.

Josua crouched behind a barrel standing against the cog's starboard side, gazing in alarm at Mordechai's wound. "Do something," he pleaded.

Ciarán grasped Caladbolg's hilt. The stone in its pommel had turned as dark and gray as the sky above. *I can't just stand behind the sail and summon the wind, I'll be dead in a heartbeat.*

The next arrow that struck the bulkhead flamed at the tip. The fire licked the wood and smoke hissed into the air. Ciarán glanced between the arrow and Josua. "The planks are wet, they shouldn't burn."

"The planks are caulked with pitch," Josua said, "and I assure you, pitch burns."

To his left, Ciarán heard the crackle of flames. Fire crawled up the sail where a flaming arrow had pierced the sailcloth.

"Buckets!" Évrard cried from the sterncastle.

"Get water!" more crewmen hollered from the bow.

Arrows sped overhead trailing smoke, while others pounded into the hull. Flames kissed the cog's gunwales. Khalil burst from the hatch and dumped a wash bucket on two fire arrows jutting from the deck.

Ciarán's heartbeat was racing. *If I don't do something, everyone is going to die.* He looked hopelessly to the sky. The clouds had grown darker, nearly the color of the smoke that plumed from the burning sail. *Another storm is brewing—and a sword is the symbol for air . . .*

He prayed to Saint Columcille his plan would work, before clearing his thoughts and whispering into the gemstone. White light spilled from the scabbard as he drew the blade. As soon as he stood, he knew he would be a target for the *Reaver's* bowmen. Yet he hoped the smoke from the burning sail might obstruct their aim.

Ciarán inhaled the light's warmth, praying it would give him the power to speak the ancient words. Another arrow whizzed through the tattered sail into the bulkhead behind him. He felt the light's warmth within his throat, filling his lungs as if they would burst. Rising to his feet, he pointed the sword toward the clouds. "God in Heaven, bring a storm—and bring them ruin!"

A shout ripped from throat as he released the force gathering within him. Heat surged from his lungs, up his arm, and into the blade before a lance of white light sped toward the clouds. Ciarán gasped for breath, but did not take his eyes off the sky, where the storm clouds began to rumble and boil. High above the longship, a flash seared from the clouds a breath before a torrent of lightning and the peal of thunder. The blinding bolts struck the longship at its highest point, blasting *Reaver's* mast into a thousand shards. Ciarán gaped in awe. As the thunder faded, the longship rocked violently, smoke hissing from the ruins of its mast, while cries rang from her hull.

Ciarán could hardly believe what he had done. Elation overwhelmed him as the hail of arrows ceased and rain began to pour from the clouds onto the flames that licked the cog's deck planks. *Blessed rain,* he thought with a smile.

"You . . ." Josua muttered, staring wide-eyed at the wreckage, "did it."

Khalil wrapped Ciarán in a bear hug. "We are saved," he said, beaming.

"Well done, lad!" Évrard called from the sterncastle. "Now man those buckets men!"

Khalil and the crew scrambled to obey the captain, while exhaustion hit Ciarán like a breaking wave. He dropped to a knee, leaning on his sword, and watched Josua and two crewmen tear the smoldering remains of the sail from its yard. Ciarán's heart sank. "How are we going to get anywhere without a sail?"

Mordechai clutched his wounded arm, but smiled despite the pain. "Don't fret," he said. "Évrard always keeps a spare in the hold."

~

THE HARBOR TOWN WAS NAMED BREST, A ONE-TIME FISHING VILLAGE that had blossomed into a trading port at the western tip of Brittany. The longship rowed into the sheltered harbor guarded by a stone tower where spearmen peered down upon the battered vessel.

Only half of *Reaver's* crew could man the oars. Another third were maimed so badly by shards from the ravaged mast that Naberus doubted they would survive more than two days onshore. The rest of the Varangian's crew had perished in the searing bolts that struck the longship moments before the sudden storm drove the hapless craft eastward. Naberus's leg still stung where a shard of timber had ripped through his thigh, though he fared far better than the Varangian. When the lightning struck, its heat had seared the left side of the pirate's face and turned half his beard to ash. The blast left the pirate more hideous and fearsome than before, turning his wicked scar black as it stretched to his cheek. Naberus had expected the man to die from the pain, but the Varangian just screamed defiantly to whatever gods he claimed and endured the agony, albeit with the help of copious amounts of grappa he kept onboard.

That Naberus had even survived such a calamity gave him hope his cause was not lost, though he would have to find new passage to England—and soon, for Midsummer was less than a week away.

He stood on the ship's bow as the cold morning breeze wafted across the water. Hermes perched on the prow, while Set and Grimm, who had miraculously survived the explosion with barely a scratch, sat at his feet, ignoring the Varangian as he clomped up beside them.

The Varangian pointed toward the ramshackle wharf crowded with cogs and fishing boats. "You're in luck, consigliere."

Naberus squinted as he looked to the place where the Varangian was pointing. A pair of longships docked among the other vessels, their masts swaying with furled sails. "Do you recognize those?"

"I bet they belong to Danes, and the Rus and Danes are like brothers." The Varangian flashed a cruel smile. "It will come with a price, consigliere, but you might finish your voyage yet."

29

ALBION

L a *Margerie* reached the channel between England and France under gray skies and favorable winds, and by Évrard's esti-mation they would arrive at the English coast three days before Midsummer.

Ciarán was no longer concerned about being pursued, for the *Reaver* was so damaged it seemed unlikely the mastless vessel had even made it to shore. With the winds blowing off the coast of Brittany, Ciarán saw no need to use Enoch's device to speed up their travel, allowing him to tend to Mordechai's wounded arm and Alais' shoul-der. Mordechai's wound was healing well, though he would have to stay away from the rope ladders for the rest of their voyage and take a respite from his fencing lessons with Khalil. Alais' wound would leave a scar by the time they reached England, though her injury appeared deeper than the gash on her skin. After the attack, she began wearing the close-fitting mail tunic she had been given in Rosefleur. Évrard had cautioned her about that, for were she to fall overboard, the armor would sink her like a stone. Yet she resisted his sound advice, insisting the armor made her feel more secure, even though the danger posed by the *Reaver's* crew was long past.

The next morning, Ciarán found himself alone with her on the bow. Although he wished she had heeded Évrard's advice and stowed the mail tunic, he found the silver of its featherlike scales matched her storm-gray eyes, making her appear as strong and beautiful as ever.

She gazed at the dark-blue sea rippling with waves. "It's so different from the Mediterranean," she said.

"That's because the water's as cold as Saint Brigid's Day," Ciarán replied. "But it reminds me of home."

"If Évrard sailed northwest," she said with a smile, "you could be home."

Ciarán shrugged. "I do long for Ireland, but then I'd miss all the merriment on Midsummer."

Her smile melted. "I've begun to wonder about this Giant's Ring."

"How so?"

"Do you think it was built by the Nephilim?"

Ciarán thought about that. "Dónall once told me that long before we Irish settled our own island and the Celtic Britons arrived on theirs, Britannia was called Albion. He claimed, according to the myths, Albion was a land of giants, and you know what Dónall always said about myths?"

"There's truth in those old myths," she recalled. "But if the Giant's Ring is some Nephilim ruin, how do we know it's safe to go there?"

"The riddle from the Book of Giants is our only chance to find the Key before the enemy does. It's a risk I'll take, safe or not." He cocked his head. "But I suppose I should ask, have you been having any dreams about this place you're not telling us about?"

Alais shook her head. "I've not foreseen it. The entire voyage, my dreams have stayed the same. On the Palatine Hill or with the woman in the Temple of Venus and Roma, and in the gray wasteland with the hill of skulls."

"That settles it, then," he said with a grin. "Stonehenge must be perfectly safe. And we might be there as early as tomorrow."

Alais rested her head on his shoulder. "I hope you're right."

For the rest of the day, Ciarán wondered if he had mistaken her affection for Khalil, only to remind himself again and again of his monastic vows. Though with his wispy beard, full head of hair, and salt-stained tunic, he imagined he looked nothing like the monk who left Ireland just eight months ago.

An hour before sunset, he spied white cliffs in the distance, rising from the sea and crowned with green. Ciarán stood with Évrard and Josua on the sterncastle, where the two merchants studied their nautical charts. "Those cliffs must be the island of Vectis," Évrard said. "On the other side of her, there's a channel to England and an estuary that will take us as close as we can get to this Stonehenge of yours." After some debate, Évrard and Josua decided they would look for a natural harbor on Vectis and drop anchor for the night. In the morning, they would sail east around the isle until they reached the channel. And for once, Ciarán thought, everything was going as planned.

CIARÁN WOKE THE NEXT MORNING TO DARK SKIES AND A STEADY drizzle. By first light, Évrard and his crew had *La Margerie* sailing eastward around the rugged coastline of Vectis. At times the rain seethed and the sea boiled, rocking their vessel and blasting her deck with spray. Ciarán had to hold on to the rigging to keep from losing his feet on the soaking deck, while Alais clung to one of the rope ladders, still wearing her mail tunic over her dress.

"You should stow that mail in the cabin," Ciarán called through the driving rain. "It's not safe!"

She shook her head defiantly. "I have better sea legs than half the men on board!"

Ciarán ran a hand through his rain-soaked hair and glanced away, knowing how stubborn she could be. He wished she would come to her senses, for every wooden plank on the vessel was slick with rain and seawater, and it would not take much for someone to slip overboard in these angry seas.

By midday, the cog was sailing west, heading towards the mouth of the estuary. Through the pelting rain, Ciarán could see the gray beaches and white cliffs of Vectis on the larboard side, while on the starboard side, the faint outline of land emerged—the coastlands of England.

The rain ceased that afternoon. Ciarán was standing with Josua on the bow when he spotted the mouth of the estuary where the shoreline curved northwest, fringed by marshlands. "Some of the crew," Josua said, "are wary of entering that estuary. They've heard there are sea serpents in the rivers and lakes of this land."

"The only sea serpent I know of," Ciarán said, "is in a lake in Scotland. Saint Columcille wrote of the monster, but that's nowhere near here."

"Tell them that," Josua said, before uttering a curse.

"What is it?"

Josua pointed toward the marshlands, where dense fog wafted off the water. "Fog is the bane of every sailor," he said. "Évrard won't be pleased."

Ciarán soon understood why. By the time the cog reached the estuary, thick white fog drifted in waves around the vessel, obscuring any view of the shoreline. From the sterncastle, the fog even veiled the bow. Ciarán donned his baldric and scabbard and offered to summon the wind to blow the fog away. But Évrard disliked the idea, concerned that a strong wind might drive them into the rocky shore. Instead, the captain ordered the crew to reduce the sail and maneuvered the cog slowly through the murk. In time, he let Mordechai man the tiller and took watch on the bow, barking orders to his first mate. "Steer larboard," he cried at times, then "Keep her steady, lad." Ciarán found it unnerving near the stern, where one could barely see the mast, so he accompanied Évrard on the bow. Alais soon joined them, along with a third of the crew, until Évrard ordered his men to stand along the sides and keep lookout for rocks and shoals.

Aside from the shouting between Évrard and Mordechai, it was eerily quiet in the cold, damp fog. Ciarán peered into the white vapor, hoping to glimpse anything amid the murky waves. Ahead, he caught the faint sound of a splash. "Something's out there," he whispered to Évrard and Alais.

The rotund captain leaned over the prow. "I don't see anything."

"Listen." Ciarán heard it again, a vague splashing, almost rhythmic in sound. Up ahead, he saw the shadowy crest of something, a tree perhaps. *We're heading straight for shore!*

"Larboard turn!" Évrard cried.

Ahead, the shadowy form took on a golden hue and an ominous shape, ten feet tall. Alais gasped. Emerging from the fog, black eyes glistened above a wide-open mouth with jagged teeth, atop a serpentine neck reared back and ready to strike.

"Sea serpent!" a crewman cried.

Ciarán's blood ran cold. The serpent surged toward the cog's starboard hull. Then behind the serpent's head, a wall of color materialized through the fog: a square sail striped in red and gold. And beneath it sat the hull of a longship. Men with painted round shields crowded behind its gunwales.

Ciarán turned to Alais. "To the cabin—run!"

Alais stared wide with terror. "Ciarán—"

"Just go!" he shouted.

Panicked cries erupted from the stern, an instant before the cog rocked violently, throwing Ciarán hard into the hull's side. A second longship had burst through the fog and rammed *La Margerie's* stern. From the attacking vessel's prow rose a dragonlike head.

His heart pounding, Ciarán glanced between the two longships, just as the first vessel slammed against the cog's starboard hull. Grapples hooked over the gunwale, lashing the cog to the longship, as a fierce roar sounded from its hull. *"Odi-i-i-n-n-n!"*

The attackers flooded onto the cog like a hellish wave. They howled as they leaped with swords and axes, their faces half-hidden beneath conical helms, their teeth bared like wolves, framed by savage beards. Évrard raised his arms as if to ward off the raging horde, a breath before an ax cleaved into his skull.

"No!" Ciarán gasped. A sudden coldness settled in his core as he watched his friend flung lifeless to the deck. Évrard's blood stained the mailed chest of his killer, a massively tall warrior with a braided beard and a merciless gaze. Ax in hand, the Viking spun toward Ciarán, who fell back and ripped Caladbolg from its scabbard, in time to parry his attacker's blow. Steel clanged against steel and the Viking staggered backward for a breath. The Viking heaved his ax, but Ciarán struck quickly. Caladbolg sheared into the Viking's mail straight through his stomach until his gut rested against the sword's cross-guard. The ax tumbled from his grasp, as he looked at Ciarán wide-eyed as if he sensed his life seeping from his wound.

Ciarán wrenched the blade free. He thought of pressing the sword's pommel to his lips and infusing the gemstone with his soul light, but in the time it would take to clear his mind and utter the word, the Vikings would shear his head from his neck.

Warriors crammed the cog's deck as far as Ciarán could see through the curtain of fog. Two paces away, a red-bearded Viking chopped an ax into Bero, one of the Christians who had been with the crew since their first voyage. Ciarán's mind screamed. *It can't end like this!*

Filled with sudden rage, he swung at Bero's killer. The Viking caught the sword blow with his round shield, but Caladbolg rendered a deep gash in the wood. Ciarán's next strike split the shield in two. The Viking grimaced, white teeth clenched amid his red beard. Ciarán roared as he lunged, bringing Caladbolg down with all his might. The chopping blow severed the Viking's arm above the elbow. The stunned Viking collapsed onto the deck, as another took his place. Ciarán parried his new attacker's sword and Caladbolg cut the blade in two. Realizing his advantage, Ciarán retaliated with a backhanded strike. Caladbolg tore through the man's jaw. The Viking collapsed onto the deck planks, only to be pushed aside by a towering man with a mail hauberk draped over a black tunic, his long-fingered hands gripping a spear with a spike-tipped blade. Ciarán's eyes flew wide. Through the frame of a half-helm, Naberus da Roma stared back, malice simmering in his gaze.

How is this possible! Ciarán thought in alarm as he dodged the first spear thrust, then answered with a wild swing that missed its mark. The Roman moved with remarkable speed, but Ciarán stepped back and readied his blade. "The Key," Ciarán huffed through gritted teeth. "Why do you want it?"

Naberus's eyes narrowed. "For my salvation." He struck with fierce speed, but Ciarán sidestepped the thrust and knocked the spear away with the flat of his blade. He had reared Caladbolg back for a cutting blow when a screech pierced his ears. Black feathers filled his vision, reeking of carrion, as talons dug deep into the flesh of his face. He cried out in pain. A beak lanced his forehead, just missing his eye. He swatted the creature away with his left arm as the spear thrust toward his torso. Ciarán spun to the side, nearly losing his footing, as the spear passed a hair from his chest. Grimacing, the Roman jerked his spear up. Its tip bit into Ciarán's right hand, just below his thumb. The gash stung like fire as the Roman whipped the spear sideways. Its tip rammed into Caladbolg's cross-guard and ripped the sword from Ciarán's grasp. Ciarán lunged to grab the blade as it tumbled over the larboard gunwale, but his fingers closed on nothing but fog.

A hopeless cry burst from Ciarán's lungs.

With a fiendish grin, Naberus da Roma drew back his spear for the death blow.

ALAIS SLAMMED THE CABIN DOOR SHUT, HER HEART POUNDING IN HER chest. She rummaged through the cabin until she found her dagger. With the cries of men roaring outside, she huddled in the corner, gripping the blade.

This can't be happening! Alais had long tried to wall away the memories of her rape at Selles-sur-Cher, but now they surged back like a raging flood. Bile rose in her throat as she recalled Adémar of Blois holding her down, his body between her legs.

Her head became light, and she feared she might faint, then the door exploded inward. A giant of a man stepped through the portal looking as if he had crawled from the depths of Hell. Merciless eyes stared from a hard, weather-burned face surrounded by wild, red hair and an untamed red beard. Bloodstained mail covered his broad chest, and serpentine rings adorned his heavily muscled arms. He let his battleax fall to the plank, as a lecherous grin spread across his face.

Bellowing an order in some foreign tongue, he gestured for her to drop the dagger.

As he stepped toward her, Alais lunged with the dagger and aimed for his gut. With surprising speed, the huge man whirled aside and the dagger glanced off his mail. Then his massive hand smashed into her face, slamming her to the deck. The dagger slid across the planks. The giant Northman was yelling—or laughing—when he picked her up as if she were a child and slung her over his shoulder.

She hung there, her limbs numb, her vision still blurred. He carried her from the cabin and over the gunwale onto one of the long-ships, before throwing her onto a rowing bench while a crowd of men erupted in a triumphant roar.

Blinking until her vision cleared, she found herself surrounded by Northmen huddled around her like drunken villagers at a cockfight. In the center stood her red-bearded attacker, hiking up his mail skirt to reveal the bulge in his breeches. Two of the men grabbed her dress and tore its skirt from her waist, exposing the white of her undertunic and the bare flesh of her legs.

Her mind screamed. *Never again!* She kicked the next man who reached for her in the face, breaking his nose. Another grabbed her arm, but she wrenched it free. She knew she could never fight off this horde. *But there's another way.*

As her red-bearded attacker lunged for her, Alais sprang off the rowing bench and slipped over the ship's side. She plunged into the icy sea. The dark water enveloped her, the cold stabbing like a thousand knives. Alais wondered how long she could hold her breath, then she glanced down at the mail of her tunic snug across her chest.

And just as Évrard warned, she began sinking like a stone.

PART III

And now my soul is poured out within me; days of affliction have taken hold of me. The night racks my bones, and the pain that gnaws me takes no rest.

—Job 30:16-17

30

THE HUMILIATION OF JOHN THE GREEK

Two days before Midsummer, Pope Gregory summoned all of Rome's clergy to the plaza outside the Lateran Palace to witness the humiliation of John the Greek.

Thousands of monks and priests gathered there beneath a cloud-laden sky, along with a sea of Roman citizens that filled the plaza's every flagstone. From the vaulted balconies of the adjacent basilica, a throng of bishops and lords looked on, while in the plaza's center the massive statue of Constantine astride his mighty stallion loomed above the crowd. With his right hand raised, it seemed as if the legendary emperor was addressing the people of Rome.

Gregory looked upon the crowd from the papal balcony, catching a whiff of sweat in the humid air. Rumeus joined the pope between the balcony's thick marble pillars, along with Emperor Otto, Chancellor Heribert, and Margrave Eckard. Otto, his face sullen, had barely said a word since his arrival. Gregory knew it was best to ignore his cousin's fits of melancholy, and he was not about to let Otto's mood darken this triumphant day. The pope turned to Rumeus. "Will more than a third of the Romans respect my papacy now?"

Rumeus regarded him with a somber gaze. "Is this the showing of mercy you mean to give them?"

"Must you always judge me, Rumeus?"

In the plaza, a herald dressed in the gold and red of Breisgau worked his way into the center of the plaza. "Citizens of the Holy Roman Empire," he hollered, "behold John the Greek, who dared to play pope!"

Count Berthold emerged from beneath the papal balcony to usher the false pope through the crowd to the base of the statue. Dressed in episcopal vestments, John the Greek stood hunched and shaking. Berthold drew a dagger from his belt and held it above the false pope's head. Grabbing him by the collar, Berthold slit the back of his robes, then with a violent yank, tore half the garment from his prisoner, causing the false pope to lose his footing and crash to the ground. Berthold ripped the remnants of the robe from the mauled creature at his feet, leaving John Philagathos garbed only in a stained undertunic. As Berthold jerked the antipope to his feet, the herald cried again, "Behold John the Greek, who dared to play pope!"

The crowd roared as a monk entered the plaza holding a rope tethered to a donkey. Berthold hauled the false pope onto the beast and positioned him so that he sat backward in the saddle, facing the donkey's hindquarters. The false pope's hands quivered as the count handed him the donkey's tail, as if it were the beast's reins.

The donkey responded by dropping a heaping stool onto the plaza. A young boy darted from the crowd, grabbed a fistful of the dung, and flung it into the face of John the Greek. The crowd erupted in laughter. The monk led the donkey through the plaza, while the false pope's head lolled from side to side with the herald's repeated call: "Behold John the Greek, who dared to play pope!"

The mob pelted the wretched figure with rotted fruit amid a flurry of curses and jeers. "Heretic!" some cried.

"False!" others yelled.

"Traitor!"

Beside Gregory, Otto averted his eyes. Eckard's rugged face was a mask of stone, while Heribert of Cologne could not take his eyes off the spectacle. Rumeus winced as a cabbage lobbed from the crowd hit the antipope's head so hard his neck snapped back like it might break.

226

When the antipope began to retch in his saddle, Gregory felt a pang in his stomach. *Have I let this go too far?* As if in answer to his own question, he kept his hands clenched on the balcony's rail, never raising them to stop the humiliation.

The mob whipped into a frenzy. A man tried to rip the undertunic from the false pope, but one of Berthold's burly Germans kicked him away. The shouts and curses took on a rhythm—"False!" "Traitor!" "Heretic!"—while the herald's refrain sounded above the jeers. "Behold John the Greek, who dared to play pope!"

As the monk urged the donkey to make a second pass through the plaza, the sun broke through the clouds, casting a shaft of sunlight upon the mob gathered beside the statue. Among the crowd, a hooded figure stood a half head above the surrounding citizens, staring at the papal balcony instead of the donkey and its rider. Gregory narrowed his gaze as the figure drew back its hood, revealing a woman's face and long, platinum hair that spilled to her shoulders.

"Theodora!" the pope gasped. "Eckard, seize that woman!"

The margrave furrowed his brow. "Even if that is the countess, Your Holiness, she's committing no crime."

"She was Crescentius's whore, for God's sake!" Gregory growled. "She should have never been released in the first place."

Eckard looked to Otto, who just shook his head.

Heat flushed up Gregory's neck. "Rumeus, take as many guards as you need and go get her!"

Rumeus gave a faint sigh. "As you wish, Your Holiness."

When Rumeus left the balcony, Gregory glared at his cousin. "I swear to you, she's up to no good." He glanced back at the crowd, but the woman was gone. He searched for her among the masses, yet scores of them wore the same drab color as her cloak.

By the time Rumeus returned, Gregory was fuming. "Do you have her?"

Rumeus shook his head. "We could not find her among the mob, Your Holiness. But someone found me—the Archbishop of Ravenna. He asked to speak with you privately."

"Gerbert? Why in heaven isn't he in Ravenna?"

"He says it's important," Rumeus explained. "Will you see him now?"

"I want that woman, Rumeus, not a visit from that insufferable cleric. Let him wait."

Rumeus obliged and Gregory returned to the spectacle until the monk led the antipope to the palace stables. After bidding his cousin a curt farewell, he followed his archdeacon into the palace, wondering why Gerbert did not ask to speak with Otto, too.

They found Gerbert in the study, gazing at the shelves of leather-bound tomes and Psalters behind a carved, black oak desk neatly organized with a quill, inkpots, and a stack of rolled parchments. When Gregory entered, Gerbert regarded the pope with disapproving eyes.

Gregory pursed his lips. "To what do I owe this visit?"

"Tidings of a sort," Gerbert said, holding a letter in one hand.

Gregory waited until Gerbert bowed and kissed the Fisherman's ring.

"Was that necessary, what you did to Philagathos?" Gerbert asked.

"The man's a traitor. He planned to subjugate the papacy to the patriarch of Constantinople. A message had to be sent."

"A message that you're merciless?"

Gregory grimaced at the words. "You weren't there two years ago when they stormed this palace crying, 'Down with the Saxon pope!' Had I not escaped, they would have thrown me in Castel Sant'Angelo, where I'd have been strangled like Pope Benedict. But you've not come here because of Philagathos. Tidings of his capture would have barely reached Ravenna in time for you to plan your journey."

Gerbert raised the letter in his hands. "You're right. I've come about something more important."

"More important than treason against the Holy See?" Gregory sneered.

"Very much so," Gerbert replied gravely. "It concerns the End of Days."

31

THE LIVING AND THE DEAD

Ciarán's eyes froze wide. The spear tip sped toward his heart, then the air flashed with steel. A sword blade splintered the spear shaft in two.

A broad-shouldered Viking nearly as tall as Naberus da Roma gripped the sword in his left hand, his muscular arm adorned with serpentine rings. Golden hair spilled over the Viking's mailed shoulders, and his bearded face burned with rage. With his right hand, he threw Ciarán to the deck as if he were a child, bellowing words to the Roman in a foreign tongue.

Naberus bared his teeth. *"Han er mine til at dræbe!"*

"Vores pris var slaver, og denne mand er min thrall!" the Viking shouted, his face flushing red.

Naberus glanced over the larboard gunwale where Caladbolg had tumbled into the sea. *"Fint!"* he snapped, as he held out an arm for the fat raven to land.

"Fint!" the bird cawed, its beak still red with Ciarán's blood. Naberus shot Ciarán a parting glance. "Your God has failed you, and your cause is lost."

Ciarán watched as the Roman retreated to one of the longships, then glanced up at the Viking, whose chest heaved with each breath beneath his mail coat. The Viking regarded Ciarán, almost as if he were studying him. The look in his eyes was more reasoned than cruel, but Ciarán could not ignore the sick feeling in the pit of his stomach. For he had recognized one of the Viking's words. A word the monks of Derry were taught to fear. *Thrall*. The Viking word for slave.

Gritting his teeth, the Viking grabbed Ciarán by his bloodstained tunic and yanked him off the deck. With a grunt, the Viking hammered the pommel of his sword into the side of Ciarán's head. A thousand stars exploded in Ciarán's vision, then melted into darkness.

Ciarán awoke to the rocking of a ship and the smell of brine. The light of a half-moon seeped through a break in the clouds, though wisps of fog still lingered in the air. He lifted his hands to rub the sleep from his eyes, only to find his wrists bound tightly with rope and a cloth bandage wrapped around his wounded right hand. He found himself slumped down on damp wooden planks; cold iron bit into his ankles. As his vision cleared, he saw the manacles and the short iron chain linking his bare feet.

His cheek burned from the wounds inflicted by Naberus's raven and his head throbbed, to a rhythm of sorts. The haze in his mind began to clear, and he realized the rhythmic sound was a man chanting. Pain flared as Ciarán turned his head and found himself looking down the length of a longship where round oaken shields lined the ship's starboard and larboard sides. Down its open hull ran pairs of benches, maybe twenty, maybe more, each one manned by a bare-chested Viking pulling a long wooden oar. They rowed to the beat of a song sung by a rotund man with a face as ugly as a boar's, working an oar in the second row.

Ciarán wondered if he had awoken into a nightmare, when a voice whispered over his shoulder. "Are you all right?"

Ciarán craned his neck to find Khalil, huddled in the prow, bound, manacled, and barefoot. Blood and sweat stained his linen tunic, and an iron slave collar hung around his neck. Though the sight of his friend brought only a moment of hope.

"Where are the others?" Ciarán asked. "Where is Alais?"

Khalil shook his head. "They must have taken her on the other ship with the rest of the crew."

Ciarán shuddered. He did not want to imagine what they would do to her, though deep down he knew what that was. He swallowed hard, as tears welled in his eyes. "Évrard fell, and Bero, too."

Khalil grimaced as if stung by the news.

"There's more." Ciarán choked on the words. "Caladbolg . . . it's gone, into the sea."

Khalil's eyes flew wide. "Merciful Allah."

Ciarán breathed a long sigh as Naberus's parting words echoed in his mind. *Your God has failed you, and your cause is lost.*

Boots clomped down the deck planks. Ciarán looked up into the wolf-gray eyes of another Viking. The hulking man stood bare-chested, his torso rippled with muscles and scrawled with patterns made of oak gall ink. White-blond hair hung to his midchest, framing a bearded face battered by wind and age. *"Vær stille!"* he growled, before cracking the back of his enormous hand into the side of Ciarán's head.

Ciarán's skull slammed into the hull, and his mouth filled with the coppery taste of blood.

"Thrallene taler ikke!" the Viking snapped, then broke into a chuckle.

Ciarán sat still as a deer until the man clomped back to his rowing bench. As a lad, Ciarán was taught the Vikings were the scourge of God, heathen sea-wolves who had terrorized Ireland's monasteries for the past two hundred years. Derry, however, had been spared during his lifetime, so Ciarán had never witnessed these heathen warriors until now. He could not tell if his captors were *fin-gall* or *dubh-gall*, Norsemen or Danes, but what did it matter? Enoch's device was gone, and so was Alais. Her terrified face was the last that he saw of her. Ciarán clenched his jaw and fought back a tear.

231

While on the nearest bench, one of the Vikings laughed under his breath.

~

By the time the remnants of fog faded away, the longship had entered the mouth of a river flanked by dark rolling hills.

The Vikings near the fore of the ship drew in their oars, and two of them lumbered to the prow. One was the older Viking who had silenced Ciarán with the back of his hand. The Viking glanced down at him, then shoved him to the side with a nudge from his muscular thigh sheathed in woolen trousers and tucked into a goatskin boot. With the aid of a younger-looking, yellow-haired Northman, the two lifted the massive dragon-head from the prow and set it down between Ciarán and Khalil. The beast's head, painted red and gold, stared back at Ciarán with lifeless black eyes.

More Vikings began pulling in their oars, before donning short woolen tunics and coats of mail or studded leather. Most strapped belts around their waists and slung cloaks over their shoulders and pinned them with brooches. On their heads, some of the Vikings placed iron helms, slightly pointed at the top, with triangular nasals or broad metal guards with just holes for the eyes. *Are they preparing to fight?* Ciarán wondered, unsure of what that meant for him and Khalil.

Ciarán peered over the starboard side. The ship glided toward a settlement with a timber wharf filled with twenty or thirty longships. Beyond the wharf, a log palisade surrounded the settlement, where peaked roofs rose above the enclosure, bathed in moonlight. Outside the palisade loomed thick, dark woods, as if the settlement had been carved into a forest on the river's west bank. *Not a fight,* Ciarán realized, *they're taking us to their home.* He whispered a prayer to Saint Columcille that one of the longships moored at the wharf had carried Alais, Josua, and the crew's survivors to this place, wherever it was.

After the Vikings guided their ship into the wharf, four of them tied the vessel to the moorings. Some of the men lit torches, placing them into holders on the tall timber columns that flanked the docks.

From the rows of benches, a Viking with a half-shaven head crowned with a shock of yellow hair approached them holding two lengths of chain. His beard was close-cropped, and he watched Ciarán with bright blue eyes that seemed common to this Northern race. Ciarán felt a tightness in his chest when he realized the Viking was wearing the hauberk of polished mail that once had belonged to Maugis d'Aygremont, as well as the leather baldric with a Viking sword sheathed in Caladbolg's scabbard.

The thieving Viking barked something to Ciarán in the Northmen's tongue and hooked one of the chains to the iron collar around Ciarán's neck. He hooked the second chain to Khalil, whose dark eyes regarded the Viking with a defiant look.

Another Viking stepped toward Ciarán from the crowd of Northmen who were pulling their shields from the ship's sides and gathering axes and swords beneath the benches. Ciarán stared back at the huge, golden-haired warrior who had saved him from Naberus's spear. The warrior, whose sculpted face showed few lines of age and not a fleck of winter in his beard, regarded Ciarán with curious eyes. Over his mail, the man wore a bear-fur cloak pinned at the shoulder with a round, golden brooch shaped like a serpent with its tail between its jaws. The brooch, as well as the gold and silver rings on his arms, led Ciarán to suspect the man must be the Vikings' lord. He grabbed Ciarán's chin with a powerful hand, and turned his head from side to side as if measuring the worth of his new slave. Then he took the chain around the slave collar that bit into Ciarán's neck, and with a Nordic command beckoned him to stand. Ciarán did as he was told and followed the golden-haired Viking in the footsteps of Khalil and his captor.

The docks led down a plank road across the muddy bank to a large timber gate through which the crew returned home. The stench of mud and refuse hung in the air, and the barking of hounds heralded the Vikings' return. Torches flared beyond the gate, which opened into a crowd of wattle-and-daub houses roofed with birchbark and turf. The houses surrounded a huge timber hall with a peaked roof and Y-shaped finials decorating its gables. Men and women, and even some children, poked their heads from the doors of houses. Some of the villagers stared as the two Vikings led Ciarán and Khalil toward one of the largest houses, which Ciarán assumed belonged to the lord. A pen of black sheep stood near the house, the air thick with their dung, and beside it was a timber hut no larger than the corbeled stone cells that Ciarán had lived in as a monk at Derry. The only entrance to the hut appeared to be a short wooden door that could be barred from the outside. That hut, Ciarán realized, would be their prison.

The Viking with the half-shaven head removed the chain leash from Khalil's and Ciarán's collars and pushed them one at a time into the hut. Crude benches lined three of the four walls, and the damp floor reeked of urine. The Viking lord left them with their half-shaven jailer, who held a perverse smile on his face. Ciarán wanted to lunge at the man, to overtake him and flee this place. But Ciarán's wrists were still tied and the manacles on his feet would not allow more than a half stride. Meanwhile, the Viking had a longsword in Caladbolg's scabbard, and judging by the jagged scar that ran down the left side of his face, he was a seasoned warrior. Ciarán knew he could not fight the man, but there was one thing he could do. The Norse and Danes had settlements in Ireland, and with luck his jailer might have spent enough time there to learn the language.

"Are you *fin-gall* or *dubh-gall?*" Ciarán asked in Irish.

His jailer raised a brow. "Irish, eh?" he replied fluently, much to Ciarán's relief.

"Are you *fin-gall* or *dubh-gall?*" Ciarán asked again. "Norse or Dane?"

The Viking smiled, revealing a mouth full of straight white teeth. "We are the men of Svein Forkbeard, the great king of Denmark, and you are a thrall of Jarl Holger Horiksson, a mighty Danish lord. He is generous and good to his thralls—at least to the ones who don't betray his trust. To those who do betray him, he's not so kind. Has a temper like Thor the Thunderer."

Ciarán noticed the hammer-shaped pendant hanging on a leather cord around the Viking's neck. *Thor's hammer.*

"I am Magnus, the jarl's hirdman. He's asked me to look after you, which I will so long as you don't betray my trust. I may not have a temper like Thor, but I'm quicker with a sword than most men, so don't give me a reason to use my blade. Her name is Life Taker, and she always strikes true." He jerked his head toward Khalil. "Does he understand what we're saying?"

Ciarán shook his head. "He doesn't speak Irish."

"He looks like a Moor, so he wouldn't, would he. Tell him what I said."

Ciarán nodded. "What happened to the other longship that attacked us?"

"Jarl Orn's ship? They carry the Roman who paid us to attack your cog. He bribed Jarl Orn to take him somewhere." ﹀

Ciarán grimaced. He knew where Naberus was going—to the Giant's Ring, on the summer solstice. *Your God has failed you, and your cause is lost.* Ciarán shook off the thought. "There was a woman. She would have been brought to the other longship."

"Raven-haired? A fine-looking wench, but I heard she leaped overboard, scared at the size of Orn's cock. So she gave herself to Aegir of the Seas and drowned."

The words hit Ciarán like a blow.

"She was your woman then?" Magnus asked with a shrug. "But she's with Aegir now." As if punctuating his words, the Viking shut the door and slid the bar in place.

Khalil spun toward Ciarán. "What is it?"

Ciarán stared back blankly. "Alais is gone."

"Gone?"

Tears welled in Ciarán's eyes. "Drowned."

The Persian closed his eyes. "Merciful Allah."

"God's shown no mercy," Ciarán scoffed. "And He's forsaken us now."

32

AEGIR'S REALM

The frigid waters swallowed Alais. As she sank into its depths, she wondered what would happen when her breath ran out and the icy liquid filled her lungs. Would everything go black? Or would she feel whisked to another realm? If there was an Otherworld and an Underworld, there must be a Heaven, she thought. She wondered whether her late husband Geoffrey would be waiting there.

Her face and limbs began to numb. Death would come soon. But then Alais realized she was no longer sinking.

She wondered if she had reached the seabed, but there was nothing beneath her feet. With her arms outstretched, she felt a vague sensation of floating in the watery void. It was not the Fae mail that had pulled her down, just the momentum of jumping from the ship. Whatever Otherworldly metal the mail vest was made of, it seemed to weigh no more in the water than her linen dress. Alais kicked her legs, propelling her body. *I can swim . . .*

A surge of hope quelled any thought of dying. Growing up on the River Clain, Alais had swum her whole life, and she knew her skill would not fail her now. As she neared the surface, she saw the dark outline of the longship's hull, and spun away. *They'll be looking for me.*

She swam as hard and as far as she could before breaking the surface, just long enough to steal a breath.

Above the water, the night was filled with the Vikings' clamor. She ducked beneath the surface as her mind settled on a terrible realization. *It's nighttime, I cannot see the shore.* She doubted her body could endure much more of the icy waters, and knew fatigue would claim her if she accidentally swam into the channel.

She poked her head out of the water, only to find herself staring at the oak hull of the second longship. A swell of panic sent her below the surface again. Around her, the water was black, save for a faint light below her toes. She turned toward the glow. It emanated from the seabed, a mote of light no larger than an ember within a dying cook fire, though its color shone white like a star in the midnight sky.

Alais swam toward the light. Through the glow, she saw the outline of a sword, its blade jutting from the sea bottom with a gemstone burning in its pommel.

She could hardly believe her eyes. *Caladbolg . . .*

She stroked toward the sword, unwilling to think what this omen might mean for Ciarán's fate. The gemstone's warmth surrounded her hand as she reached for the hilt. She wrapped her fingers around the leather grip, and pulled. The blade slid from the silt. In the gemstone's light, she could see an area before her less dark than other places. *The shore.*

She kicked to the surface, cupping a hand around the sword's pommel to shield its glow from the Vikings above, and took a deep breath. With Caladbolg's warmth invigorating her limbs, she believed she could make it to shore. She swam with all of her will until her muscles burned and she felt slick rocks beneath her fingers. Her knee sank into the wet gravel and she crawled over the rocks until her whole body rested on the shingle beach.

Laying there, she heaved for breath, clutching the sword. The light from its gemstone faded away. When her breathing finally calmed, she closed her eyes and uttered a prayer to Saint Radegonde. And let the exhaustion claim her.

~

ALAIS WOKE TO THE HISS OF THE TIDE AND THE TOUCH OF A HAND against her face. With a startled breath, she scrambled back, her eyes wide with panic.

"Héo sy lifiendee!" exclaimed a woman kneeling before her in the wet sand. She was a skinny thing, no older than Alais, with big brown eyes and a pale face, wearing a nun's veil. A woman as burly as a woodsman towered over the nun, staring down at Alais with a blunt nose and a humorless expression. Three more nuns huddled behind the burly woman, casting furtive glances at the longsword by Alais' side.

Alais exhaled. She found herself sitting on a beach of brown and copper rocks, thick with puffs of foam left by the outgoing tide. "Where am I?" she asked in Latin, hoping the nun spoke the language.

"You speak Latin?" the nun asked with a look of surprise. "Were you on the ship?"

Alais nodded, cold in her damp dress. "Have you seen it?"

"We saw it burning like a bonfire on the water last night. That's what the sea-wolves do. They always burn the ships. Our prioress sent us to look for survivors, and here you are." The nun furrowed her brow. "Is that armor you're wearing?"

"Of a sort." Alais glanced toward the water. The sun shone on its surface like quicksilver, but there was no sign of *La Margerie.* "Were there other survivors?"

The nun frowned. "We found only you."

Alais swallowed hard as a tightness gathered in her chest. She had not stopped to think long enough for her worst fears to take root, but now, if what the nun said was true . . . The pain of losing Eli, Dónall, and Isaac had stung like a knife twisting in her gut. But Ciarán and Kahlil, and Josua and Évrard? That pain felt like cold fingers had wrapped around her heart, crushing it with all their might. Her breath wavered and a pair of tears trickled down her cheeks. She wiped them away with a sand-caked hand, smearing a streak of silt across her face, which was sore and swollen where the Viking had struck her.

The nun gave her a weak smile. "Are you hungry?"

The last thing Alais could think of was food, but she nodded just the same. The nun helped Alais up, then glanced down by her feet. "Whose sword is that?"

Alais brought a shaky hand to her forehead; she had forgotten about the blade. "It was my husband's," she lied. "It's all I have left of him."

The nun's eyes narrowed, and Alais could not tell if the woman believed her. "I'm sorry for your husband, but that's good to know. With the vest you're wearing and that sword, I feared for a moment you might be one of those Danish shieldmaidens. But then I told myself, I've never heard of a Dane with hair as dark as yours. Where are you from?"

"France."

"Well, you're safe in Wessex now," the nun said. "Our priory's not but a mile away. We'll get you some food and get you to Prioress Euphemia. She'll know what to do, she always does."

The nun introduced herself as Sister Leofflaed, and Alais followed her and her four companions over hillocks thick with bracken. They walked for a healthy mile, though the soreness in Alais' limbs from swimming the night before made it feel like ten miles, until the priory emerged over a hillcrest. The priory was a group of stone buildings with slate roofs standing beside a ramshackle stable and rickety pens with pigs and gray sheep. If a wall ever surrounded the priory, it had long ago collapsed, and existed now only as moss-covered rock piles. Downhill from the priory was a village, smaller than Selles-sur-Cher, of thatch-roofed cottages surrounded by furlongs and fields, but with no manor house for a lord or lady. Alais suspected the prioress played that role.

"Welcome to the Priory of Saint Frithuswith," Sister Leofflaed said. "We're not as well endowed as our sister house in Oxford, but we make do."

Sister Leofflaed escorted Alais to a sparsely furnished refectory and asked the woodsman-sized woman, whom she called Lay Sister Agnes, to scrounge up some food while Sister Leofflaed fetched the prioress. As she waited for the women to return, Alais sat at a trestle table with Caladbolg propped against the bench, while wind whistled through cracks in the stone walls where the mortar had crumbled away. She gave a long sigh and sank her head into her hands. All her companions—men whom she adored—were gone and likely dead, leaving her alone and their journey in shambles. Suddenly, the words Orionde had spoken before she set Ciarán and Alais upon that journey took on a grave new meaning. *"You have yet another role to play . . ."* *Could that be what she meant, that I would have to finish the journey alone?*

Lay Sister Agnes returned with a cup of ale and bowl of pea pottage topped with almonds. She handed it to Alais with a grunt and a half smile. The lay sister, whom Alais suspected was from the village and could not speak Latin, let her eat in silence. The ale tasted sour and the pottage salty, but as she ate, her mind began to churn. Before the attack, Évrard had said they would arrive three days before Midsummer, so there was still time to reach Stonehenge. When last she saw Naberus da Roma, he was on the deck of the crippled *Reaver,* and a ship without a mast would never make it to England in time. She could finish the journey, she realized. *If only I can find my way to Stonehenge.*

While Alais pondered how that might happen, Sister Leofflaed entered the refectory with a woman who had to be Prioress Euphemia, along with a little, pug-faced dog scurrying at her feet. Short and thickset, the prioress had a weak chin and a round face with a pinkish complexion amid her white veil, though her stern eyes beneath sharp plucked brows suggested she was not a woman to be trifled with.

"I give you the Reverend Mother Euphemia," Sister Leofflaed said before Lay Sister Agnes hurried to meet the prioress with a wooden chair.

The prioress plopped onto the chair's grease-stained cushion, then the dog hopped on her lap. Her nose wrinkled into a pinched expression before she spoke. "Sister Leofflaed tells me you're the lone survivor," the prioress said in a slightly accusatory tone. "Yet they find you on the beach dressed in what looks like a coat of mail, with a longsword no less, like one of those shieldwomen the heathen sea-wolves sing about in their poems. But Sister Leofflaed assures me you speak Latin. Everyone knows the Danes are apostles of Satan, and not a one speaks the language of the Church. Where did you learn Latin?"

"In Poitiers," Alais said. "I am cousin to the Duke of Aquitaine."

"Is that so?" The prioress raised one of her plucked brows. "Is it customary for ladies in France to armor themselves like soldiers before crossing the channel?"

Alais did not like where this was heading. "No, it's not customary. Before we were attacked by Vikings, we encountered a ship full of pirates in the Basque Sea. An arrow grazed my shoulder, so I donned the coat for protection. But we never anticipated the Vikings."

"No one ever does." The prioress's pinched expression melted away. "May they all roast in Hell, though I question whether our good King Ethelred has the stomach to put them there anytime soon. A hundred years ago King Alfred the Great drove the Danes from our shores, but now they're back, and breeding like rabbits if you ask me. More arrive every spring, hoping the king will pay them the Danegeld, else they ravage our abbeys and burn down our towns. I've heard they've left France alone, so why would a French woman ever come to England?"

"There's a place here," Alais replied, weaving another lie, "a ring of standing stones, I believe, called Stonehenge. My companions were scholars and friends of my late husband. They theorized the stones act like a giant sundial, and wanted to be there on Midsummer to test their theory. The least I can do now is complete their journey. It's what they would have wished."

"Stonehenge?" The prioress looked as if she had chewed into a lemon. "A dreadful, pagan place."

"But a magical one," blurted Sister Leofflaed. "The Welsh believe a white wizard is trapped beneath the stones."

The prioress glared at the young nun. "All magic is black, and only the Danes are worse than the Welsh."

"Can you show me the way to get there?" Alais pressed.

"It's not far," the prioress scoffed, "but a woman traveling the roads alone—I dare to even think what might happen to you along the way."

"I could show her," Sister Leofflaed offered eagerly. "Lay Sister Agnes could come, too. With three of us, we'd be fine."

"Not a chance!" The prioress's face was turning a shade of red. "There's too much work to do around here to go off chasing fantasies. Have you seen the stables? The whole roof might collapse by Sunday if we don't shore up the beams."

Sister Leofflaed bowed her head and glanced away, then a gust of wind whistled through the cracked walls. It gave Alais a sudden thought.

"This mail coat," she told the prioress, "is made of the finest metal ever forged. You could build a whole new stable for what it's worth in silver, and repair these walls, too. Even then, you'd have money left over. It's yours if you want it. All I ask is that you let Sister Leofflaed and Lay Sister Agnes take me to Stonehenge."

The prioress peered at the armor, then pursed her lips. "What about the sword? It looks like it's worth more than the coat. I'll take that, too."

Alais felt the blood drain from her face. "I cannot. It belonged to my late husband. It's all of him I have left."

The pug glanced up at his mistress as if awaiting her verdict. She scratched the dog's head. "Perhaps paupers shouldn't be choosy," she said with a shrug. "We've long been in need of a patron, and I suppose when a French woman washes ashore offering an expensive coat of mail, who am I to turn her down?"

Sister Leofflaed glanced at Alais, unable to hide a smile.

"In exchange for the mail, they can take you to Stonehenge," the prioress said as Alais tried hard to suppress a grin. "But I warn you"—the prioress jabbed a finger to punctuate her words—"that is a very unchristian place, and I doubt very much you'll like what you find there."

HOLGER HORIKSSON

Ciarán woke in the slave hut shivering on a crude bench. He found Khalil on the dirt floor, prostrate in prayer. The Persian quietly uttered verses from the Qur'an, bowing and then prostrating himself a second time.

Ciarán's wrists were still bound and he had not eaten in nearly a day, though, as a monk, he was used to fasting. "What do you pray for when God has forsaken us?"

"Last night," Khalil told him, "I went to sleep believing all is lost. But the Qur'an teaches that Allah does as He wills. So I woke wondering why He has willed this fate upon us. What is His purpose?"

Naberus's words still echoed in Ciarán's mind. *Your God has failed you, and your cause is lost.* "Maybe on this millennium, God's decided to let it all end."

"Then why did He bring us together, myself devoted to the poetry of Fierabras, and you a student of the mysteries of Maugis d'Aygremont? It took both of our knowledge to find Enoch's device, and Alais' too, each of us with a connection to Charlemagne and his paladins and the secrets they preserved."

Ciarán sank his head in his hands. "The device is lost . . ."

"Perhaps it was the demon's words that led us astray," Khalil said grimly.

Ciarán swallowed hard. He had feared the same thing last night, in the darkness of the hut. "If so, then I've doomed us all."

"Yet what if we can find our way back to the right path?"

Before he could answer, the bar scraped against the door. As it opened, Magnus stood in the threshold holding a wooden cup and a hunk of bread. Behind him loomed the hulking, older Viking with the long white-blond hair, looking no less ornery than the night before. He stood nearly a head taller than Magnus, and his sleeveless tunic revealed four silver rings on each massive arm, both of which were tattooed with oak gall patterns.

"Hello, Irish," Magnus said with a feral grin. "It's time for the day meal and your first chance to earn my trust. I have some watered ale that tastes like swine piss for you and a slab of stale bread."

From a sheath at his belt, the older Viking drew a long knife. He gave them a look like a cat toying with a bird.

"This is Jorundr," Magnus added. "He does not plan to kill you, but he will if you make trouble. Some of the crew want you dead for the Danes you two killed, though Jarl Holger would not hear of it. You owe your lives to him, so you should be honored to serve him as thralls."

Jorundr stepped into the cell and grabbed Ciarán's arm with a crushing grip. Then he slid the knife beneath the rope that bound Ciarán's wrist. With a jerk of the sharp knife, the bonds came free.

While Ciarán rubbed his wrists, Jorundr cut Kahlil's bonds.

"We need to keep the chains on your ankles," Magnus said, "until we know you won't try to run away. Of course, where would you go? You're on an island, after all."

Ciarán took a bite of the bread, which was so hard he feared he might break a tooth, and washed it down with the ale, which had gone as sour as a lemon. But still, it was food. He broke off another morsel of bread and handed the rest to Khalil. This time, Ciarán soaked the bread in the ale in the hope of softening it. "Are we in England?"

"No," Magnus replied, "but England is why we are here. Ever since he won his throne, King Svein has vowed to conquer the kingdom. Jorundr and I were with him, drunk in his mead hall, when he made that vow. So we sailed to England with ninety-three ships, and some Norse, too, who served Prince Olaf Trygvesson. We were three thousand strong at the Battle of Maldon, where we cut off the head of Byrhtnoth, the defender of England, and killed so many English the ravens were fat for weeks."

"Yet you left England?"

"The English paid us to leave. After Maldon, the English king, Ethelred, paid King Svein and Prince Olaf a ransom, ten thousand pounds of silver, to go home and leave the English be. But Svein had vowed to conquer England, and a vow is sacred, no? So four years ago he and Prince Olaf attacked the English again. The battle began at an old Roman town called London, and led to the coastlands, where we plundered and burned every village along the way. So once again, the English king paid the ransom from a tax the English call the Danegeld, but this time he gave more of it to Prince Olaf because Olaf had asked King Ethelred to have some Christian priest baptize him in a river. I suppose it did not matter to the English king that Svein had been baptized long ago at the insistence of the German emperor, but, then again, King Svein knows that Thor and Odin are more powerful than the Christian god, so they are who he honors.

"Anyhow, Prince Olaf took his silver and his men and sailed back to Norway, but we Danes are lingering here to remind the English king that when he paid over the Danegeld, he should not have slighted King Svein. So we have settled here on the Isle of Vette, and that's where you are, Irish. But someday King Svein will keep his vow and we will conquer England, and Svein will rule as king." Magnus clapped Ciarán on the shoulder. "Now eat up. You thralls have work to do."

After they finished the bread and ale, Magnus led the two captives from the cell. Wisps of fog hung in the chill morning air, and the muddy ground was cold and wet against Ciarán's bare feet. In the morning light, the turf roofs shone green atop the homes of timber and daub, and the plank roads that ran between the structures were alive with Danes. Women wearing dresses of blue, green, and gray strolled about with children at their sides, who gave long stares as Ciarán and Khalil passed. The men, most of whom were tall, bearded, and fair of hair, watched, too, though some shot hostile looks toward the two new slaves. *We killed some of their friends,* Ciarán thought. *But they killed some of ours too.*

As Jorundr and Magnus led them down the plank roads, Ciarán discovered the Danish settlement was far larger than it had looked the night before, and as bustling with animals as it was people. Geese pecked the ground and dogs sniffed around the narrow alleyways, where stray hogs rummaged through the mud and roosters and chickens roamed free. Along the way, he counted more than fifty houses, and guessed there might be ten times that, or more, within the palisade. A half score of timber homes stood larger than any others in the settlement, save for the peak-roofed hall in the center. *Jarl Holger is not the only lord in this place,* Ciarán realized.

Beyond the houses, the settlement gave way to planted furlongs where the forest had been cleared, extending hundreds of yards to the back of the palisade. More men and women worked around the fields —and all wore iron collars around their necks.

"Time to work, Irish," Magnus commanded.

Ciarán set his jaw and trudged into the furlong. Dozens of other slaves, most of whom looked like Saxons—English men and women, Ciarán guessed—knelt between rows of cabbage, leeks, and grain weeding and tending to crops. None spoke the Irish tongue, so Ciarán never learned how they had been enslaved or for how long, but they all shared the same fate serving their Danish lords.

After midday, when the sun beat down on the fields and sweat soaked Ciarán's dirt-stained tunic, Magnus summoned him. "Come, Irish. Jarl Holger will see you now."

Ciarán nodded toward Khalil. "What about my friend?"

"Not the Moor, just you."

Magnus led Ciarán back down a plank road to one of the largest houses in the settlement with a Y-shaped finial at the peak of its gabled roof covered in birchbark shingles. Six timber columns supported a lower, pitched roof above a pair of sturdy double doors. The columns and the shape of the rooflines reminded Ciarán vaguely of the ancient buildings in Rome, but where the Romans were masters of marble and stone, these Danes knew only wood planks and logs.

Beside the entrance stood the fierce-looking Jorundr, who opened one of the oaken doors as Magnus and Ciarán approached.

A wave of apprehension washed through Ciarán's gut. "Why does Jarl Holger want to see me?"

"It's not a thrall's place to ask why. Jarl Holger will tell you if he wishes."

As Ciarán stepped through the doorway, his eyes had to adjust to the dimness of the hall. It had no windows, but oil lanterns hung from the rafters and a hearth crackled in the center wafting smoke through a soot-blackened hole in the roof. Rushes of calamint and restharrow covered the floor and their scent mingled with the smell of smoke and a lingering odor of roast meat. Beyond the hearth stood a raised platform with two tall chairs, and in them sat a man and a woman holding hands. An enormous boarhound lounging at their feet glanced up as Ciarán approached.

He recognized the golden-haired lord as Jarl Holger, but it was the slender woman in the other chair who caught Ciarán's eye. Her hair was as red as an autumn leaf and her face was pale and as beautiful, yet fierce as any woman he had ever seen, like a warrior goddess from the old Celtic tales.

"Who is she?" he asked Magnus under his breath.

"Breda," he said. "She's your lord too."

The woman must have noticed Ciarán's stares, for she leaned over and whispered something to the jarl.

"Do you recognize my wife?" The jarl spoke in thickly accented Irish.

Ciarán swallowed hard. There was no mercy in the jarl's eyes. "No lord," he said.

"Where are you from?" the woman asked. Her Irish was flawless, erasing any doubt about her homeland.

"From Derry," Ciarán said.

The woman smirked. "Are you a monk?"

"I was, at the abbey there."

"He doesn't look like one of the shaven men," the jarl said.

"He means a priest," the woman explained. "You don't look like one, you know."

The jarl glared at Ciarán. "It would be bad if you are a priest, for everyone knows that the sea gods, Aegir and Rán, hate the shaven men, so it's very bad luck to take one to sea. Had my crew believed you were a shaven man, they would have thrown you overboard and let Rán take you to a watery grave."

Ciarán sucked in a breath. "It's been more than a half year since I served in the abbey. Since then, I've lost my robes and broken my vows."

"So you are no longer a shaven man?" The jarl cocked his head. "That makes sense, for your hair is not shaven, and priests do not fight with swords. You cut down two of my crewmen, and maimed one of Jarl Orn's kinsmen. His name is Sigurd, and he'll want your head."

"I regret killing those men," Ciarán lied.

"At least they died with swords in their hands." The jarl stroked his golden beard as if he were pondering something. "The tall Roman wanted us to kill you and your Moorish friend. Now, why would he want me to do that?"

Ciarán wondered where this was going, and he did not know what Naberus da Roma had told the Dane, so he chose his words carefully. "The Roman and I were rivals. We were both sailing to the place the Saxons call Stonehenge. It has a certain religious significance to us."

The jarl glanced at his wife, who answered him in Danish. With a furrowed brow, he looked back to Ciarán. "I have seen that ring of standing stones, but it is not a Christian place. They say it was built by giants or the old gods of that land. I have often been curious about the Christians, and I know enough to know that giants and gods are not Christian things."

Little do you know, Ciarán thought, recalling the now familiar verse from Genesis. *The Nephilim were on the earth in those days—and also afterward—when the sons of God went into the daughters of men . . .* "There are elements of my religion that are older than the birth of Christ, dating back to creation and the time before the Great Flood. I needed to be there by Midsummer."

"That is the day after next, on Thor's day, so it seems your rival will win," the jarl said. "But it is no matter now. Tell me, on that ship, did you learn to sail?"

"Aye," Ciarán said. "I was not always a sailor, but I became one."

"And you like being at sea?"

"I do, lord,'" Ciarán admitted.

The jarl gave him a nod. "Then maybe Aegir and Rán don't hate you, and maybe we shall sail together someday, you and I." He turned his head and said something to Magnus in the Danish tongue.

"Bow to your lords, Irish," Magnus said. "They've seen enough of you."

Ciarán did as he was told and left with Magnus, all the while wondering why Jarl Holger was so curious about him and his religion, and whether he could sail a bloody ship.

The following day, he and Khalil mended fences surrounding the furlongs and sheep pens, slopped hogs, and chopped firewood, all under the watchful eyes of Magnus and Jorundr. The Vikings made them stack the wood in open fields, arranging them in pyramids, each a man's height. Ciarán knew by tonight those pyramids would be lit with birchbark torches, and he knew the reason why. The thought of it churned his stomach.

After sundown, the whiff of smoke from those fires invaded the slave hut, along with boisterous laughter and sounds of revelry. "What are they doing?" Khalil asked.

"Burning bonfires and getting drunk," Ciarán said bitterly. "We Irish do it, too. On Midsummer Eve."

Khalil gave a long sigh. "To celebrate the solstice."

Ciarán nodded grimly. He knew by sunset tomorrow, Naberus da Roma would be at the Giant's Ring, solving the riddle to find the Key to the Abyss. What would happen if he discovered it? Would the fallen angels rise from the bottomless pit like locusts sent to torture and destroy all that lives? In Revelation, John of Patmos wrote that in those days, when the smoke from the bottomless pit choked the sky, people would seek death and long to die. If so, Ciarán brooded, had his decision to follow the demon's words condemned them all? And had Dónall and Isaac, and Remi and his parents, and Eli, Niall, and Évrard—all died for nothing? Bile gathered in Ciarán's throat. *I cannot let their sacrifice be in vain . . .*

As he sat in the cold darkness of the cell, with the pagans' music and laughter filling the air outside, he wondered if they would still be laughing if they knew how close they stood to the precipice of the Apocalypse. Yet how close were they, really? Even if Naberus found the Key, Ciarán reasoned, who was to say he knew the location of the bottomless pit?

Ciarán looked to Khalil. "The other day, you wondered if we could find our way back to the right path. Do you believe that?"

"Allah brought us together for a reason. He would not bar all doors now. Some path must remain."

"But we cannot find it shackled and locked within this hut."

"What are you getting at?"

Ciarán thought about that, then set his jaw. "We'll need to earn Magnus's trust, and the jarl's too. And we'll need numbers, more than you and I. But at some point, the other longship will return here with Josua and Mordechai and the others."

"And what, when they do?"

"We'll find a way to free them," Ciarán swore. "And together, we'll make our escape."

MIDSUMMER

idsummer morning brought fair skies and a breeze that hissed across the fields of the village of Amesbury, where the remnants of bonfires still stood, gray and ashen.

The night before, young boys had run through those fields with burning branches to drive away evil spirits, while the villagers of Amesbury drank and danced to the music of mummers and musicians with reed pipes and bowl lutes. The affair reminded Alais of the festivals she and Geoffrey hosted at Selles-sur-Cher on the eve of Midsummer. Those festivals had been born of the old ways, the Frankish ways and the Celtic ways, long before the Church came and renamed the feast Saint John's Eve. They were nights of gaiety and merrymaking, celebrating the end of the sheep shearing and the beginning of the hay harvest. With the tragedy of the Viking attack weighing heavy on her, Alais had found last night a welcome respite.

Sister Leofflaed had been among those dancing around the bonfire, wearing a necklace of yarrow blossoms and even dragging Alais into the revelry at one point. The young nun smiled like a pixie as she twirled and clapped, while Lay Sister Agnes sang arm in arm with the villagers, enjoying cups of spiced ale and sweetcakes. The two seemed overjoyed, if for no other reason than to be free of the strictures imposed by Prioress Euphemia, and Alais could not help but share some of their delight.

They had spent their second night since setting out from the Priory of Saint Frithuswith in the guest house of a stout abbey in Amesbury dedicated to Saint Mary and Saint Melor. In the morning, Alais insisted they leave there before Terce, for if they did not reach Stonehenge before sunset, their journey would be for naught. Sister Leofflaed claimed the stones were not that far from the village, but she seemed as eager to see the henge as Alais. So, an hour before Terce, the trio left the abbey and passed through the fields of Amesbury until they reached the road which ran west through green meadows, fringed by woodlands.

Back at Saint Frithuswith's, Alais had traded her ruined dress for a gray, woolen habit and the simple white headdress that the lay sisters wore. She cradled Caladbolg in her arms wrapped tight in a dun-colored blanket, while Lay Sister Agnes hefted a pack with their provisions and a walking staff made of hard ash. She stood as tall and imposing as most men, and with that staff in her hands, it was no wonder they had traveled unmolested along the English roads. As they walked, Alais rehearsed the riddle of the Giant's Ring in her mind.

> *As the sun sets on a thousand years, seek the Giant's Ring,*
> *On the Solstice, at the Altar Stone, with blood the Spirit brings . . .*

If this was the role she was meant to play, as Orionde's words had foretold, then she would need to solve that riddle, and without any help from Ciarán or Khalil this time around. The puzzle might be referring to a sacrifice of some kind, yet was it speaking of animal blood—or a human's? The thought made her shudder, and she wondered if Caladbolg's razor-sharp blade would have a role to play, too. But first, she would have to find this Altar Stone.

Alais turned to Sister Leofflaed. "Did Stonehenge used to be a temple of sorts?"

252

Sister Leofflaed cocked her head, as she tended to do when thinking. "Don't think so. Grandmother used to call the stones the 'Giant's Dance.' Said it was a magical place, brought to England from Ireland across the sea, by a white wizard named Merlin. He was a Welshman, some say, the wise man to a great Welsh king named Arthur."

Alais had heard the names before in Archbishop Turpin's journal. Merlin was the druid whose tomb Turpin and the paladins had visited when they retrieved the sword Flamberge. Like Excalibur, it was another name for Caladbolg. "Tell me more about Merlin."

"I only know what Grandmother told me. She had the finest stories, you know." Sister Leofflaed blushed. "She said he was a dashing man and silver of tongue. And he even had a *lover*, a fair and wanton maid who might have been one of the Fae folk."

"Truly?"

"'Tis true!" Sister Leofflaed grinned like a castle gossip. "She was one of the damsels of the lake, on the Isle of Avalon. A place of magic if there ever was one."

Avalon . . . Alais recognized that word too from Turpin's journal.

"Anyhow," Sister Leofflaed went on, "the damsel promised Merlin her maidenhood if he would teach her all the magic he knew, which was a lot, I reckon. He was so smitten by her beauty, he did as she asked. And so she gave him her maidenhood, but then she tricked him. Used his own magic to trap him beneath the stones, so she could take a new lover, it's told. Quite the scandalous affair. But that's why Stonehenge is such a magical place. Because Merlin still lives there, just where the damsel of the lake put him."

Alais pondered this story as the three of them continued down the road. Leofflaed's story was just another myth, but as Brother Dónall was fond of saying, there's truth in those old myths. Whatever truth was buried in this myth, Alais did not know; nor was she any closer to learning more about the Altar Stone, though she prayed silently to Saint Radegonde that its meaning would become apparent when they reached Stonehenge.

An hour before midday, they caught their first glimpse of the megalith. The road led to a wooded valley where, through a break in the tree line, a meadow stretched far and wide. And in its center, like a solitary crown upon an emerald quilt, stood a jagged cluster of upright stones. "There it is!" Sister Leofflaed held a look of wonder in her eyes.

Alais drew a long breath and rehashed the riddle one more time. Her destination lay but a mile away, and Orionde's words echoed in her thoughts. *You have yet another role to play . . .*

Lay Sister Agnes pointed to the road, which turned north, away from Stonehenge. The nearest route to the meadow was through the woodlands, for the break in the tree line was another half mile away. "Those woods don't look thick," Sister Leofflaed said. "We'll find a path."

They set off from the road toward the woods, where beech trees formed a canopy of green leaves over a carpet of woodland duff. Finding a natural pathway through the woods was not hard. Sunlight trickled through the branches, and before long the light grew brighter as the first hints of the meadow emerged through gaps between the trees. Lay Sister Agnes led the way, but stopped in her tracks when something moved beyond the tree line. It was large and roan-colored, and for a heartbeat Alais feared they had stumbled upon an aurochs—until she saw the big brown eyes of a mare staring back. They were horses, about a half dozen or so, grazing at the edge of the woods. Alais wondered if wild horses roamed this valley.

Then she noticed the saddles.

Leather saddles, and bridles and reins, on each mount. She glanced frantically through the woods, then Sister Leofflaed grabbed her arm. "Look," she whispered.

Ten paces away near a broad beech tree stood a man with his back to them, clearly relieving himself. He was tall, broad-shouldered, and long-haired, and above the waistline of his woolen breeches were tattoos scrawled across his naked skin. Sister Leofflaed withdrew a step. Her foot fell on twig, snapping it in two.

At the sound, the man turned. Hard eyes and a full beard marked a vaguely familiar face—a Northman's face. Alais' stomach hardened into a rock. She had seen the man before, on the deck of the longship, moments before she leaped overboard. Her mind screamed. *This isn't possible!*

The Northman's mouth twisted into a lecherous grin. He held up his hands, gesturing that he meant no harm, but stepped deliberately toward them. Lay Sister Agnes brandished her staff. The Northman took another step, motioning with his hands for her to put the staff down. Instead, Lay Sister Agnes swung. The tip of the ash staff careened toward the man's head. To Alais' horror, the Northman caught the staff with both hands and wrenched it from Lay Sister Agnes's grasp. He hammered the staff back. She shielded her face, but the blow sent her crashing to the ground. Sister Leofflaed lunged for her friend, but the Northman batted her away into a pile of leafy duff. He yelled something in his Northern tongue, leering at Alais.

He was calling for the others, she realized. Alais glanced down at the sword in her arms, still wrapped the blanket. She had never swung a blade, but knew their lives depended on her doing it now. She pulled off the blanket and grabbed hold of Caladbolg's hilt with two hands.

The Northman cocked his head, an amused expression settling in his face. Clutching the staff, he sauntered toward her, while through the trees came the sounds of more men. Men who would rape and enslave them. Alais' heart pounded in her chest. With a cry, she swung the sword in board arc. The Northman raised the staff to parry the blow, but Caladbolg cleaved through the hard ash like it was a wheat stem. The blade's tip continued on, cutting into the flesh of the Northman's stomach and through the waist of his trousers until it sliced clean through where his manhood should have been. The Northman wailed and doubled over, clutching his groin.

In the woods, men were yelling now. Sister Leofflaed shot Alais a panicked look. Alais pointed to the edge of the woods. "The horses!"

The three women clambered toward the woodland's edge. Holding Caladbolg in her left hand, Alais climbed onto the saddle of the nearest mare. Sister Leofflaed mounted another, and Lay Sister Agnes a third. Alais gazed out at the meadow. Scores of Northmen gathered around tents and half-built cookfires, while others hurried into the woods. Farther away, at the ring of standing stones, a tall, black-clad man turned his head toward the commotion. He was not dressed like the Northmen, and even from this distance Alais suspected who it was. How Naberus da Roma had come with these Vikings, she did not know, and there was no time to search for answers. The men closest to the horses had spotted them and were calling to the others in their foreign tongue.

With her right hand, Alais grabbed hold of the reins and kicked her heels hard into the mare's side. The horse broke into a gallop as the Vikings barreled toward them, swords and axes in hand. With the woods to the east, the only place free of Northmen was to the south and west of Stonehenge, so that is where Alais spurred her mount.

Sister Leofflaed and Lay Sister Agnes rode desperately beside her. Alais glanced over her shoulder. A half-dozen Northmen had mounted horses, yet they were hundreds of yards behind. Alais knew that if their mares rode strong, the Northmen would not catch them. But whatever secret to the Key lay in the Giant's Ring, it was lost, and so was any hope for their journey. For at sunset, Naberus da Roma would stand at the Altar Stone, and perhaps find his way to the Key.

And Alais saw no way now to prevent whatever hell would follow.

NABERUS DA ROMA CIRCLED THE GIANT'S RING AS THE SUN BEGAN ITS descent. The sarsen stones loomed thirteen feet tall, forming what remained of the monolith's outer ring. In places, other stones, speckled green with moss, surmounted pairs of sarsens, creating rectangular gateways into the inner ring. Fewer of the blue-gray stones remained upright there, the rest having joined the other fallen sarsens as rubble on the grassy plain. Naberus stepped between two massive standing stones into the monolith's center, where another stone lay on its side. A smooth stone, flat like an altar.

Naberus could sense the aura of this ancient place, older than the pyramids of Egypt and the Great Sphinx of Giza, and far more hallowed. Long before the Celts had arrived at the island's shores, his ancestors had infused the great standing stones with power and arranged them with sacred geometry to draw upon the energy of the Otherworld. So that on the sabbats, when the curtain between dimensions grew thin as mist, the spirit of the stones might divine a glimmer of the future for those capable of mastering the ring's mysteries.

As he waited for sunset, he recalled each verse of his grandfather's instructions:

> *As the sun sets on a thousand years, seek the Giant's Ring,*
> *On the Solstice, at the Altar Stone, with blood the Spirit brings,*
> *The answer to the mystery forged when Atu sank into the sea,*
> *The way to our salvation, the revelation of the Key.*

Naberus drew a deep breath. *Salvation* . . . That was what the voice had promised, and at no time in history had the stars so aligned for victory. His people's enemy, weak to begin with, was already defeated and their precious weapon cast into the sea. Their God had abandoned them like he had abandoned the rest of mankind, and now no one could stop him from finding the Key. With it, he would free his forefathers, the gods of old, trapped for eons in Dudael, and together they would forge a new world. One where his kind would emerge from the shadows, to rule as they had in antediluvian times. And for this triumph, he would receive the gift promised to him in Orcus's shrine—eternal life.

The sun neared the horizon, painting the sky in its orange-red glow. It descended until it shone like a blazing eye between a pair of sarsens, casting a ray of light on the Altar Stone. *It is time.* Naberus slid the dagger across the palm of his left hand. The blade stung and his blood welled. He cleared his mind and placed his bloodied palm on the Altar Stone. *Spirit, guide me now.*

From the altar, ethereal fingers clawed hold of his consciousness, as if they were pulling him into the blue-gray stone. The air sizzled as his spirit passed through the ancient rock until he found himself in a reality beyond his imagination. By the time he returned, he was slumped on the Altar Stone, sweat clinging to his brow, huffing for breath. The huffs became a cough, and then a laugh. As he rolled onto the grass, running his fingers through his hair, he could hardly believe his good fortune.

For the spirit had shown him what he needed to see, and Naberus could never have fathomed how easy his task would be.

Sister Leofflaed knew of a monastery west of Stonehenge, so that is where the three women rode. Its former abbot had become the Archbishop of Canterbury, and the abbey had become so famous, one of the kings of Wessex had been interred there. The abbey was rich and fortified, so it would be safe from the Northmen, even though the women had seen no sign of the Viking riders since Stonehenge vanished over the horizon.

They arrived at twilight, but not to what Alais had expected. For the abbey was built on an island in the middle of the land. Marsh water from peat bogs created the curious inland sea where four green hills rose from the water. Foremost among them was a rounded tor, one of the oddest things Alais had ever seen. The tor appeared to be comprised of a series of terraces carved into the earth, one atop the other, narrowing to its apex where a stone tower stood proudly against the dusky sky. A pathway zigzagged down the tor's terraces, toward its western base, leading to the island's shore. There stood the abbey, as large as the monastery of Saint-Hilaire-le-Grand in Poitiers, built of stone and slate, with a formidable church that loomed over a nearby wharf crammed with fishing boats and a ferry stand.

From the saddle of her mare, Alais shook her head. "What is this place?"

"It's Glastonbury Tor," Sister Leofflaed said.

Alais recognized the name. The isle of Glastonbury, yet another reference from Turpin's journal. Although he had another name for the place too: Avalon, the home of the Lady of the Lake. Turpin wrote of Avalon as if it were in the Otherworld, like Rosefleur, and from the look of the odd-shaped tor, Alais could only imagine where the gateway to such a place might be hidden.

Sister Leofflaed pointed to the tower atop the tor. "That's the monastery of Saint Michael, but it's the larger one at the base where we're headed: Glastonbury Abbey. The whole isle is crawling with monks, but they'll take in a nun and two lay sisters from Saint Frithuswith's for sure. So we'll be safe for the night."

They crossed a timber bridge that led to the island and the abbey's gatehouse, where Sister Leofflaed told the gatekeeper what had happened to them at Stonehenge. The gatekeeper, who looked no older than sixteen, with a pockmarked face and bulbous ears, was aghast when he learned about the Northmen. He hurried off to warn the abbot, but not before giving them the key to a room in the guest-house and directions to the kitchen where they could sup on the left-overs from the night's meal.

The frightened gatekeeper had not noticed Caladbolg, which Alais tried hard to conceal behind her back until she could stow it in the guest room. Once that was done, they found the kitchen. The left-overs consisted of three pieces of herring pie, cold pea pottage, and three cups of ale, but it was plenty. None of them were particularly hungry, for the harrowing encounter with the Northmen was still too fresh in their minds.

"You saved us, you know," Sister Leofflaed said, cupping her ale in her hands.

"The sword saved us," Alais replied.

"But you swung it." Sister Leofflaed's eyes widened. "You gutted one of the bloody heathens! Even if he lives, he won't be making any little Danes, now will he? Though I suspect he's gone and the Devil's welcomed him with open arms."

Alais swallowed her ale. She had not thought about whether the man survived. But if he had not, she felt nothing. The man had been going to rape them. "Maybe the world's a better place with one less of them in it."

At the table, Lay Sister Agnes nodded and smiled, as if sensing the gist of the conversation, even though Sister Leofflaed and Alais were speaking in Latin.

Sister Leofflaed set down her cup and frowned. "I'm sorry you weren't able finish your friends' journey, and figure out whether it was a sundial or whatnot. But what will you do now? The priory could always use a new lay sister, and I'm sure Prioress Euphemia would approve."

Alais sighed. "I don't know what I'll do now, and I'm too tired to think of it."

"A night's rest we'll do you good," Sister Leofflaed said with a smile.

When they returned to the guest room, Lay Sister Agnes wrapped Alais in a bear hug and wiped a tear from her eye before settling into one of the room's three wood-framed beds. Sister Leofflaed climbed into another, and Alais took the third. Lying on the feather mattress, she felt sleep taking hold. And soon, she was lost in her dreams.

She found herself standing between the Roman Coliseum and the towering Arch of Constantine, its white marble reflecting the light of a full moon. She glanced west, where the ruins of the Temple of Venus and Roma stood on the grassy hill with its shadowy warrens. Behind the ruins, the bell tower of the Church of Santa Maria Nova rose into the night sky. A familiar and haunting song echoed from the temple's ruins, beckoning Alais.

She climbed the hill, passing broken columns, as the foreign words of the song grew louder. She followed the tune to the nave hidden behind the towering remains of a once vaulted chamber. There, amid the remnants of porphyry columns, the woman in white danced gracefully across the ancient patterned floor, painted in moonlight. Fireflies twinkled around her, flitting with the motion of her arms and her silvery hair, like leaves wafting on an autumn breeze. The woman's eyes were closed as she danced, as if she was lost within the melody of her song. She never seemed to notice Alais, who could not bring herself to set foot on the ancient tiles. Nor did the woman notice the movement in the shadows, but Alais saw it well. Something shifted in the darkness near the entrance to the nave.

In a breath, the fireflies scattered and vanished. The woman opened her eyes. Alais wanted to cry out, but the scream caught in her throat. From the shadows emerged a towering figure in a cowl and black robes. Like a wraith, it reached for the woman in white, enveloping her within the folds of its cloak. This time, the scream burst from Alais' lungs.

She bolted awake, only to find herself in the darkness of the guest chamber. In the beds beside her, Sister Leofflaed and Lay Sister Agnes slept soundly. Alais breathed a sigh of relief, but then felt a tingle crawl across her skin. As if she was being watched. Alais froze. *There's someone else in the room . . .*

As if her nightmare had sprung to life, a looming figure stepped from the shadows. A broad cowl obscured any image of its face. Alais tried to scream, but a long-fingered hand flashed before her eyes and clamped over her lips. She clawed at the intruder's arm, but its hand held her with a grip like a blacksmith's. As she struggled for breath, her head began to spin.

Then everything faded to black.

OBLIVION

lais woke naked on a cold stone floor, covered only by a blanket of undyed wool. A faint glow illuminated the otherwise dark chamber in which she lay. She looked to the ceiling, though where she expected to see rafters, she saw thick branches sprawling for hundreds of feet in every direction. The coarse bark on the boughs was the color of stone, gray and lifeless, as was the nearest wall. Even stranger, it was the only wall in the chamber. The rest were not walls at all, but crumbling parapets, as if she lay on a terrace carved into a gigantic oak.

I must be in a dream . . .

She had heard of petrified forests, where the trees had literally turned to stone eons ago, but nowhere had she seen a tree this enormous. Especially one with stairs in its trunk. For that is what she found herself staring at, a stairwell hewn into the stone of the twisted tree.

This cannot be real . . .

She rose to her feet, pulled the blanket around her, and padded to the parapet. Peering over its edge, her eyes flew wide. The terrace overlooked a lake that surrounded the titanic tree, and the water glowed as if moonlight emanated from the lake bed. And on its surface, something was moving. It looked like a boat with a curved prow, and as it neared, the image of its oarsman came into clearer view: tall and black-robed with a broad cowl.

Her mind reeled. She glanced at the stairway carved into the tree trunk. It seemed the only way out, but the stairwell had no rail. She darted for the stairs, clinging to the trunk, cold and rough like the rock of a cave wall. She glanced down, then jerked her head back. The blanket slipped from her shoulder and fell, fluttering forty feet to the lake below. Gripping the bark so hard her fingers turned white, she forced herself to ascend the narrow stairs. Ahead was another terrace. She willed her limbs to move. When she reached the terrace, she found another parapet, though half of it had collapsed. Yet across from it stood a wooden door: ironbound and hinged into the side of the petrified tree. She sprinted toward the door, grasped the handle, and pulled. The door did not budge. *Dear God, let this be a dream!* She pinched herself, praying she would feel no pain.

But the pinch stung.

The only escape was over the parapet, which plunged fifty feet to the lake below. Wrapping her arms tight around her naked breasts, she stood there trembling. At the curve of the stairway emerged the point of a hood. Alais gasped as her abductor strode onto the terrace. The figure stood a head taller than Alais, its cowl hiding any glimpse of her abductor's face.

Alais cringed. "Who are you?"

Her abductor drew back the cowl. Silvery hair spilled to her shoulders, and eyes as gray as Alais' own peered from an ageless face. "My name," said the woman, "is Nimue."

Alais shook her head in disbelief. The woman had the look of the dancer in her dreams. She looked like Orionde of the Fae, though this woman's cheeks were more sunken and her skin was pulled tight over her skull. That skin, however, was pale and flawless, and her silvery hair shimmered in the light from the water below.

"Are you. . ." Alais asked, "the Lady of the Lake?"

The woman's thin lips spread into a faint smile. "Once I was called that, a long time ago."

"Then this is . . ."

"Avalon." The woman's smile vanished. "This is *my* purgatory." She drew a swath of cloth from her robes and handed it to Alais. "You can wear this."

Alais took the cloth. It was a chemise, flint colored and as soft as silk. She pulled it over her head. The neck of the chemise was cut to the center of her chest. An immodest thing, she thought, before her mind returned to a more pressing question. "Why did you bring me here?"

"I sensed your arrival when you brought Caledfwlch close to its home, and I knew you would never find your way to Avalon on your own."

Caledfwlch . . . Alais had heard that name before. Brother Dónall had said that was the Welsh name for Caladbolg. Then a panicked thought struck. *I left Caladbolg in the abbey's guest room!*

"The sword is here," the woman said as if she could read Alais' thoughts. "Safe, where it belongs."

Alais prayed the woman was telling her the truth, but there was an unnerving coldness in her gaze. "Why not just take the sword and leave me be?"

"Because I know Orionde gave you that sword before she died, and I suspect the reason why."

A chill prickled Alais' skin. "You know Orionde died?"

"I know many things, child. Neither past nor present is hidden from me, and sometimes not even the future."

"But you weren't at Rosefleur."

Nimue's eyes narrowed. "I did not need to be. I will tell you more, but first you must eat." She strode barefoot past Alais toward the door in the side of the petrified tree trunk. After removing a ring of silver keys from her robes, Nimue unlocked the door and beckoned Alais to follow.

The door led to more stairs that climbed through a tunnel within the tree trunk. Alais followed Nimue up the spiraling stairs, wondering if she was walking with the damsel of the lake from Sister Leofflaed's tales. They emerged on a broad stone terrace set atop one of the enormous branches of the petrified oak. Romanesque columns surrounded the terrace, where a table stood, also carved from stone and adorned with silver goblets, bowls, and platters. A high-backed chair was set at each end of the table.

Nimue glided to the table and reached out to an unlit candle near one of the goblets. At the touch of her finger, the candle hissed into flame. "Eat, child," she said. "I will return shortly." With that, Nimue disappeared up another flight of stairs at the far end of the terrace, leaving Alais alone.

At the sight of food, Alais' stomach began to growl; the meal she had shared with Sister Leofflaed and Lay Sister Agnes in the kitchen of Glastonbury Abbey seemed an age ago. On the table, bowls were piled high with red apples, the platters were crammed with cheeses speckled with green mold, and the goblets were filled with a dark red wine. She tasted the wine, strong and rich with black currant. She chased it with one of the apples, as sweet as any she had ever eaten, and then picked enough mold off a hunk of cheese to make it edible.

As she ate, Alais attempted to make sense of her situation. She had little doubt she was in the Otherworld, for like Rosefleur this alien place held an aura of desolation. Even the surrounding columns had cracks in the marble and wisps of cobwebs strewn between the gaps. The Fae woman had found her hours after arriving at the abbey, which meant the gateway between worlds must be near Glastonbury, just as Archbishop Turpin had written in his journal. Maybe even beneath Glastonbury Tor.

The thought brought back stories of the old faerie mounds her grandmother used to warn her about when she was a child. They were hollow hills, and dangerous places, where the faeries would lure girls and boys with tricks, or trinkets, or tinkling bells. As Alais swallowed another sip of wine, she recalled a part of those tales that sent a shiver down her limbs. Faeries, Grandmother had warned, enticed their guests with food and wine, but whoever ate or drank became enslaved, never to return to the outside world. Alais took a deep breath. It was too late to worry if Grandmother was right. Besides, those were stories to frighten children, and Orionde and her sisters were nothing like the wicked faeries of those tales.

By the time Alais put her mind at ease, Nimue returned. Gone were her black robes and cowl, replaced now with a dress of silvery gauze that clung to her hips and breasts. The dress's material was vaguely opaque, highlighting the perfection of the Fae woman's body, and leaving no question in Alais' mind that ancient man once viewed such women as goddesses. Nimue claimed a chair and took a long drink of wine. "Sit, child."

Alais did as she was told, while Nimue gestured toward the massive boughs above them. "The Celts," she said, "who ruled this land ages ago, believed this to be the Tree of Life, home of the mother goddess of the earth. Yet as you can see, there's nothing living in this place, only gloom made bearable by our arts."

Alais thought for a moment. "Why do you live here? Clearly you can leave. You found me at the abbey."

Nimue steepled her fingers. "Because damnation comes in many forms. We were among the rebellion that led to the Great War, and when that war was lost, the Creator's archangels sentenced each of us to our fates. Most were imprisoned within the Abyss, in a place called Dudael, while Samyaza, who led the rebellion, was bound in a prison all his own. For the rest of us, the archangel Michael argued for clemency, for when the war began, we turned on Samyaza. We were forbidden to return to our celestial realm and condemned forever to this Otherworld in between. I can roam the whole of the Otherworld, yet if I were to leave the shadows for long, Michael and his brethren would find out, and then I would wear chains in Dudael."

"So you came here, and Orionde went to Rosefleur?"

"That is not how it was." Nimue drained her goblet. "In the age of Atlantis, we lingered close to that great city of men. But when Samyaza was released from his prison, war returned and Atlantis became one of its casualties. After the war ended, those of us who survived settled in the shadows of Éire. There we reigned for a millennium as the Tuatha Dé Danann, until war returned again, and shattered our realm. Some of us fled to Albion, where you sit now, in Avalon. Here we remained until Orionde left with our sisters and made Rosefleur, where you found them."

"Why didn't you go with them?"

Nimue pressed her lips into a thin smile. "Because, child, in Avalon I am queen. Orionde was covetous of my title, and like Samyaza, she convinced our sisters to join in her own rebellion, one that allowed her to be queen of her own piece of purgatory. But now war has returned again, and her realm is no more. She should have stayed in Avalon."

"I saw that war," Alais said. "I was part of it, and it was horrible. Why does God or Michael or whoever let it go on?"

"Only the Creator knows, but suffice it to say, Samyaza is both powerful and persuasive, and in every war, surrender has its terms."

As she listened, Alais felt numb. Brother Remi had believed the prophecy was a test to determine if mankind deserved to live another thousand years. She had not contemplated that all of this might be the Devil's terms. Nor had she ever expected to encounter another like Orionde. While there was no love lost between these two Fae women, Nimue had knowledge of everything Ciarán, Dónall, and Remi had searched for. Yet now, Alais realized, she was the only one who could learn the answers to their questions. *You have yet another role to play...*

Alais set her jaw. "What is the secret of the journey?"

"Orionde did not tell you, did she?"

Alais shook her head. "She died before she could reveal it."

Nimue frowned. "That's not true, is it? I saw what happened. She had time in Rosefleur to tell you. She fancied herself the keeper of our secrets, yet when it mattered most, at the moment of prophecy, she failed."

"Can you tell me the secret?" Alais pressed.

Nimue leaned back in her chair. "Better yet, child, I can show you."

Nimue led Alais down a series of stairs that wound around the tree's enormous trunk. As they descended, the surrounding darkness began to fade. They were heading toward the tree's base and the luminescent water surrounding it. The closer they came to the water, the more the petrified trunk reflected the lake's light.

"Why does the lake glow?" Alais asked.

"The lake is formed from the waters of the River Lethe, one of the five rivers that flow through the Otherworld. Some, like the Styx, are black like cuttlefish ink, but the Lethe is filled with millions of tiny creatures whose bodies have a natural luminescence. Their effect is beautiful, but to consume them is dangerous. Most who drink of the Lethe begin to lose their mind and eventually succumb to madness. 'Tis no wonder the river's name means *oblivion*."

Alais clung more tightly to the petrified trunk. "Then why are we heading toward the water?"

"We are not going to the lake, but to the scrying pool. We shall be there soon."

Alais wondered what this scrying pool was as she carefully descended the stairs, which ended in what looked like the roots of the titanic tree. Each root was a dozen yards wide, fanning out like a small island before submerging beneath the luminescent waters of the Lethe. Nimue climbed over one of the massive roots, and Alais followed. They descended into a dark hollow where at its shallowest point lay a broad pool of water glowing like a pale moon.

"Behold the scrying pool of Avalon," Nimue said. "It's a nexus between worlds and can reveal the past and the present, and sometimes the future. Let a thought of what you wish to know settle in your mind, and then stare into the pool. You will begin to recognize shapes in the water. Focus on one and close your eyes. You will see the image in your mind, and the power of the Lethe will do the rest."

Alais saw only still, glowing water.

Nimue reached down and picked up what looked to Alais like a dead sapling's branch. "First we must disturb the pool. Then you shall take my hand. This is your first time scrying, so I shall join you and tell the pool what you wish to know."

Nimue dipped the branch into the pool, causing ripples in the water. Then she ran the branch around the edge of the pool, causing the water to swirl. She grabbed Alais' hand. "Now, gaze into the pool and think of nothing but what you see."

Alais stared into the pool, focusing on the gently whirling water. Within its current, a shape began to form. Circular, with smaller orbs appearing beneath a creased brow, and a gaping mouth like a screaming skull.

"Now close your eyes!" Nimue commanded.

Alais did, and in her mind's eye, the glowing skull crystallized into a more definite shape. It was not a man's skull, but a beast's, and it was not the only one. Alais gasped. For before her rose the hillock of boulderlike skulls, and atop it loomed the glassy, black obelisk etched with spidery runes. *Dudael* . . . The gray wasteland surrounding the hill of skulls was a tapestry of carnage. Dead men in antique armor sprawled across the field amid the white-skinned corpses of giants. As a woman emerged on the hillock, Alais' jaw dropped. The figure was the woman in her dreams. Long silver hair spilled over a tunic of feather-like mail. She seemed so like Orionde, but Alais sensed it was not her, for this woman's features were even fairer, and she moved even more gracefully as her slender legs scaled the skulls. A longsword belted to her hip swayed with each step.

Behind the woman, a second woman emerged dressed in similar armor and also one of the Fae, for her hair was a fiery mane of copper and her features were sharp, yet beautiful. As the silver-haired woman gazed up at the towering obelisk, the other woman slipped a dagger from its sheath.

Studying the obelisk, the silver-haired woman seemed oblivious to the dagger behind her back. Alais wanted to cry out and warn her as the copper-haired woman pulled back her knife. But as she thrust the blade, the silver-haired woman flinched, as if sensing the danger, and spun. Instead of plunging into her back, the blade sliced across her ribs. The silver-haired woman cried out, grasping at the wound. Her attacker moved to strike again, but the silver-haired woman ripped her sword from its scabbard. The sword struck the dagger hard, and the lesser blade flew from the attacker's grasp.

The silver-haired woman advanced with her sword, while the other backed away, arms outstretched. A bluish glow flashed from her hands, its light reflecting on her fiery hair. The hill shook as an enormous serpent burst from the skulls, translucent and as blue as the glow emanating from the attacker's palms. The serpent coiled around the silver-haired woman, its mouth gaping with fangs. The woman grimaced as the serpent constricted, while the copper-haired woman watched with gleeful rage.

Then fire struck like lightning.

The torrent of flame roared from a staff topped with an ankh, a white gem blazing in its loop. A man wielding a staff stormed up the hill, bearded and handsome, clad in antique armor similar to the battlefield dead. Alais had no doubt what this weapon was, for the gemstone was Caladbolg's own. *Enoch's device,* Alais recalled, *has taken many forms . . .*

Engulfed by the pouring flames, the copper-haired woman writhed in pain, her flesh blistering and blackening. Howling with fury, she leaped from the hill into the carnage below. As she fled, the ghostly serpent melted away. The man rushed to the silver-haired woman's side. When they embraced, the scene began to fade . . .

Where the wasteland had been, a river bank emerged. Silvery sand spilled into luminescent waters similar to Avalon's lake. The silver-haired woman stood barefoot on the shore, clad in the silken white dress from Alais' dreams. She stepped into the glowing water and waded toward a boat with a prow carved like a heron's head. An oarsman stood in the hull, tall and dressed in ivory robes that held a luminescence similar to the river. Its glow reflected off his hair, the color of beaten bronze, and wreathed his face, as ageless and perfect as the Fae woman who approached him. Then the image began to fade again.

"Open your eyes," Nimue said.

Alais felt light-headed as she found herself standing before the scrying pool. "Who were those women?"

"The silver-haired woman," Nimue explained, "is named Sirra, though she's sometimes known by her Greek name, Andromeda. Both names mean 'the chained woman,' for she is bound to the Key to the Abyss, and she is its keeper. The other's name is Lilith, and she sought to seize the Key from Sirra and free the Watchers from their prison."

"Then the journey *is* about the Key to the Abyss."

"Yes, child, and it has remained so ever since that day. I was there when it happened, three thousand years ago in Dudael, after my sisters and the survivors of Atlantis defeated the Nephilim of Gog and Magog. To this day, I do not know why Sirra went so close to the obelisk that seals the Watchers' prison. Curiosity, perhaps. Or perhaps at Lilith's suggestion, but that is of no mind. No one knows what made Sirra hesitate and turn, just as Lilith's dagger should have pierced her back. But her hesitation saved her life, and then Arcanus of Atlantis and the power of Enoch's device drove Lilith away."

Alais shook her head. "But Lilith was one of you. Why would she turn on her sister?"

"Some believe Lilith had been Samyaza's lover. Though I don't know that to be true. Others think she fell under his spell. Or perhaps she had just tired of the purgatory to which we all had been condemned."

"Does she still live?"

Nimue shook her head. "Lilith was destroyed in the next millennium, when the time of prophecy came 'round again and war returned once more. Yet until then, she had only one desire—to kill Sirra and claim the Key."

"Is that why Sirra left with that man, at the end of the vision?"

"That was no man, it was *Michael*." Nimue spoke his name with a hint of scorn. "Sirra believed he had the power to help her forge a solution, yet one that would require her to sacrifice her immortal form. For just like Caledfwlch changes shape in each millennium, so too does Sirra change her skin, never appearing again as she was the time before, to make it near impossible for Lilith to locate her and the Key. For a thousand years, Sirra's solution worked, yet eventually Lilith found her. Though before Lilith could claim the Key, she was slain by Solomon of Israel. When the war ended, Sirra took a new form, and the Key went with her."

Alais' mouth fell open. "Are you suggesting Sirra still holds the Key?"

"That is precisely what I'm suggesting. To find Sirra is to find the Key, and that is the journey's purpose."

Alais shook her head in disbelief. "How do you find one of the Fae who does not wish to be found?"

"The answer to that question is the secret of the journey, and like the prophecy itself, it is etched in the heavens." Nimue stepped away from the pool. "Follow me."

Nimue guided Alais to the base of the tree's trunk, where the faint outline of a door appeared in the petrified wood. Carved into the door was a familiar symbol: the ring of the Zodiac with a seven-pointed star in its center. All that was missing was the ankh, the symbols of the planets, and the Greek words scrawled along the star.

"You have seen this symbol before?" Nimue asked.

"Yes," Alais replied. "In the Book of Maugis d'Aygremont."

"Then you know the journey began with a sacrifice, symbolized by Capricorn. The journey moves forward like the waters of the Lethe, embodied by the constellation Aquarius, but it is in Pisces where the secret lies. In the heavens, the twin fish of Pisces are linked to two other constellations, as if bound by chains. The first touches the neck of Cetus, another name for the great monster Leviathan. It is a symbol of the Watchers bound in Dudael beneath the hill of skulls. The second fish touches the constellation Andromeda, the chained woman, who holds the Key to their prison. Through these constellations pass the great planets, and when Venus passes through Andromeda and comes within Aries, the journey is at its end and the Key's location shall be revealed to both the enemy and the champion of prophecy."

Alais shook her head again. "How long until this happens?"

The ghost of a smile touched Nimue's lips. "There is still time until the end. As you are the prophecy's champion, there is much I can show you about the power, forged from the language of creation. It shall serve you well in the tribulations to come."

"But I'm not the champion," Alais said. "Brother Ciarán is the one who answered the call, even Orionde said so."

Nimue raised a brow. "One of your companions on the ship?"

A chill washed over Alais. "How do you know?"

"The pool told me before you arrived. I saw you jump into the sea when the Northmen attacked, and then I saw them round up the survivors among your crew. The Northmen bound them to the mast and set the cog afire."

Alais clutched her chest. Although she had suspected the worst, she felt unready to face the truth.

"Child," Nimue said softly, "your friends burned to death on that cog. I saw the flames blacken their flesh until nothing but bone remained, lost within the fire. You are the only survivor, which means the prophecy is yours to fulfill. Do you wish to be prepared for what lies ahead? I can teach you, but only if you are ready."

Tears welled in Alais' eyes. *I know my role . . .*

Nimue stepped forward and embraced her. The Fae woman's arms were as hard as stone and as cold as ice. "Are you ready?" she whispered.

Alais drew a shuddering breath. "I am."

36

THE WIND SERPENT

Dark-gray skies and a damp mist greeted Ciarán and Khalil the morning that Magnus and Jorundr led them down the plank road to the compound's wharf. Ciarán had lost track of how many days had passed since their enslavement, and nothing had changed. The longship carrying Josua and the rest of *La Margerie's* surviving crew had not returned to Vette, and the iron manacles still bit into his ankles.

At the wharf, thirty longships swayed in the river. While on the docks, a host of Danes and slaves prepared boats for fishing. Magnus directed Ciarán and Khalil toward a copse of hazel and chestnut trees that framed thicker woods of oak and beech. A hundred paces from the woods, a boat lay overturned on the river bank. "That one belongs to Jarl Holger," Magnus said. "Her bottom needs a good scraping."

The longboat hull was speckled with mussels and caked with mud. For a moment, Ciarán wondered if they could use a boat like this to make their escape, but the sight of a wharf full of longships made him think otherwise. He could never outrow one of those. He glanced at the surrounding woods. A man could hide there, but the Danes were fond of dogs, and boarhounds in particular. *We'd be hunted in that forest.*

Magnus gave Ciarán and Khalil each a dull knife and insisted they begin scraping. Ciarán did as he was told, working the mussels free from the oak planks, all the while thinking about how they might escape. The boats might be too slow, but if enough of Josua's crew survived, they could sail one of the longships. They would just have to be patient until an opportunity presented itself.

Ciarán's hand was still sore from the wound he had suffered from Naberus' spear, and by midday it began to blister from working the knife through the caked mud and stubborn mussels. From the wharf, a horn sounded. Ciarán looked up to see the curved prow of a long-ship heading toward the docks. The beast head had been removed from the prow, though shields lined its sides and at least twenty oars dipped into the river.

Magnus sauntered up beside Ciarán. "That's *Wind Serpent,*" the Dane said. "Jarl Orn's ship."

Jarl Orn. Ciarán recognized the name. *The other ship that attacked us.* He drew in a breath. *Blessed Columcille*, he prayed, *let them be aboard that ship.*

He watched as *Wind Serpent* glided to its dock. Three Danes secured the ship, and then helped lower the gangplank. The first man to disembark was a red-haired giant clad in a fur cloak. His right arm grasped a stout chest, while his left held an ax slung over his shoulder. A woman and two small boys rushed down the dock to embrace him. As more Danes disembarked, they too were greeted by their families, gathered outside the palisade's gate. The Danes unloaded more chests, weapons, and crew until the last man left the ship. Naberus da Roma was not with them, but neither was anyone else.

Ciarán felt a weight in his chest. "Where are their thralls?"

Magnus answered with a grimace. "You haven't heard? Jarl Orn was going to sell your crewmates to the Rus who sailed with the Roman before their ship was struck by lightning. They're to replace the dead among his crew, so wherever the Rus and the Roman have ventured, that's where your friends have gone." He clapped Ciarán on the shoulder. "Now get back to work."

Ciarán slumped onto the overturned boat. After a long sigh, he began stabbing at a patch of mussels fixed to the hull. Khalil leaned over, an urgent look in his eyes. "Where are Josua and the others?"

As he answered, Ciarán felt hollow inside. "With the Varangian and Naberus da Roma."

~

THAT NIGHT, CIARÁN'S SLEEP WAS HAUNTED BY NIGHTMARES ABOUT THE fate of Josua and their crew. He imagined them chained to benches, pulling a longship's oars, while Naberus's raven pecked at their flesh until its beak was red with blood. He woke to the grating sound of the bar to the slave hut's door. As he rubbed the sleep from his eyes, not a rooster crowed and no sunlight seeped through the door's tiny window. *It's still the middle of the night . . .*

As the door began to open, he grabbed Khalil, who lay sleeping on an adjacent bench. The flicker of torchlight illuminated the half-open doorway where a man stood, yet it was not their jailer. The torch-bearer was taller than Magnus, more sinewy than Jorundr, and darker than both of them. Bathed in the torchlight, his face had a hellish appearance, with a chest-length beard ending in a thick braid.

"Who are you?" Ciarán jumped from the bench, reminded of the cold shackles around his ankles.

"I am Grimr Grimsson," the man replied in ill-spoken Irish, "hirdman to Jarl Orn Skullreaver, and one of the last men you'll see before you feed the raven." In his left hand, he gripped a double-edged sword. "Naberus the Roman paid me to kill both of you, but I'm only going to kill the Moor. My cousin Sigurd will kill you for what you did to his arm." The Dane stepped aside to allow a red-bearded warrior to peer into the hut. He bore a vengeful look on his face, and the stump of his right arm was covered in a stained bandage where Caladbolg had claimed it.

A lump settled in Ciarán's throat. "We belong to Jarl Holger. If you kill us, he'll kill you."

The dark-bearded Dane flashed a cruel smile. "The Roman has already paid us the wergild, the blood price for your lives. We shall pay it to Jarl Holger, and under our law, it will settle the matter of your deaths."

The red-bearded warrior stepped into the hut wielding a short sword with his good arm. *"Forbered dig pa dø svin!"* he hissed in the Danish tongue.

Ciarán felt as if his feet were mortared to the floor, unable to take his eyes off the red-bearded warrior and his pointed blade. Then Khalil exploded from the adjacent bench, ramming his body into the one-armed Viking. The warrior flailed and fell into the dark-haired Dane, who slammed into the hut's plank wall. The torch, still in his left hand, grazed the birchbark roof, its flames licking the dry wood.

Grimacing, Khalil looked to Ciarán. "Run!"

Ciarán bolted toward the doorway. As soon as he could taste the brisk night air, the chain around his ankles snapped taut. His momentum sent him face down into the mud.

Khalil shuffled past him, taking no more than a half stride to avoid Ciarán's fate. With a roar, the red-bearded Viking burst from the hut, swinging his sword. Khalil spun to avoid the blow, but one foot caught in the manacle's chain, sending him tumbling onto the ground. The Viking thrust his sword straight down, but the Persian rolled to the side just as the blade sank into the wet earth. Kahlil's hand flashed for the hilt and, in a heartbeat, the two men were wrestling for control of the sword.

Ciarán scrambled to his feet. Around him smoke hissed into the air as flames curled from the hut. Embers wafted to the ground as Grimr emerged from the hut's doorway, his face a portrait of fury.

A fierce barking drowned out the crackle of flames as an enormous boarhound bounded toward them. Grimr's eyes flew wide, then he bolted into the night. Abandoning the struggle for his blade, his one-armed cousin clambered behind him. The boarhound rushed beside Ciarán, barking ferociously into the night. Trailing it was the hulking Jorundr with a broadax in hand, and a stride behind was Jarl Holger, bare-chested and armed with his sword.

Jorundr bellowed a Danish curse at the fleeing Vikings. Jarl Holger knelt beside Ciarán, looking over him like a merchant inspecting his wares. "You're unhurt?" he asked in his thickly accented Irish.

"They tried to kill us," Ciarán said. "The Roman paid them to do it."

Jarl Holger's eyes narrowed. "Then they were Jarl Orn's crewmen. Was Sigurd among them?"

"Aye," Ciarán said. "And his cousin, Grimr."

"A treacherous pair," the jarl said. "And this is about more than coin. You Christians may be taught to turn the other cheek, but we Danes are taught to seek revenge. Orn, Grimr, and Sigurd are kinsmen, so this is a blood feud now, and they will not rest until you have paid for maiming Sigurd." He scratched the chin of his golden beard. "I have been hoping to get back out to sea, so now you and I will sail together sooner than expected. Until then, you and the Moor will sleep in my hall, but in two days we will leave for Dublin."

Ciarán could hardly believe his ears. *Dublin.*

"Yes, lord," he responded, but in his heart the promise of the situation had already taken hold. *We're going to Ireland.*

And then, come hell or high water, I'm going home.

PAPAL SECRETS

Theodora stretched her arms along the sides of the pool as the steam from the bathwater kissed her face. The *balneae* was one of the hidden treasures within the ruins of Trajan's Market, a private bath built by some wealthy merchant long ago who adorned its walls with mosaics of naked nymphs and mermaids, now aglow in the dancing light from candles burning in each corner.

The *balneae* was hers alone within the sanctuary of the Brotherhood of the Messiah, a benefit of her newfound role. Before he left Rome, Naberus had convinced the brothers of the need for a new leader after Crescentius's death, and that she, as a descendant of Marozia and Senatrix Theodora, was the one destined to lead their resistance against the foreign pope and his imperial cousin. Some of the brothers abhorred the thought of a woman in power, but Theodora reminded them how the matriarchs in her family once ruled Rome, when those who refused to come around ended up floating in the Tiber. Ever since, she had viewed the brotherhood as her weapon, and often only needed her words to wield it. When that failed, she relied on her allure, which even the most devout monks found hard to resist. For whether cleric or true rogue, many of these men saw her as a goddess made flesh, and they would kill for a chance to worship at her altar.

As she lounged in the bath, Theodora heard the slap of sandals on the marble floor. "My lady," a man said. The voice belonged to Brother Simeon, the handsome young gatekeeper she had encountered on her first visit to the brotherhood's sanctum.

"Yes, Simeon," she answered. "You can come in."

Simeon tried not to look at her, but despite his efforts, his eyes seemed drawn to her body beneath the bathwater. "I have good tidings," he said, blushing. "Our messenger reached Nilus da Rossano on Monte Gargano, and has sent word. He said Nilus was horrified to learn of Pope John's fate at the hands of the emperor and the Saxon pope."

"Nilus da Rossano is nearly ninety years old. Are you certain he'll come to Rome?"

"Yes, my lady. Pope John and Brother Nilus are both Calabrian, and I'm told Nilus loved His Holiness like his own son."

Theodora ran her fingers through her platinum hair. "Will his visit be enough to drive a wedge between the Saxon pope and his cousin?"

"I swear it will," Simeon said. "Nilus is revered as a living saint. His judgment shall carry tremendous weight, and you saw the emperor's face at Pope John's defrocking."

Theodora had indeed seen the horror in the emperor's eyes. John Philagathos was Otto's godfather and his mothers' lover, if the rumors proved true. She could tell he had no stomach to see his godfather so humiliated and mutilated. The emperor's reaction revealed a fissure between the cousins, and now she needed to widen that rift. "So we pray that Nilus's judgment so shames the emperor he turns on his cousin?"

"Yes," Simeon said, "and once emperor and pope are driven apart, we pray the emperor returns home."

"Leaving the Saxon pope all alone." She took a deep, satisfied breath. "Tell me, Simeon, do you like what you see?"

Simeon stuttered. "Y—yes, my lady."

"Then what are you waiting for? Take off your clothes and join me."

～

POPE GREGORY HAD BEEN SUMMONED, AND THE ARROGANCE OF HIS summoner annoyed him to no end.

When Rumeus told Gregory of the summons, he had half a mind to refuse it, if for no reason than to prove a point. *Only emperors summon the pope, not archbishops.* Yet Rumeus insisted this was important. Gerbert had been rummaging through the papal archives for nearly a week, and finally he had discovered something that warranted this insufferable summons.

The papal archives contained the most sacred writings and artifacts in all of Christendom. Centuries ago, they were kept in a series of rooms set off from the papal library. Then in the fifth century, to protect the archives from Attila and his Huns, Pope Leo had them moved to the cellars beneath the palace.

As Gregory followed Rumeus down the hidden stairwell that led to the archives, he pursed his lips. "If this turns out to be the waste of time I expect it will, I'm of a mind to strip Gerbert of his archbishopric in Ravenna and make him the Bishop of Malta."

"Malta is overrun by the Saracens, Your Holiness," Rumeus said.

"Exactly my point. To think, all this nonsense was caused by a letter written by some Irish monk. The whole island is infested with drunken Celts."

"Gerbert claims he knew the monk's superior back in Reims," Rumeus replied. "He vouched for his credibility. Also, the monk's account of the blood rain in Aquitaine has been confirmed by a number of sources, including the Duke of Aquitaine and the Prior of Saint-Hilarie-le-Grand."

Gregory shook his head. Two months ago, tidings of a blood rain in Aquitaine had reached Rome, inciting panic among many of the clergy that the end times had begun. Gregory was skeptical, so he set a team of scholars from monasteries throughout Rome to research the history of blood rains. The findings were telling. In antiquity, the Greek poet Homer wrote of a rain of blood in two instances around the fall of Troy. In the year 582, Saint Gregory of Tours reported a blood rain in the city of Paris, the same year a great plague killed many in France. A copy of the English annals contained another account of a blood rain in the year 685, when one of the Saxon kings fell victim to disease and passed away. The world had not ended after any of these events, so an account of a blood rain was hardly proof the end times were imminent. At best, the results confirmed a blood rain portended some public disaster, and in this case it was likely Duke William's doomed campaign against the Viscount of Limoges and his ally, the Count of Anjou. Even more, the prophecy of Daniel had ensured the world would not end now, and in Gregory's mind that was the end of the debate. "The account of a blood rain means nothing," he said. "My scholars proved it."

Rumeus looked away. "As you say, Your Holiness."

The stairwell ended in a passageway hewn of earth and reinforced with brick, where the air smelled of dust and age-old vellum. Rushlights glowed down the corridor, illuminating the alcoves along the walls where the popes kept the most sacred treasures. Gregory passed a broad alcove containing a massive golden menorah. It had been the finest of spoils when the Romans sacked the temple in Jerusalem. Other alcoves held golden reliquaries containing more treasures from the ancient temple, including the vestments of the Hebrew high priest. Farther down, the archives' largest alcove held a full-sized crucifix plated in gold and studded with jewels. Both Rumeus and Gregory made the sign of the cross as they passed, for the crucifix was actually a gigantic reliquary containing the remains of the true cross of Jesus Christ. Constantine's mother, Saint Helena, had discovered the cross in the Holy Sepulcher during her travels to Jerusalem, and it remained one of Christendom's most sacred relics.

The pope and his archdeacon bowed before the next alcove, where a statue stood like a sentinel. The statue depicted a beautiful and slender woman wearing a crown of thorns and cradling a cross over her breast. Beyond her, the alcove held a silver chest containing the

Veil of Saint Veronica, the cloth used to wipe Christ's forehead as he hung upon the cross. Legend held that the cloth bore the image of the Savior's face, although Gregory had never confirmed this. He was afraid to open the vessel and expose the holy relic to the stale air. At least that is what he had told Rumeus the first time he ventured into the secret archives. Left unsaid was the fact that if the legend proved untrue, Gregory did not want to know it.

The passageway ended in a long room filled with wooden shelves crammed with books and scrolls. This is where Pope Leo had moved the palace's secret collection to protect it from the Huns. A wheel-shaped candelabrum hung from the ceiling, its candles shedding light on a long table cluttered with inkwells and open tomes. Gerbert looked up as they entered. "Ah, Your Holiness, it's good you arrived."

"What is it, Gerbert?" Gregory asked tersely.

"An astounding discovery." Gerbert glanced at the nearby shelves, his eyes as wide as a child's. "I never imagined the breadth of works kept down here. There's an actual copy of the Gospel of Mary Magdalene and the Sophia of Jesus Christ. And copies of Porphyry, Iamblichus, Plotinus—all deemed forbidden by your predecessors, but preserved nonetheless. I could stay down here a year and not finish them all."

Gregory crossed his arms. "I assure you that won't be happening. What have you discovered?"

"Oh, yes," Gerbert said. "You see, I read the research you commissioned on the blood rain of the type reported in Brother Ciarán's letter. While the research appeared thorough, and I cannot disagree with its conclusions, it did overlook the most prominent reference to a rain of blood—the one in the Apocalypse of John."

"I thought you believed the Book of Revelation to be a *metaphora*, not a literal account of things to come."

Gerbert held up an index finger. "True, but that didn't stop me from investigating, and you'll never imagine what I found."

"What?" Gregory said, growing more annoyed.

Gerbert shot him a witty smile. "The original. The Book of Revelation written by Saint John himself." He gestured toward a scroll partially unfurled on the table, held open by four stones. "It's right here."

Gregory raised a brow. "Does it say anything different from the copies?"

"No, but rolled up inside it, I found this." Gerbert held up a small, curled sheet of vellum. "A letter, from apparently the last pope to read Saint John's scroll."

Gregory glanced at Rumeus, who just shrugged. "Who?"

"Saint Sylvester, who served as pope during Constantine's reign." Gerbert handed Gregory the letter. "Read it."

Gregory unfurled the vellum:

To whoever finds this letter before the millennium and the End of Days:

Seek the mysteries Solomon bore,
Through sacred ring from Enoch's lore,
In Pontifex's gift to the bishop of Rome,
The secret lies in sacred tome.

I write in riddles so only those who are worthy may learn of these mysteries.
~ Sylvester

Beneath the name was the papal seal pressed in red wax.

Gregory looked up from the letter. "A riddle?"

"Yes, and one that speaks of the very same things in Brother Ciarán's letter." Gerbert cocked a brow. "An unlikely coincidence, wouldn't you agree?"

"Saint Sylvester lived six hundred years ago," Gregory scoffed. "It's hard to believe one could have anything to do with the other. And how are we to even know what this riddle means?"

"Let's start at the top," Gerbert said. "The mysteries Solomon bore. Legends have long held that King Solomon possessed power over demons through a device called the Seal of Solomon."

"And what exactly was that?"

"A stone set into a signet ring—just like the ring referenced in the riddle's second verse—and given to Solomon by an angel, no less, according to the legends. Incidentally, that same ring is referenced in Brother Ciarán's letter."

"How?"

"In his explanation of Enoch's device, a thing referenced in the Book of Enoch, which I believe is what Sylvester meant by 'Enoch's lore.' According to Brother Ciarán, the device took different forms in different millennia, and at the time of King Solomon, it took the shape of a gemstone set into the royal signet ring. Another coincidence? Doubtful, and the reference to the Book of Enoch all but proves it."

Gregory shook his head. "The Book of Enoch?"

"It is not part of the biblical canon, Your Holiness," Rumeus explained. "A legendary thing at best. But if the Book of Enoch ever existed, it has been lost to time."

Gerbert smiled back. "That's not entirely true. It was rumored Saint Augustine had every copy of the book destroyed, but it appears some copies survived. Brother Ciarán claims there was one in Charlemagne's library, which was eventually hidden by the lay abbots of Selles-sur-Cher in France until my old colleague Dónall mac Taidg discovered it. The Caliph of Córdoba also kept a copy in his secret collection."

"How do we even know these accounts are true?" Gregory pressed. "Did Brother Ciarán show you a copy?"

"No, he claimed both were taken from him. Fortunately, I found another one myself."

Gregory's mouth fell open. "How?"

"Down here, of course." He pointed to a gilded scroll case on the table lying next to a stack of tomes. "It seems Saint Boniface, who was pope in Augustine's day, must have secreted one away. I found it among a collection of forbidden works, right next to a copy of the Book of Jubilees. It took some time to read, but it corroborates everything in Brother Ciarán's letter. The stories of the Watchers and their desires for the daughters of men, just as the Book of Genesis tells. It also speaks at great length of the Nephilim and their punishment by God, all in the time leading up to the Great Flood. The Watchers were imprisoned in a place called Dudael, a fact noted by Saint Peter and referenced in the Book of Job. And it tells how the Archangel Uriel showed Enoch the way to a great and glorious device at the ends of the whole earth, just like Brother Ciarán described."

"So you think everything this Irish monk wrote may be true?" Gregory threw up his hands. "We're to believe that a secret race of Nephilim is seeking the Key to the Abyss to bring about the End of Days? What on earth happened to the skeptic in you, Gerbert?"

"There's plenty of skeptic left," Gerbert replied with a wink, "but I'll not disregard such evidence without weighing it first. Brother Ciarán wrote of a prophecy that speaks to averting the end times at a point of crisis in each millennium. Three times, he claims, the champions of this prophecy have accomplished this task. Now, we've found proof that centuries earlier, Pope Sylvester wrote a letter referring to a secret to be sought before the End of Days. What if this secret pertains to the prophecy of Brother Ciarán's letter? One that speaks to the same device from Enoch's lore?"

Gregory glared at Gerbert. "Am I to believe you've solved Sylvester's entire riddle?"

"Am I not a learned man?" Gerbert asked with a smug expression. "Let's go to the third verse. *Pontifex* in Latin is formed from *pons facere*, which means 'bridge builder'—"

"I know the title. *Pontifex Maximus.*"

"The very title you hold. Supreme Pontiff, the bishop of bishops. So don't you see? Sylvester is describing a gift from one pope to another."

"That hardly narrows things. There have been one hundred and thirty-seven popes before me."

"True," Gerbert admitted. "But which was the first to use the title *Pontifex Maximus?*"

Gregory smirked. "I don't know."

"You really should get down here more often," Gerbert chided. "The history of every pope is kept in these archives. The answer, it turns out, was Pope Callixtus, who lived in the early third century about a hundred years before Sylvester. Callixtus's successor was none other than Saint Urban. So I began by searching for something Callixtus may have passed down to his successor."

"And I suppose you found it?"

"It was here all along, in the *vita* of Pope Urban. It appears Callixtus's gift was a Psalter written and illuminated by his own hand."

"A Psalter . . ." Gregory realized aloud. "A sacred tome."

"Precisely! Solomon's secret lies in a sacred tome. So can't you see? We're looking for the Psalter of Saint Callixtus, for somewhere in its pages, Sylvester must have hidden Solomon's secrets!"

Gregory ran his fingers through his hair. "And how do you suppose we find that?"

"Truly, you have no idea of the knowledge kept beneath your palace. There's an index here of every relic in Christendom. It's hundreds of pages long, but there indeed is an entry for the Psalter of Saint Callixtus. It was kept in these archives for seven centuries until Pope Paschal unwittingly gave it as a gift to the abbot of Fleury. It's remained at Fleury ever since."

"In France?"

"Yes, and that's where I'm going," Gerbert said, "even if I have to contend with that insufferable Abbo of Fleury while I'm up there. I intend to leave for Ravenna tomorrow, and then set off for France within a fortnight."

"So soon?" Gregory's thoughts were still swimming with everything he had heard.

"If there's truth to Brother Ciarán's words, and those of Saint Sylvester, then time is not with us. Besides, the last time I summered in Rome, the fever nearly killed me."

Gerbert furled the scrolls and put them back on their shelves before bidding Gregory a hasty farewell, leaving him with Rumeus in the archives. Gregory found himself troubled by the notion that there could be truth in the Irish monk's account. "Do you believe any of this, Rumeus?"

"I don't know what to believe, Your Holiness," Rumeus replied. "It makes my old head ache, if truth be told. But why would Saint Sylvester hide a letter in the Apocalypse of John if he did not believe there was a threat of the end times a millennium after the Savior's birth? Did not Saint John write, 'When the thousand years are ended, Satan will be released from his prison'?"

"But a thousand years after what? And still, we cannot ignore Daniel's prophecy."

"Which one, Your Holiness?"

"The one about the dream of a giant statue with a head of gold, a chest of silver, a midsection of bronze, and legs of iron. Daniel claimed each part of the statue represented a great empire, and he foretold all four must fall before the End of Days. The golden head was the empire of Babylon, the silver chest was that of Persia, and the bronze waist was that of the Greeks, all long gone. But the iron legs were the Roman Empire, the very one which persists to this day under Otto, as Holy Roman Emperor. So Otto shall live and his empire shall survive beyond this millennium, proving the words of Revelation cannot have a literal interpretation. Whatever end it predicts shall happen long after we're gone."

Rumeus pressed his lips together. "Ah, *that* prophecy. Unfortunately, not everyone views the empire's history the same way you do. In the year 480, Julius Nepos Augustus was the Western Roman Emperor. Then one night, his own men stabbed him to death. Afterward, a soldier who had declared himself the first king of Italy annexed what remained of the Roman Empire into his new kingdom. Three hundred and twenty years would pass before the word *empire* would have meaning again, when Pope Leo the Third put a crown on Charlemagne's head."

"What are you saying?"

"That with the assassination of Julius Nepos, the Roman Empire died, and with his death the statue of Daniel's prophecy should have crashed into a thousand pieces. So, perhaps the thousand years are indeed ending."

Gregory narrowed his gaze. "If they are, what would you do?"

Rumeus clasped his hands. "I would prepare for what comes next."

WHISPERS OF RAGNAROK

The night before they sailed for Dublin, Ciarán lay awake on the rushes of Jarl Holger's hall. He kept his eyes closed, pretending to sleep, for the jarl had his boarhound, Rosta, sleep in the hall, too, so the beast could wake the Danes if the thralls made any trouble. Ciarán had no intention of causing trouble tonight, but as he feigned sleeping, he worked through the details of their escape plan.

The plan was simple. They would continue to earn the jarl's trust on the voyage to Dublin and convince him to remove their manacles, just like Magnus had promised. At Dublin, Magnus said the thralls would stay with the ship, and Ciarán was counting on that, for in the dark of night it would not be hard to slip overboard and swim to the nearest shore. That would be their most dangerous moment. Dublin was ruled by a *fin-gall* king named Sigtrygg Silkbeard, so it would be crawling with Norse and Danes, and their dogs. But Dublin was less than ten leagues from Kildare, the home of his late mother in the Irish kingdom of Leinster. If they made it there, they would be safe and could venture north to Meath, and then to the abbey at Armagh. There, they could travel by curach to Lough Neagh and up the River Bann, and ultimately to Derry's shores. Khalil could find passage to the continent, or perhaps they might enlist men to help them find Josua and the others. But at least they would be freemen, and if the end times did arrive, they would die knowing they had broken the yoke of their Viking captors.

The morning of the voyage, Magnus and Jorundr rousted Ciarán and Khalil from the jarl's hall. They led them outside through a cold mist to a storehouse behind the hall, where a roan mare harnessed to a long wagon waited by the open doors. Ciarán glanced around for any sign of Grimr or his cousin, but neither was evident, and Ciarán hoped it would stay that way until they left Vette.

Magnus pointed to a cluster of casks and crates inside the storeroom. "That is what we will trade in Dublin," he said, "so get them onto that wagon."

Heat rushed up Ciarán's neck as he recognized the markings on the barrels. "Those were Évrard's and Josua's," he told Khalil under his breath. The Persian nodded grimly, before helping Ciarán heft the cargo onto the wagon. By the time they were done, the wagon looked to hold half of *La Margerie's* wares: barrels of olive oil from Barcelona, casks of red wine from Rome and Spain, and two crates of African spices procured in Malaqha. When the job was done, a bitter taste lingered in Ciarán's mouth. "As soon as we get to Dublin," he said, "we'll be rid of these pirates."

"The hour cannot come soon enough," Khalil replied.

Accompanied by Magnus and Jorundr, they led the horse and its wagon to the wharf where more than a dozen Danes readied the jarl's longship. Some secured lines made of seal hide to the mast with its furled sail striped with crimson and white, while others arranged iron-bossed shields on strakes along the ship's sides. The shields, painted with patterns of blue, red, black, or gold, or images of serpents, ravens, or wolves, overlapped one another down each side of the longship. Beneath the row of shields, Ciarán counted twenty oar ports.

Magnus grinned as they approached the ship. "This is the *Lindworm*, Irish. She's the fastest longship to ever sail from Denmark. She needs forty men to row her, but you slew Kjartan Half-Giant and

Snorri Snorrison, so now you and the Moor will take their places on the benches."

The reminder that he had slain the Dane's brethren made Ciarán's stomach churn. "Won't these men kill me for the lives I took?"

"Several of them would love to," Magnus said with a shrug. "But Jarl Holger has forbidden it. Besides, you were defending yourself as any man would, and you gave them a gift, for they died in battle with a sword in their hand."

"Why does that matter?"

"Because they died as warriors, so when the Valkyrie came for their souls, they were taken to golden Valhalla. It is Odin's mead hall, the most glorious place in all Asgard, where they will feast on wine and mead and food fit for kings. And then they will don their armor and fight in the battlefield until the next mealtime, where they will drink and eat and brawl every day until Ragnarok comes."

Ragnarok. Ciarán recalled the word. Back at Saint-Germain-des-Prés, Brother Remi had equated it to Armageddon.

"Kjartan dreamed of Valhalla," Magnus continued, "and now he's there, and Snorri's biggest fear was dying a coward, so you saved him from that. We'll miss them both, but you gave them a far better fate than dying in some bed, without a sword in their hands. They'd be condemned to an afterlife of torture and misery in Niflheim with the goddess Hel and the souls of the damned."

Ciarán could barely imagine the afterlife these pagans dreamed of, for it seemed so different from the choirs of angels and saints he imagined would greet the souls whom the Savior lets into Heaven. And he wondered where the slain men's souls had truly gone, for the Church preached that heathen souls were damned, and if so, Magnus's beliefs were but fancy. *But what about the soul that took their life,* Ciarán wondered. *Is mine damned, as well?* As he boarded the longship, he silently prayed for God's mercy, though based on the icy stares from several of the Danes, he doubted he would receive any forgiveness from the ship's crew.

After he and Khalil hauled the cargo onboard and lashed it with ropes beside the ship's sturdy mast, Magnus showed them to their places near the aft on the last pair of benches. The ship's beam was no more than ten feet in width, and with all forty rowers on board, the ship was crowded with Danes. Most of them were tall, bearded, and long-haired, though a few shaved their heads, leaving only shocks of hair near their foreheads, and even fewer wore no beards at all. Each one bore the trappings of a warrior: armor of leather or chain mail; helmets, some bossed, others conical in shape with nasals or cheek plates; and daggers and axes or longswords, making them look as fierce a lot as Ciarán had ever seen.

Despite the wet and dreary weather, most of the Danes seemed in good spirits this morning, boasting in their foreign tongue, until Jarl Holger appeared on the pier. The Danish lord stood resplendent in his polished mail with his bear-fur cloak and a bossed helmet tucked under one arm. To his left padded Rosta, but it was the figure to his right that surprised Ciarán. Clad in a mail vest under a fox-fur cloak, Breda strode beside her husband. Her red hair was piled atop her head, a round shield was strapped behind her shoulders, and a Danish sword hung at her hip.

"She's coming with us?" Ciarán asked Magnus, who stood before the bench in front of him.

He answered with a grin. "Breda often comes. She may have been born Irish, but she's a shieldmaiden now, as feisty as any in Denmark. I would not want to be the man who told her to stay home."

Once they boarded, Jarl Holger, Breda, and Rosta made their way down the aisle between the rows of benches. The jarl paid Ciarán and Khalil no heed as he strode toward the steering oar, nor did the boarhound, but Breda cast a brief glance at Ciarán. For the first time, he noticed the pale green of her eyes set within her untamed and beautiful face.

Before the curved sternpost, Jarl Holger stood with his hand on the steering oar and bellowed commands to his men. In no time, they had pushed the longship from the pier and threaded the pinewood oars through the ports, each of which was rimmed with leather. "Follow my rhythm," Magnus called back, gripping his oar. "The jarl hates it when men row out of rhythm, and if you start to, I'll have to clap you upside your head."

Ciarán watched Magnus, pulling the oar when he did, trying to match his rhythm. The longship sat low in the river and the planks of the oak hull creaked as men worked the oars. One of the Danes began a song and its words provided a beat to match each stroke of the blades. Other Danes joined in the song and soon the longship glided down the river against the incoming tide. By the time it reached the river's mouth, Ciarán's arms and shoulders burned. Most of the men had removed their tunics, rowing bare chested, for despite the morning chill and mist, the labor of rowing had already slickened many a back with sweat.

When they reached the channel between Vette and England, the Danes removed the shields from the ship's flanks and affixed the golden-scaled head to the prow, giving the *Lindworm* the frightful appearance of its namesake: a mighty serpent riding the seas. The longship rocked with the chop of the waves and water slapped against the hull. Jarl Holger bellowed another command, summoning a trio of Danes to unfurl the massive square sail. The sailcloth bulged in the wind. With another of the jarl's commands, the Danes drew in their oars and stopped the oar ports with wooden plugs. "Now you shall see how fast *Lindworm* is," Magnus said, glancing back with a grin.

Ciarán had never experienced anything like it. Unlike the cumbersome cog or the Irish curach hulled in ox hide that had taken him and Dónall to France, the longship glided through the sea. As it sped forward, spray blasted over the gunwales and the salty wind whipped through Ciarán's hair. Occasionally, a wave would pitch the ship from side to side, but most of the time it knifed through the rippling waters like an arrow set on its course. He imagined what it would be like to travel the world in such a ship, but once the wind died and the rowing began anew, he reminded himself that he was still a thrall to these Viking slavers.

At dusk, the longship sailed into a bay surrounded by gray cliffs and a shoreline piled with rocks. Two of the Danes reduced the sail, while Jarl Holger and Magnus moved to the prow and searched for a beach to take the ship ashore for nightfall. Across the aisle, Khalil sat on his bench with his eyes closed, though whether he was resting from the oar work or lost in silent prayer, Ciarán could not tell. He touched his hands to his lips and whispered his own prayer to Saint Columcille—one to be rid of these Danes as soon as the ship reached Dublin.

Before he could finish, a woman's voice called in Irish from behind. "You should not be so bitter."

He turned to see Breda holding the steering oar with Rosta lounging on the deck against her fur-trimmed boots. As close as she stood, Ciarán could see the freckles dotting her cheeks and cascading down her neck to the *V* of her tunic and the swell of her breasts. She held a wry smile between her thin lips, before sipping from a horn of ale.

"Because you have no reason to be," she said. "You are lucky to be with Jarl Holger. He is a great man, a descendant of Sigfred, the second Danish king, and Kings Gudfred and Horik. The descendants of Ragnar Lothbrok may rule the Danish throne today, but the day may come when the House of Sigfred again holds the title. And it may even be Jarl Holger, or the son I will give him someday. He's the finest jarl you could ever hope to serve."

The word *serve* sent a flush of heat up Ciarán's neck. "You don't know what it's like to be a thrall."

Breda's eyes narrowed. "Oh, I know. Like you I was born Irish, the second daughter of a chieftain of Meath, but later I became a thrall."

Ciarán shook his head. "How?"

"When I was thirteen, my father wed me to one of his rivals, a drunken pig of a man named Áengus mac Áed, twenty years my senior. Some days he beat me. Most nights he raped me. That was my life for four years, beatings and rapes by my *noble* Irish husband. Every night he lay upon me, I wished him dead, but I lacked the courage to kill him myself. Then one day, Áengus was trading with the Danes, and in his thick skull he thought he could cheat them. But the Danes discovered his ruse, so he did the only thing he could think to do. Fight them and kill them. So that's what he ordered his men to do.

Fortunately, the pig's men were weak as milk cows and no match for the mighty Danes, and most of all their leader, Jarl Holger. The pig tried to escape and take me with him, but that's when I found my courage and cried out to Holger. He captured the squealing pig, but he let me kill him. So I cut off his cock, then stuck a dagger through his eye. That was the day I became Jarl Holger's thrall."

Ciarán ran a hand through his sweat-crusted hair. "But he freed you?"

"Aye. He did after a time, and then we wed. Now, I am a jarl's wife and the equal to any man under the Dane's laws—a far cry from the way you Christian priests treat the women who bring life into the world. My husband has freed many a thrall, but even if he never frees you, he will still be a good and just lord."

"Yet I'd still be a damn thrall."

Breda's eyes flashed with fury, and she flung her ale-horn at Ciarán's head. He raised his arm and blocked the horn, but the ale drenched his face and chest. Rosta looked up from his slumber and cocked his head at the horn, rocking on the deck planks.

"If that's how you want to view it, then I'll treat you like one." She glared at the ale pooling on the deck beneath Ciarán's bench. "Now clean that up, *thrall.*"

Around him, the Danes broke out in laughter. Jorundr bellowed the loudest, throwing back his head with its white-gold hair. As Ciarán pulled off his wet tunic to wipe the ale from the deck, the bitterness hardened in his mouth like a blacksmith pounding iron into steel. He could not wait to see the first cliffs of Ireland. And once again taste freedom.

SIX DAYS LATER, CIARÁN SPIED HIS HOMELAND. THE SUN WAS BEGINNING to set, coloring the western sky red, but the only color he cared about was green. Lush and emerald, it crowned the cliffs that sprawled along the rugged coastline. Beyond those beautiful crags lay the kingdom of Leinster, and to the north, the abbey of Kildare. Ciarán made the sign of the cross and whispered a prayer. *Blessed Columcille, guide us to safety.*

According to Magnus, they would be at Dublin before the next dusk. Anticipation welled within Ciarán, but there was still the problem of the manacles around his ankles. Magnus had promised they would be removed, though Ciarán began to fear his insult to Lady Breda might be the reason they were still shackled to his legs. Since she had thrown the ale-horn in his face, he had tried to be on his best behavior around her, but the woman would hardly look at him, and the few times she did, her eyes were like daggers. He wondered if he and Khalil could swim in those manacles. It would take more effort with his arms, but he imagined it could be done. Though what would they do if the Danes spotted them on shore and released their dogs? There would be no outrunning boarhounds in the woods with chains around his legs.

By the morning, the thought of the manacles left him as sullen as the gray sky above, and his mood was not brightened by the still winds, which meant hours of hard rowing. The rowing was back-breaking work, but Ciarán tried to ignore the pain in his limbs, for each stroke brought them closer to freedom.

After another tug on the oars, Khalil leaned over from the bench adjacent to Ciarán. "What's troubling you?" the Persian said under his breath.

"These bloody manacles," Ciarán replied. "We need them off."

Khalil nodded. "If Allah wills it, it will be done."

Ciarán gritted his teeth as he pulled on the oar. *What if God's no longer on our side?*

At midday, as *Lindworm* glided past emerald cliffs on the larboard side, the wind picked up and the crew drew in their oars and lowered the striped sail. Ciarán slumped on his bench, letting his sore arms dangle and throb. Then he heard the sound of scraping metal behind him. He glanced back. Jarl Holger was seated in the shadow of the curved stempost, drawing a whetstone down the length of his sword blade.

Khalil leaned over, his eyes wide. "*Look* at that blade."

Ciarán shook his head as if to ask why, but then glanced back. Squinting, he spotted what Khalil must have seen, for down the gleaming blade were etched a series of runes. Ciarán's own eyes widened when he focused on their shapes. They were not like the harsh Viking runes he had seen carved on Irish stones. Those were crude, sharp, and sticklike, but these were more graceful and flowing, and strangely more familiar. "Those runes aren't Nordic," he answered under his breath. "They look Celtic."

"They're like the symbols in Maugis' book," Khalil insisted.

Ciarán took another glance. *By God, he's right!* The artistry was not identical, but the flow of the runes appeared similar to the Fae script hidden in the Book of Maugis d'Aygremont.

Khalil nodded toward the jarl. "Ask him about them."

Ciarán turned to face Jarl Holger as he ran the whetstone down the edge of the blade. "Pardon, lord," Ciarán said in Irish. "May I ask about your sword?"

The jarl peered up with his keen blue eyes, wind breezing through his long golden hair. "What do you wish to know?"

"Those symbols down your blade, I've never seen such markings on a sword. Do you know what they mean?"

Jarl Holger responded with a curious expression. "Why do you ask?"

"They don't appear Danish, but I've seen symbols like these before in an old Frankish book."

Holger narrowed his gaze. "I'm told the best blades come from France. This one was taken from that land by my forefather Sigfred, who was king of the Danes. When I inherited it upon my father's passing two winters ago, I too had questions about the runes."

"Did you ever learn to read them, lord?"

"I did, but I needed a gothi to teach me."

"A gothi, lord?"

"A priest of our gods," Holger explained, "but they are nothing like your shaven men. I sailed to the Temple at Uppsala, where I found one who could interpret the runes. He was old, and blind in both eyes. The gothi ran his fingers down the blade and told me the letters were ancient, from the time before the Great Flood, but that the blade itself was only a few centuries old. Yet he said it was a mighty blade with mighty brothers, and then he told me what the runes said. *My name is Curtana, of the same steel and temper as Joyeuse and Durandal.* The gothi also said it is a sword of kings, before he told me its destiny. That I would fight with Curtana at Ragnarok."

That word again, Ciarán thought. *Ragnarok.* "The End of Days?"

"Aye. The time when Loki the trickster god shall break free of his bonds and summon his children Fenrir, the wolf, and Jörmungandr, the Midgard Serpent, from the boiling seas. Loki shall sail on *Naglfar,* the ship of the dead, with his daughter Hel to make war against the gods. The war to end all things. The skalds speak of it often, and I sense these times may be near. You were one of the shaven men, do all Christians believe these times will soon be upon us?"

"Not all," Ciarán said, "but many do, for the millennium nears, one thousand years after the birth of Christ."

"Do you believe that?"

Ciarán drew a deep breath. "I do, lord."

Holger replied with a wink. "Then maybe you too will fight at Ragnarok." He stood up and slid Curtana into her scabbard. Without giving Ciarán a parting glance, he strode toward the bow where Breda awaited. As soon as the jarl had passed, Khalil grabbed Ciarán by the arm. "You heard those names—Curtana, Joyeuse, Durandal?"

"Perhaps I read about them in Turpin's journal, but—"

"They are the swords of Charlemagne and his paladins," Khalil insisted. "Can't you see? Our fate is now as clear as the sky after a summer storm!"

"What do you mean?"

"I mean we can't flee at Dublin."

"Why the hell not?"

"Because in those runes, Allah revealed our destiny—and it lies with Jarl Holger."

LABYRINTH

Thousands of tiny spiders crawled up and down Alais' skin, biting and filling her with their poison. She scratched and clawed at them, but it did nothing to stop their assault. A scream burst from her lungs, filling the cave—until she bolted awake, heaving for breath. She was still in the caves and her limbs were free of spiders, but scared and smeared with blood. The same blood caked black beneath her nails.

The spiders, they're in my mind . . .

She wrapped her arms around herself, trembling. "Must . . . find a way out." Talking to herself in the solitary cave was the only thing keeping her sane. The only ward against total darkness was the sparse patches of lichen on the cave walls, dimly alight with a phosphorescent glow. The only sound was the growl of her stomach. She could not remember the last time she had eaten, though it had been sometime before Nimue gave her the goblet. Its contents tasted like wine, but the drink made her head spin and the walls tremble. *It will prepare you for your trial,* Nimue had said, her words echoing in Alais' skull. They were the only words she had heard in days, other than the sound of her own voice. The drink had robbed her of her consciousness, until she awoke here, in the labyrinth.

"You must find your way through the labyrinth," Nimue had told her. "To shatter the barrier between the mind and the spirit. Only then can you wield the power."

"It's my mind that's breaking," Alais whispered to herself, as another bite stung her arm. She slashed at the creature with her nails, leaving bloody red lines where nothing had been. She sucked on the wound until her lips were dry, then pulled at her hair, ready to scream.

"Get up," she told herself, shaking.

She struggled to her feet with the ground swaying beneath her toes. Leaning against the cold stone wall, she tried to keep her balance. Three tunnels led from the cave, each into darkness. She could not remember how many times she had gone down those paths, but each time she ended back up in this cave. *Or was it one just like it?* All seemed the same—cold, quiet, and desolate. *Must try again or I'll starve . . .*

Despite the cool cave air and the cold stone floor beneath her bare feet, sweat beaded on her forehead as she chose the middle tunnel. She steadied herself as she walked, her legs trembling with each step. The lichen was sparser in the tunnel, the darkness nearly all-consuming. When the tunnel forked, she took the left path. Or was it the right? She shook her head to clear the cobwebs from her mind, but that reignited the pain within her skull. Down the tunnel echoed a voice.

"Alais!"

She gasped at the sound. *Sister Leofflaed?*

"Alais!" a second voice called. Her mouth hung open. *Lay Sister Agnes—they're searching for me!*

"In here!" she cried, though the words came out like a croak from her raw throat.

"Alais!" the voices called again.

She clambered toward the sound, only to find herself facing another fork. The voices echoed from the passage to the left. She took a step, and then stopped. The tunnel was filled with a smoky mist. Huffing for breath, she tried to remember Nimue's words.

Without the light, you'll be lost in the mist . . .

A memory surfaced, one of a forest with skeletons covered in moss, a graveyard within the mists that surrounded Rosefleur. *Khalil almost became one of them. I'd be next . . .*

"Alais!" Sister Leofflaed and Lay Sister Agnes called again.

She longed to go to them, but stifled her tears. "Good-bye," she whispered. Then she took the pathway to the right. The tunnel meandered on, twisting and forking and breaking into more new pathways like a spider's web. When her legs finally gave out, she found herself once again in the cave with three tunnels, beneath the lichen's phosphorescent glow.

"No!" she screamed.

"Nooooo!" the tunnel answered in echoes.

She broke down in sobs and would have retched had there been anything in her belly. As she sat on her knees, her head became light and the cave began to spin. Only closing her eyes made it stop.

Alais lay down, without a care whether her eyes ever opened again.

EVENTUALLY, SHE WOKE. THE CAVE WALLS WERE GONE, AND IN THEIR place was nothing but sand. Beneath the sun's light, sand blasted through the air with a deafening howl. Alais shielded her eyes. Whipped by the wind, the sand bit into her ankles and tore across her shins.

Through the sandstorm, she glimpsed three men riding the most absurd-looking horses she had ever seen. They were lanky and loping creatures with golden coats and twin humps on their backs. The riders wore black robes and scarves like hoods around their heads, shielding their faces from the storm. *Saracens . . .* One of the men pointed at Alais.

"Where am I?" she cried, but the wind drowned out her words.

The man gestured fiercely, urging her to go away from them.

Alais turned to where the man was pointing. Through the blasting sand stood the ruins of an ancient structure. An outer wall of limestone featured an open gate, its frame scrawled with symbols. She glanced back at the three men on their absurd horses. Their leader was pointing at the gate, screaming at her to do something, though she could not hear his words through the howl of the storm. *He wants me to go inside . . .*

She darted through the gate, only to find herself within a forest of rectangular columns, each of limestone ten feet tall and etched with hieroglyphs of birds, scarabs, and ankhs. Many were broken at the top, their crowns strewn like rubble in the sand. The structure had no roof, so sand whipped through the ruin, obstructing her vision past a dozen yards. The only way forward lay through the shrieking sand and the sea of columns, which extended in every direction from the gateway.

I'm in another maze.

Shielding her eyes, she maneuvered around the columns, but stopped dead at the sight of something slithering up ahead. Black and glistening, the serpent snaked through the sand, with two more crawling in its wake. She bolted away, then stopped again. More serpents slithered in the path ahead as if the ruin had been built on a nest of asps. Her heart began to pound. Everywhere she looked, more serpents writhed from the sand.

Summoning her courage, Alais darted around the nearest column and dodged another serpent, hissing at her heel. She rushed down a corridor of columns, only to encounter another brood of asps. One sprang at her legs. She spun away, but felt something strike. She jumped back, glancing at her ankle. Twin trickles of blood would mean certain death. But the only thing marring her flesh was sand.

With a relieved sigh, she hurried around another pillar, sidestepping a pair of hissing asps. Past twin columns stood another gate— and it was open. Beyond, she could not see through the blasting sand, but at least she'd be free of this asp nest. She sprinted through the gateway. Sand blasted against her limbs, strafing her flesh. Shielding her eyes with her arms, she tried to peer through the storm. Something large lay up ahead. Something massive.

As she approached, its shape emerged through the savage storm.

More than sixty feet tall loomed a titanic statue of a sitting lion. Yet instead of a beast's head, a massive human head sat on its shoulders. Behind it stood a trio of mountain peaks, though, oddly, they looked perfectly smooth and triangular in shape. She walked closer toward the statue, finding herself at the foot of one of its gigantic paws.

There's something inside. Alais did not know how she knew this, but she felt certain of it. *That's why the Saracen wants me to go here.*

She pressed up against the statue's side, built of enormous limestone blocks. Working her way around its perimeter, she searched for any sign of an entrance. The statue stretched hundreds of feet in length, and it would be a long journey through the roaring sand. As she neared the portion of the statue were the tail should be, the skin on her limbs began to blister. Then the sand gave out beneath her feet.

She screamed as she plunged down a shaft. She slid down silt and stone until landing on a bed of sand within a limestone passageway barely three feet wide. The storm's roar was but a whisper down here. Through the slivers of light piercing the sandstorm, she peered down the passageway. A dozen feet down, it ended in what looked like a door carved into the limestone wall. She padded toward the door, which had a symbol carved into its face: large and oval-shaped with limbs like a crab or an insect. A scarab, she realized. Throwing her weight at the door, she pushed. With the grinding of limestone, the door opened into darkness save for a tiny mote of light, like a solitary firefly. She reached for it, but the light flickered. And then exploded. White and blinding, it surrounded her, drowning her in its heat.

Alais bolted awake. She found herself face down on the cold floor of the cave. The weakness in her limbs, the agony in her stomach, all of it came crashing home. She began to shake. *It must have been another dream.*

On the ground ahead, something was moving. She stared at it, black and oval-shaped, and no bigger than her thumb. It was a beetle, with six tiny legs. Like a scarab. The insect scrabbled away from her, toward the rightmost tunnel.

She decided to follow it, crawling behind the creature on her hands and knees. The beetle soldiered on, seemingly oblivious to the human behind it, moving with purpose down the winding tunnels, beneath the lichen's dim glow. Alais lost track of how long she followed the insect, or down how many tunnels, but she sucked in a breath when she saw a white light emanating from the cave ahead.

She rose to her feet. The beetle was heading toward a pool of water that filled half the cave, a spring perhaps bubbling up through the ground. As dry as her throat was, her heart sank, for it was the water that glowed, pale and white like the River Lethe. *Its name means oblivion, I can't drink it.*

The beetle crawled to the water's edge. *What if Nimue was lying, what if I take just one sip?* She dropped to her knee, licking her chapped lips. She touched the cool water, following the ripples as they spread out from her finger toward the far end of the pool. Something rose from the water, carved into the cave wall. *A pedestal.* Ignoring her thirst, she stood and waded through the pool, the water no higher than her ankles. An object sat atop the pedestal. Round and opaque. A crystal no larger than a hazelnut. Nimue's words echoed in her mind.

The crystal reveals the soul's light.

Her hand trembling, Alais reached out and grabbed the crystal. She took a long breath as she placed it at her lips, recalling the Fae word Nimue had taught her. Alais uttered it with a whisper of breath. *"Eoh."*

Like the solitary mote of light in her dream, a spark flared within the crystal and then burst ablaze, brighter than the Lethe. Once again, she recalled their journey through the mists to Rosefleur. *I know the way out . . .*

She wandered back down the tunnel, taking whichever passage caught her eye. Eventually they would lead to the mists. They always did. In time, she came to a tunnel filled with the smoky mists. *Without the light, you'll be lost in the mist. But now I have the light.* As she thrust forth the crystal, its light cut a pathway through the mists, just as Isaac's had done during their journey to Rosefleur. She followed the path forged by her light, winding through the tunnels until she could see the lakeshore in the distance, where the Avalon's great tree rose from the Lethe. Nimue stood waiting in its glow.

"Child," the Fae woman said, a gleam in her eyes, "your time in the labyrinth was your baptism of fire, and through it, you have been reborn, a wielder of the light. Yet there are many mysteries still to learn." She opened her arms as if offering an embrace. "So come to me, and let your apprenticeship begin."

THE TRAITOR'S ROCK

Atop the Capitoline Hill, two prisoners stood gagged and shaking in their black robes at the edge of the Tarpeian Rock. The rock was a tree-topped precipice amid the ruins of some of the city's most prominent temples, and it had been a place of death for the most notorious criminals in ancient Rome.

A hundred armed Lombards, Germans, and Saxons crowded the clifftop as an afternoon breeze carried the scent of wormwood from the pale-yellow flowers growing on the hillside. At their forefront stood Otto in his shining mail and purple cloak, beside Rumeus and Gregory, who glared at the prisoners.

Both were under twenty, and despite their monastic tonsures, Gregory guessed they were more rogue or cutthroat than true monk. It was a miracle either could still stand, having endured days of torture at the hands Gregory's papal guardsmen. Yet neither man had broken and confessed the name of the brotherhood's leader or the location of their hideout. Their fanaticism, it appeared, infused them with an unbreakable spirit. But even that would not save them from the punishment they faced.

Otto turned to Gregory. "Are you sure this is appropriate, cousin?

As a method of execution, it's quite unorthodox. A hanging would have been sufficient."

"It wouldn't send the right message," Gregory replied tersely.

"The people have seen what we did to Crescentius, and that thing you did to John Philagathos. I hardly think another message need be sent."

Gregory grimaced. "Canon Goswin was Bavarian, and one of the most promising young priests at the Archbasilica. These men hung him from a tree in the ruins of the Forum. The sign around his neck said, 'Death to the Saxon pope.' What if that were to become the will of the mob? There are hundreds in Rome who view Crescentius as a martyr. He's become more dangerous in death than he was in life. So it's time you start treating these people like the traitors they are. In antiquity, execution at the Tarpeian Rock was reserved for the worst traitors and murderers in Rome. It was considered a fate worse than death, a shame above all others. These men deserve no less, and the mob will understand the symbolism behind their deaths. It's what the Caesars would have done. And if you want to be Caesar to these Romans, then show them you can be one."

Otto glanced at Rumeus. "Is it true the Caesars did this?"

"The practice is older than the Caesars, Your Majesty." Rumeus pointed to the ruins of a temple closest to the precipice. An arcade of columns remained, surrounded by brick and stone fragments of what must have been an impressively large structure. "That was the Temple of Jupiter. During the Republic, it was the high priest of Rome who held the title *Pontifex Maximus*. The high priests were the first to employ this method of execution with the blessing of the Senate. Julius Caesar was *Pontifex Maximus* before he became ruler of Rome, and every emperor since has kept that title, administering punishment the way the high priests did hundreds of years before."

Gregory raised a brow. He had not known the title *Pontifex Maximus* once belonged to the emperors. Though it was hardly surprising, given the Church's penchant for adopting pagan concepts as their own. The winter festival of Yule had become Christmas, and Easter had been named after Eostre, the Saxon goddess of spring.

Pontifex Maximus evidently was just one more thing taken in the name of converting pagans to Christianity.

Otto gave a halfhearted shrug. "Very well, let's send a message and get on with it."

At the emperor's word, Ulrich, the royal executioner, strode toward the prisoners. Ulrich was a bear of a man, nearly six-and-a-half feet tall, and as fat as he was strong. He positioned himself behind the first prisoner, then looked to Gregory and nodded.

Gregory delivered the prisoners' sentence in his most commanding voice. "You are guilty of murdering the blessed and most holy Canon Goswin and of treason against your emperor, your pope, and the Holy See. You are anathema to God. May your souls burn in the Lake of Fire!"

Rumeus made the sign of the cross as Ulrich hurled the first prisoner over the cliff. Gregory rushed to the edge. The prisoner flailed through the air as he plummeted eighty feet to the rocks below, landing with a sickening thud. Behind Gregory, the horde of men erupted in cheers.

The second prisoner was ashen. Gregory could see the panic in the man's eyes, and for an instant hoped his will might crack. But the prisoner sucked in a breath and waited as Ulrich wrapped his thick hands around the back of the man's robes and hefted him off the ground.

He barely resisted when Ulrich threw him off the Tarpeian Rock.

Deep within Trajan's Market, Theodora listened to the tidings Simeon brought her. She sat in the candlelit chamber, eating her evening meal with a carafe of red wine. As Simeon spoke, her muscles tensed, but she took a long breath to soothe her temper.

"They threw them off the Tarpeian Rock?" she asked in disbelief.

"Yes, my lady," Simeon replied. "It was meant to mark them as traitors, like the emperors did in antiquity."

"The young pup is not worthy to act like an emperor of Rome. Nor that false pope." She took a long sip from her goblet. "But that may soon change. When do you expect Nilus da Rossano to arrive?"

"Shortly, my lady. Nilus is old and travel is hard for him. But he is coming."

"Good." She eyed the handsome young monk from his tonsure to his sandals. "Join me for a drink."

Simeon answered with a smile. "As you wish." He had begun to pour himself a goblet of wine when someone rapped on the chamber door.

Theodora pursed her lips. "Who is it?"

The door opened and Brother Bene poked his head in. The plump-faced monk blanched as if he had disturbed something untoward. "My lady," he said meekly. "There is someone here to see you."

"Whoever it is can wait, Bene."

The door opened wider as a black-robed man pushed past Brother Bene. The intruder towered over the monk. "I don't like to wait."

Theodora gasped.

Naberus da Roma stood in the doorway, regarding her with a savage gaze.

A chill washed down her limbs. "Simeon, Bene, leave us."

Wide-eyed and nodding, Simeon backed away from the table, then hurried with Bene from the chamber. Naberus pulled up a chair and took Simeon's goblet. He studied the wine. "Falernian?"

"Yes," she said, her mind racing with the implications of his sudden return.

He took a long sip. "Theodora, as beautiful as ever. And quite the leader, it seems. Don't fret, I'm not here to take over your precious brotherhood."

Theodora felt a weight lifted off her shoulders. She reached for her wine. "Then why have you returned?"

"Rome was on the way. Besides, I need something here."

"What?"

"For you to be patient with your plans for Pope Gregory."

Heat rushed up her neck. "For God's sake, why? I have a plan to drive a wedge between the Saxon pope and the boy-king, and our cause has captured the hearts of the people. They view Crescentius as the marble horse who died fighting the German oppressors. And we have one of our most loyal brothers stationed within the Lateran Palace. Once the pup leaves Rome—"

"I'm not asking a favor," Naberus said sternly. "There are plans afoot that you cannot know and this pope is part of those plans."

"You would keep secrets from me?"

Naberus placed a long-fingered hand on his chest. "I am but a messenger. I sail for Byzantium in the morning. And when I return with reinforcements, as my new master desires, no one who stands in my way shall survive. Not you or this pope. But if you wait for me, you shall have your revenge. I swear it."

Theodora could hardly believe her ears. Had Naberus reached some agreement with Emperor Basil? Could the Byzantine aid Crescentius had longed for be on its way?

Naberus reached across the table and caressed her face. Her skin tingled at his touch. "Do I have your word?" he asked.

Theodora's jaw quivered. "Yes," she said softly. His hand fell to the base of her neck and she sucked in a breath.

Naberus rose from his chair. "A long journey lies ahead, but if we take it together, a future awaits more glorious than anything you can imagine. It requires just one more sacrifice along the way."

Her heart began to pound as he took her hand and helped her off her chair. As he drew her close, she let herself be kissed, surrendering like a prisoner to his will.

TO FEED THE RAVEN

A month had passed since Khalil convinced Ciarán to abandon any thought of escape and stay with Jarl Holger, though as summer gave way to harvest time, Ciarán began to suspect once again they had chosen the wrong path.

Weeks earlier, when they had sat beneath the stars in *Lindworm's* hull while most of the crew reveled in Dublin's mead hall, Khalil could not have been more steadfast in his conviction. "I believe in my heart," he said, "this once again is kismet—*fate*—the will of Allah guiding us on His intended path. Kismet brought us together, me a disciple of Fierabras, who wrote a poem with the same words as the verse in the Book of Maugis d'Aygremont, which you happened to possess. Both were paladins of Charlemagne, and we know they sought to preserve the prophecy's secrets until the threat of the end times was upon us. And now, we find ourselves in the company of Jarl Holger, who wields Curtana, the sword of Ogier the Dane, another of the twelve paladins of Charlemagne. Jarl Holger's ancestor was King Gudfred, who was Ogier's father. So not only do they wield the same sword, but they share the same blood. Are we to believe it was but chance that brought the three of us together? No, it was kismet, for Allah does as He wills."

"Are you suggesting this is all predestined?" Ciarán asked incredulously. "That we were meant to be enslaved by a Danish lord, and now we must do his bidding in accord with some divine plan?"

"No." Khalil shook his head. "We are human, so we have free will, but Allah has shown us a path. We must recognize His signs and travel down that path. Which means our quest has not failed."

"How can you say that? Enoch's device is lost."

"You needed the device to survive the conflict at Rosefleur. Perhaps it served its purpose."

Ciarán let out a sigh. The similarities between Ragnarok and Armageddon lingered in his mind, and Jarl Holger believed himself destined to fight in that battle. Ciarán ran his fingers through his hair. "What would you have us do?"

"Stay with Jarl Holger and do as he bids. If I am right, Allah will give us another sign, and once we understand it, we shall know what to do."

But since that night in Dublin, God had given them no signs. They remained thralls, though upon their return to Vette, Jarl Holger had ordered their manacles removed and given them leather shoes for their feet and clean tunics and woolen trousers, so they looked more like the Danes they served. Though the jarl left the iron collars around their necks, perhaps as a symbol of their lowly place among the Danes. But they were treated more like servants than slaves, sleeping on benches in the jarl's hall, tending to his horses and livestock, and serving food and drink to him, Breda, and their household men. The Danes ate twice a day, once at the morning meal, or *dagverthr*, and again at sunset for the night meal, or *náttverthr*, as Ciarán and Khalil came to call them as the weeks passed and they acquired proficiency with the Danish tongue. Magnus and Jorundr remained their overseers, and the rest of the jarl's crew seemed to have accepted their presence, but that was not true of the other Danes on Vette.

Jarl Orn and the crew of *Wind Serpent* remained ever present. The jarl himself was an ogre of a man, as tall as Jarl Holger and as broad too, but a decade older. His face was blunt and wind-burned, made all the more fearsome by the wild mane of red hair and unkempt beard streaked with gray. His hair was the one feature he shared with his kinsman Sigurd, whom Ciarán had spied more than a few times lurking with Grimr Grimsson, peering vengefully from the alleyways between the timber houses. The only thing keeping Orn's kin at bay was the frequent presence of Magnus, Jorundr, and Rosta, the massive boarhound who had grown particularly fond of Ciarán. Meanwhile, the Danes loyal to the other jarls on Vette wanted nothing to do with Ciarán and Khalil, having heard rumors of the blood feud between Orn's kinsmen and Holger's two thralls.

Each day had become the same for Ciarán and Khalil, laboring for Jarl Holger while looking over their shoulders, hoping Grimr or Sigurd were not hiding in the shadows, knife in hand, willing to settle their feud in exchange for the wergild. And each day, the millennium drew closer, with no signs from above. Ciarán began to wonder if they would have been better off escaping at Dublin, and at least living as free men. Yet through all this, Khalil kept his faith. "Allah *will* give us a sign," he insisted, "though we must keep our eyes open to see it."

By the time the harvest moon appeared over Vette, the only sign that things might change was the horde of longships arriving from Denmark, which crammed the wharf and brought a thousand more Danes to the island. Magnus revealed the reason for their arrival one night in Holger's hall. "King Svein wants us to remind the English to pay us the Danegeld, so we're to go a-viking," he said. "Two days from now will be the seventh year since we defeated the English at Maldon, and on that day we are to take sixty-seven ships to the English land of Dorsetshire and convince the lords there to implore King Ethelred to pay over the Danegeld. Otherwise, we'll take their crops and their gold and their women, and if the English choose to fight us, they'll go to feed the raven."

"Feed the raven?" Khalil asked him.

Magnus grinned. "Have you ever seen a battlefield, my Moorish friend? What do ravens feast on but the corpses of men? See, that even rhymes. We Danes are great poets too, you know."

"Poetry, a wise man once said, is a language common to mankind," Khalil replied, "so I have no doubt."

Ciarán, however, could not care less about the Danes and their poems, for he found no joy in the thought of traveling with these Vikings to ravage and kill fellow Christians. And of one thing, he was certain: If Khalil was expecting some divine revelation, this most certainly was not it.

~

THE DANISH RAIDS IN DORSETSHIRE LASTED SO LONG CIARÁN LOST track of the days.

Just as Magnus had promised, the fleet sailed eastward into the mouth of the river Frome on the seventh anniversary of the Battle of Maldon. There, some of the longships rowed upriver, while others beached on the gravelly shores. Hordes of Danes stole English horses and rode inland through the rolling hills, only to return laden with sacks of coins, food from the English harvest, and more livestock than the Danes could eat. During the raids, Magnus ordered Ciarán and Khalil to stay and protect the ship, for while the English defenders would often flee at the sight of a Viking horde, they were known to sneak up beside ships and burn them. This was the worst damage the English could inflict, according to Magnus, for the longships were precious to the Danes. Yet while the raids lasted, Ciarán and Khalil never saw any ship-burners, though often they saw smoke stain the sky as villages and monasteries were set aflame and ravens circled for their feast.

At times, the Danes would return with gilded reliquaries and crucifixes inlaid with copper or bronze. These were the hardest sights for Ciarán to endure, for he could only imagine how many monks and priests might have died trying to defend God's treasures. Yet here he was, a monk by vow, guarding Danish ships from English Christians who sought only to defend their homeland.

By all accounts, the English were as timid as Magnus had predicted. Forces would gather against the Danes, only to flee in the face of a Danish shield wall thorned with spears and swords. Some of the English took refuge in a walled burh called Wareham, perhaps hoping the English king would send more men, but none came. That is until news arrived that an English force was advancing on the harbor of Poole, where near half the Danish fleet had beached their ships. That was the first time Ciarán tasted fear since the raids on Dorsetshire began, for judging by the conspiracy of ravens gathering in the nearby trees, there would be plenty of dead men today for their feast.

The sky above Poole Harbour was gray and the air was still, as if nature herself held her breath waiting for the battle to begin. Thirty longships were moored on the gravel beach flanked by salt marshes and mudflats to the west, where the heather and moor grass grew thick. To the east stood woodlands of birch and oak, their branches a fiery collage of red, orange, and gold, save for the black ravens waiting on the branches. Between the woodlands and the salt marsh was a swath of grass more than a hundred yards wide, climbing to a hillock where the Danes had assembled to meet the English.

At the beach, ninety Danes guarded the longships, and Ciarán and Khalil stood among them. Before the raids began, Jarl Holger had returned Khalil's scimitar and scabbard, which the Persian wore as if the blade had never left his side. Ciarán was given an unadorned double-edge sword of the type the Danes used, though neither he nor Khalil wore armor over their woolen clothes. The two stood by the prow of the beached *Lindworm,* gazing up at the fifteen hundred Danes assembled atop the hillock. "If anything happens," Khalil told Ciarán, "let me take the lead. You are still more scholar than swords-man, and that's not Caladbolg at your side."

"Aye," Ciarán replied as a wave of apprehension washed through his gut. *At least this is better than being trapped in that siege tower,* he reminded himself.

Behind them, pebbles crunched under a pair of leather boots as Breda joined them with Rosta. She looked like the embodiment of a Danish shieldmaiden. Red hair spilled from a conical helm down to the mail on her shoulders, and she had slung her leather-covered shield over her back. At her side hung a Viking sword, and her right hand gripped the ash shaft of leaf-bladed spear. "The bravest men stand in the front of a shield wall," she told them, "and Holger is there at its center. Jorundr will guard his left side, while Magnus stands at his right. The three are like kinsmen, and they always fight alongside one another."

Horns sounded in the distance, and Breda smiled. "The English have arrived."

Over the wall of Danes many rows thick, Ciarán spied the English banners. One bore a red cross on white, while others featured a white cross over gold and a wyvern on a gray field. Next came the thunderous din of swords beating on shields. Ciarán's heart began pounding with the beat, which went on for an eternity before it stopped, replaced suddenly by the thudding of arrows. A hail of shafts fell on the Danes, who hid under their shields like a tortoise in its shell. A moment later, with a chorus of battle cries, the Danish wall surged forward. The armies collided with a crash that shook the ground beneath Ciarán's feet. Then came the cries of men, war cries and death cries, amid a flurry of swords and spears bristling from the husk of shields.

Ciarán stood transfixed on the battle until another horn sounded from the woods. A Dane burst frantically from the trees. "Archers!" he cried. "In the woods!"

Breda's eyes flew wide. "They'll outflank us!"

Already, Danes were running from the ships with spears and swords into the dense woodlands. "Come on!" Breda commanded, charging off with the other Danes, Rosta barking fiercely by her side.

Ciarán grabbed Khalil's arm. "If the English win, they might free us."

"Or they might mistake us as Danes and slaughter us both," Khalil hissed. "Besides, our path lies with Jarl Holger, and if the English win, he most certainly will die. Now let's go, and remember what I said!" He ripped his scimitar from its sheath and set off after Breda.

Ciarán stood for a moment, wishing he shared Khalil's faith, but knowing he did not. Yet he could not let Khalil go into those woods alone. "Bloody hell!" Ciarán spat as he drew his own sword.

The crunch of dead leaves and twigs filled the woods as Danes darted through the maze of trees, getting lost among the foliage. Ciarán searched for Khalil, but could not find him. The woods were too dense for any organized force to move through. Out of the corner of his eye, Ciarán thought he glimpsed the Persian an instant before he disappeared behind a thick birch. Ciarán tried to follow, just as an arrow whizzed by his ear. His heart pounding, he ducked behind a broad oak as more arrows thudded into the bark and the screams of men rose from the woods. Ten paces ahead, he spied an old conifer tree and waited until his breathing calmed. He scurried behind it as another shaft sank into the leafy duff.

As he poked his head out from behind the tree trunk, he saw a Dane engaging an English archer twenty paces away. A bow lay at the archer's feet beside a trio of arrows sticking up from the ground. The Dane's shield bristled with shafts, but his sword was free, clashing with the archer's blade. The Dane made a furious swing, but the archer swerved and the blade glanced off the side of his mail coat. The archer hammered back with his blade. The Dane tried to parry the blow, but he slipped on the dead leaves and skidded onto his arse. That was all the advantage the archer needed to backhand his sword through the Dane's exposed neck. Ciarán's stomach hardened. *If we don't stop them, they'll slaughter us all.* So he charged.

The archer spun to meet him. Ciarán roared, unsure what he would do next except swing as hard as he could. His blow was wild and his sword clanged against the flat of the archer's blade. The archer struck back, ramming an elbow into Ciarán's chest. The blow sent the wind from his lungs and knocked him to the ground. The archer looked down with piggish eyes, his mouth widening into a brown-toothed grin.

As Ciarán lay there struggling to breathe, boots pounded through the duff, followed by another battle cry. The archer turned as a Dane barreled into him with an iron-bossed shield. The archer slammed onto the turf. Ciarán's eyes flew wide, for glaring down on the archer stood Grimr Grimsson, who, without hesitation, drove his sword into the archer's skull.

Ciarán's blood turned to ice. He clambered to his feet, still gripping his Viking blade.

Grimr peered back, a fire in his eyes. "Saw you run in here. Let's finish our feud."

"There's a battle going on!" Ciarán pleaded.

"And the Danes are winning," he replied with a wolfish grin. "It's time you fed the raven." He struck fast. Instinctively, Ciarán parried the blow, but its force sent a shudder down his arms.

Grimr began circling like a wolf around its prey. He swung again, but this time Ciarán jumped back and the sword sliced through air. Ciarán returned the attack, though Grimr blocked it with his shield. The Dane's next blow hammered Ciarán's sword above the guard, wrenching it from his grasp.

He backed toward a pair of birch trees. When Grimr made a cleaving strike, Ciarán ducked behind the nearest tree. The Dane's blade sank deep into the bark. He tried to pull it free, but the sword did not budge. As Ciarán scrambled to the side, Grimr cast off his shield and drew a long dagger from his belt. He lunged toward Ciarán, who darted back, but dead leaves slid beneath his shoes. He tumbled backward, landing hard on the archer's yew bow and nearly impaling himself on one of the arrow shafts jutting from the ground.

In a breath, Grimr was upon him. Ciarán tried to roll away, but the Dane's dagger arched across his chest, slicing through tunic and flesh. Grimr pinned Ciarán to the ground and slapped a hand on his wounded chest. As Ciarán gasped in pain, the Dane raised his dagger, his eyes filled with fury. Beneath him, Ciarán lay helpless, though his fingers grazed the shaft of an arrow stuck into the duff. With a desperate thought, he ripped the shaft from the earth and plunged it into Grimr's face. The Dane whipped his head back to avoid the strike, but the arrow's tip pierced his left eye.

Grimr howled, both hands flying to his face.

Using all the strength, Ciarán shoved the Dane off him, his chest throbbing with pain.

"I'll kill you!" Grimr screamed as blood oozed between the fingers over his ruined eye. "I swear it to the gods!"

Huffing for breath, Ciarán clutched his bleeding chest and fled.

～

Ciarán heard the account of the Danish victory from Magnus and Khalil as he sat inside *Lindworm's* hull, slumped against the larboard side. Once the skirmishers were discovered, any hope the English had of a surprise attack died with the archers in those woods. Many of the archers fled, as did half the English host. The rest were slaughtered by Danish axes and Danish swords, their corpses left on the battleground to feed the ravens. The English commander was cut down by Orn Skullreaver, who fought like a berserker, leaving heaps of English dead in his path. He chopped off the commander's head and hurled it at the fleeing English so they could remind King Ethelred what might happen if he did not pay over the Danegeld.

Magnus and Khalil left Ciarán with Breda and went to claim the corpses of the fallen Danes. She tended to the wound across Ciarán's chest. The cut was not deep, but it was broad, and she told him it would be weeks before he could pull an oar.

"Hot wine will clean the wound," she said while pouring steaming liquid into the gash. The liquid burned and Ciarán grimaced, but he knew it was for the best. Next, she took a needle and thread and began stitching the wound closed. "Jarl Holger is happy you lived," she explained as she carefully worked her needle through his flesh.

"Why does he care that much about a thrall?"

Breda shot him a harsh look and tugged the thread so hard Ciarán winced. "Do you wonder why he asked if you can sail?"

"Aye," Ciarán said.

Her green eyes narrowed. "Because he sees you sailing with him in his dreams. They haunt him at night, dreams of you and him standing at *Lindworm's* prow, sailing through darkness into battle. A gothi told him he would fight in Ragnarok, and because of these dreams, he thinks you must be there by his side."

Ciarán shook his head, struggling to believe what she just said.

Isaac had dreams, and Alais, too . . . "Why me?" he asked, though he already knew the answer.

"I wouldn't have picked you," she said with a hint of a smile. "But that's for the Norns to decide."

"Norns?"

"The three spinners who stand at the Well of Fate, weaving the destiny of both men and gods. The Norns are cruel, but Holger believes they have chosen you to stand with him in battle."

Ciarán closed his eyes. He refused to believe that three pagan women would decide his fate. But Khalil thought God would grant them a sign, and sitting in *Lindworm's* hull, Ciarán could not help but wonder if this was it.

JUDGMENT

W hispers hissed through the great hall of the Aventine Palace where a horde of clerics gathered beneath the frescos of Hector and Hercules. Flanked by marble columns, a clear aisle ran down the center of the hall to a dais at the far end where a finely carved throne sat empty. A step below the throne stood two less-ornate chairs where the pope and the emperor sat awaiting the arrival of Nilus da Rossano.

Gregory took a deep breath, sensing the anticipation on the faces of the assembled clergy. They waited eagerly to witness the Calabrian hermit whom many deemed a living saint. Over Gregory's objection, Otto had insisted on leaving his throne for this old man, elevating his status far higher than warranted. *This hermit should bow to his emperor and kiss the Fisherman's ring,* Gregory thought, *not sit above us like some overlord.* Otto, however, would not listen to reason, for ever since word arrived of the hermit's coming, he had agonized over what Nilus's visit would bring.

The young emperor fidgeted in his chair, gripping the hem of his purple cape. "You shouldn't have treated Philagathos so harshly," he said under his breath.

"Me?" Gregory replied in a hushed tone. "Count Berthold was your man."

"Why did you tell him that verse from scripture?" Otto shuddered. "The mutilation . . ."

Gregory's eyes narrowed. "That was the Holy Word of God. And, need I remind you of your godfather's treachery?"

Otto bit his lip and looked away. They waited until a knock arrived from the towering doors at the end of the hall where Count Berthold and his men stood guard. The murmur quieted. As Otto commanded the doors to be opened, Gregory felt a lump of apprehension in the pit in his stomach.

Through the double doors emerged a figure as hoary as any beggar found scrabbling in the filth-ridden alleyways of Rome. Clad only in a goatskin tunic, the hermit moved at a tortoiselike pace, barefoot and hunchbacked, walking with a cane made of driftwood. His skin was as brown as a hazelnut, creased with deep wrinkles, and his beard wisped to his knees. Though beneath thick, tangled brow, determination shone in his eyes.

Otto clambered from his chair to kneel before the hermit, then reached to kiss his gnarled hands. In return, Nilus placed a hand on Otto's head. *"Pax tibi filium meum." Peace be with you, my son.*

"We are honored by your visit, Holy One," Otto said, his voice cracking.

He helped the hermit to the dais, but the old man stopped at the base of the steps. "I've not come to sit above emperors or popes," Nilus said. "I have come to plead for the life of John Philagathos."

"He is alive, Holy One." Otto clasped his hands. "I swear it."

"Alive, yes," Nilus said. "But what has been done to him?"

Otto blanched; Gregory realized it was time to seize control. "John Philagathos is a traitor," he announced. "He sought to depose me, the rightful pope, and rule as antipope while conspiring with Emperor Basil and the patriarch of Constantinople to place the Holy See within Byzantium's yoke. Perhaps his punishment was severe, but it was warranted."

323

For a moment, Nilus closed his eyes. "I warned him not to set himself up as pope. But he did not listen."

"And he has paid for his insubordination," Gregory assured him.

The old hermit clasped his hands. "All actions come with a consequence, but did not the Savior preach pity? John Philagathos was once my student, a good and thoughtful man back then. Release him into my care and I shall take him to my Basilian community in Serperi and shepherd him through penance to redemption."

Otto fell to his knees. "Whatever you demand—"

"We shall do to a point," Gregory interrupted, shooting his cousin a cross look. "We will leave him in your care, but you must stay with him here in Rome. I will not have this traitor brought so close to Constantinople lest he be tempted to continue his treachery."

The hermit glared at Gregory. "I hear he has no tongue. So how could he speak of treachery?"

"He has become a pawn of the Devil," Gregory insisted. "There is no telling how the Devil could use him to his wicked ends."

"So you know how the Devil works?" Nilus asked.

Gregory glared back. "Do you?"

The hermit sighed. "This is your verdict?"

"This is my judgment," Gregory said, "as *Pontifex Maximus* and Vicar of Christ."

The hermit lowered his head and stood silent for a moment, as if in prayer. "May I see him?" he finally asked.

Otto shot Gregory a horrified look, but the pope pursed his lips. "Bring us Philagathos," he commanded Count Berthold.

As they waited for the count to return, Gregory simmered in his chair. *This vagabond shall not have his way, even if Otto has lost his backbone.*

Arms crossed, Otto sat in his chair gazing solemnly at the hermit who seemed to have fallen asleep at the base of the dais. Whispers filled the hall until Berthold returned with the prisoner.

Nilus came awake as if he had sensed his pupil's presence. But when he turned to see Philagathos, the hermit gasped. Time had done little to mask the false pope's wounds. Scars had sealed the holes of his eye sockets, and scabs covered what had been of his nose, though the remnants of his ears remained but wisps of flesh. The rest of him, clad only in a filthy tunic, was skeletally thin, his skin dull and gray after weeks in the dungeon.

A tear spilled down Nilus's face and Otto's jaw began to quiver. The old hermit made the sign of the cross, then turned toward Otto and Gregory. "This is how you've treated this man?" The hermit's expression flashed from sadness to defiance. "He who held each of you lovingly when he lifted you as newborns from the baptismal font!"

Otto's hands flew to his lips; Gregory clenched his jaw.

Nilus pointed a crooked finger, glaring beneath his age-worn brows. "Our Savior demands mercy, yet is this how an emperor, anointed by God, and a pope, who is His servant, meet that demand? You showed no mercy on this man. And so the Lord shall show no mercy on you when you stand before His judgment!"

Heat flushed up Gregory's neck. He opened his mouth to rebuke the hermit, but Otto grabbed his arm. Gregory glanced at his cousin; the rebuke died in his throat.

For as Nilus stood there pointing in judgment, Otto stared wide-eyed and shaking like a man condemned to Hell's fire.

THE SECRET OF AVALON

Alais could no longer keep track of the days and weeks that had passed since she emerged from the labyrinth. Perhaps a month, perhaps two. There was no dusk or dawn in Avalon, no sun and no sky. Only the perpetual gloom created by the cavern's darkness mixing with the pale, glowing waters of the Lethe. Down here, events were the only mark of time. Some had seared into her memory; others she barely remembered at all. Yet her most vivid recollection was the day she learned the language of creation. The day her life forever changed.

Her first lesson back then took place in a hollow between two massive tree roots that slid into the Lethe like twisted serpents. Within the hollow, a small fire burned in a stone brazier, its light dancing over the ancient roots. Nimue stood near the brazier, holding a staff, blackened with soot and flaxseed oil, and carved from an alder she claimed had been felled by lighting. The staff reminded Alais of the one Brother Remi had wielded at Selles-sur-Cher. "Take it," Nimue demanded.

Alais took the staff. It was smooth to the touch and as heavy as a quarterstaff.

"Point it toward the fire," Nimue commanded. As Alais did, Nimue put a hand on the staff and wrapped her other arm around Alais' waist. The Fae woman's touch sent a shiver across Alais' skin. "Listen to the words," Nimue said, her breath kissing Alais' cheek. "And feel the air around you."

Nimue uttered a verse that sounded to Alais like the beginning of some beautiful yet alien song. Around Alais, the air sizzled and a subtle bluish glow, like Saint Elmo's fire flaring off a ship's mast, streaked up the staff. From the brazier, the fire surged. As if summoned by Nimue's words, the blaze leaped from the brazier to the staff's tip. Alais gasped as the staff flared like a birchbark torch. Another verse of Nimue's foreign song sent a pulse up the shaft and through Alais' palm, causing a jet of flame to burst from the staff. Alais watched wide-eyed as the fiery mote sparked and splintered into a score of flaming embers. The embers wafted skyward like burning stars, before dying within the tree's highest branches.

"The words I spoke," Nimue said, "are part of the language of creation, a language as ancient as time itself, used to weave the fabric of this world. When spoken in the right order, with the right voice, the words can affect the sacred elements, bending them to the speaker's will."

"You'll teach me these words?" Alais asked.

"Yes," Nimue hissed. "Now that you can use them. The human mind erects a barrier that prevents mortals from wielding this power. But your initiation in the labyrinth shattered that barrier, and when you spoke the word that filled the crystal with your soul light, your spirit was freed to learn these ancient mysteries."

She took the flaming staff from Alais' grasp and arched it through the air. As more words rolled off Nimue's tongue, the air thrummed. She brought the staff full circle, creating a ring of fire that lingered in the air, punctuating it with a fiery cross that transected the circle. Alais recognized the blazing symbol. *A wheel cross.*

"All power," Nimue instructed, "comes from the spirit. Power over the four sacred elements, each mastered by an object that symbolizes its essence. Ancient man had an apothegm for it. *Stone cuts earth, staff kindles fire. Sword parts air, cup binds water. Spirit incites the power.*" With her final word, the blazing wheel cross hissed into smoke and was gone.

"Throughout the ages," Nimue continued, "men and women have sought out the Lady of the Lake to learn these secrets, but only the most worthy ever received my teachings. Men and women such as Taliesin, Morgaine, and Merlin, who shaped the history of Albion." She drew Alais close, pressing her cheek to Alais' ear. "Now, Alais of Poitiers, it is time to see if you are worthy."

In the passing weeks—*or was it months?*—Alais had felt worthy, even though she had endured failure aplenty when it came to Nimue's lessons. Some were oppressively hard; others were disturbing in their nature, and the Fae woman's moods had been perhaps the most troubling of all. They changed like a weather vane in a storm. At times she was kind and caressing, sometimes almost too close and too kind for comfort. In a breath, however, she could turn as cold as a winter stream or become as demanding as a prioress. As a teacher, she was wickedly stern, and on many a day, Alais dreamed of fleeing her tutelage. But each lesson, and each failure, eventually gave way to triumph. For Alais learned the words. She understood their meaning and tasted their power. Her words had sent wind howling through Avalon, molded rock with only a crystal in her palm, and made waves in the Lethe that crashed against the shore. Yet even as she honed these newfound skills, she knew if she were to use them to fulfill whatever remained of the journey, she had to leave this place. Her only mistake was sharing this thought with Nimue.

The Fae woman glared at Alais, her eyes like daggers. "You are not ready to leave."

"But I'm passing your tests," Alais insisted. "I can speak the words and wield the power."

Nimue grimaced, then her lips twisted into a smile. "I have not pushed you hard enough. Had I done so, you would know you are unready."

"Your tests have been plenty hard."

Throwing back her head, Nimue laughed. "No, child, they have not. But tomorrow's will be." A gleam flickered in her eyes. "Tomorrow's test shall be the mother of all tests. And if you pass, perhaps I'll continue this debate."

Alais felt a tightness in her chest, then clenched her jaw. For whatever gantlet Nimue intended for tomorrow, Alais was determined to prove her worth.

~

THE MORNING OF THE TEST, IF ANYTHING COULD BE CALLED MORNING in the gloom that was Avalon, Alais stood on the shore, the gray sand cool beneath her toes. Beside her, Nimue faced the Lethe. The water's ghostly glow glistened off the ancient tree rising from the lake, although its highest branches remained lost in the shadows.

Over her chemise, Alais wore a leather belt and scabbard, sheathed with a leaf-shaped sword similar to the one Brother Dónall used to wield. Over her shoulder hung a burlap sack with her crystal and her pewter chalice, and her right hand gripped her blackened staff. These had been Alais' tools since returning from the labyrinth, and they would be needed for the day's test, whatever it turned out to be.

Alais sucked in a breath. "What would you have me do?"

Nimue held the ghost of a smile on her lips. "Listen."

From high above in the branches came a noise, like an animal's squeal at first, until its familiar sound caused Alais to gasp. The squeal was an infant's cry. "What in the name of God have you done?"

"The child belongs to a milkmaid who works in the abbey," Nimue replied with a feral gleam in her eyes. "The mother undoubtedly is frantic, searching for her daughter. You will decide if she ever sees her again."

Alais spotted the child, in a cradle of thatch nestled in a branch fifty yards above the lake. "This is madness!"

"This is your test," Nimue hissed. "And that child is prey."

Alais' jaw fell slack. "For what?"

Turning her attention to the lake, Nimue grinned. From its glowing waters, a shape emerged, slithering onto one of the branches sunk into the lake. Free of the water, the serpent was a dozen feet long and as thick as a melon, glistening like the ghostly waters of the Lethe. Its diamond-shaped head peered up at the child.

"Some say the venom of the Lethe serpent is deadlier than the Egyptian cobra's," Nimue said. "Others believe the serpent is as clever as a man, making it one of the most dangerous predators in the Otherworld."

As she spoke, the serpent slithered up the root and began crawling up the tree's trunk, faster than any snake Alais had ever seen.

Alais' pulse quickened. "No . . ."

"Your time is wasting," Nimue snarled.

Alais felt the world closing around her until another shriek from the child spurred her to act. Removing the chalice from her sack, she rushed to the lake. *Cup binds water.* She filled the chalice and uttered a verse, feeling the surge of power that came with each syllable as she hurled the contents onto the lake's surface. As it landed, the water froze, spreading like ripples in a pond until a sheet of ice extended from the shore thirty yards across the lake. Above, the serpent slithered across a branch two dozen yards from the screaming child.

Alais hurried onto the ice, ignoring the frozen liquid beneath her bare feet. Her gaze fixed on the cradle made of thatch, praying it was thick enough to hold the child's weight. She dropped her staff and unsheathed her leaf-shaped sword. *Sword parts air.* Words flowed from her tongue as a thrum of power surged up her arm through the leaf-shaped blade. She whirled the weapon as she spoke, summoning a breeze around her that surged into a gale. As she recited more words, the funnel of wind climbed skyward, her voice guiding it toward the cradle. Alais sensed the breeze surrounding the thatch, cupping it in its swirling grasp. The serpent hissed as the wind carried the cradle from the branch like a leaf caught in a storm.

Alais ignored the child's cries as it spun in the cradle, borne aloft by the wind. Her arm shook as she used the sword to guide the cradle toward her until she could catch it with both arms. The child looked up at her with panicked eyes. "You're safe," she said. Then the sound of scales scraping across petrified bark caused her to look up.

The serpent was descending the tree with reckless abandon, dropping from the stairwells carved into the bark and careening down the trunk until it neared the gigantic roots. It launched itself, soaring over the roots, and landing on one just twenty yards from where Alais stood on the sheet of ice. Its jaws wide, the serpent gave a hiss so ferocious she could feel its wind on her face.

With the infant in her arms, Alais realized they would never make it to shore. She set the cradle and the sword on the ice, and retrieved the crystal from her sack. The serpent slithered to the water's edge, coiling for another spring. Alais touched the crystal to her lips and spoke the Fae word. *Eoh!* Light erupted in the crystal as she thrust it toward the snake. As she spoke a new verse, power pulsed through the crystal in her fingers. The light exploded into a beam that struck the serpent like a lance of sunlight.

The serpent writhed in the light, whipping its head from side to side. But then it steadied itself as if recovering from the blindness—and sprang.

Alais grabbed the child and the chalice as the serpent landed on the ice, its eyes cold and black.

I've one last chance. She backed toward the water's edge. The serpent raised its head as she knelt and plunged the chalice into the water. She began uttering the verse when the serpent reared back and launched. She tore the chalice from the lake, sending a torrent of water at the snake. The liquid stuck to its skin and expanded, slowing the creature as it hardened into ice. The icy coating glistened over the serpent's scales. Huffing for breath, Alais traded the child for her sword. She approached the frozen serpent, gripped the hilt with both hands, and swung. The blade shattered the frost and sliced clean through the serpent's neck. Its head thudded onto the ice, its eyes as black in death as they had been in life.

The infant was still wailing when she scooped it up and strode toward the shore. As she stepped onto the sand, she flung her sword at Nimue's feet. "Damn you!"

Nimue pushed away the blade. "Temper your anger, child. You needed high stakes to reach your potential. Soon you may be ready."

"No," Alais said, shaking her head. "I'm ready now—and I'm leaving."

Nimue's eyes narrowed. "Where would you go?"

"There's another who can help," Alais said. "The Archbishop of Ravenna. Before we left Rome, Ciarán wrote a letter to him, telling him everything about the prophecy and our search for the Key. He has resources."

"And yet what good would you be to him? You are unready. But there is still time to complete your lessons, and *that* is what you must do. For you are the only hope, the only one left. All your companions are gone, drowned when the Northmen threw them into the sea."

Alais blinked. "You said they burned. The Northmen burned them on the cog."

Nimue's nostrils flared. "Burned or drowned, it's all the same. They're dead, and you—you are *unready!*" She grabbed the child from Alais' arms. "I'll leave this for its mother, and when I return, I expect you to be here and to be more obedient. For no one leaves Avalon unless I say so."

As Nimue stormed away with the wailing infant, Alais stood there stunned. *She lied . . .* The thought sent a quiver through her stomach. It brought to mind a question, something she had not contemplated since her arrival in Avalon.

What if they're still alive?

THAT NIGHT, ALAIS DID NOT SLEEP. INSTEAD, SHE LAY SILENT, WAITING.

She did not know where Nimue slept—or if she ever slept, so there was no way to know where the Fae might be lurking, save for the portions of the tree visible from the terrace. Hours passed before she dared to stand and start down the stairway that descended to the tree's base. She padded down the stairs, glancing back, praying she was not being watched.

When she reached the bottom, where the broad roots splayed toward the water's edge, a chill pricked her skin. She climbed over roots until she spied the soft glow of the scrying pool in the dark hollow between two of the largest roots. She approached the pool and found the old branch that Nimue used to disturb the water. She ran the branch around the edge and focused her mind on the swirling waters. "Show me Ciarán mac Tomás and Kahlil al-Pârsâ."

Staring at the pool, she saw a shape emerge among the ripples. A shape curved like a swan. She closed her eyes. In her mind's eye, the shape remained but took on new features, swanlike but fierce. A terrifying shape that harkened back to the Viking attack, the dragon-shaped prow of the longship. Yet this one was not ramming the cog but cutting through the water, blasting spray down each side of the prow.

Northmen filled the ship's hull, rowing to a song sung by an obese Northman with a face as ugly as a boar's. Her consciousness pressed down the aisle between the oarsmen. Then she sucked in a breath. On a bench near the aft sat Khalil. His beard was thicker, but there he was, *alive*, pulling an oar and laughing with the Northman sitting across from him. Behind him sat another man in the aft. His beard was full, and his hair long, but there was no mistaking those eyes. *Ciarán!* He sat next to a beautiful but savage-looking woman with red hair, with a huge boarhound lounging at her feet. Alais could not tell whether Ciarán was enjoying the Northwoman's company or merely tolerating it as her captive, though a stained bandage ran across his chest. *He's wounded . . . but, by God, he's alive!*

Suddenly, the image shattered. Alais' eyes flew open. The pool was boiling, and through the steam glared Nimue. "Betrayer!" she screamed.

Alais' heart began to race. "You lied to me—my friends are alive."

"And you will never see them again!" Nimue thrust out her hand. Alais felt the air thrum as a burning filled her veins. She wanted to run, but her legs would not move. The burning spread through her limbs. She tried to scream, yet her jaw would not budge.

Nimue's hand cracked across Alais' face. The force of the blow knocked her sideways. She landed hard on the petrified root. All feeling had left her limbs.

With little effort, Nimue plucked Alais off the ground. "You'll join the rest of them now."

She carried Alais to the boat and set her in its hull. Alais' mind raged like a swarm of bees, but the burning in her veins had paralyzed her body. The Fae rowed the boat to shore and carried Alais from the vessel. She headed toward one of the caves that pockmarked the cavern beyond the lakeshore. For a moment, Alais feared she was being taken into the labyrinth, but Nimue chose a different cave. The tunnel was dark, though tiny patches of the phosphorescent lichen speckled the rocky walls. By the time the tunnel ended in a round, iron-bound door, Alais could feel a tingling in her limbs. She wriggled her toes, then twitched a finger. *The paralysis is wearing off . . .*

Nimue inserted a key beneath an iron latch. She opened the door to the scream of its hinges. "What about the prophecy?" Alais croaked. "If you keep me here, you know how it will end."

"Yes child, I know how it will end. This place, this loneliness, all of it shall be gone." She dropped Alais through the doorway. "I need it to end."

The door slammed like a boom of thunder.

The cell stank of piss and rot. Alais pulled herself off the cold ground, her limbs shaking. The faint glow of lichen outlined something at the far end of the cave. As the shapes came clearer into view, she gasped. Heaps of corpses and skeletons were piled against the far wall. *This is not a cell, it's an ossuary!*

Some of the dead were still clad in the black robes of monks or the habits of nuns, while others wore remnants of chainmail or boiled leather. *You'll join the rest of them now . . .* The implications of Nimue's words crashed down like the heavens.

And Alais screamed.

44

KING OF THE DANES

By the time the Danish fleet returned to Vette laden with English plunder, the blood feud between Jarl Orn's kin and Jarl Holger's thrall had grown from a cook fire to a bonfire, and it threatened to engulf the entire Danish settlement in its flames.

Orn demanded that Ciarán be killed for maiming a jarl's hirdman, even though Holger insisted Ciarán was fighting in self-defense. Regardless, Holger paid Orn the wergild for Grimr's eye and Sigurd's arm, but Orn spit on the coins and tossed them into a swine pen. According to Magnus, this was a great insult. Under the law, an offer to pay the wergild obligated Orn to stay his hand. But if Holger had a temper like Thor, then Orn had a temper like Surt, the fire giant whose flames would consume the world at Ragnarok.

One night in the mead hall, Orn's fire for vengeance flared when he challenged Holger to the holmgang—a duel to the death between the hazel rods. The only thing that prevented that duel was Jarl Ulf, the eldest jarl on Vette, who insisted the Danes should not lose one of their finest warriors to a feud over a thrall, and a hand, and an eye. The holmgang was averted, but the mead hall erupted in a raucous brawl which left six of Holger's crewmen with black eyes and broken bones. Orn left so enraged that Ciarán and Khalil had to spend the ensuing weeks barricaded in Holger's hall, while Jorundr, Magnus, and Rosta kept watch for any sign of Orn or his kin.

During their seclusion, on a night when Ciarán sat beside Holger at his hearth sharing a skin of ale, Ciarán decided to ask about the jarl's dreams. "Lord," he said as embers crackled in the hearth, "Breda told me about your dreams. May I ask when they started?"

Holger swallowed a quaff of ale from his drinking horn. "An odd question, but I still remember the night, in the spring month, the fifth night after the new moon."

Ciarán thought about that. *The spring month,* March by the Julian calendar, and the new moon was on the first. The fifth was the night Ciarán had claimed Enoch's device at Rosefleur and killed Adémar of Blois. *Alais' dreams began around that time, too.* "Tell me what you saw, lord."

"It's often the same," Holger said, running his fingers through his golden hair. "You and I stand at *Lindworm's* prow sailing in darkness. There are no stars in the sky, but we've lit braziers while the others row. I've come to believe we are on a river in a chasm. You are dressed as a warrior, and you have a sword with a round pommel. Within it is a gemstone that burns like fire, not red like these embers, but white, like Thor's lightning. And always, I know where we are heading—to Ragnarok, just as the gothi foretold."

Ciarán shook his head. "That can't be."

"Why do you say that?"

"Because I recognize the sword. It belonged to me once, but I lost it on the night your ships attacked our cog. It was cut from my hand by Naberus the Roman and fell into the sea. So whatever you are dreaming, it cannot be your future."

Holger raised a brow. "The gothi was a great seer, and I know what he told me. And I know what I dreamed. It haunts me so often, I knew your face the moment I saw it. That's why I saved you from the Roman, because of my dreams. Not because I needed another thrall. And just look at the trouble you're causing me! I have to keep poor Jorundr up half the night to make sure Orn does not kill us in a hall burning. But I feel it in my bones, you and I will sail together in that chasm, and the sword will be at your side." He gulped more ale. "The gemstone in its pommel, what causes its light?"

Ciarán had watched Caladbolg tumble into the sea, so there was no way Holger could be right. Yet he answered him nonetheless. "The gemstone, I was told, is etched with the one true name of God."

"The Christian god, nailed on a tree?"

"The only God."

Holger cracked a smile. "Tell that to Odin, Thor, and Frey. The Norse gods are many and strong, and as proof, they favor us when we raid Christian lands. Yet still, you Christians would deny them?"

"I'm not denying them," Ciarán replied, recalling what Remi had said about his father's theories. "But I would not call them gods. They were the Watchers, angels who came to our world and ruled for a time. It was the same with the old Celtic gods, and the gods of the Germans, too. What many think of as religion is just a legend—the memory of the time when the Watchers ruled like gods among men."

"You're lucky I'm no zealot," Holger said. "A man could be killed for speaking as boldly as you, and I can recall a few black-robed priests who were. I believe in the gods, though they can be cruel, and the Norns most of all. Yet I wonder if the Christ-god is not growing stronger. Our last king, Harald, was a Christian, and King Olaf of Norway follows the Christ-god, too. Even on Vette, there are Danes who wear the cross instead of Thor's hammer. The gothis view you Christians and your priests like a plague, but I'm beginning to think the plague is contagious." He tipped his horn to Ciarán. "When you find your sword, show me its magic. Then I may think about your one God."

Ciarán made that promise, though he had no hope of ever seeing Caladbolg again. Yet in the passing days, he thought more about these Northern myths, and Remi's theories, and Dónall's old saying: *There's truth in those old myths.* Ciarán wondered if there was anything in Norse mythology akin to the Key to the Abyss. He decided to ask Magnus one morning while plucking feathers from a goose they planned to cook for the *dagverthr.* "In your myths, what causes Ragnarok to happen?"

Magnus cocked his head. "Do I look like a gothi to you?"

"No, but you told me about Niflheim. I thought you'd know."

Magnus scratched the side of the half-shaven head. "They say Loki, the trickster god, escapes from the cave in which he had been bound. After that, the wolf Fenrir breaks free, the world serpent Jörmungandr rises from the sea, and their sister Hel sails up in her ship of the dead. Then Ragnarok begins. But why do you bloody care?"

"How was Loki bound?"

"The god Frey made a chain from the guts of Loki's son, or something like that. But like I said, do I look like a gothi?" He cuffed Ciarán upside his head. "Now get back to work. I better not see a feather on the goose before we cook her."

Ciarán continued plucking. "Is there a gothi I could ask?"

"On Vette? No."

"Where did Jarl Holger find his gothi?"

"At Uppsala."

"Where's that?"

"Far away in Sweden," Magnus said, "so stop thinking about it, and finish that bloody goose."

Ciarán did as he was told, unable to fathom crossing the North Sea for answers. But a week later, on the eve of the *Winterfylleth,* the winter full moon, Magnus arrived with news they would in fact cross that sea. For King Svein had heard of the bountiful raids on Dorsetshire and summoned the victors to his hall for a grand celebration. So, *Lindworm* and its crew were going to Denmark, and Ciarán and Khalil were going with them.

FORTY LONGSHIPS LEFT VETTE FOR DENMARK. THE NORTH SEA WAS savage and cruel, and at times Ciarán wondered if it might claim them all. But *Lindworm* was built to withstand the fierce waves, cresting the monstrous swells and plunging back into the sea. The curved prow struck the water like thunder, blasting a fury of frigid spray over the hull. No man rowed shirtless, for the wind was bitter and ruthless, and the sea mist stung like ice.

Breda was worried Ciarán would rip the stitches in his chest if he tried to row, so she insisted Holger recruit another oarsman to take Ciarán's place. On most days, Ciarán sat in *Lindworm's* aft, with Rosta resting his head on his lap, alongside Breda, who liked to be near Holger when he manned the steering oar. For the first time, Ciarán felt at ease around the Danes, despite the harrowing voyage, which seemed to invigorate him each time *Lindworm* bested the angry sea.

When the sea calmed, Holger would call for oars in the water, and the crew would oblige with vigor. As fearsome and fearless as these Danes could be at times, Ciarán found them to be rollicking and adventurous men, and competitive too, especially when it came to poetry. Breda spoke of the "mead of poetry," and if poetry was drink to these Danes, Magnus and Jorundr were among its most ardent imbibers. Often it led to contests on the weeks-long voyage to Denmark. Khalil fit in well among these men, and even though he lacked coin to wager, more than a few Danes were willing to sponsor him if it meant winning silver from two of the jarl's most boastful men.

Such a competition broke out one afternoon when the sea was less ornery and the wind fair enough to have *Lindworm* at full sail. After much bluster and bravado, wagers were set, before Magnus answered the challenge with a rhyme about their victory at Poole.

> *With reddening spears we Danes arrived*
> *And the English host was scared alive.*
> *For they knew they'd die in pools of blood*
> *When the Danes charged forth like a roaring flood.*
> *They crawl on earth while ravens fly*
> *To make their feast on those who died.*
> *The English were a fitting meal*
> *For ravens' beaks and Danish steel!*

A roar erupted from the Danes, but Jorundr stood, waving his hands dismissively. "The hirdman's good," he jeered, "but he's still a pup. Make way for the big dog! *Woof, woof, woof!*" Jorundr patted his barrel chest and cleared his throat.

> *King Ethelred won't take the field*
> *Too scared to carry sword or shield.*
> *Instead of horse, he rides a mule*
> *Which he buggers daily like a fool.*
> *So fond was he of that poor beast*
> *He never saw the Danish fleet*
> *That raided lands 'til hulls were heavy.*
> *No wonder he's known as Ethelred the Unready!*

The huge Dane punctuated his rhyme with a booming fart, to the groans of his benchmates and the howls of the rest of the crew. Then over the laughter rose a chorus. "Moor! Moor! Moor!" Khalil's supporters stomped their boots on the deck planks. The Persian stood up and bowed.

> *Lindworm's crew sails off to fight*
> *Sleek serpent in the seas.*
> *Spear tips gleam in morning's light*
> *Woe to their enemies.*
> *Bright shields like an iron wall*
> *And the dancing of their swords,*
> *With graceful art their foes shall fall—*
> *All hail the battle lords.*

The crew gave a rousing cheer, and Holger clapped the loudest. *That's Khalil,* Ciarán thought, *ever the master of flattery.*

"Who wins?" one of the Danes cried.

Holger stood to his full height. "It's as close as a sword to its sheath," he said with a sly grin. "But I'll give it to the Moor!"

Jorundr threw back his head as if wounded, while a chorus of cheers and jeers filled the air. Khalil shot Ciarán a wink as Magnus glowered on a nearby bench, paying off his wagers.

The mood among *Lindworm's* crew was light that day, and it remained so for most of their voyage, despite the travails of battling the wintery sea. But moods darkened the morning they spied Denmark's shores, for abaft of *Lindworm*, *Wind Serpent* approached. Her serpentine prow crested the waves like Midgard's Serpent rising from the sea, and beyond it stood Jarl Orn, his hands gripping the gunwale. He glared at Holger's ship as the wind whipped his fiery hair, and Ciarán could feel the weight of his wrathful stare. The Danes might have come for a celebration, but *Wind Serpent's* captain had come for something else, and Ciarán did not need to guess what it was.

Jarl Orn had come for vengeance.

THE FLEET ROWED BENEATH A SLATE-GRAY SKY UP THE MOUTH OF THE river that would take them to Jelling, home of the Danish kings since the days of King Svein's grandfather, Gorm the Old. The ships moored at a modest wharf teeming with longships, forcing many of the captains to beach their ships on the riverbank. Much to Ciarán's relief, Jarl Holger kept his crew onboard until *Wind Serpent's* crew had made their way across the pale-yellow fields that led to the massive timber palisade surrounding Jelling.

By the time *Lindworm's* crew disembarked, there was no sign of Jarl Orn or his kinsmen among the scores of Danes heading into town. The peaked roof of a gigantic mead hall loomed above the palisade, along with wood-shingled longhouses with smoke wafting from their hearths. The crew carried chests filled with gifts for King Svein, along with the tents that much of the crew would use as shelter, for even a king's palace was not large enough to hold so many men.

Jarl Holger led the crew through the city's gate, a huge timber struc-ture with oak columns topped with finials carved in the shape of twin ravens. Beyond the gate, ribbons hung from birch trees beside golden winter furlongs where shaggy black sheep grazed alongside longhorn cattle. Shepherds and cowherds stopped to watch the arriving crews, as did a throng of Danes from a cluster of turf-roofed houses east of the gate. Some even formed musical troupes, welcoming the victors with drums and lutes and horns. Ciarán surveyed the square-shaped palisade, concluding Jelling was three times larger than Vette, but much smaller than the great Frankish cities of Paris and Poitiers, and nothing but a neighborhood in sprawling Córdoba or within Rome's Aurelian Walls.

Ahead stood the king's palace, a massive structure with timber columns supporting gabled roofs with finials shaped like birds and beasts. Around the main hall stood a barracks, a brew house, a cook house, and a sleep house. Between the palace and the clusters of turf-roofed homes, where more ribbons dangled from the trees, crews from Vette had begun erecting striped tents, their colors as varied as the sails of the longships in which they rowed. Within a nearby swale between two small hills stood a pair of standing stones beside another timber structure. The building had a gabled roof, but in place of a finial was a wooden cross. Ciarán could hardly believe his eyes. "Is that a Christian church?"

Magnus cracked a smile. "What other kind would it be? King Harald Bluetooth built it, but don't get excited, there are none of your shaven priests there."

"There must have been at one time."

"Aye. King Harald became a Christian to appease the German emperor, Otto, but he must have liked your Christ, for he invited a gaggle of shaven men here to convert the Danes. But his son Svein hates the shaven men, ever since they forced him to be baptized. None of them could sway Svein, for he favored Odin and Thor, and they favored him, too. Eleven years ago, he took a fleet of thirty ships and challenged his father for the throne. King Harald had fifty ships, but even with twenty more than Svein, it was not enough because the gods were on Svein's side. They battled at sea, but the fight broke off at dusk. King Harald was warming himself by the campfire when he took an arrow from one of Svein's men. The arrow hit him in the arse and poor King Harald bled to death like a stuck pig. When Svein returned to claim his crown, the shaven men fled Jelling, for they knew he would kill them. But he never burned the church because King Harald had put the remains of King Gorm there, so Svein let it be."

Ciarán did not like what he was hearing about this Danish king. At least the king had the decency to spare his father's church, he thought, before Holger approached them.

"We must pay our respects to King Svein," Holger said. "Ciarán, you and Khalil go help the crew set up the tents, though make camp as far away from *Wind Serpent's* crew as you can."

Ciarán and Khalil helped the crew build campfires and raise a score of striped red and gold tents, while keeping a lookout for *Wind Serpent's* crew. At dusk, *Lindworm's* crew drew straws to determine who would have to stay in camp tonight, for though the king's hall could hold six hundred men, more than two thousand had sailed from Vette. Some of those men hailed from Jelling, so they had warm houses here, and women too, but several hundred Danes from Vette would have to remain at the encampment each night, their only comfort being that the celebration would last five days, so there would be other nights of feasting to partake in. This evening, six men from *Lindworm's* crew drew the short straws and cursed their terrible luck. Their moods grew darker as sounds of laughter and music echoed from the king's palace, but their spirits improved once the king's servants arrived with barrels of ale, baskets of bread, and cauldrons of cabbage and mutton stew.

After they ate, Ciarán and Khalil sat with Rosta and the other six crewmen warming themselves by the campfire, bundled under wool cloaks and sealskin blankets. The air grew frigid once the sun went down, but Ciarán found the king's ale and the crackling fire helped him endure the night. Khalil had forsaken the ale, and Ciarán knew his Persian friend would be colder for it. As they talked about retiring for the evening, Rosta looked up alertly when a man approached their camp.

The fire's glow revealed him to be Magnus, looking a bit glassy-eyed and reeking of the king's ale. "Irish," he said. "You and the Moor need to come with me."

"Whatever for?" Ciarán asked.

"Because I bloody said so," Magnus snapped.

Khalil shot Ciarán a concerned look, which did nothing to ease the feeling in his gut. They shed their sealskin blankets and followed the hirdman. "The king has summoned you two," he finally said.

"Why would a king care about two thralls?" Ciarán asked.

"Because you two have caused a shait-full of trouble!" Magnus stopped and let out a huff. "We were having a grand good time until Jarl Orn threw his drinking horn onto the king's table. He's drunk, and he demanded that Jarl Holger engage him in the holmgang, right now, in the middle of the king's mead hall. All because *you*,"—he pointed angrily at Khalil—"killed two of his crew, and Irish here maimed two of his kin. Of course, Jarl Holger told King Svein that he had offered to pay the wergild for the maiming of his kinsmen, and that under the law that should be enough. But Jarl Orn insisted that because the maimed men were kin, he's bound by blood to avenge them. The king—who, trust me, has had *plenty* of mead—said both Orn and Holger had fair points, but before he let two of his mightiest jarls try to gut each another between the hazel rods, the king wanted to see the two thralls who've caused all this trouble. So now you're going before Svein Forkbeard, one of the most feared kings alive, and only the Norns know what he's going to do."

Khalil glanced at Ciarán. "This is bad."

Ciarán sucked in a breath. "Very bad."

Magnus led them up a flight of wooden steps that climbed to the palace, which looked like a giant mead hall. The thick timber columns supporting the hall's lower roof were carved with reliefs of serpents and dragons, while the image of a dragonship and an eight-legged stallion galloping through the sky embellished the broad oaken doors that led into the hall. As Magnus opened the doors, Ciarán's muscles tensed.

The roar of banter and the aroma of ale washed over him as he entered the hall. It was larger than Duke William's hall in Poitiers, but instead of stone pillars, timber posts supported the thick wooden trusses that buttressed the lofty ceiling. Oil lamps hung from the trusses, illuminating the hall with their flickering blaze. Down the length of the hall ran trestle tables littered with the remains of roasted hogs and geese, half-eaten loaves, pots of stew, and a myriad of cups, goblets, and drinking horns in the hands of a host of Danes, hundreds in number. Many ceased their banter, greeting the thralls with dark glances. From benches along the walls, adorned with painted shields and battle axes, more Danes stared, as did the servant girls in their embrace, each one in a shameless state of undress.

A hush settled over the hall as Magnus led Ciarán and Khalil down an aisle between two long tables. At the largest table, where the most richly clad Danes sat, Jarl Orn stood at his mead-bench, his weather-burned face a mask of hatred, maned by his fiery hair and beard. Across from him stood Jarl Holger, his arms crossed and face stern. Breda sat beside her husband, glancing nervously between the approaching thralls and the king of the Danes, who lounged in a high-backed chair at the head of the table. Svein Fork-beard was a large man with a long face and auburn hair spilling beneath a golden crown. His eyes had a cunning look, and his ruddy cheeks masked his age, as did his grayless beard, which was plaited in two, like the prongs of a fork. His left hand gripped a gilded drinking horn, and his red tunic, embroidered with golden thread, was stained with grease and mead below his beard, adding to his surly appearance.

The king's eyes narrowed as Ciarán and Khalil approached. Then King Svein began to laugh. "These are the two who have caused such trouble among my jarls? A Saracen and this Irish pup? It's a wonder they killed even one Dane, let alone four. Jarl Orn, what was the matter with your crew?" he asked, slapping the table with his free hand. "Were they all drunk?"

Laughter followed the king's words, but a chill washed through Ciarán's gut.

"Let me kill them now!" Orn demanded.

"No!" Holger yelled, pounding a fist on the table.

Orn grinned viciously. "Then let's settle this matter with the holmgang!"

The king slapped the table again. "Why should I allow that and lose one my jarls because of two slaves? And both of you are mighty warriors. Who's to say you two won't kill each other, and then I'd lose two jarls."

"That's what I told 'em back on Vette!" Jarl Ulf slurred from the table, froth sticking to his gray beard.

"Then how shall we settle this?" Orn growled.

Beside him, Grimr Grimsson rose to his feet, a patch covering his maimed eye. "Let me fight in the holmgang—against him!" He pointed to Ciarán.

When the king smiled, Ciarán swallowed hard.

"Now that is more like it," the king said. "Let's add some spice to our feast. By Thor, get more mead, and bring out the hazel rods!"

Holger began to protest while most of the Danes roared in acclaim, raising their cups and horns. But Khalil's words cut through their cheers. "I'll fight you!"

"I don't want you," Grimr snarled. "I want the Irishman!"

Holger glanced at Khalil, who cocked a brow. "Grimr Grimsson," the Persian said, "I recall a poem about a man like you:

> *Unlike tempered steel engraven,*
> *There was a man who was most craven.*
> *Even though he wore fine mail,*
> *He always knew that he would fail.*
> *And fall much worse than any fellow,*
> *For beneath his mail, his belly was yellow.*

With each verse, Grimr's face grew redder. The Danes howled in response, while Grimr clenched his fists. He pointed to Khalil. "You die now!"

The king raised a brow, his gaze fixed on Khalil. Holger gave the Persian a subtle nod, though Ciarán whispered into his ear, "You don't have to do this."

"It's already done," Khalil said.

While Magnus fetched Khalil's scimitar, two of the tables were pushed to the walls and a space was cleared before the king's table. The Danes marked the space, about ten feet square, with hazel branches stripped of their leaves. Holger explained the rules of the holmgang in simple terms. "The duel is a fight to the death," he said. "Both men are confined between the rods, and if anyone steps out, their life is forfeit."

Khalil nodded. He was eying Grimr, who had pulled on a coat of polished mail and donned a helm with a broad nasal that gleamed in the lamplight. He stood a half head taller than Khalil, and his dark beard fell to his chest, ending in a thick braid. Sigurd One-Arm handed him a round shield painted with twin ravens and a pointed iron boss that made the device as much a weapon as a sword. Grimr strapped it to his right arm, before Orn handed him his longsword, announcing its name, "Neck-biter." Grimr gripped it in his left hand, then kissed the blade.

The Viking stepped into the square marked by hazel rods, his mail chinking as he walked. Khalil had no armor, and stripped off his tunic to fight bare-chested, his torso chiseled from weeks of rowing. Magnus handed him his scimitar. Khalil reached out with his right arm, still badly scarred from the Greek fire, and took the curved blade.

Men began cheering as soon as Khalil stepped into the square, but Ciarán's stomach churned when Grimr struck the first blow, an angry, vicious swing, fueled by rage. Khalil parried it with his scimitar, but the force of the blow staggered him back toward a hazel rod.

The Dane is bigger and stronger, Ciarán realized in dread.

With catlike speed, Khalil struck before Grimr could raise his blade, but Grimr caught the blow with his shield and the scimitar banged off the oak. Howling with rage, Grimr swung again. Khalil parried, then whirled behind the Dane, landing a broad slice across his back. The mail saved Grimr's life, but he reeled, before spinning hard and ramming his shield into Khalil's left shoulder. The pointed boss gashed the Persian's flesh, sending a stream of blood into the crowd. Grimacing, Khalil backed away. Grimr gritted his teeth and hacked again. Khalil ducked and parried the blow. He retaliated, striking the inside of Grimr's shield hard enough to open a gap. Khalil whipped his blade to the side and thrust at Grimr's shoulder. The blade missed its mark but sank deep into Grimr's right arm.

Over the holler of the crowd, Grimr roared. He swung wildly, forcing Khalil to back off. Blood spilled down the Dane's right arm, and he was forced to shake off his shield and toss it outside the hazel rods. As Khalil readied his blade, Grimr grabbed a dagger from his belt with his blood-soaked hand. He fought now with a blade in each hand, circling Khalil like a wolf eyeing its prey. He swung again, but Khalil jumped back. Grimr huffed for breath. As if sensing the man's fatigue, Khalil came alive in the sword dance, striking quickly, landing blow after blow on Grimr's sword. The clang of steel filled the hall.

He's tiring him out, Ciarán realized, and it was true. Grimr's moves were becoming more lumbering as he parried Khalil's incessant strikes. Like a fire devil, Khalil whirled again, once more spinning behind the Dane, though this time, Kahlil aimed for Grimr's legs instead of his back. The Dane screamed as the scimitar ripped through his wool trousers into flesh, buckling his knees. Khalil's next strike severed the sword-hand from Grimr's wrist. The Dane fell onto his back, and Khalil lunged. The tip of his scimitar pierced Grimr's mail below his chest. Khalil dropped to a knee, putting all his weight on the blade. The scimitar tore through the metal links and plunged into Grimr's gut.

Khalil heaved for breath as blood gurgled from Grimr's wound. Ciarán's mouth widened in elation, but then his eyes flew wide. Grimr's injured right arm was moving—and he still gripped the dagger.

"Look out!" Ciarán screamed.

With a desperate gasp, Grimr thrust the blade between Khalil's ribs. Khalil jerked and glanced at the wound. The dagger's hilt pressed against his skin, its blade sunk deep within his flesh. He clutched the hilt with both hands and stared hopelessly at Ciarán.

"Khalil!" Ciarán cried as the Persian toppled sideways onto the bloodstained floor.

Ciarán tried to lunge for his friend, but Breda clung hard to his arm. "No—there's nothing you can do. He's gone. They're both gone."

The hall grew silent as Khalil and Grimr lay bloody and unbreathing on the floor. Ciarán clutched his chest as if something had ripped out his soul.

"Let this be it," Holger said.

"Never!" Orn cried, ripping his own sword from his sheath. "Let me kill the Irishman!"

Ciarán's anguish surged to rage. He wanted to grab Kahlil's scimitar and plunge it through Orn's heart, but Breda held him tight and Holger grabbed his shoulder.

"Enough!" the king roared, slamming his drinking horn on the table. "The thrall is dead, the debt is settled."

"No!" Orn replied. "The Moor killed two of my crew, so perhaps that debt is settled. But not the debt of Sigurd's arm or Grimr's eye."

Ciarán stood shaking. *If I do one thing in this life, it will be to send you to Hell.*

Holger's grip tightened on Ciarán's shoulder. "Grimr now sleeps in the corpse-hall. Let Odin have his eye."

"But what of my arm!" Sigurd shouted from the crowd. The crew of *Wind Serpent* joined his protest.

"Silence!" King Svein roared.

"My king," Orn said, "I have also heard that the thrall is one of the shaven men."

"Is it true?" the king asked.

Ciarán clenched his jaw against the fury and grief boiling within him, refusing to betray any weakness before this pagan king. "It's true."

The king's gaze hardened. "There are few things the gods hate more than a shaven man. Very well, I'll kill the bloody thrall myself. But Orn, you will pay Jarl Holger the wergild for his life, and then I'll have no more quarrels between you two."

A bead of sweat ran down Ciarán's forehead.

"But, my lord—" Holger pleaded.

The king slapped his hands on the table. "I'll hear no more of this! By Thor, I'm tired. We'll do this on the morrow."

"Do it now!" Orn insisted.

"On the morrow!" the king bellowed. Then he stormed from the hall.

45

THE SUNKEN PALACE

At midnight, beneath the faint light of a half moon, Naberus strode through the streets of Constantinople. He glanced at the Hagia Sophia, the centuries-old seat of the Byzantine patriarch and the crown jewel of Emperor Justinian's creations. Barely a candle flickered in the windows of the hulking structure, with its massive dome and high walls that made it look more like a fortress than one of the largest basilicas on earth.

Not a soul ventured down the marble streets at this time of night, so Naberus walked unmolested to the squat, tomblike structure that housed the entrance to the Sunken Palace. Many believed the palace to be haunted by evil spirits, which kept even the most brazen thieves clear of this place. Naberus, however, knew the true reason why trespassers rarely returned to the land of the living. The Sunken Palace was part of the dark underworld of Byzantium, ruled in secret through the centuries by the race of Magog.

The entrance to the palace was a door carved from a foot-thick marble block, too heavy to be moved by a normal man. Naberus, however, had little trouble pushing the door open, its marble scraping against the stone floor.

He lit a torch, illuminating the stairwell that led down to the palace. As he descended, the rhythm of dripping water echoed in the stairwell, and the air grew damp and thick. At the bottom, fifty-two steps below the surface, he passed beneath an engraved archway to the edge of a cavernous chamber flooded by water. From the dark liquid rose more than three hundred marble columns with Corinthian capitals, each supporting archways more than thirty feet high. A barrel vault ran down the chamber's center toward where a gilded altar once stood, illuminated by oil lamps. Their flames danced across the water. The place had once been a basilica before Emperor Justinian flooded the chamber and turned it into a cistern. Above-ground, the basilica would have been impressive with its flurry of archways, hundreds of columns, and intricate stonework. Yet beneath the city, flooded by water, the basilica took on the haunting beauty of its namesake, a sunken palace.

At the water's edge, Naberus paused. More than a century had passed since he'd set foot in the palace, and the last time he was a wanted man. He had been condemned for murdering the Prior of Stoudios, and the elders feared his crime would draw unwanted attention on the House of Magog from the emperor of Constantinople. Once upon a time, Naberus imagined he might return home like the prodigal son. But now his arrival was more like John the Baptist, announcing the coming of a new messiah. Naberus was aware that when John had challenged the king, the prophet lost his head. He hoped his own head would stay on his shoulders tonight, but there was something more than fear of reprisal preying on his thoughts. *What if she is here?*

Drawing a deep breath, he stepped into the water to a depth just beneath his knees and waded down the ancient nave. Halfway down the aisle, a warrior emerged from the chancel, rising from the water a full seven feet in height. His armor looked ancient, like that of a Roman legionnaire, with a steel breastplate and helm that concealed most of his face. His hands gripped a spear nearly twelve feet tall. "Who seeks a council before the elders?" His question echoed through the columns.

Naberus stepped forth. "Naberus of the House of Magog."

"Why do you seek the council?"

"Because I bring tidings from the Otherworld."

The sentinel stood silent, but from the ancient chancel a voice answered. "Come."

The warrior waved Naberus into the chancel, which served as the audience chamber of the Sunken Palace. Oil lamps hung from the archways, washing the chamber in a faint reddish glow. Along a curved dais that rose five feet from the water stood nine thrones, and on them sat black-robed figures, the elders of Magog. Each elder wore a broad cowl and a golden mask forged in the image of a god or goddess of ancient Greece, six men and three women. Four more sentinels positioned themselves around the chamber, each casting wary glances at Naberus as he approached.

Naberus eyed the women wearing the goddess masks. *She could be any one of them.*

An elder leaned forward wearing a mask of Zeus with an angry brow and pleated beard. "Naberus," the elder said, his voice hoary with age, "when last you lived in Byzantium, you stood accused of murder, subject to a death sentence. A sentence we can still impose. Why would you dare return?"

"I've not come to relive the sins of the past." Naberus surveyed the elders. "The spirits are stirring. How many of you have spoken to one of late and heard the whispers? A new voice has arisen, speaking words of prophecy long ignored by our kind."

Several elders nodded, but one in the mask of Ares crossed his arms. "Speak plainly," he demanded.

"As you wish," Naberus replied. "I often communed with the demon Orcus in a shrine beneath the Palatine Hill, but when last I sought him, a new voice answered in his place. A voice more ancient and awe-inspiring than any before it. A voice of absolute truth, deserving absolute obedience, with the power to grant absolute salvation. This is the prophecy he relayed:

The Morning Star has awakened, Gog and Magog heed his call.
The sacrifice is ready, the heir of Constantine shall fall.

The Prince of Rome holds the path to the Key.
The pillar will be broken, the Watchers shall be freed.

"These things," Naberus continued, "will happen soon, and the Prince of Rome shall be the apostle through which they come to pass."

"You?" Zeus scoffed. "You are but a murderer and thief, unworthy of your family's name."

Naberus forced a smile. "Dismiss my cause at your peril."

"You dare threaten us?" Ares cried.

"I merely warn that my master's memory is long, and he's not known for his penchant for forgiveness. The time shall soon come to separate the believers from the blasphemers, and woe be to anyone who stands on the wrong side."

Zeus bolted from his throne. "You are the blasphemer!"

His condemnation was cut short by a female elder masked as the goddess Hecate. "Stop!"

The sound of her voice sent a flutter through Naberus's stomach.

"I have heard these whispers from the mouths of demons," she said. "And I too have heard this prophecy. What is it you seek, Naberus of Rome?"

Naberus exhaled, looking her in the eyes. "I seek warriors. Men to serve as the tip of my spear, to become the soldiers of our salvation."

"That is out of the question!" Zeus growled.

Hecate rose from her throne. "No, that is for the council to decide by equal vote."

Several elders grumbled, but none raised a challenge. "And that is how it shall be settled," Hecate said. "Leave us, Naberus, and await our verdict."

He did not know how she would react to his return. He had stopped writing her decades ago, before his liaisons with Senatrix Theodora. He feared her anger, but her words gave him a semblance of hope as he left the chancel.

He waited in the vestibule, beneath the archway through which he'd entered, as the council's arguments echoed through the palace. So many voices spoke at once, he could not make out what as being said, but he could tell the debate was fierce. When the arguments finally ceased, a lone figure sauntered down the aisle. Lithe and feminine, with a golden mask bearing the image of Hecate.

Naberus held his breath.

She spoke dispassionately. "The council grants your request."

He breathed a relieved sigh. "How many men?"

"Nine," she said to Naberus's disappointment. "Eight of them will be chosen from among finest warriors of Magog, bred from the purest bloodlines to preserve the great strength of our legendary race. The ninth shall be Antaeus of Gog. He has been in our service for two years now, a giant like Goliath reborn and more than a match for the other eight who shall serve you."

"Then it's more like sixteen," Naberus observed. "They will do. And I thank you."

"I should have forsaken you as you had forsaken me so long ago," she said, anger in her voice. "But how could a mother forsake her own son?"

Naberus set his jaw, unwilling to accept the emotions her words stirred. "I'll not let you down again."

Through the golden mask, his mother's eyes held a longing gaze. "You have the tip of your spear, Naberus. The one your grandfather died wanting you to wield. Now go and wage your war."

46

THE PRISONER'S FATE

The fetid smell of death hung in every inch of King Svein's dungeon. One of the earlier inhabitants of Ciarán's cell was now a mound of dry skin and bones, slumped in a corner where rats scurried in the shadows. A flicker of torchlight seeped through the small barred window in the oaken door. It was the only thing keeping Ciarán from utter darkness.

He sat there, numb, his mind tormented by the memory of Khalil's hopeless stare and Grimr's dagger plunged between his ribs. Khalil had joined Évrard and Alais, Dónall and Isaac, Eli and Remi, and Niall and all their friends at Derry among the dead. And for what? For all Khalil's faith, he died mistaken. There was no kismet, or fate, or signs from God pointing them in the right path, unless their destiny was to die in Jelling before a horde of Danes. The only words that rang true anymore belonged to Naberus da Roma. *Your God has failed you, and your cause is lost.* All Ciarán could do now was wait for his jailer to return and take him to meet the king's ax. He glanced up at the corpse across the cell. *At least my death will be swift.*

Hours passed before he heard the bar scrape free of the door. He looked up at his jailer, but Jarl Holger stared back.

"Come," he said, "we must be quick." He pulled Ciarán off the earthen floor and hurried him into the timber-walled chamber where the jailer lay unconscious. Jorundr loomed over him, ax in hand, beside Breda holding a torch.

Ciarán shook his head in disbelief. "Why are you doing this?"

"I believe in my dreams," Holger replied.

"But your king?"

"Will have my head, too, if he catches us, which is why we must hurry."

Ciarán followed them out of the stockade, into the bitter night air. Jorundr and Breda led the way, through the alleyways between the turf-roofed houses of Jelling until they came to a postern gate. A pair of Danish guardsmen sat bound and gagged at the base of the timber palisade, near two more of Holger's crewmen. Gunnar Boar's Head hurried them forward, while a young Dane they called Strong Bjorn held open the gate.

Outside, they made their way around the palisade, hugging its timber walls, until they were out of sight of Svein's guardsmen and could safely traverse the fields that led to the wharf. Breda extinguished her torch, and they fled under the light of a half-moon until they came upon *Lindworm,* rigged and ready, with oars in the water and shields lining its sides. The six of them had to wade up to *Lindworm's* hull. Holger nudged Ciarán toward the longship, and Magnus helped him aboard.

The hirdman had a sour look in his eyes. "We'll all be outlaws because of you," he growled. "I would've let the king take your head."

Many of the crew gave Ciarán dark stares as he made his way aft, where Rosta sat waiting for him. The boarhound's wet kisses were the only warmth Ciarán felt among the crew, until Breda joined him and handed him a horn of ale.

"Drink this," she said.

As Holger ordered his men to row, Ciarán noticed the man-sized shape lying near the steering oar. The body was wrapped from head to toe in white linen, and Ciarán knew he was looking upon Khalil al-Pârsâ.

Breda placed a slender hand on Ciarán's shoulder. "Jarl Holger demanded to keep the body because Khalil was his thrall. Holger wanted you to be able to say good-bye to him."

A tear stung Ciarán's eye; he clenched his fists to fight it. "Will we bury him?"

"When we make landfall tonight," she said.

"Where are we going? Vette won't be safe."

"We're going to Uppsala. With all that's happened, Holger seeks guidance. So we are sailing to see his gothi."

TWILIGHT DESCENDED ON THE RUGGED COASTLINE WITH ROCKS THE SIZE of a man's head colored in orange and brown and every shade of gray at the place where *Lindworm* beached for the night. Beyond the shore rose a steep, green-covered hill, and at its summit Ciarán dug the grave.

He worked alone at first, in the shadow of an ancient yew, until Jorundr lent his own shovel to the task. "He was a fine poet," Jorundr said.

"Aye," Ciarán replied with a nod, "and a great friend."

Over the many voyages he had shared with Khalil, Ciarán had learned enough about Muslim customs to try to honor his friend's faith. The grave had to be deep, Ciarán recalled, and dug in a way so that the body's head faced southeast, toward an Arabian city named Mecca.

They dug to the sound of the waves striking the Danish shore until Jorundr hit rock. Then the two of them climbed out of the grave with aid of the crewmen who stood to watch the burial. Most of the Danes present had been fond of Khalil, having profited greatly in the poetry contests thanks to the Persian's expertise. Holger stood there as well, as did Breda, with Rosta at her side. Only Magnus was absent, still bitter over the events that had put *Lindworm's* crew in trouble with the king of the Danes.

Before they lay Khalil into the grave, Ciarán knelt. "I never learned your prayers, yet I know your God and God the Father are one and the same, and you have served him well." Then he spoke a Gaelic prayer, pieced together from the few he could remember.

May the waves rise to greet you,
May the birds bring music to your ears.
May the sun shine warm upon you,
May the rain fall softly on your grave,
Until we meet again, in the holy light of God.

After Khalil was buried, Ciarán used a dagger to etch Khalil's name onto the stone that Jorundr fetched as a grave marker. Ciarán placed the stone at the head of the grave, finding it hard to hold back tears. But he fought them to appear strong in the face of the Danes. That proved more difficult, however, when each of them came up and clapped him on the shoulder or offered words of comfort. Holger was the last to approach.

"He died a warrior," Holger said, "with a sword in his hand."

BEFORE THEY SET SAIL THE NEXT MORNING, HOLGER SPOKE TO HIS MEN. He acknowledged that some of them disagreed with the way they had left Jelling and did not wish to be at odds with King Svein. To those who wished to return to Jelling, Holger offered them coin to find a ship to take them back to the Danish stronghold. The jarl announced he was sailing to the hall of King Olaf of Sweden, an enemy of Svein Forkbeard. Ciarán knew this was a lie, though few among the crew understood that Holger was taking *Lindworm* to the Temple at Uppsala. Nine of *Lindworm's* crew accepted the jarl's offer, but Magnus was not among them. The hirdman swore Holger was like an older brother, whom he would follow wherever he sailed, even though it was a bad decision to risk so much for the life of an Irish thrall, and a shaven man no less.

With a quarter of the crew gone, Ciarán took his place once again on an oar bench, his chest having healed enough that Breda felt comfortable with him pulling an oar. In the days that passed, *Lindworm* sailed into a vast body of water the Danes called the East Sea until it reached the rugged crags of Sweden. The winds had grown frigid by the time the longship entered the fjord that led to a large, forest-lined lake called Mälaren. By the time *Lindworm* arrived at the mouth of the river Sala, daytime snow flurries had coated the pines white.

The Sala snaked northward through dense, snow-flecked woodlands until *Lindworm* arrived at a frost-covered wharf where a trio of longships was moored. Two pale-gold banners hung beside the wharf marking the temple grounds, and there Holger revealed to his crew their true destination. The crew appeared to accept the necessity of Holger's deception, and none seemed to mind a visit to the sacred temple, though several worried aloud that they had not brought an animal to sacrifice on the altar of Thor.

The Temple at Uppsala stood a half mile from the river in a grove of towering pines. The temple itself soared near the treetops, and was by far the tallest building Ciarán had seen among the Northmen. Each gabled roof gave rise to another, such that the peaked roofs rose skyward, one upon the other, ending six stories above and crowned with a stout spire. The wooden structure was broader than King Svein's palace, and more elaborately adorned, with runes carved upon the timber columns and a huge golden chain hanging from the first-story gables that wrapped around the entire temple. More pale-golden banners draped from posts set around the temple, while the corpses of deer, horses, and even dogs hung from tree limbs in every direction, as if the Northmen honored their gods with this macabre wreath of slain creatures.

Ciarán felt a chill as he followed the Danes past the hanging corpses, thick with the stench of death. Ahead, oil lamps burned beneath the gables of the heathen temple, illuminating the structure amid the shadows of the pines. As the crew climbed the steps that led to the great oak doors beneath a birchbark roof, Magnus sauntered up to Ciarán, still wearing Ciarán's hauberk and baldric. "Now you will see a temple to mighty gods, Irish," the hirdman said. "There are no suffering gods in here."

Ciarán held his chin high though he subtly made the sign of the cross before stepping into the heathen temple. Inside, the temple was enormous and laid out similar to a church. Carved columns were spaced down a nave-like area, adorned with boughs of mistletoe and blackthorn. Between each column, arched trusses etched with golden runes ran down the nave, giving Ciarán the feeling that he was standing within the rib cage of some titanic beast. Oil lamps hung from the arches, their smoke carrying the scent of incense and herbs as it wafted to the lofty ceiling, where it became lost in the darkness above. Northmen moved about the temple, while some gathered around shrines along the walls of the nave, decorated with paintings of dragons and beasts. Holger led the way toward what looked to Ciarán like a chancel, dominated by three gigantic statues seated on elaborate thrones inlaid with more golden runes. The towering statues were crude compared to the sculptures in Rome, but in the blazing lamplight of the pagan chancel, they were savage and frightening to behold.

"That is Odin, the Allfather, wisest of the gods," Magnus said, pointing to the leftmost statue, carved of wood to look like a bearded king clad in armor whose plates were forged of polished bronze. A patch covered one of his eyes, and he cradled a human-shaped skull in his hands. Next, Magnus pointed to the middle statue, a ferocious bearded warrior resting his hands on an enormous hammer inlaid with gold and bronze. "That is Thor, the strongest of all the gods," the hirdman said. The third statue was of a naked man with a pointed beard and pointed helm, but his most prominent feature jutted from between his legs: an erect phallus as thick as a barrel and as longs as a lance. "That is Frey," Magnus explained, "the god of fertility. You pray to him if you are with a woman and want her to bear you a good son."

At an altar before the statue of Thor, a group of Northmen huddled around a black ram standing on the stone slab. A white-cowled figure held a knife in the air before slitting the bleating ram's

361

throat. Its blood soaked the altar, where the men touched the sanguine liquid with their hands and smeared it over their faces and chests.

Another man dressed in a white cloak and cowl, with a scarred face and gray beard, stood near the statue of Frey, watching Holger and his retinue approach. The gothi pointed at Ciarán. "His kind should not be here!"

Ciarán's muscles tensed, as he wondered how the gothi knew he was not a pagan. "He's my thrall," Holger responded.

"Then he can wait in the grove," the gothi snapped.

"We shall leave," Holger said. "But first, I seek Blind Mikkel."

The gothi narrowed his gaze. "He comes and he goes. Yet if he is here now, you will find him in the cave, by the spring that flows by the great tree."

Holger gave the gothi a nod, then turned on his heel. "Follow me." He grabbed Ciarán's arm and ushered him back down the nave. They emerged into the wintery air, and Holger led his crewmen down a side path away from the temple, toward a massive pine. "The great tree," Holger observed aloud.

The tree looked ancient, standing at least twenty feet taller than the nearest pine, with a moss-encrusted trunk thirty feet around. Its bark was as thick as breastplates, and its branches so wide and full that only slivers of light pierced through its foliage. A ring of dead animals hung from the boughs, including a bull, three boars, two rams, a horned sheep, a horned buck, and three mares, their black eyes sad and lifeless. Ciarán swallowed hard. The more he witnessed these sacrifices, the more he wanted to flee from this heathen place.

"There's the spring," Breda said, pointing to a stream flowing near the massive tree, down from one of the hills that surrounded the grove.

Holger scratched his beard. "Last time, he was in the temple. I wonder what caused him to retreat here."

The spring emerged from the hill near a small cave, nearly covered by the surrounding brambles and blackthorns. Ciarán swore he saw a faint mist in the mouth of the cave. Perhaps it was caused by the bubbling spring, but he felt a strange sensation as he neared the opening like he had when he entered the primordial forest at Brosse.

"Wait for me here," Holger said.

Ciarán sucked in a breath. As much as he disliked this place, he had to know the answer to his question. "Take me with you."

Holger turned, his eyes narrow. "Why would you want to go?"

"Because I seek answers, too. And remember your dreams."

The jarl ran a hand through his golden hair and thought for a moment. "Then come."

Ciarán followed Holger to the mouth of the small cave. Holger pushed past a thicket of blackthorn, growing like claws around the cave, and ducked his head before stepping inside. Ciarán watched Holger disappear through a curtain of mist that hung beyond the cave's threshold. Making the sign of the cross, he followed Holger inside, only to be struck by the heat within the cave. Ciarán wondered if that was creating the mist from the moisture of the stream, for the cave was humid and its rock walls were slick and wet. He drew a deep breath before stepping into the vapor. The mist surrounded him, and for an instant he thought he might drown in its murk. But then he emerged through the other side, into darkness. His foot splashed in a deep puddle of water, and he swore he heard something slither along the walls—and the hiss of something breathing. A chill raced down his limbs, just as a hand grabbed him from the darkness.

"We're here," Holger said under his breath. "Blind Mikkel?" he called out.

From the darkness came a rasping sound, followed by a dim glow of light, as if someone had lit a candle. Though Ciarán could see no candle or flame, just a faint glow, like the light of a crescent moon, emanating from the puddles of water clinging about the cave floor. The glow illuminated a sitting figure, robed and cowled, though if the robes were once white, they now were as gray as ash. A tangled beard spilled from the broad cowl, and from the sleeves of his robes emerged gnarled fingers tipped with clawlike nails. Ciarán could not see the man's face in the shadow of the cowl, and he feared the gothi must be a ghastly thing to behold.

"Welcome, Holger Horiksson," the gothi said in a coarse and ancient voice. "Yet I sense another in my cave. You have brought your shipmate?"

"Aye," Holger replied. "The one I saw in my dreams, sailing through a cavern into darkness."

"Ah, your dreams," the gothi said with a hiss. "Myths are but memories of the past, yet dreams are portents of the future."

"Is that still my fate?" Holger asked.

"The fate that has been spun or the fate to be won?" The gothi stretched out a bony arm and touched the cave wall with one of his wicked nails. The glow followed his movements, and now illuminated a portion of the wall, revealing scores of Nordic runes and astrological symbols carved into the stone. The runes, which appeared to cover every inch of the wall, reminded Ciarán of the sanctum sanctorum in Rosefleur, and he wondered now if he stood within another of those sacred places.

The gothi traced a pattern down the runes, his nail scraping against the rock. "Your fate is unchanged, Holger Horiksson." His fingers crawled like a spider across the wall. "You shall be there when the great horn sounds, and the giants march forth from Jotunheim, and the beast of the land, Fenrir, charges across the barren land, howling in triumph. You shall stand beneath the starless sky when the demons spill forth from Niflheim at the behest of Hel, their queen, and Jörmungandr, the beast of the sea, erupts onto the battlefield, where the Sly One marshals his forces of chaos. And there you shall stand at the side of your shipmate, just as your dreams have foretold. For this is your fate, Holger Horiksson. All other plans and oaths are like dust."

Holger sucked in a breath. "Then let it be so."

The gothi reached out his other hand and traced a nail down a series of runes scrawled across the low ceiling of the cave. "And what do you wish to know, Ciarán mac Tomás?"

A chill melted down Ciarán's spine. "How do you know my name?"

"Blind I may be," the gothi rasped, "but one needs not eyes to see."

"Then you already know my question."

The answer came like a serpent's hiss. *"Yes."* The gothi's fingers scrabbled over the runes, his nails clattering across the rock. "You wish to know about the Key to the Abyss."

Sweat beaded on Ciarán's forehead. "Can you tell me about it?"

"The Key is a mystery. The men of the north speak in stories, so I shall tell you a story. The enemy of the gods is Loki, the Sly One, the Father of Lies. One day, the gods learned that Loki was responsible for the murder of Baldur, Odin's favorite son, so the gods sought to punish Loki for his crime. When they captured him, they took him to a cave deep within the earth, and that cave was to be his prison. Among the Asgardians was Frey, a lord of the Vanir, ruler of the light elves. To Frey alone, the power of binding had been given, so the gods left it to him to bind Loki in the cave. Frey took the entrails of Loki's son, Narfi, and bound the Father of Lies, making the entrails into a chain as hard as iron. Frey bound Loki beneath a serpent whose venom dripped upon the Sly One day after day, and the earth quaked with Loki's torment.

"But Frey, it turned out, was an unworthy caretaker for his power. For the lust of forbidden love, he had given up his sacred sword, so at Ragnarok he lacked the weapon to fight Surt, the fire giant of Muspell. Surt slew Frey, and seized his power, for to the victor go the spoils. But Frey had a twin, his sister Freya, the most beautiful of the gods and leader of the Valkyrie. Freya avenged her brother and killed Surt, but she could not stop his fire from burning the Nine Worlds. Yet unlike Frey, Freya escaped Ragnarok, hiding in the tree Yggdrasil, until she was reborn as Lifthrasir in the new world that rose from the ashes."

Ciarán's mind was churning, working through any connections between this story and what he knew of the prophecy. "What of the chain that bound Loki?"

"That is the mystery," the gothi said. "Did Frey truly turn Narfi's entrails into a chain as hard as iron? In the same vein, did Pandora truly open a box?"

"It's not literal," Ciarán realized, recalling the word Gerbert had used. "It's a *metaphora.*"

The gothi drew in a hissing breath. "You are learning to see through the mists. Perhaps by Midwinter, your vision shall be clear."

"Midwinter?" The word brought to mind the riddle from the Book of Giants. *On the solstice, at the Altar Stone, with blood the Spirit brings . . .* "The winter solstice—that's when I'll find the answer?"

"Enough," the gothi growled. "You have seen what you were meant to see."

"Yet I'm not finished," Holger pleaded. "I've betrayed my king, and know not what to do. Where must I go to realize my destiny?"

The gothi pointed a curved nail at Ciarán. "He already knows, and the time is nigh for the servant to become the master. Now be gone, Holger Horiksson, and take your servant with you." With his final word, the strange glow vanished, leaving Ciarán and Holger in darkness.

"Come back!" Holger demanded. He jostled Ciarán, groping for the gothi. "Where are you?"

"He's gone," Ciarán said, somehow knowing it was true.

"He was just here!"

Ciarán placed a hand on the Dane, trying to calm him. "Whatever he was, he's not here anymore."

When they returned through the curtain of mist into the daylight, Holger grabbed Ciarán by the shoulder and shoved him against the cave wall. The Dane's teeth were clenched. "What did he mean?"

Ciarán grimaced. "He knew of my quest, before my enslavement."

Holger narrowed his gaze, pressing Ciarán hard against the wall. "Who are you?"

"I am the keeper of a secret," Ciarán told him, "one preserved by the paladins of Charlemagne, including the Dane whose sword you wield. That secret was passed down through my father and my mentor, and it concerns the event you call Ragnarok. I thought all had been lost when I became your thrall. But perhaps there's still time."

"For what?" Holger snarled.

"To reach the place the English call Stonehenge. I thought we had to be there by Midsummer, to discover the path to an artifact we would need before the end times. But the riddle spoke only of a solstice, so that could be Midwinter as much as Midsummer. *That's what the gothi meant.*"

"What are you saying?"

"That I must get to Stonehenge by Midwinter." Ciarán looked Holger firmly in the eyes. "And given what the gothi just said, you're the one who's going to take me there."

4 7

THE SIGN OF THE CROSS

Alais' nightmare knew no end. She awoke on the cold stone floor of her cell, as she had for weeks. Or was it months? She had lost track of time.

Her gaze crawled across the floor toward the round, iron-bound door. In front of the door lay a cup of water and hunk of bread. These would appear often when she awoke, but not always. Some days passed with nothing, parching her throat, and adding to the pain in her stomach. Already, her limbs were skin on bones, and her ribs protruded from the remains of her chemise. She glanced at the heap of skeletons. Their hollow eyes stared back in death, amid the rotting corpses who looked more like their skeletal brethren every day. *Soon I'll look like one of them.*

She scrabbled toward the food and bit off a hunk of bread. The bread was stale, but Alais did not care. After she finished it and the water, she visited the makeshift latrine she had been using beside a mound of dead. She had grown numb to the stench of urine and waste.

When she was done, she crawled back to the spot on the floor that had become her bed. Lying there passed the time, and sleep was better

368

than being awake. For when she was awake, she sometimes heard the sounds.

They echoed down the tunnel, barely audible through the heavy door. Sometimes it was singing, a haunting tune like the one the Fae danced to in Alais' dreams. Other times it sounded like moaning, as if two voices joined in the throes of pleasure. Nimue must have taken a lover, for often the sounds were those of a man. At times, Alais would try to call to him, to warn him. But only faint whispers or hacking coughs sprang from her bone-dry throat. When she heard the man's voice, she would glance back at the heaps of the dead, wondering how many of them had been Nimue's lovers.

One night, Alais awoke to the sound of Nimue's voice, loud and full of fury, echoing through Avalon. The man's voice mixed with hers. Then the man screamed—until his scream went silent.

Alais waited, feigning sleep as the key scraped in the lock. The iron hinges squealed, followed by a thud, just inches from Alais' head. She opened her eyes. The man lay next to her, unmoving.

After the door slammed shut, Alais came to life. The man was a monk, dressed in a Benedictine habit, and he was young. Perhaps eighteen or nineteen, with a fair complexion and comely face. *Had all the dead here once looked like him?* Alais crawled toward him and tapped his cheek. "Wake up," she hissed.

The monk did not stir. She tried to lift his head. It moved too easily, and a sickening feeling settled in her stomach. When she let go, his head sloughed to the side, his neck clearly broken.

Sniffing back tears, she grabbed the man by his ankles and dragged him toward the mound of corpses. He was heavier than she expected. *Or have I become that weak?* It seemed a shame to add such a beautiful man to this mound of death. She ran her fingers across the man's smooth cheek, then stopped upon noticing a cross, worn on a leather strap around his neck. It was a fine pendant, made of beaten bronze with a stone in the center where the crossbars met. *He must have been a lord's son to own a cross like that,* she thought, her gaze lingering on the stone. Opaque, like a crystal.

"*My God,*" she realized aloud.

Her hands shook as she took the pendant from around the dead man's neck. She brought the cross to her lips. *Blessed Radegonde, let this work.* Alais drew a deep breath and cleared her mind of thought. As she exhaled, she whispered the word, each syllable pulsing with power. *"Eoh."*

Light flickered in the gemstone, like a wick accepting a flame, and then flared into a brilliant glow. Her head felt light as she held up the cross, gazing at the glow of her soul light blazing in its center. A verse from the ancient apothegm came to mind.

Stone cuts earth . . .

Her limbs tingling, Alais kissed the cross. *I've found my way out.*

ALAIS WAITED, HER EAR PRESSED AGAINST THE IRON-BOUND DOOR, UNTIL a quiet settled over Avalon.

She prayed once more to Saint Radegonde before uttering the words to transform the rock surrounding the door's lock into mud. The verse rolled off her tongue, followed by a thrum of power. She pressed the cross's gemstone to the rock, feeling the heat that each word brought. The air around the lock shimmered with blue fire as the rock's surface began to glisten, becoming more liquid than solid. She threw her weight against the door. It took three times, but the rock slowly gave way. She pushed carefully, praying that doing so would dampen the screech of the hinges. The lock's iron bolt slid through the muddy rock, and with only a slight creak the door cracked open enough for Alais to slip through.

Free of the cell, she doused the light, though kept the cross clutched in her hand. *Darkness is my friend now.* She tiptoed down the tunnel, listening for any sound of Nimue. Hearing none, she continued into the cavern of the lake, with the tree of Avalon rising from the Lethe into the shadows above. To her surprise, the boat was moored on the lake's shore. Alais sucked in a breath. She would need the boat, but that meant Nimue was up and about, away from the ancient tree. Alais glanced over her shoulder, searching for any sign of her captor, but found none. *Maybe she's wandering the Tor?* Alais suspected Nimue did so from time to time, haunting the outside world like a wraith in the night.

The titanic tree stood awash in the lake's eerie glow. As much as she wanted to flee from here, she had to return there—to retrieve Enoch's device. She had a hunch as to where Nimue had hidden the sword, and prayed her hunch proved true.

Steadying her nerves. she unmoored the boat and stepped inside it. She rowed until the boat reached its mooring where the water met the tree's massive roots. It did not take long to find the door in the base of the tree's trunk. She hoped the symbol of the seven-pointed star and the Zodiac carved into the door meant what she thought it did. The door had no handle and no lock, so Alais pushed.

The door did not move.

Undeterred, she took the cross and whispered again into its gemstone. *"Eoh."* The glow erupted in the gem, and this time it spread to the symbol, illuminating the star and the ring of astrological signs one by one. She pushed again and the door gave way.

A rush of cool air washed over Alais as she stepped inside, while the gemstone's glow illuminated the stone-tiled floor. Each flagstone bore an alien symbol, astrological perhaps, though Alais did not know for sure, and that pattern repeated on the stone bricks of the chamber's curved walls. She gaped at the chamber's size, nearly half as large as Rome's Pantheon, complete with a domed ceiling etched with more glyphs.

Shadows obscured two large objects in the chamber's center, though as she approached, the shadows dissolved in the gem's light. Alais breathed a relieved sigh, for next to a sarcophagus was a stone the size of a boulder. And protruding from its top was Caladbolg. It looked as if the sword had been stabbed into the rock. In her soul light, the gemstone in the pommel glittered like a diamond.

Alais glanced at the sarcophagus. Carved atop the lid was a relief of a handsome man wearing robes like a priest's. The image brought to mind an account from Turpin's journal. *They traveled to Merlin's tomb to retrieve the sword . . .* And here it was. Nimue had returned Caladbolg to the very place where the paladins had discovered it.

Standing on her toes, she wrapped her fingers around the cross-shaped hilt. With a jerk, the sword slid free of the stone, its steel scraping against the rock. The sound echoed through the chamber, and her stomach hardened. *What if Nimue heard that?* Alais did not wait to find out. She put the cross on like a necklace and let its light die. Then she gripped the sword with both hands and hurried from the chamber onto the sprawling roots that sank into the Lethe.

As she neared the boat, she spied the hollow of the scrying pool. She glanced around for Nimue, but all seemed quiet in the cavern. *Perhaps there's still time.* She descended into the hollow, where the pool glimmered like a pale moon. Beside the pool, she found the old branch and stirred the waters. Then she drew in a breath. *Show me Ciarán mac Tomás and Khalil al-Pârsâ.*

Within the pool's whirling water, a circular shape emerged. Alais closed her eyes. In her mind's eye, the shape took on a more elaborate form: a vast ring built of towering stones, half of which lay in ruin. Snow dusted the ancient stones and blanketed the grassy plain on which they stood. She recognized Stonehenge at once, and the vision could mean only one thing. Ciarán and Khalil were going to the Giant's Ring, and they aimed to be there by the Midwinter solstice.

When she opened her eyes, the image faded. But she knew now where she had to go. She figured one of the passages in the labyrinth must to lead to the outside world, for how else had she heard Sister Leofflaed and Lay Sister Agnes searching for her after her abduction? With luck, Glastonbury Abbey would be near. All she would need is a horse.

She returned to the boat and rowed to the lake shore. Across the cavern, the cavelike entrance to the labyrinth stood but fifty yards away. As she stepped off the gray sand to the cold cavern floor, a voice boomed like thunder. *"That does not belong to you!"*

From the entrance to the labyrinth emerged Nimue. Alais feared the thrum in the air, the burning in her limbs, and the paralysis that would follow. But in a breath she realized she could still move. *She must be too far away to wield that power.* If so, Alais knew she had only seconds, for the Fae woman was moving fast with her long-legged strides, her face a mask of fury. Without further thought, Alais pressed the sword's pommel against her lips and uttered the Fae word. *"Eoh!"* The gemstone flared. Its fire seared down the blade, exploding with the light of a thousand torches. Heat surged through her arms as she raised the sword.

Nimue recoiled in the blade's light. "You would fight me?"

"Only if I must." Alais leveled the sword at Nimue. "If you stop me, you'll become like Lilith. And what was her fate? Torment in the Lake of Fire the priests speak of? Compared to that, your purgatory will seem like paradise."

Nimue's eyes narrowed.

"Yet if I leave," Alais said, "and find my companions, there may be another thousand years before your day of judgment. In which case, you may have a millennium to seek your redemption. The choice is yours."

Apprehension tinged Nimue's gaze. She watched as Alais strode toward the entrance to the labyrinth, giving the Fae a wide berth and keeping Caladbolg's fire between the two of them. The sword's light danced across the Fae's pale skin; she turned her head to avoid looking into the flames.

By the time Alais reached the entrance to the labyrinth, she knew she had won. Whatever Enoch's device was, Nimue feared its power. Or perhaps she felt the weight of Alais' words. But the Fae did nothing to stop Alais as she entered the labyrinth.

When she encountered the first passage filled with mist, she thrust Caladbolg into the vapor. The white flames flickering off the blade cut through the mist like a scythe through wheat. Mist hissed into steam, revealing a damp tunnel with cool air carrying the scent of hawthorn. Twenty yards in, a spring bubbled from the rocky floor. Alais stepped into the water, cold and fresh, rushing through her toes. Ahead, moonlight spilled through the mouth of a small cave, perhaps three feet in height. She dropped to her knees and crawled through the water, only to emerge from a moss-covered cave mouth into a stream that trickled along the base of a rising hill. *The foot of Glastonbury Tor.*

Alais rose to her feet and let the light fade from Caladbolg's gem. In the distance, torchlight flickered from Glastonbury Abbey. She took a long breath and looked up to the heavens. Somewhere among the glimmering stars, Aquarius and Pisces remained, and so did the journey.

All she needed to do now was finish it.

MIDWINTER

T he voyage through the North Sea brought angry waves, freezing rains, and frigid gales, but *Lindworm* survived the brunt of their fury by the time the longship reached England's shores. Magnus blamed the weather on Rán, believing the sea goddess to be furious because the crew had betrayed King Svein and cast their lot with a Christian thrall. Jarl Holger insisted he would hear no such talk, leaving his hirdman to glower through the voyage home. Still, that did not stop Magnus on more than a few occasions from threatening to throw Ciarán overboard and deliver him to Rán's nine daughters before the worst weather passed.

By the time *Lindworm* entered the channel, Magnus's mood had brightened a bit, along with that of many of the crew. Soon, their voyage took them near Vette, and crewmen asked about stopping home to resupply and allow those who had family there to visit their wives and children. Jarl Holger resisted at first, concerned about the presence of Jarl Orn, and even Jarl Ulf, now that Holger had defied King Svein. So instead, Holger moored the longship upriver and let anyone with family on Vette sneak into the settlement at sunset so long as they promised to return before sunrise. Only one failed to report back, a young Dane named Ingvar who had a pretty wife and a newborn son. While Holger dismissed this as the actions of fool boy following his heart, Magnus cursed the tiding as more bad luck, for Ingvar's decision had left the ship with ten fewer oarsmen since departing Denmark.

The tidings from Vette proved more concerning. While Jarl Ulf's ships had returned three days prior, the *Wind Serpent* had not, and there were rumors Jarl Orn was hunting the seas for Jarl Holger and his crew. When *Lindworm* returned to the channel that morning, everyone on board kept watch for *Wind Serpent* prowling the horizon.

Before midday, *Lindworm* entered the Solent, the strait that led north to the river which snaked inland toward the plain where Stonehenge stood. Ciarán recognized the estuary by its curved shoreline and surrounding marshlands, and the memory of this place left a bitterness in his mouth. For here, in this estuary, *Lindworm* and *Wind Serpent* had rammed *La Margerie*, leaving Alais and Évrard dead, and many of the crew enslaved. Ciarán glanced over the larboard gunwale, knowing that somewhere beneath those dark, blue waters lay Caladbolg, never to be found again.

While a half year had passed, he remembered the attack as if it happened yesterday, and it was hard to believe now he sailed as a crewman on one of those longships, with the very men who carried out the murderous raid. But the Lord, as Abba used to preach, works in mysterious ways. So perhaps Khalil had been right. Maybe God had not forsaken them, and this gothi, despite his pagan trappings, had been one of His signs. Whatever the truth, by tomorrow Ciarán would stand within the Giant's Ring. And there, he would learn for certain whether he could salvage any hope of fulfilling the prophecy.

After rowing upriver until the waters curved east, the crew moored *Lindworm* on the riverbank and made camp for the night. Stonehenge remained a full day's journey by foot, and to reach it by sunset, Jarl Holger determined they must to set out before dawn.

Ciarán awoke on Midwinter to snow blanketing the riverbank and glistening on the pines. He had expected to travel with a small group to the henge, but most of the crew wished to go and see the Giant's Ring they had heard so much about since leaving Uppsala. Jarl Holger decided that three men and Rosta should stay with the longship, and the rest could venture forth to appease their curiosity. So before first light, Ciarán set off with Breda and twenty-eight Danes laden with packs, weapons, and shields to find the Giant's Ring.

Snow covered the countryside northwest of the river, making the party's trek more daunting than expected under cold gray skies. Yet as the day wore on, the clouds gave way to a crisp blue sky, and by the time the sun was cresting west, the first glimpse of Stonehenge emerged on the horizon. From the distance, it looked like a crown atop the snowswept plain, but as the party neared, the shape of the standing stones came into view. Set upon a gentle hill, some of the sarsen stones loomed taller than others, surmounted with capstones that Ciarán figured must have formed a circle atop the monument in the ancient times. Portions of the ring had collapsed into ruin, though what remained preserved a sense of grandeur. For while he had seen plenty of standing stones in Ireland, he had never witnessed any as large and awesome as this. *No wonder men believe it was built by giants.*

Magnus scratched the side of his head. "No man could have moved those stones."

"No, I think not," Holger said, before turning to Ciarán. "What do we do now?"

Ciarán took a deep breath. "The reference I discovered about the Giant's Ring spoke of a ritual that had to be performed at sunset on the solstice. So, I suppose, we wait until sunset."

"Then what?" Holger asked.

"Then maybe, like the gothi said, I'll learn more about this mystery that binds you and me."

Breda shook her head. "Why do I get the sense neither of you know what in Hel's name you are doing?"

"The gothi sent us here," Holger insisted. "I have faith in his words."

Ciarán glanced at the sun. Within the hour, it would sink beneath the horizon. "It's almost time."

Together, the crew advanced on the henge, while several of the men wondered aloud about the possibility of gold buried under the stones. "If there was treasure buried here, don't you think the bloody English would have found it by now?" Magnus asked Haki, a boyish, fair-haired Dane and chief among the speculators.

"Maybe they never thought to look," Haki said. "After all, these Christians are scared of—"

An arrow ripped through Haki's throat. Then the twang of bowstrings and the hiss of shafts filled the air.

Beside Ciarán, a Dane fell backward, an arrow jutting from his chest. As Ciarán dropped to the snow, two more arrows slammed into Magnus's shield. In front, another crewman collapsed, an arrow protruding through his back. Two more shafts sank into the ground, paces from Ciarán's face.

Archers emerged from behind the sarsen stones. The attackers numbered more than a dozen.

"Shields!" Holger cried. "Form the wall!" *Lindworm's* crew scrambled backward, gathering in close formation and raising their round shields. Wood clattered as shields overlapped one another in the front, with another layer of shields formed overhead by men in the second row. Ciarán scurried behind the wall, just a man away from Breda, as arrows thudded into shields like hailstones in a storm. "Reveal yourself!" Holger bellowed.

From within the henge, a voice answered—the voice of Jarl Orn. Ciarán peered out from the edge of the shield wall. Orn strode from between two sarsen stones dressed for battle in his mail and helm, with a broadax clutched in his hand. More than thirty Danes joined him on Stonehenge's gentle hill, spear-Danes and sword-Danes. Among them stood Sigurd One-Arm.

"You are a wanted man, Holger," Orn roared. "When the Roman hired my kinsmen to kill your thralls, he told them that if the thralls ever escaped, we would find them here at Midwinter. And lo, here you are, and with your Christian thrall, too! Our king commanded me to capture you, but I think I'll kill you instead. Then I'll ravage your wife while drinking mead from the skull of your precious thrall!"

As the shields of *Wind Serpent's* crew clattered together, forming

378

their own wall, Magnus glared at Holger. "They outnumber us by ten, maybe more. Are we to all die now because of this thrall?"

"Orn's blood feud goes beyond any thrall," Holger growled. "He wants me dead too, and when a jarl falls, his hirdman is never far behind."

Magnus grimaced "Then may we all feast in Valhalla tonight."

Wind Serpent's crew slammed their swords and axes against their shields, like war drums before a battle. "Kill! Kill! Kill!" Orn's voice rose above the noise. "Kill them all!" Jorundr began pounding his ax on his own shield. *Lindworm's* crew joined him, the drumming din filling the air.

Slowly, the two walls advanced on each other. The more they neared, the more Ciarán felt the weight of his own breath. "Ready!" Holger yelled as *Lindworm's* wall surged forward until the two walls collided with a sound like a thunderclap. The ground shook beneath Ciarán's feet, then horror followed. Sword tips flashed through gaps between the shields. Men screamed as the blades struck flesh, drenching the snow in blood. Axes chopped at shields, splitting the wooden panels. A spear flashed through one gap and impaled the crewman in front of Ciarán. As the crewman slumped to the ground, Ciarán lunged for his shield, though nearly lost his footing in the slick snow. Another spear plunged into the gap, grazing Ciarán's shoulder. Ignoring the pain, he raised the shield in time to meet a hammering ax blow that sent shudders through his very bones. The ax struck again, and the shield boards began to splinter. The force of the blow drove Ciarán backward. He tried to brace himself with his right leg, though this time the slush gave way and he slid awkwardly to his knee. He could see his attacker through the hole in the shield wall, a thick-bearded Dane whose eyes burned with the madness of battle. His attacker raised his ax, then someone knocked Ciarán to the ground. Breda's shield met the attacker's blow, before she knifed through the gap with her sword. Their attacker howled as she drew back the blade, slick with his blood. "Back on your feet!" she yelled. Ciarán clambered to his feet and raised his half-broken shield behind Breda's, just in time to meet another sword blow. He grimaced with the pain of each strike, while beside him Breda screamed in rage, stabbing her sword through the gap. Around them, the air stank of sweat, and blood, and piss, as men screamed and men died. Ciarán wondered how the assault would ever end, when Holger shouted a command: "Fall back!"

The Danes shuffled backward, leaving their dead and those of the enemy before them on the battlefield. *Wind Serpent's* crew made a similar retreat, forming a tight shield wall in front of Stonehenge.

Ciarán counted at least six men lost as *Lindworm's* shield wall had shrunk in size, and the survivors huffed for breath. Blood trickled down the side of Holger's face and seeped from a long cut on Jorundr's arm. Only Magnus looked unscathed. "We'll not rest long," Holger huffed.

"How many of them?" Breda asked.

"Four, maybe five dead," Magnus said, "but the bastards outnumber us by a dozen now."

Ciarán glanced at the battered crew. *We'll not survive another round.*

As if to remind him of that, the enemy resumed drumming their shields. Ciarán's nerves tensed. Another sound joined the cacophony —the pounding of hooves. He spun toward the sound. A rider thundered down the plain, the hooves of its charger churning up snow.

The rider headed for *Lindworm's* shield wall. As it neared, the horseman came more clearly into view. Skeletally thin, with long raven hair that flowed behind a familiar face, sunken yet beautiful. Ciarán's eyes flew wide.

For galloping toward them was a ghost.

"KEEP YOUR SHIELDS UP!" HOLGER COMMANDED HIS MEN AS THE RIDER slowed her mount behind *Lindworm's* crew. "They won't charge a shield wall," he told them, glancing at the rider.

Across the battlefield, the drumming ceased. "Jarl Holger!" Orn roared. "Has a woman come to save you? When you're dead, I'll have her, too!"

Ciarán barely heard the laughter erupting from *Wind Serpent's* crew as he stared breathlessly at the apparition before him. As she rode nearer, his shield slipped from his grasp. His head became light, and he dropped to his knees. "Sweet Jesus," he muttered. Her limbs were caked with dirt, and her dress was little more than rags beneath a drab woolen cloak, but her storm-gray eyes were all he needed to see to assure him it was her. "By God, Alais."

A tear ran down her cheek. "It's me," she said with a faint smile.

He scrambled to his feet and ran to her. She reached down to caress his face. "Where's Khalil?"

Ciarán swallowed hard. "He fell."

Alais winced, while another tear streamed down her face. She sniffed it away. "You'll need this." She unwrapped a bundle resting between her and the saddle. Free of its wrapping, steel gleamed from Caladbolg's blade.

Ciarán staggered. "How?"

"After I jumped overboard, I managed to save it. There's more to tell, but not the time."

On the other side of the field, *Wind Serpent's* crew started banging their weapons on their shields. Alais glanced at the enemy shield wall. "Are they the Vikings who attacked our ship?"

"Some of them."

She handed him Caladbolg. "Then use this well."

He took the sword, feeling its cold steel in his hands. Holger gasped at the sight of the blade. "The weapon from my dreams!"

Ciarán nodded, barely believing what he held in his hand—and how much their fortune had changed. "Lord," he told Holger, "prepare to charge."

"Are you daft, Irish?" Magnus called back. "It's suicide to charge a shield wall. They'll cut us down like pigs to the slaughter!"

"Their wall will break, I swear it."

Holger hesitated, then gave a nod.

Ciarán watched as Alais guided her horse a safe distance behind their shield wall, then he turned to the crew. "Remember, no matter what you see in the next moment, do not be afraid. I and my sword are on your side." He cleared his mind and put the sword's pommel to his lips, whispering to the gem. *"Eoh."* The sensation that pulsed from his lips to his limbs, through the hilt and the steel, was more welcome than anything he could imagine. White fire surged up the blade.

Lindworm's shield wall broke first. Many of the Danes fell back, abandoning any attempt at keeping their shields in place. Before Ciarán, Magnus's mouth hung open in disbelief; Jorundr gaped at the blade. Yet Holger's eyes stared the widest.

"Follow me," Ciarán commanded, his muscles tense.

He stepped out, raising the sword into the air, its blade awash with fire. Glaring at *Wind Serpent's* shield wall, he shouted an Irish battle cry. *"Columcille!"*

Behind him followed a roar of Danes. Ciarán charged the enemy wall. The shield wall held fast, but as he advanced, cracks began to form, like he knew they would. As the shields parted, *Wind Serpent's* crew looked on in terror. Some dropped their weapons, others fell back. But at its center, Jarl Orn stood fast, his gaze a mix of fear and rage.

"Odi-i-i-n-n-n!" Orn cried, barreling toward Ciarán with his broadax raised high.

With gritted teeth, Ciarán swung. Jarl Orn caught the blow with his shield, but the blade sheared through the wood as if it was parchment. Orn roared, hacking furiously with his ax. Caladbolg parried the blow and sundered the broadax where the iron met the shaft. His face a mask of fury, Orn swung a fist at Ciarán's head, but Ciarán severed the fist from Orn's wrist. As Orn staggered, Ciarán's next blow caught him in the chest. The blade cleaved through mail and bone; white fire spilled into the wound.

"That was for Khalil," Ciarán said.

Jarl Orn gave a wheezing gasp, his eyes in a disbelieving state of shock. Smoke curled from his chest; then he toppled backward onto the blood-splattered snow.

Around Ciarán, *Lindworm's* crew continued the slaughter. Sigurd One-Arm lay dead at Holger's feet, while a half-dozen corpses littered the ground around Jorundr and Magnus. The fight ended quickly, with the surviving members of *Wind Serpent's* crew kneeling in surrender.

Alais rode up to them, gazing on Orn's corpse with grim satisfaction. Ciarán sank Caladbolg into the snow and helped her dismount. He wrapped her in his arms and kissed her forehead, then her cheeks, and then her lips, letting that last kiss linger. When their lips parted, tears stung his eyes. She kissed him once more, then let go as Holger approached.

Blood splattered the jarl's mail and his face glistened with sweat. "That magic," he asked, his eyes filled with wonder, "was it from your god?"

"Aye," Ciarán replied, "the one true God." He looked at Alais, whose gaze fixed west, where the sun threatened to set.

She glanced back with an urgent look. "It's time."

WITH BLOOD THE SPIRIT BRINGS

T he sarsen stones along the outer ring of Stonehenge loomed over Ciarán, each thirteen feet tall and crowned with snow. An icy breeze whistled through the standing stones, erected long before the first Celt arrived at Albion's shore. Ciarán touched one of the stones, sensing the weight of this ancient place, just as he had in the forest that marked the gateway to Rosefleur.

As he stepped through a gap between two of the massive stones, he wondered who had built such a place. The Irish believed monoliths like this were built by the Tuatha Dé Danann, who ruled Ireland before the days of men. Perhaps this one was created by the Faefolk of Albion as a device like Brú na Bóinne to mark the passage of time along the Wheel of the Year. Or maybe it was built by the men who roamed these lands before history was written, though it seemed impossible men could move such massive stones. Or perhaps the Britons Archbishop Turpin wrote of were right, and the ring indeed was built by giants. Though the thought that Nephilim had created this place sent a shiver through Ciarán's limbs.

Within the outer ring, only three pairs of sarsen stones still stood, surmounted by snow-dusted capstones. Several more standing stones jutted within the ruin, while smaller stones lay on the ground, caught within the shadows cast by the setting sun. Alais followed behind him. "It reminds me of Avalon," she said.

"Avalon?" Ciarán could hardly believe his ears. "You've seen it?"

"I found it, along with Merlin's tomb, just as Archbishop Turpin wrote in his journal."

Ciarán glanced at Caladbolg, gripped in his right hand. It too had been found by Turpin in Avalon, and he wondered for an instant if that place, this ring, and the sword were somehow all connected to what must occur here. He turned back to Alais, noticing a sadness in her eyes. "What happened there?"

"Many things," she replied. "Some were good, most were terrible. But there will be time for stories later. The sun's beginning to set."

Ciarán nodded, but froze when he heard footsteps in the snow. He craned his neck as Jarl Holger emerged from the shadows between two of the stones. "This is where you perform the ritual?" he asked.

"Aye," Ciarán said, relieved it was just him. "If we can find the Altar Stone."

"Here," Alais said, clearly recognizing the meaning of the Danish word *alteret sten*. She stood before a flat sandstone among the rubble, larger than an oxcart. She brushed off a coating of snow, revealing the stone's purplish-green surface. "It's the only one lying flat like an altar, and it faces the two tallest stones, with that capstone atop them." She was right: the flat stone was aimed at a pair of sarsens, and the sun seemed poised to set through the gap between the stones. As he watched the setting sun, he recalled the words of the riddle from the Book of Giants:

> *As the sun sets on a thousand years, seek the Giant's Ring,*
> *On the Solstice, at the Altar Stone, with blood the Spirit brings,*
> *The answer to the mystery forged when Atu sank into the sea,*
> *The way to our salvation, the revelation of the Key.*

Ciarán knew what he must do. "Be careful," Alais said softly behind him.

"I will." He stabbed Caladbolg into the snow beside the Altar Stone, then touched the cut where the spear had grazed his shoulder. With no time to bind it before sunset, the wound still oozed blood, and Ciarán rubbed it until his palm was slick. He waited until the sun blazed like a red orb between the pair of sarsens, then drew a deep breath. Clearing his mind of thought, he set his palm upon the Altar Stone. At first, his fingers tingled as his blood made contact with the sandstone. The sensation crawled up his arm, growing into a thrum by the time it reached his shoulder. It continued up his neck, into his skull, cold and powerful, as if fingers were pulling on his consciousness. Around him, the air sizzled as he felt himself being drawn into the stone.

His vision faded, and for a moment Ciarán felt like he was floating in the sea. But then the tug of gravity pulled him down, drifting toward the ground. Black turned to gray, and as his vision cleared, he found himself standing within Stonehenge. Before him, his bloody handprint stained the Altar Stone, while all around the monolith stirred a thick mist. Its tendrils wafted between the sarsens and curled over the capstones. He glanced around, realizing he stood alone. "Alais?" he called out.

A voice answered from the mists like wind groaning through a forest. *"You seek prophecy . . ."*

A chill washed through Ciarán as the phrase *with blood the Spirit brings* took on an ominous meaning. It was not referring to the spirit within a man, but something else. Something here in the mist, and Ciarán had no choice but to speak with it. "Yes," he answered.

"There is only one prophecy," the voice said. Ciarán struggled to determine where it was coming from. All he could see was mist through the sarsens, and whatever was speaking was moving around the circle.

"The Morning Star has awakened, Gog and Magog heed his call," the voice continued. *"The sacrifice is ready, the heir of Constantine shall fall."*

The chill in Ciarán's veins turned to ice. *Those were the demon's words . . .*

"The Prince of Rome holds the path to the Key. The pillar will be broken, the Watchers shall be freed."

"Who are you?" Ciarán reached for Caladbolg at his side, but the sword was gone. His heart pounded.

"Who am I? I am called Wise One and son of Baraq'el, seer of dreams and maker of wings. Lord of the sky and prophet of doom. I lived when the world was young. I watched it end, and saw it reborn. I am the diviner of mysteries, the keeper of secrets, and the oracle on the path to salvation."

Ciarán swallowed hard. He had seen the Fae and the Nephilim, and the terror of demons before them, yet he could only imagine what this thing might be. "I've come for the answer to a mystery. Where is the Key to the Abyss?"

"That is for me to know, and me to tell. But not to you."

Ciarán grimaced. "Then why did the riddle bring me here?"

"To deliver you to me." A shape began to emerge between two of the sarsens, gaunt and manlike, nearly as tall as the stones themselves. "The demon of the abbey guided you to the prince's tome, which brought you here." It stepped from the mists, a giant taller than two men, its flesh rotted and blackened, with eyes like embers in its wasting skull. "To Mahway."

Ciarán felt as if his feet were rooted in place as he recognized the name from the Book of Giants.

"So you see," the corpse giant said with a fiendish grin, "the demon lured you here to die!"

The creature moved faster than Ciarán could process. Its massive hand wrapped around his waist, hefting him effortlessly into the air. Ciarán clawed at its fingers, digging his own into Mahway's rotting flesh. But the creature's grip was as firm as steel. Ciarán felt a flutter in his gut as Mahway hurled him like a child's doll toward one of the sarsens.

Ciarán cried out as he slammed into the stone. He slid to the ground, numb from the impact, as the giant bounded forward. He tried to scramble away, but the giant caught his leg and whipped him across Stonehenge. He crashed into the earth and snow. Lying there, he could no longer feel his limbs. He feared the bones were shattered.

With two massive strides, Mahway was upon him. He pinned

Ciarán under his enormous foot. A carrion stench filled Ciarán's nostrils as the weight of the giant pressed down on his chest.

Mahway's eyes burned in his skull. *"Now die."*

ALAIS WATCHED IN HORROR AS CIARÁN CONVULSED UPON THE ALTAR Stone. The Danish lord was shouting something in his foreign tongue. He shook Ciarán as if to wake him, but Ciarán just wheezed for breath, blood trickling from his nose.

Alais' heart pounded. "He's dying!" In her desperation, the apothegm came to mind. *Spirit incites the power . . .* Without a second thought, she pulled Caladbolg from the snow and sliced her palm. As the blood welled, she put the sword's pommel to her lips, then uttered the word. *"Eoh."* With the sword's power surging through her limbs, she held Caladbolg in her good hand and slapped her bloodied palm onto the Altar Stone.

As her blood touched the stone, she felt a force grab hold of her consciousness, drawing her downward as if into a chasm. Around her the air sizzled as she let the force take her, knowing it was the only way to save Ciarán. Closing her eyes, she gripped Caladbolg tightly, praying it had the power to move between this world and wherever the Giant's Ring was taking her. When she felt her feet touch ground, she found herself within the circle of standing stones. The sunset was gone, replaced by a storm-darkened sky and a ghostly fog wafting through the sarsens. The handsome Dane was nowhere to be seen, but, as she had hoped, Caladbolg blazed in her hand.

She spotted Ciarán at once, but gasped at the sight of his monstrous attacker. "Leave him alone!" she cried.

The corpse giant turned toward her, stepping off Ciarán's limp body, its burning eyes fixed on her flaming sword. *"Not that,"* the creature groaned.

She took a bold step and raised the blade. "This is Caladbolg and Excalibur and Flamberge. This is Enoch's device and the power of the Urim, etched with the one true name of God. I can see you fear it."

"But I don't fear you!" The giant sprang, raking a massive clawed hand.

Gritting her teeth, Alais swung the blade. With a flash of white fire, its steel met the giant's hand, severing four huge fingers from its palm. The giant howled like a sandstorm and leaped backward, away from her blade. With its one good hand, it reached for one of the toppled stones. The giant roared as it ripped the stone from the earth and hurled it at Alais. A scream stuck in her throat as the stone whizzed by her head, exploding behind her.

The giant shrieked with frustration. *"You don't belong here!"*

It raised its arms and thrust them at Alais. As if summoned by this gesture, billows of mist rushed from between the stones. The mist crashed over Alais like a wave, obscuring her vision and filling her mouth and nose. She feared she might drown within it, but fought the panic. *Sword parts air . . .* She choked out a Fae verse, each syllable pulsing with power. A faint breeze swirled around her ankles, curled up her body, and surged down her arm. The blast of air cleared the mists and gathered around the sword. The flames dancing along the edge of the blade were caught up in the wind. Reciting more words, she aimed the sword at the giant. Fire and air rushed forward like a gale.

The roar from the giant's throat shook the ground beneath her feet. The torrent of fire washed over its already rotting flesh, searing through to its bones. The giant writhed, flailing its arms, fire consuming its ruined hand.

"Where will the Key be revealed?" she demanded.

"That is not for you to know!" the giant screamed.

"Tell me, damn it!"

Within the firestorm, the giant wailed. *"Venus and Roma!"*

Alais stopped for a breath. *The Temple of Venus and Roma.* Her dreams, she realized, had been telling her so for months.

"Now leave," the giant pleaded.

Alais grimaced. "It's you who doesn't belong in this world." With a cry, she willed fire and air forward with all her fury. The flames rose to a deafening roar. The giant howled as its flesh became ash, blasting off its skeletal form until bone fragments followed, torn apart by the flames. As the wind died, only a blackened silhouette of the giant remained on a sarsen at the far end of Stonehenge.

Alais ran to Ciarán. He wasn't breathing. "No," she said softly, "not here."

She dragged him to the Altar Stone, dropped to a knee, and set Caladbolg's pommel against Ciarán's chest. Then she cleared her mind and focused her spirit into the gem. "You can't die here," she said. "You have too much left to do, and I refuse to lose another I love."

As her spirit flowed into the gemstone, the sword's glow surrounded Ciarán. She set her palm on the Altar Stone, still stained with her blood. Caladbolg's light spread until it filled the inner ring like a blinding sun. When the glimmer faded, Alais found herself in Stonehenge at sunset, kneeling by Ciarán's body, the sword clutched in her hand. The Danish lord held Ciarán in his arms. Ciarán's chest heaved with breath.

"Thank the Lord," she said.

Beside her, the Dane was muttering like a fool, his wide eyes darting between her and Ciarán. Of the Dane's words, she could recognize only a single one.

"*Mirakel.*"

AFTER THE SUN VANISHED BENEATH THE HORIZON, CIARÁN'S EYELIDS fluttered and he slowly came to consciousness, lying on the Altar Stone. Alais caressed his face until he looked ready to talk. "Did that creature speak to you?"

Ciarán nodded weakly. "It was a trap." He sucked in a long breath. "The demon led me here, to be killed by that thing."

"That thing will never kill anyone ever again," she said.

"How did you do it?" he asked. "How did you save me?"

"At Avalon, I learned from the Lady of the Lake. I can use the power, and I can use Enoch's device. Its fire destroyed that monster."

Ciarán gazed at her with wonder in his eyes. "I suppose a lot *has* changed. But we still don't know anything more about the Key to the Abyss."

Alais took Ciarán's hand. "I know where the Key's location will be revealed. I made that thing confess, only to realize my dreams have been showing me the place ever since we left Rosefleur."

"Where?"

"The Temple of Venus and Roma, on the night when Venus passes through the constellation Andromeda into Aries. We still have time, but not much. And we have a long way to travel."

A ghost of a smile crossed his lips. "As luck would have it, I happen to be an oarsman on the fastest ship in the sea. I'll need to convince the captain, of course," he said, nodding to the Dane who still knelt by his side, looking as if he was trying to understand their conversation. "But I suspect he'll come around."

Alais drew a deep breath, thinking how strange this journey had become. Yet at last, their path forward looked clear, even as she was struck by the irony of it all.

For once again, all roads led to Rome.

PART IV

Then I saw an angel coming down from Heaven holding in his hand the key to the bottomless pit and a great chain.

—Revelation 20:1

THE EMPEROR AND THE POPE

On the eve of the Roman New Year, in Saint Peter's Basilica, Pope Gregory presided over mass on the feast of Saint Sylvester. The day honored the pope who had founded the basilica during the reign of Emperor Constantine. Yet it was not lost on Gregory that this was the same pope who had authored the cryptic note about the End of Days that sent Gerbert on his faraway quest to find the Psalter of Pope Callixtus. Or that tomorrow would bring the first day of Anno Domini 999, which meant the millennium was but a year away.

An array of bishops and canons joined the pope in the chancel where, atop columns from Solomon's Temple, a silver canopy stretched above the high altar. Down the length of the cavernous nave, beneath glittering oil lamps and amid rows of towering marble columns, knelt the thousands who attended the mass. First among them was Otto kneeling in a white tunic and cloak, flanked by Heribert of Cologne and Eckard of Meissen. Dozens of nobles, both Saxon and Roman, knelt behind them, followed by a host of the emperor's guard, an assemblage of the papal Curia, and a crowd of monks, priests, and nuns. Beyond them genuflected throngs of pilgrims from across Christendom and hundreds of common

Romans. Only the strong scent of incense masked the stench of so many people crammed beneath the basilica's lofty roof, all awaiting the pope's blessing at the end of the mass.

Gregory stretched out his arms and the congregation bowed their heads. *"Benedicat vos omnipotens Deus: Pater et Filius et Spiritus Sanctus." May almighty God bless you: the Father, and the Son, and the Holy Spirit.* "Amen."

Upon the dismissal, he followed the procession of bishops and canons down the center aisle to a psalm of joy chanted by a monastic choir. When the procession reached the vestibule, one of the canons announced in a booming voice: *"Ite missa est!"*

"Deo gratias," the congregation replied. *Thanks be to God.*

As the congregation filed out of the basilica, Gregory gathered with the rest of the clergy in the atrium known as the Garden of Paradise. Among the garden's ferns and fountains, he greeted nobles who wished to offer their respects and kiss the Fisherman's ring, all the while keeping an eye out for his cousin. Otto's behavior of late concerned Gregory, for ever since their audience with Nilus da Rossano, his cousin had become prone to fits of melancholy. And it was becoming harder to shake him from those moods.

Gregory craned his neck toward the vestibule's open doors, only to have his view eclipsed by a hulking priest with bearded jowls. "A mass most excellent, Your Holiness," the priest said, before bowing to kiss the Fisherman's ring. "I am humbled to be in your service."

"Father Ugo," Gregory replied, deeming it futile to try to peer around the giant man's shoulder. "We've been blessed to have a quaestor of your talents in the Lateran Palace. In the months since you joined the Curia, I cannot recall a priest who could get more done in this wretched city."

Ugo Grassus gave a sly grin. "I've been ferrying through its channels for a lifetime."

"Of course." As the quaestor bowed again, Gregory spied Margrave Eckard emerging from the vestibule. Otto was not with him. "Excuse me, Father." Gregory strode to the margrave's side. "Where's the emperor?"

Eckard sighed. "Praying, Your Holiness."

With a furrowed brow, Gregory stepped back into the vestibule. He peered down the nave, where a white-clad figure lay prostrate at the crossing. The congregation had thinned to small groups of pilgrims admiring the mosaics along the walls, and a contingent of guardsmen lingering in the shadows of the left transept with Heribert of Cologne.

Gregory walked toward the prostrate figure, his footfalls echoing through the basilica. Otto stood when Gregory reached him.

"Why are you lingering?" Gregory asked.

Otto's face was pale, his eyes red. "Because I thirst for absolution."

"I can grant you that."

"No, cousin." Otto shook his head. "Your sins are equal to mine. Both of us stand condemned."

Gregory grimaced. "That hermit was just a man, sympathetic to Byzantium and partial to a traitor. His words hold no sway over an emperor and a pope."

"Nilus da Rossano is a living saint."

"Anointed by whom?"

"By God Himself." Otto gazed at the mosaic gracing the massive archway over the crossing. At its apex, Christ in all His glory sat on a gilded throne with Saint Peter to his right and Constantine to his left. A silver nimbus surrounded the emperor's head as he presented a miniature version of the basilica to the glorified Christ.

"Constantine," Otto said, "built the bridge between emperor and pope when he gave Pope Sylvester this place. As emperor, he was the defender of Christianity and the protector of the Church. That obligation now falls to me, cousin, for we are both servants of Christ on earth. Yet Constantine and Sylvester were holy men, while we have fallen into sin."

Heat rushed up Gregory's neck. "You've let that hermit fill your head with poison."

Otto shook his head and gave an odd smile. "Saint Nilus has shown us the wickedness of our ways. John Philagathos gave us love as children, as a godfather should, and yet we repaid his love with violence. So now we stand condemned."

"Yet you refuse the absolution that's within my God-given power to grant," Gregory said, arms crossed. "So how shall you get it?"

"I'm leaving."

Gregory blinked. "What?"

"I have lands to the south," Otto said. "I shall leave for them in a fortnight, and once there I'll walk barefoot up Monte Gargano to prostrate myself before Nilus da Rossano and beg for absolution."

A knot tightened in Gregory's gut. "You can't leave, the city's still not safe. The Crescentii lurk like rodents in the shadows and the Brotherhood of the Messiah lingers, too. If you're the defender of the Church, then stay here and defend it!"

Otto gave a sigh. "So long as I stand condemned, I'm unworthy to defend God's Church. Your papal guard can protect the Holy See."

"Now is not the time to test them while you're off on some witless pilgrimage!"

"This is no fool's journey, but a quest for salvation." Otto started down the nave, then stopped and looked at Gregory. "While I'm gone, cousin, perhaps you should think of your own salvation."

THE MORE GREGORY THOUGHT ABOUT OTTO'S DEPARTURE, THE MORE the knot tightened in his gut. He too had felt the sting of Nilus's rebuke, but he had long concluded it meant nothing. The hermit was no saint, just another pawn of the patriarch of Constantinople. But now, that old man had become more dangerous than a serpent, luring Otto and his guardsmen away from Rome. The Crescentii could not have done a better job had they done it themselves.

Standing in the basilica's nave where Otto had left him, Gregory whispered the words of a psalm. "Lord God, save me from the arrows that fly by day." With a sigh, he knew he needed a solution to this problem. He felt certain he could persuade Eckard to leave some men behind, for surely the margrave would appreciate the mistake Otto was making. And he could force the bishops to lend him soldiers, and double the size of the papal guard. But what of the Crescentii, he wondered, before a voice called from the vestibule.

"Your Holiness." Rumeus strode down the nave, where only a few canons lingered. "We should return to the palace."

Gregory pursed his lips. "The emperor is leaving Rome."

Rumeus furrowed his brow. "Whatever for?"

Gregory gestured toward the mosaic of Constantine. "Because that hermit convinced him he was unworthy to fulfill Constantine's role as protector of the Church. So now he's determined to walk barefoot up Monte Gargano so the hermit can absolve him of his sins."

Rumeus set his jaw. "Over your treatment of John Philagathos."

"John the Greek was a traitor! Even the great Constantine would have understood that in his day." Gregory glanced at the mosaic of the hallowed emperor handing the miniature basilica to the Savior with his right hand, while his left hand clutched a prayer book. Gregory's gaze lingered there. He had not noticed that detail before.

"Monte Gargano is on the east coast of Italy," Rumeus said, "less than a two-week ride. I doubt his absence will—"

"Wait." Gregory held up a hand, still staring at the mosaic. *Otto said Constantine built a bridge with the Church—a bridge builder.* "Didn't you tell me the Roman emperors once held the title *Pontifex Maximus?*"

"Yes, Your Holiness," Rumeus said. "Until that title passed to the popes."

Gregory shook his head. "The answer's been staring us in the face. In *Pontifex's* gift to the bishop of Rome."

Rumeus scratched his head. "Are you referring to the riddle Gerbert found from Pope Sylvester?"

"Yes." Gregory repeated the riddle from memory:

> *Seek the mysteries Solomon bore.*
> *Through sacred ring from Enoch's lore.*
> *In Pontifex's gift to the bishop of Rome.*
> *The secret lies in sacred tome.*

"Look at the mosaic," Gregory said. "Constantine, as *Pontifex Maximus,* gave this basilica to the bishop of Rome." He pointed at the prayer book clutched in Constantine's left hand. "But that may not have been his only gift to Pope Sylvester."

"The Psalter?"

"A sacred book."

Rumeus' eyes widened. "The secret lies in sacred tome!"

"And if Pope Sylvester built this basilica . . ." Gregory tipped his head, estimating the gabled roof was nearly a hundred feet high, and the archway over the crossing stood more than half that height. *That's taller than the Aurelian Walls.* He spied a canon straightening up a shrine to Saint Evasius halfway down the nave. "Rumeus, grab that canon and ask him how they clean this mosaic."

"Of course," Rumeus said, scurrying after the canon.

The nervous canon informed them of a series of wooden stairs that climbed to the rafters and of the platform the canons could attach to ropes and a system of pulleys. Anchored to the rafter above the crossing, the platform allowed lay servants to polish the mosaic. Gregory demanded that the canons set up the contraption. When they had secured the platform with ropes, just as the canon described, Gregory insisted on being the one to climb out on it. The canons watched with ashen faces as Gregory stepped out onto the platform, which creaked and swayed under his weight. He touched the mosaic, marveling at the skill of the artists who created it. Tens of thousands of golden tiles made up the background on which Saint Peter and Constantine knelt before the Savior, while white-robed angels waited in the wings. Thousands of more-colorful tiles comprised the robes of the three figures in the center of the arch, artistry so fine it took Gregory's breath away.

As the canons pulled the platform toward the massive figure of Constantine, Gregory realized the Psalter within the emperor's hand was larger than a Saxon shield. When he could touch the tiles that comprised the Psalter, he began searching for some that were loose. He found none among the brown tiles that formed the book's cover, but the tiles that made up a silver cross on the face of the book shifted slightly at his touch. While the entire cross was mortared together, there was no mortar between it and the rest of the Psalter. Working his fingers into the unmortared space, he wriggled the cross free of the mosaic. He set it on the wooden platform and reached into the space where the cross had been. His fingers touched something cold and metallic, and cylindrical in shape.

He pulled the object free, and found himself staring at a scroll case. The vessel was made of burnished gold decorated with gemstones of lapis and emerald, ruby and amber. Each cap featured a pentagram inlaid in silver, and the cylinder had a helical shape, like a twisted rope. The shape reminded him of the twisting columns that framed the high altar. Constantine had brought them to Rome from the temple in Jerusalem. *King Solomon's Temple.* "The mysteries Solomon bore," Gregory said under his breath.

He returned the cross to its rightful place in the mosaic, then urged the wide-eyed canons to bring the creaking platform back to the landing where Rumeus waited with the pale-faced canons. "Rumeus," Gregory announced, "we have work to do. I'll deal with the mess my cousin created, but in the meantime I need you to do something."

"What, Your Holiness?" Rumeus asked.

"Find me Gerbert of Aurillac."

51

THE PALACE SPY

At twilight, Theodora hurried to the Basilica of Santa Maria in Domnica at the base of the Caelian Hill, a half mile from the Lateran Palace. The basilica, with its gabled roof of terra cotta tiles, basked in the rose-hued sky between a copse of oak trees and the massive ruined arches of the Claudian Aqueduct. For months now, the basilica had been the place where she conspired with the brotherhood's spy within the palace, and today she was hungry for the secrets he would bring her.

She opened the twin oak doors and stepped into the deserted basilica. Inside, the air was thick with the smell of tallow candles illuminating a columned nave and a chancel with an apse bearing a mosaic of the Virgin Mary and infant Jesus. She scurried down the nave and ducked into a confessional in one of the transepts.

At the screen dividing the confessional, she knelt and bowed her head. "I confess to almighty God, and to you Father, that I have sinned and desire absolution. For the thousand years are ending, and the Savior soon returns."

"And when he comes," answered the familiar voice beyond the screen, "may no foreigner sit on Saint Peter's throne."

"Amen, Father. What tidings do you bring?"

"Good ones," the spy replied. "Tomorrow, the emperor and his entourage will leave Rome for Monte Gargano so the emperor can seek absolution from Nilus da Rossano. Margrave Eckard and Heribert of Cologne shall travel with him, as will most of the warriors of Meissen and Breisgau. Only a small contingent will remain in the Aventine Palace, leaving the Holy See to fend for itself."

Theodora's eyes widened. "So the pope's efforts failed?"

"The pope tried mightily to convince his cousin to stay, but the young emperor is especially pious and fears terribly for his soul. He believes God will not spare him on Judgment Day without Nilus's forgiveness."

She tipped her head back and allowed her elation to wash over her, for everything was unfolding as planned. "How long will he be gone?"

"A month, my lady," the spy said. "Maybe two. But it won't matter if we act with haste."

Theodora sighed. "There is a complication."

"Oh?"

"Naberus is waiting, for some reason," she explained. "And he has yet to tell why."

"Has he not heard? The early bird catches the worm. The pope is shaken by Otto's decision. There's no cause to wait."

Theodora shook her head. "He can be obstinate."

"And *you* can be persuasive. You are beautiful, Theodora, and few men can resist your allure. Now go with God, for He is good."

"May His mercy endure forever," she said, closing her eyes. If only her spy knew what he was asking. Naberus seemed immune to her charms, and each time she tried to oppose him, it was she who fell under his spell. He was unlike other men, strangely sensual and primal in his passion. Afterward, she would hate herself for it, for each time felt like a betrayal of Crescentius, who might be alive today had Naberus not turned against him. Yet kneeling in the confessional, she reminded herself that the pope and his cousin were the ones who killed her lover. And it was that for which she craved vengeance. This time, Naberus would have to listen.

Darkness had fallen by the time she reached the ruins outside

Trajan's Market. She stole through a maze of archways to the door to the brotherhood's lair, where she was greeted by Simeon.

"Where is Naberus?" she asked tersely.

Simeon frowned. "In his observatory."

She bid Simeon a brisk farewell and headed for the stairwell that climbed five stories to the topmost reaches of the market. She ascended the torchlit stairs, only to be met by one of Naberus's towering Greek warriors guarding the door to the observatory. Naberus had returned from Constantinople with eight of these Greeks, each of whom stood closer to seven feet than six, muscled like Roman statues and as stoic as Basilian monks. That was a shame, for they were handsome men with long black hair braided so that it fell like a horse's tail from beneath the polished iron helms that covered all but the center of their faces. Along with these eight warriors, Naberus had brought one more: a pale-skinned monster of a man who loomed a full head and a half above the already towering Greeks. She had never seen that one's face, for he concealed it behind a great helm with a crown shaped like the head of the Nemean lion and a burnished facemask cast in the image of Hercules. Only the holes through which his dark eyes stared, and his breath through the slit for his mouth, gave proof of a living man behind that mask. That one unnerved her, and she was grateful it was not he who guarded the observatory.

"I must speak with Naberus," she told the warrior.

He nodded and knocked on the door, opening it when a voice announced: "Come in."

She stepped inside an antechamber where a dozen amphora stood against a wall. These were more gifts Naberus had brought back from Byzantium, filled with enough Greek fire to burn the Lateran Palace to the ground. She did not know the true purpose for which he intended to use them, for he kept that detail as secret as his plans for the pope.

After passing through an archway into the observatory, she found Naberus clad in his black cassock. He stood, wine goblet in hand, before one of the windows where a brass sighting tube sat surmounted on a tripod. His raven Hermes perched on an armillary sphere on a nearby table, while his two mastiffs, Set and Grimm, lounged in the chamber's center beneath a wheel-shaped candelabrum that illuminated tapestries of the known world and the constellations on the far wall.

"To what do I owe this pleasure?" Naberus asked.

"I have tidings from our spy in the palace," she said. "Tomorrow, the emperor will leave Rome for Monte Gargano. The Holy See will lie unprotected, and we've been urged to strike quickly against the Saxon pope."

Naberus set down his wine. "The time's not right."

"Why not?" she snapped. "Why give the pope time to find a new protector?"

"When the time comes, there shall be no one who can protect him, I assure you. Until then, we must be patient."

Theodora crossed her arms. "I've waited seven months for my vengeance. If I am to wait more, I deserve to know why."

"We wait for the stars to align." Naberus glanced at his sighting tube. "At the Giant's Ring, I foresaw the very moment you shall taste your vengeance."

"When?" she demanded.

"Five weeks from now, on the night of the Feast of Saint Simeon of Jerusalem, when Venus passes through the constellation Andromeda into Aries. A great portent will occur that night in the Temple of Venus and Roma, and on that night the world as we know it shall forever change. And Pope Gregory's life shall be the instrument of that transformation."

"Enough!" Theodora's face grew flushed as her anger rose. "Why on earth must we wait five weeks for stars and portents while you talk in riddles? Our spy in the place insists we should strike as soon as the emperor leaves Rome."

"Is this spy your master or your servant?" He reached for her cheek. She pulled away, but his fingertips grazed her skin, sending a tingle down her neck. "I serve only one master, and his will shall not be denied."

"Who is it?" She pressed her lips thin. "Have you made some arrangement with the Byzantine emperor?"

"Basil the Bulgar-Slayer?" Naberus scoffed. "My master has slain far more than Bulgars. Mine is the one who started it all, when the sons of God went into the daughters of men. His seed gave life to a bloodline that has lived in secret for centuries, as empires grew and empires crumbled. A bloodline which even more than you yearns for vengeance. This is the blood of my ancestors, and it's similar to the blood I believe flows through you."

Theodora threw up her hands. "What are you saying?"

"That I believe you are special," he said, reaching for her hand; this time she let him take it. "There's a reason you have the face of an angel and the figure of a goddess. I'll learn for certain if I'm right at the Temple of Venus and Roma, on the very I night I swear to you Pope Gregory will die. And then, we all shall have our revenge."

He drew her close and kissed her.

"I don't understand," she said, her lips trembling.

"You will in time, and I will be the one who helps you see." He kissed her again. She wanted to push him away and demand more answers, but with each kiss the barrier between them crumbled like a wall of sand. As she fell deeper under his spell, she let him have her, and then nothing else seemed to matter.

Not even that, once again, Naberus had won.

THE RETURN TO ROME

E ver since *Lindworm* entered the Mediterranean Sea, God's foul weather had stalked her like a school of sharks. Storm clouds brought seething rains and pounding waves, and at times the storms forced the crew to beach the vessel until the weather passed. Other times, the crew fought through the rain and the swells, bringing curses from Magnus, who swore that Rán and her daughters were furious at *Lindworm's* crew.

"Rán's a jealous bitch, Irish," he spat one morning as brine blasted over the hull. "We're paying the price for having that woman of yours onboard."

"We're lucky to have her," Ciarán said. "Or have you already forgotten how she saved us from Jarl Orn and his crew?"

Magnus flashed a smile. "We would've beaten those bastards with or without her. Though she's not hard on the eyes, I'll give you that." His smile turned to a grimace as a swell swamped the starboard side, drenching them both. "But that's what makes Rán such a jealous bitch."

Ciarán did not believe in Rán and did not care what Magnus thought, for all that mattered was that Alais was with him. She huddled in the aft, wrapped in the midnight-blue cloak that Jarl

Holger had purchased for her in Brest, along with a like-colored dress, a pair of leather boots, a pewter chalice, and a crystal. The latter two items, Ciarán knew, were tools needed to practice the same mystic arts that Dónall and Remi had mastered from the Book of Maugis d'Aygremont. That Alais had learned the craft from one of the Fae, and survived the ordeal that followed, was hard to fathom. Yet whatever had happened in Avalon, it had changed her. She looked older now, and wiser, with fine creases at the corners of her eyes and strands of gray mixed in her raven hair. Something else about her was different, too, for the woman who emerged from Avalon was more strong-minded than before, as if the ordeal had tempered her spirit like a blacksmith forged iron into steel.

She remained, however, the same woman Ciarán loved. He knew that when they first kissed, and when he held her in his arms while she wept after hearing the story of Khalil's sacrifice. Somehow, Ciarán believed, they were bound together in their chase to fulfill the prophecy, for what else could explain the miracle by which they were reunited, or how she had saved Caladbolg from a watery grave? Khalil had been right—God had given them signs, and those signs had led him back to Alais and set them on this voyage back to Rome.

Despite the foul weather during the voyage, Alais was certain they would reach Rome before Venus entered Aries. In Avalon, she had learned that celestial event would bring a portent that would reveal the whereabouts of Sirra, a Fae who had possessed the Key for the last three thousand years. That their journey had come down to a search for some mysterious Fae was not what Ciarán had expected. But such was the nature of mysteries.

After *Lindworm* crossed the Tyrrhenian Sea and neared the mouth of the Tiber, Magnus and a red-bearded Dane named Stóri reduced the sail, while Jorundr and Strong Bjorn removed the dragon's head from the prow. Holger leaned on the larboard gunwale and gestured for Ciarán to join him. The jarl had done so often ever since they left England, where he removed Ciarán's slave collar and declared him a freeman and full member of their crew.

"The tide looks high," Holger grumbled.

Ciarán peered out at the murky sea through a drizzle of rain. In the distance loomed the ancient archways and columns of the ruined port of Ostia, half submerged by water. "The river's flooded," he realized.

"What will that mean for the city?" Alais asked.

Ciarán shook his head. "We'll know soon enough."

Once the crew dropped the oars and began rowing the longship upriver, it was clear the Tiber had overflowed its banks, turning the lowlands into shallow lakes and nearby fields into marshlands. Floodwaters obscured the river's course, so Holger positioned Ciarán on the prow to look for signs the ship might be straying beyond the Tiber's banks. After the longship brushed a sandbar, drawing a loud curse from Magnus, Alais went to Ciarán's aid. "The river snakes north here," she said, pointing in that direction.

"How can you remember?"

"I just do. It's odd, but I feel like I know this river as well as the Clain back home."

Ciarán smiled. "Then I'll let you do the navigating, and I won't have to listen to Magnus hollering at me."

Alais proved to be a capable guide, allowing Ciarán to focus more on their surroundings. After a while, he spied a fishing boat upriver. At the sight of the longship, the trio of fisherman onboard began scrambling to pull in their nets, and Ciarán heard more than one panicked cry.

"*Pax vobiscum!*" he called out. *Peace be with you!*

The fishermen hesitated.

Ciarán held up his arms. "We mean you no harm."

A jowly fisherman with a potbelly nodded back.

"Is the city flooded?" Ciarán asked.

"Been flooded for five days," the fisherman called back. "You picked the wrong time to sail to Rome. Half the city's underwater, and the fever's running rampant."

Alais flashed Ciarán a concerned look. He'd almost forgotten about the Roman fever that Évrard had warned about the last time they were here.

Holger joined them on the prow. "What is it?"

"The city's flooded," Alais answered in Danish, having learned the language on the six-week voyage. "And stricken by fever."

Ciarán sighed. "All we need is a good famine, and it'll truly feel like the end times." He called back to the fisherman, "What's the emperor doing about it?"

"Nothing," the fisherman replied. "The emperor's left the city and the pope's holed up in the Lateran Palace. If you're hoping for law and order, you've come to the wrong place."

Ciarán glanced at Alais. "Seems a bit's changed since we left."

"In my dreams," she said, "I didn't see a flood."

"Maybe the ruins aren't flooded." Ciarán thanked the fisherman for the news, while Holger returned to the steering oar.

When they reached the Aurelian Walls, they saw that water had risen a third of the way up the great stone walls; and when the ship rowed through the gap between the two towers, the water completely obscured the great chain that could seal off the river. Inside the walls, the city was gray and murky, and even the terra-cotta tiles of the buildings and churches appeared dull amid the persistent drizzle. Treetops rose above the floodwaters, which submerged the first floors of the cramped houses and shops crowded around the Tiber. Between the homes, the narrow streets and alleys had turned into canals, where a few Romans paddled on skiffs. But other than these few and the occasional egret and heron skimming for fish, there was an eerie quiet to Rome, as if the citizens had abandoned the city for higher ground.

At the Porto di Ripa Grande, floodwaters submerged the wharves, and what few boats remained were moored with ropes to the port's square tower, which rose like an island from the river. As *Lindworm* approached, Ciarán spotted the dockmaster peering out from the tower's window.

"Who's the old geezer?" Magnus asked.

"The dockmaster," Ciarán said. "He was here the last time we were in Rome."

"He's not the only one," Alais said, her eyes narrow. "Look." She pointed to the tower's peaked roof, where a fat black raven perched, watching them.

Magnus squinted. "So what? It's a bloody raven."

"Naberus da Roma had a raven," Ciarán reminded him.

Magnus scratched his close-cropped beard. "It could be any raven."

"No." Ciarán touched the scar beneath his eye. "I know that one. That's the raven who gave me this."

"Which means Naberus knew we were coming," Alais said.

"And he had his bird waiting for us," Ciarán realized. "But that doesn't mean we can't stop the messenger. Magnus, grab your bow!"

Magnus rushed to the weapons rack and strung his bow. But as he pulled an arrow from its quiver, the raven sprang from the tower, beating its great wings.

"Hurry!" Ciarán yelled.

Magnus drew back an arrow and let it fly. The shaft sped forward, but with a flap of wings, the raven banked. The arrow missed its mark, arching harmlessly into the water while the raven disappeared in the charcoal sky somewhere over the heart of Rome.

Where Naberus da Roma waited.

THE MYSTERIES SOLOMON BORE

lais did not blame the dockmaster for hiding behind one of the tower's dilapidated windowsills, gazing warily at the longship filled with violent-looking Danes as they began mooring *Lindworm* to the tower.

The dockmaster did not budge from the windowsill when Ciarán tried to speak with him, and Alais realized the old man no longer recognized the Irishman. Ciarán appeared nothing like the clean-shaven monk who left Rome a half a year ago; rather, with his shaggy hair and brine-seasoned beard, he looked more like a Northman now, which did little to quell the old man's apprehension. Alais worked her way through the Danes mooring the vessel and called to the dock-master in Latin. Recognition dawned in his eyes. "Milady," he said.

After she told him Brother Ciarán was on board, the dockmaster's eyes grew wide. "A priest," the dockmaster said with a gap-toothed grin. "There's a priest waiting for you. He was hoping you'd come back. He promised me ten denarii for word of your return. I send for him now!"

For a moment, Alais wondered if the priest was Father Michele. She had thought about the kindly old canon of the Basilica of Santa Maria Nova often since learning about the portent that would supposedly happen in the ruins of the Temple of Venus and Roma. Had Father Michele been waiting for her to return there? Yet why would he do so?

At dusk, she learned the answer to her musings. A skiff crossed the flooded Tiber propelled by two oarsmen clad in scarlet tunics and crested helms. A black-robed priest stood at the bow holding a lantern that cast a yellow glow across the gray waters. He was not the height of Father Michele, and instead of the old priest's broad-brimmed hat, a deep cowl hid the man's face. As the skiff neared the longship, Alais noticed chainmail beneath the oarsmen's tunics and swords at their sides. Several of Holger's crew rested their hands on the pommels of their own blades, while the jarl stood, arms crossed, at Ciarán's side.

"Who comes here?" Ciarán asked.

The priest drew back his cowl revealing a ginger goatee and an aquiline nose. "The Archbishop of Ravenna," said Gerbert of Aurillac. His gaze flitted from Holger to the crew of armed Danes. "You continue to keep curious company, Brother Ciarán. And I see you've undergone a change in grooming, too."

Alais glanced at Ciarán, who looked surprised at the appearance of the man who had helped murder his parents. Though she saw no anger in his expression. "Pardon my appearance, Your Excellency, but we've been on a rather long journey."

Gerbert nodded slowly. "It appears so. Did you find what you were expecting at the Giant's Ring?"

"No." Ciarán shook his head. "It was a trap. The demon's words lured me there to die."

"Yet here you are alive," Gerbert replied with a ghost of a smile.

"Aye," Ciarán said. "We learned enough there to know we had to come back here if we're to find the Key. But how did you know we'd return?"

Gerbert clasped his hands. "I merely hoped you would. I have something to show you, but you must come with me."

Alais whispered to Ciarán in Danish. "Can we trust him?"

"We've no choice but to trust him," Ciarán said under his breath, before turning back to Gerbert. "Where are we going?"

"To the Lateran Palace," Gerbert said, "for an audience with the pope."

Alais shot Ciarán an astonished glance. Ciarán too appeared astounded by this news, and when Holger learned of it, the jarl insisted on joining them. Gerbert seemed dismayed at the idea of a Northman entering the heart of the Holy See, but he acquiesced once Ciarán assured him Holger was a lord of great repute.

Holger shifted his brawny form onto a bench in the skiff's stern behind one of the oarsmen, while Alais settled in the bow next to Ciarán. He wore his old baldric over his weather-stained tunic with Caladbolg in its sheath. After they'd left England, he had retrieved the baldric from the hirdman Magnus, who surrendered it only after Ciarán agreed the Dane could keep the fine mail hauberk that once belonged to Maugis d'Aygremont.

Sitting across from them, Gerbert eyed the gemstone in Caladbolg's pommel. "Is that what I think it is?" the archbishop asked with a hint of awe in his voice.

"Aye, Your Excellency," Ciarán said.

"Dear God." Gerbert made the sign of the cross. "Everything you wrote about is true, isn't it?"

"I fear so," Ciarán said.

As the oarsmen began rowing the skiff across the Tiber, Gerbert's gaze settled on the water. "I want you to know, Brother Ciarán, while you were gone I journeyed to France and visited the priory of Saint Bastian's."

The name gave Alais chills, though she sensed regret in the archbishop's voice.

"I went to the ossuary," he continued, "just as you had written. I saw the temple to the Dragon and the unholy beast that dwelt there. It took five soldiers to put it down before we burned its remains." He looked back at Ciarán. "I believe you now. Lucien of Saint-Denis had fallen in league with the Devil, and his lies misled me into that terrible situation involving your parents."

Alais put a hand on Ciarán's thigh; she could feel his muscles tense. "They died for the cause we pursue today," Ciarán said. "As did Dónall, and Brother Remi, and Khalil al-Pârsâ, and the others who lost their lives since this all began."

Hearing Khalil's name brought a pang to Alais' chest. So many had died, and Khalil's death was the worst of all. *It happened half a world away, and I never had the chance to say good-bye.* The pain lingered, and she wondered if the wound left by his passing would ever heal.

"I'm sorry for all that both of you have lost," Gerbert said.

Alais wiped away a tear as the oarsmen rowed the skiff down a street with half-submerged tenement houses crowded around a large basilica that stood across from the Aventine Hill. Past the Aventine loomed the Palatine Hill, and atop its summit, the ruins of the imperial palaces appeared haunting in the eerie gloom that pervaded Rome. A damp mist began to fall as the skiff passed between the hills, over the ruins of Circus Maximus, where charioteers and cheering Romans once reveled in Alais' dreams.

Gerbert steepled his fingers. "In all your travels, have you ever heard the name Sirra?"

Alais glanced at Ciarán, who looked as surprised as she at the mention of the name. "I've seen her," she told the archbishop.

Gerbert raised a brow. "You found her?"

"No," Alais said. "In England, I came across the isle of Avalon that Archbishop Turpin wrote about in his journal. There, I met Nimue, the Lady of the Lake. She showed me a vision, like a dream. That's how I saw Sirra. She was a warrior in battle during the first cycle of the prophecy." Alais recalled Lilith's sudden attack on Sirra, and the image of the silver-haired Fae wading toward the boat with the heron-shaped prow where Saint Michael waited. "Nimue swore that Sirra still lives, but she sacrificed her immortal form, changing her skin so that in each millennium she never appears as she did the time before. I know it sounds hard to believe, but if you had seen what I saw in Avalon . . ."

"After what I saw at Saint Bastian's, my lady, I would not doubt you." Gerbert lifted his chin. "You know, then, that Sirra is the angel who holds the Key to the Abyss. We found reference to her in an ancient text hidden in Rome by Pope Sylvester more than six hundred years ago. It was the missing link, really."

Ciarán shook his head. "What do you mean?"

"When I read your letter," Gerbert explained, "I was struck by a question. If the events of this prophecy have occurred three times before, then why was there such mystery about the journey and the Key? Why hadn't the men who fulfilled the prophecy in millennia past written lore to aid mankind in future millennia? It turns out one had. Saint Sylvester came to possess this secret and protected it. But with the turmoil that plagued Rome and the papacy in the centuries that followed, Sylvester's secret became lost and forgotten. Only through a fortuitous discovery by Pope Gregory do we have it now."

Ciarán shot Gerbert an incredulous look. "What does it say?"

"It tells how to find Sirra, and with her, the Key to the Abyss. But as you'll see, there are a few elements to this mystery that remain to be solved. Though with what you may have discovered at Stonehenge, and all the Lady Alais seems to have learned, I pray the two of you can help me find the solution."

Alais questioned whether she could help much more, for Nimue had never mentioned Sirra again after her first day in Avalon. Even more, Nimue had lied that day about Ciarán and Khalil, claiming they had burned to death. So who was to say Nimue was not spinning more lies with respect to Sirra's tale? All Alais could trust was what she saw in her mind's eye in the scrying pool, though she doubted that was enough.

As the skiff neared the Caelian Hill, Alais recalled Orionde's assurance that she still had a role to play. But what if that role had been fulfilled when she saved Caladbolg and helped Ciarán survive what happened at Stonehenge? Their journey, however, was far from over, and by the time they reached the flooded hillside, Alais could not help but wonder if there was more she was supposed to do before it ended.

SITTING IN THE SKIFF, CIARÁN WAS ASTOUNDED BY GERBERT'S revelation of a missing link. Khalil had always believed the magi who fulfilled the prophecy a millennium ago would have recorded their knowledge to aid the next generation, but Ciarán had dismissed this notion. And never once had he suspected such knowledge had been preserved by a long-dead pope. The Irish were forever wary of the papacy and the Church apparatus in Rome, so perhaps that's why he'd never given credence to the thought. Yet Maugis d'Aygremont, a Frankish Christian and paladin of Charlemagne, must not have known this secret either. Why else had he not referenced it in his writings?

Ciarán pondered these thoughts as the skiff approach the Caelian Hill. Only a scattering of structures stood amid the half-submerged trees and vineyards: a few churches, a monastery, and a vine-covered villa that appeared little more than a ruin. Where the hill rose above the floodwaters, a score of torches glowed in the fading dusk, held by horsemen clad in the same scarlet tunics and crested helms as the two oarsmen. In front of the riders waited a thin priest.

"We get off here," Gerbert announced.

As they disembarked, Ciarán recognized the priest as Father Niccolo from the day they were thrown out of the emperor's fortress. The horsemen escorted them across the hill to a stone-paved road that ran through an expanse of vineyards toward the Lateran Palace.

The Archbasilica of Saint John Lateran, crowned by twin spires, towered above the palace structures. The adjacent palace looked to be a cluster of marble-faced buildings, five and six stories high, its windows dancing with candlelight. On the top floors, pillared arcades ran beneath terra-cotta roofs, save for the most prominent structure, which featured an enormous balcony framed by marble columns supporting an elaborately adorned gable.

Holger gaped at the structure. "Your pope must be richer than a king."

"You have no idea," Ciarán said.

"It's larger than the palace at Poitiers," Alais observed in Latin.

Gerbert answered with a smug smile. "She was built with the

417

wealth of the Roman Empire, my lady. The palace and basilica were erected by Emperor Constantine as a gift to Pope Sylvester. The basilica, in fact, was Rome's first, which is why she bears the inscription, 'The Mother and Head of all churches in Rome and in the World.'"

As they entered the plaza, Ciarán marveled at the giant bronze statue of a bearded Constantine holding out his right hand while mounted on a massive stallion. Not far from it, atop a columnlike pedestal, sat a bronze sculpture of a she-wolf with feral eyes and drooping udders. "The wolf who suckled Romulus and Remus," Gerbert remarked, "the legendary founders of Rome."

Father Niccolo led the guests through the palace gates down marble halls and columned corridors adorned with mosaics and sculptures of a mastery Ciarán had never seen before. They stopped in a square vestibule with a bronze-plated door in the far wall. "We shall wait here for the pope," Father Niccolo said.

Before long, they were greeted by a portly, bald-headed priest in purple robes. "That," Gerbert told Ciarán under his breath, "is the venerable Rumeus, the papal archdeacon."

The archdeacon smoothed his robes and cleared his throat before announcing the pope. "All hail Gregory, *Pontifex Maximus, Servus Servorum Dei,* Vicar of Christ, and Lord Pope of the Apostolic See of Rome!"

The tall, blond-haired man who emerged in the hall was far younger than Ciarán expected. In fact, he appeared to be just a few years older than Ciarán himself. Dressed in a white cassock and red shoulder cap, Pope Gregory stood with a regal presence, though his skin looked pale and his face drawn, as if he had slept little the night before. Remembering his manners, Ciarán genuflected before the most powerful cleric in Christendom. Alais did the same, though Holger remained standing. "Kneel," Ciarán hissed. The Dane scowled at Ciarán, but grudgingly bent his knee to the pope.

"Your Holiness," Gerbert said, "I present to you Jarl Holger Horiksson of Denmark, the Lady Alais of the House of Poitiers, and Brother Ciarán of Hibernia."

Pope Gregory furrowed his brow. "I was expecting the Irishman, the lady, and a Moor. Not a Northman."

Ciarán sucked in a breath as Gerbert said, "Sadly, Khalil al-Pârsâ did not survive Brother Ciarán's voyage to England. But by the grace of God, Jarl Holger returned Brother Ciarán and Lady Alais to Rome."

"And this is Brother Ciarán?" the pope asked with a glare. "Has he abandoned his vows?"

"Forgive my appearance, Your Holiness," Ciarán answered before Gerbert could explain. "I've been on a long journey, and it's near a year's time since I've enjoyed the peace of a monastery."

The pope gestured at Caladbolg. "And I see you've taken up arms."

"Your Holiness," Gerbert interjected. "That's not some common sword. It's the device, the one in the Book of Enoch."

The pope's eyes widened. "The gemstone in the pommel?"

"Aye, Your Holiness," Ciarán said.

"You must understand," the pope confessed, "I find all this a bit hard to take in." He turned to his archdeacon. "Rumeus, that will be all for now."

"As you wish, Your Holiness," the archdeacon said with a nod.

After he and Father Niccolo departed, Gerbert pulled the handle of the bronze-plated door. "Pope Sylvester's secret lies inside."

Ciarán followed Pope Gregory and Alais into a candlelit chamber adorned with a mosaic on the far wall of a bearded pontiff reading a religious tome. In the center of the chamber stood an oak table, and on it lay the most ornate scroll case Ciarán had ever seen. Burnished gold covered the case, studded with emeralds, rubies, and ambers. More curious, however, was its shape, twisted like a rope in a pattern reminiscent of the four columns framing the altar in Saint Peter's Basilica.

After Holger entered the chamber, Gerbert closed the door. "This is the secret protected by Saint Sylvester and discovered by His Holiness," he said, picking up the case. He twisted off the cap and handed it to Ciarán. "Do you recognize that symbol?"

A five-pointed star inlaid in silver adorned the cap. Ciarán tried to recall all that Remi and Dónall had taught him of symbols, but realized Gerbert's question was rhetorical when the archbishop removed parchment from the case and kept on speaking. "There are seven leaves of parchment inside, all written in Hebrew."

"I cannot read Hebrew," Ciarán said.

"Fortunately, I can." Gerbert unfurled the parchment. "From the very first words, I realized the import of our discovery. 'The Testament of Solomon, son of David, who was king in Jerusalem, and mastered and controlled all spirits of the air, on the earth, and under the earth.'"

Ciarán blinked as he recognized the link between the case's shape and those words. "The scroll came from Solomon's Temple. That's why the case is twisted like the pillars in Saint Peter's, isn't it? Because Constantine brought them back from Jerusalem. Brother Dónall once told me King Solomon used his signet ring to subdue demons."

The pope narrowed his gaze and glanced at Gerbert.

"I told you he'd be of assistance," Gerbert said with a shrewd grin. "The signet ring was the Seal of Solomon, which contained the very gemstone in your sword's pommel. And the testament concerns Solomon's confrontations with demons who tormented Jerusalem during the building of the temple. It tells how he bound them and forced them to reveal their secrets. Near the end of the testament, Solomon confronts one of the fallen angels named Azazel. He, along with the rest of the fallen who suffered defeat when war broke out in Heaven, is imprisoned in a desert, beneath an object intended to seal that prison until the End of Days."

"The object's a pillar," Alais said. "I've seen it before."

"You've seen it?" Pope Gregory asked incredulously.

"It appears the Lady Alais has been having rather telling dreams," Gerbert explained, before shuffling through the leaves of parchment. "Azazel warns that the pillar shall fall upon the death of the angel who holds the key to the bottomless pit. And then Solomon writes this cryptic verse. 'Having heard this, I, Solomon, learned the angel's name is Sirra. Through this testament, with wisdom's light, may she be revealed so Azazel's prophecy never comes to pass.'"

As Gerbert finished reading, Ciarán was already working through the riddle. Two millennia ago, he reasoned, Solomon had used Enoch's device, so he must have known how to summon his soul light —*wisdom's light!* And it could reveal things otherwise hidden from the naked eye, like the secrets of Maugis' tome. "There's writing hidden in the scroll," he said.

Gerbert nodded. "A keen observation, but there's more. In the lid of the scroll case, we found a crystal, and when I infused it with the light, words appeared on the blank spaces of the seventh leaf of parchment, and on the back of it, as well."

Pope Gregory looked uneasy when Gerbert spoke of summoning his soul light, and Ciarán wondered what it must have taken Gerbert to convince the pope he was not some heretic or sorcerer who deserved to be burned at the stake.

"What did the words say?" Alais asked.

"They were instructions on how to construct a device." Gerbert reached under the table and pulled up something that looked like another of his scientific contraptions. Its frame was shaped like a pyramid made of iron rods. From its apex fell a cord attached to a diamond-shaped crystal the size of a large hazelnut. "This device."

"A pendulum?" Ciarán asked. "But what are you supposed to do with it?"

"That too was hidden within the instructions." Gerbert began placing six of the parchment leaves of on the table in two rows of three, holding their corners flat with pebbles. Then he set the pendulum on top of them. Its base aligned with the outer edges of the parchment leaves, fitting perfectly while the crystal dangled over the Hebrew words.

After blowing out several candles to darken the chamber, Gerbert turned to Ciarán. "Observe." He took the crystal and brought it to his lips before whispering a word of power. *"Eoh."* Within the crystal, a spark ignited, then settled into a warm glow. As he let the crystal go, it began swaying on its cord. With each swing of the pendulum, the crystal bathed the parchment in the light, and a shimmering image began to emerge from the Hebrew letters. After several passes, the images took clearer form, creating shapes and patterns that reminded Ciarán of Évrard's nautical charts.

"It's a map," Ciarán realized.

"Indeed," Gerbert said. "Solomon wrote that the crystal is tuned to Sirra's aura, which grows strongest when the star Ishtar—Venus in our parlance—passes through the constellation Andromeda into Aries, an event that will occur tomorrow night, on the Feast of Saint Simeon of Jerusalem. As you'll see, the way to finding her is hidden in the writings of the testament."

As the pendulum swung back and forth, the images shimmering from the Hebrew letters took on the shape of the continents: Europe, Africa, and the Arab lands. When the pendulum began to slow, the crystal's glow focused on a particular point, shining brighter than any other portion of the map. Soon, a blazing pinpoint of light fixed on the land of Italy, straight at the location of Rome.

"As fascinating as this is to watch," Gerbert continued, "it seems you already knew this, for why else would you return here at this hour? Yet this brings us to the first unsolved mystery. The pendulum shows us Sirra's in Rome. Yet it's one of the largest cities on earth. We could send the papal guard to search for her in every hovel and villa in Rome, but it could take weeks to do that. And all Solomon gave us is a cryptic clue. He wrote, 'Sirra will be found where Ishtar shines her light.' The problem, however, is that Ishtar, or Venus, is one of the *asters planetai,* a star whose light in the evening shines equally over all of Rome, and all of Italy, for that matter."

"The archbishop believes you can help solve this riddle," Pope Gregory said to Ciarán. "Can you?"

Ciarán already knew the answer, and with that knowledge it was easy to decipher the riddle in Solomon's words. "Aye, Your Holiness. As the archbishop says, Venus is one of the *asters planetai,* but she's also a goddess. That's the riddle: Venus has two meanings. So the question is, where in Rome would the light of a goddess shine the brightest?"

Gerbert raised a brow. "In one of the temples?"

"One in particular," Alais said. "The Temple of Venus and Roma.

I've seen that too in my dreams, and at Stonehenge I became certain it's where we'll find her."

"A pagan temple?" Pope Gregory rubbed his forehead. "You believe that's where we'll find this Sirra? And what of the Key to the Abyss? Saint Beatus claimed it's as tall as a man, yet there's barely anything left of the Temple of Venus and Roma, and nowhere to hide something so large."

Alais shook her head. "To find Sirra is to find the Key. That's all I was told."

Her words reminded Ciarán of something Blind Mikkel had said. *The Key is a mystery . . .* He recalled the gothi's story of Freya and the chain that bound Loki. Another myth like those of Venus and Andromeda. And now with Sirra, the answer to the mystery began to take shape like the map hidden in Solomon's scroll. "Of course," Ciarán muttered under his breath.

He glanced at the pope and Gerbert. Then, as certain as he was of anything, he told them. "I know where the Key is."

THE HEIR OF CONSTANTINE

"Where is it, then?" Pope Gregory asked, skeptical that Brother Ciarán's explanation would be any less farfetched than the woman's idea that this Key to the Abyss might be hidden in the sparse ruins of a Roman temple.

"If I may beg your pardon, Your Holiness," Ciarán said, "I believe Saint Beatus was wrong. We're not looking for a key like the one he depicted. And I think King Solomon knew that too, which is why he only has us searching for Sirra."

Gerbert gazed intently at the Irishman. "Are you suggesting there is no Key?"

"Yes and no," Ciarán replied. "Saint Beatus was describing the Key as it appears in the Book of Revelation, but as you once told me, Revelation is a *metaphora*. I didn't understand this point myself until I heard what the lady just said. It reminded me of something I learned on my journey and a theory my father and Brother Dónall long believed—that all myths, whether Roman, Sumerian, or Norse, have their origins in the events told in Genesis and the Book of Enoch, about the sons of God and the daughters of men. So beings that mythology deemed to be goddesses, like Venus, Ishtar, and Freya of the Northern myths, are one and the same. And my guess is they owe their true origins to the angel Sirra. King Solomon all but confirmed as much through his riddle about Ishtar's light."

"But what of the Key?" Gregory pressed. He rubbed the back of his neck. It was slick with sweat, even though he felt as chilled as if he were standing outside on a Midwinter Eve.

"I'm getting there, Your Holiness," Ciarán said. "When I was in Sweden, I learned the myth of Freya, a myth whose origins, I believe, lie in Sirra's history. Freya seized the power to bind Loki, the god of chaos, from a giant who killed her brother, Frey, the god originally imbued with that power. He was the god who first bound Loki, the devil in their myths, like the Dragon of Revelation imprisoned by the angel who held the Key to the bottomless pit. In the Northern myths, the power to bind is just that—a power that resided within Frey, but was stolen by the one who killed him, and then reclaimed by Freya when she slew his killer. I believe the Key and this power are one and the same. It's not a physical object, but something that resides within Sirra's veins. But if she were to die, that power would pass to her killer, who could use to it to free the Watchers, just like Azazel told Solomon. So to find Sirra *is* to find the Key, but we don't just need to find her, we need to protect her. Or Azazel's prophecy will come true, and the horrors Saint Sylvester sought to prevent will be upon us."

Gregory found all this difficult to fathom, but with Solomon's secret and this strange light, unlike anything he had ever seen, how could he dismiss any of it? All this time he had been warring against mortal enemies—Crescentius, Philagathos, and this brotherhood of fanatics—yet in the shadows, there may have been a far greater enemy waging its own secret war. A war that scripture had warned of for nearly a thousand years.

"You may have just solved our second mystery," Gerbert told Ciarán, "concerning the location of the Key itself."

"I believe it's true," Alais said, who appeared as amazed as Gerbert by what Ciarán had explained. "The theory fits with everything I learned about Sirra in Avalon."

Gregory, however, felt no sense of wonder over the Irishman's theory, for the weight of this discussion hung like a millstone around his neck. "So what do we do now?"

Gerbert clasped his hands. "We find Sirra, of course. Tomorrow night at the Temple of Venus and Roma, like Solomon's testament instructed."

"There's one thing, Your Excellency," Ciarán said. "We have to account for Naberus da Roma."

The name brought a pang to Gregory's chest. "How can you be sure Naberus has even returned to Rome?"

"Because I saw his raven, Your Holiness," Ciarán replied.

Gregory shook his head. "There are thousands of ravens in Rome."

"This one gave me these." Ciarán pointed to a trio of jagged scars beneath his left eye. "It was waiting for us at the Porto di Ripa, and it flew to its master the moment we arrived."

Gerbert pursed his lips. "If Naberus is among our enemies, we should assume the temple will be guarded. We must likewise assume he can muster the Crescentii loyalists who remain in Rome, and it's long been rumored he's aligned with the Countess Theodora and the Brotherhood of the Messiah."

"Then we'll take as many of my guardsmen as we need," Gregory insisted.

"*We,* Your Holiness?" Gerbert raised a brow. "You cannot come. Not only do you feel unwell, but you know my fear."

Gregory let out a sigh. "You give too much credence to that so-called demon's riddle."

"Demon's riddle?" Ciarán asked.

"The one you wrote about in your letter," Gerbert explained, "which warned that the heir of Constantine shall fall."

Ciarán cocked his head. "What does the heir of Constantine have to do with Pope Gregory?"

"Two words," Gerbert said. *"Pontifex Maximus.* That title belonged to every Roman emperor since Caesar Augustus until Constantine raised the Church into the position it holds today. In time, the title passed from the emperors to the popes, who used Constantine's title to supplant the emperors as the most powerful men in Rome. So you see, the heir to Constantine is none other than His Holiness, and I fear his life may be in danger."

Ciarán nodded slowly. "His Excellency is right, Your Holiness. At the Giant's Ring, I encountered another demon, more powerful than any I've ever seen. He called himself Mahway, one of the first of the Nephilim. He too spoke those words, and he called it a prophecy. Their prophecy."

"What greater target for the enemies of God," Gerbert said, "than the head of His Church?"

Gregory leaned on the table, aware of the weakness in his limbs. As much as he wanted to believe none of this was true, all this talk of demons was beginning to unnerve him. And Gerbert was right. He had not felt well in days, and the pain within his muscles and chest had been hard to bear at times. He drew a long breath, then exhaled. "What do you propose?"

"I'll find Sirra, Your Holiness," Ciarán said. "And I'll not go alone. After all, I have Jarl Holger and a shipful of spear-Danes and sword-Danes to stand by my side."

"Then it's settled," Gerbert declared. "Your Holiness will remain in the palace under the protection of the papal guard, and the rest of us will make for the temple tomorrow night." He turned to Alais. "Tell me, my lady, when you were with the Lady of the Lake, did she teach you more than the story of Sirra and the Key?"

"She taught me everything," Alais replied.

"Very well then," Gerbert said with a sly grin. "Between you and I, and the device Brother Ciarán is carrying in that scabbard, we should be more than a match for Naberus da Roma and whatever he has planned."

"I pray you're right," Gregory told him. "But a contingent of my papal guard *will* join you."

Gerbert nodded. "As you wish, Your Holiness."

Gregory closed his eyes as a wave of chills sent a shudder through his chest.

"What is it, Your Holiness?" Gerbert asked.

"It's no matter," Gregory said. "Find this Sirra, and may God be with you."

As he followed Gerbert from the chamber, Ciarán thought about the connection between the heir of Constantine and Pope Gregory, a link he had failed to recognize until now. Yet how would the death of a pope aid the fallen angels, as the demon's riddle now suggested? He did not know the answer, but felt certain Gerbert was right. The pope was in grave danger.

Father Niccolo was waiting for them in the foyer, and Gerbert turned to him at once. "Niccolo, tell Archdeacon Rumeus to double the pope's personal guard from here on out, and triple it tomorrow night. We cannot take any chances."

The thin priest nodded. "Yes, Your Excellency."

"And show our guests to their quarters," Gerbert said. "They will stay in the palace tonight."

Ciarán welcomed those words. The thought of rowing through the city this late at night seemed reckless, if not dangerous, and the thought of sleeping in a real bed instead of the longship sounded wonderful.

They bid farewell to Gerbert and followed Father Niccolo down one of the passageways. "The pope does look unwell," Alais told Ciarán under her breath.

"Aye, let's hope the palace has a good infirmarer." Ciarán remembered Évrard's warning about the Roman fever and prayed that whatever illness the pope might have was not contagious. "I liked the man more than I thought I would," he admitted.

"He was not what I was expecting, either," Alais said.

Holger scratched his beard. "This pope is the leader of your faith?"

Ciarán nodded. "And the leader of all Christ's churches throughout the world."

"There's no man like that for Odin or Thor," Holger said. "Maybe the Christian god will protect him."

"Aye," Ciarán said. "That would be good." He continued down the hall, where an immensely fat priest with bearded jowls was speaking with two other clerics. There was no mistaking a man that large. "What on earth is *he* doing here?"

"Who?" Father Niccolo asked. "Father Ugo? He's been serving in the papal Curia since Midsummer. He's a most excellent quaestor."

The fat priest's gaze flicked from the clerics to Ciarán.

Ciarán's hand fell to Caladbolg's hilt. "The man also goes by the name Charon, and he'll do anything for money. Someone's either paying him to be here, or he's stealing from your coffers."

Father Niccolo glanced at the heavyset priest, whose gaze fixed on Ciarán. Within a heartbeat, Ugo Grassus bolted down the opposite passageway. Ciarán rushed to follow the quaestor, pushing past the startled clerics.

"What are you doing?" Father Niccolo cried out behind them.

The passageway branched off in a half-dozen directions. The quaestor ducked into one of the corridors, his footfalls echoing down a flight of stairs. Moving with long strides, Holger reached Ciarán's side. "Who are we chasing?" he huffed.

"Someone up to no good." The two flew down the stairs, but the quaestor was nowhere in sight. Either he was faster than his huge form suggested, or he knew secret ways through this labyrinthine palace. They turned another corner, only to find themselves staring at a trio of papal guardsmen.

The largest of the guardsmen, stern-faced and shaven, looked as tall as the Danish lord and had already drawn his sword. He pointed his blade at Caladbolg, still in its sheath. "You bear arms in the holy palace!"

Ciarán ignored him. "The man we're chasing, you let him go!"

"That *man* is a member of the papal Curia," the guardsman growled. "Now hand me your weapon or I'll run you through!"

"Stop!" Father Niccolo yelled frantically from the top of the stairs. "There shall be no bloodshed in these hallowed halls!"

"This man," the guardsman hollered, his blue eyes blazing, "is armed."

"And he is a guest of His Holiness!" Father Niccolo hurried down the stairs, with Alais behind him.

"Father," Ciarán insisted, "you have a spy in the Lateran Palace, and they're letting him escape."

The priest answered with a huff. "Gaido," he addressed the lead guardsman, "search the palace for Father Ugo and bring him in for questioning. There has been a threat to the pope's life, and Father Ugo may have answers."

The guardsman furrowed his brow, and reluctantly sheathed his blade.

"I will escort the pope's guests to their chambers," Father Niccolo continued, "and then I shall apprise the pope of this situation, and Archbishop Gerbert, as well."

"As you wish, Father," the guardsman replied, anger lingering in his voice, before he and his companions set off.

"Let us go after him, too," Ciarán pressed.

"Absolutely not!" Father Niccolo's pale face was turning a shade a crimson. "The next guardsman you encounter may *actually* run you through."

Alais put her hand on Ciarán's shoulder. "He's right. Besides, the guards know the palace. Let them do their work."

"They'd best not fail," Ciarán said with a grimace. "There's a serpent in the palace, and my gut tells me the pope's enemies are the ones who put him here."

"If so, then his treachery's been revealed, and he's probably already fled the Lateran." She placed her hands on her hips. "Besides, we need our rest, for tomorrow night may be our only chance to find Sirra. She's the one who matters most."

Ciarán sighed. "Are you sure you'll be able to find her at the temple?"

"I'm certain of it," Alais said. "I've seen her a hundred times in my dreams. But I also fear she's in danger. We'll have to fight to protect her."

Ciarán rested his hand on Caladbolg's pommel, feeling the cut of the gemstone beneath his thumb. The war that broke out in Heaven, he realized, would once again be fought on earth, and this time he would have to lead the charge. After a long breath, he looked into her storm-gray eyes. "Then tomorrow we'll fight. And we'll save Sirra."

THE GATHERING STORM

At twilight the next evening, beneath a canopy of storm clouds growling with distant thunder, Ciarán surveyed the host of Danes assembled on the Caelian Hill.

The Danes gathered near a copse of oaks, just paces from where the floodwaters lapped against the hillside. Foremost among them stood Jarl Holger, his arms adorned in silver rings, his chest clad in polished mail, and his right hand resting on the pommel of Curtana strapped to his side. To his right, Rosta sat obediently beside Breda, who looked every bit like an Irish warmaiden with her red hair piled atop her head, her mail vest, and her shield slung over her back. To his left stood Magnus, proudly wearing the hauberk of Maugis d'Aygremont, while Jorundr, Strong Bjorn, Gunnar Boar's Head, and eighteen more of *Lindworm's* crew marshaled behind them, all decked in bossed helms and chain mail, with swords and spears and painted shields. They were the battle lords of Khalil's poem, and Ciarán imagined the papal guardsmen had never seen such a fierce-looking host.

Those guardsmen, a dozen in all, wore crested helms and crimson tunics over mail, while pulling two skiffs to the water's edge alongside four more already beached there. Gerbert of Aurillac joined the guardsmen, along with the imposing Lombard, who had guarded his chambers at the emperor's Aventine fortress. Clad in a mail tunic and sage cloak, the Lombard carried a huge spear with an immense blade. He held the weapon reverently with both hands. The spear's blade was sheathed in the center with blazing gold, just below a long, thin object affixed near the tip.

"Your Excellency," Ciarán said. He adjusted his leather baldric over the coat of mail Father Niccolo had procured for him, while eyeing the spear.

"It's the Holy Lance of Constantine," Gerbert said, "one of the greatest relics in Christendom. The emperor left it in the pope's care when he set off for Monte Gargano. I don't know what evil we may face tonight, but I thought a relic such as this may come in handy."

"Why is it a relic?"

"Ewin," Gerbert commanded the Lombard, "show him."

Ewin lowered the lance's head. Near its tip was a single long nail affixed with iron bands. "That nail is from the Holy Cross," Gerbert explained, "one of the two that pierced the Savior's hands."

Ciarán listened, though remained skeptical. He had seen too many fake relics in Rome to assume this one was real. But the weapon appeared formidable, and he agreed they might need it for the fight that lay ahead.

"We should get moving," Alais said, pulling the hood of her midnight-blue cloak over her head.

"Aye." Ciarán turned to the men and slid Caladbolg from its scabbard. As the steel scraped against the sheath, all eyes fixed on him. He raised the sword, which even in twilight had a gleam to its blade. "At the Temple of Venus and Roma, there is a woman, and we must save her. But the foes we may face tonight serve the greatest enemy of all, and if they kill her, they'll unleash the horrors of the Apocalypse." He spoke first in Latin, then repeated his words in Danish, substituting the word *Apocalypse* with *Ragnarok*. "But if we stop them, we may prevent these end times. So let us go with Godspeed, and let's save her!"

His words brought a roar from the Danish host. Holger clapped Ciarán on the shoulder. "Tonight," the jarl said, "I follow you."

The two of them claimed the rowing benches of one of the skiffs, while Ewin the Lombard, along with Breda and Rosta, piled into the stern, and Gerbert and Alais moved to the prow. As they set off, Alais summoned a pale light within her crystal to serve as a beacon for the other skiffs, who traveled without lantern or torch. Her soul light looked nothing like a flickering flame, and Ciarán prayed the enemy would mistake it for a firefly or a will-o'-the-wisp, the ghostly lights often seen at night by travelers in the fens.

Thunder rumbled over Rome as the six skiffs set off from the Caelian Hill. Ciarán's skiff took the lead, though the other five followed closely. Danes filled three of those skiffs, and papal guardsmen rowed the other two. The boats were but shadows in the falling darkness, the subtle splash of oars being the only sign of their presence.

The skiffs passed near the Palatine Hill, where the archways of the palace of Septimius Severus loomed like a haunted ruin. Ahead, the Coliseum rose from the floodwaters. Torchlight flickered in its archways, for the ruin served as tenement housing for some of the poorest in Rome. Beside the Coliseum, the Arch of Constantine stood like a lonely island in the flooded Forum.

As Ciarán and Holger rowed into the murk, one of the guardsmen's skiffs glided past them. A breath later, a voice called out from the skiff. "There's something on the water!"

Ciarán grimaced. "Hold your voice," he hissed. *Do you want them to know we're coming?*

On the prow, Alais and Gerbert peered through her crystal's light. "He's right," she said. "It's floating on the water, like lamp oil."

Ciarán glanced at Holger. "Oil?"

"Row back!" Gerbert cried.

Ciarán's pulse quickened as he reversed the course of his oars. From the Coliseum's archways tongues of flame, like a hundred candles, flared alight. Then, to Ciarán's horror, the flames took flight.

A hail of fire arrows arched through the night sky before dropping like falling stars. The shafts were not aimed at the skiffs, Ciarán realized, but at the water. As the arrows fell, the floodwaters erupted into a wall of fire, engulfing the guardsmen's skiff. The roar of flames drowned out the screams of men, while heat from the inferno blasted across Ciarán's vessel. Gerbert slammed into Ciarán; Alais cried out, fire licking her cloak.

"Great Thor!" Holger swore as he tore off Alais' cloak and cast it into the water.

Breda gaped in disbelief. "Fire on water?"

"Greek fire," Gerbert said, wincing. "It burns on water!"

Ciarán watched wide-eyed as the guardsmen's skiff was lost in the fire. His eyes grew wider as the prow of his own skiff burst into flames. "God's bones!" Ewin cried.

Alais glanced at the floodwaters behind them. "Go back!"

Holger roared as he pulled his oars, and Ciarán lent his own strength to the cause, propelling the burning skiff backward. Alais ripped her pewter chalice from her satchel and dunked it in the floodwater. Pulling it from the water, she uttered a foreign verse with the melody of a song. Then she hurled the chalice's contents onto the burning prow. Where the water landed, sheets of ice began to form, coating the front of the boat. The ice quelled the flames, turning the fire into hissing steam.

"Well done, my lady!" Gerbert said.

Ciarán stared at her in awe, until he realized a wall of fire now stretched from the Coliseum to the Arch of Titus, throwing off billowing clouds of smoke and blocking any direct path to the Temple of Venus and Roma. "What do we do now?" he asked hopelessly.

"Find the others!" Breda yelled.

The sudden thought of the other skiffs caught in that inferno brought a lump to Ciarán's throat. He searched for the other skiffs and found one, helmed by Magnus and Jorundr, who were beating flames off their bow. If the other skiffs survived, they were lost in the smoky haze.

"We can row around the Coliseum," Alais suggested, "and approach the temple from behind."

"What about the archers?" Breda pressed.

Ciarán glanced at the smoke rolling off the burning water. "The smoke will conceal us," he said. "I doubt the archers can aim through it." He turned toward Magnus's skiff. "Follow us!" he called out to Magnus in the other skiff. The hirdman nodded back, while his crew smothered the flames on their bow.

Through the smoke, Ciarán and Holger rowed around the mammoth Coliseum. They could not see any archers through the black haze, and Ciarán sensed their plan had worked. As they rounded the bend, the ruins of the Temple of Venus and Roma came into view, like an island aglow in the light of the blazing fire. A line of broken columns rose at the water's edge, and behind them the enemy waited. Some were but black shadows with pointed hoods; others were spearmen and swordsmen dressed in mail reflecting the reddish glow of the nearby inferno. There were a hundred men, maybe more.

Alais cast a worried glance at Ciarán, who swore under his breath. Then he did the only thing he could think to do.

He drew his sword.

Pope Gregory knelt at the gilded altar in the sanctum sanctorum, his private chapel in the Lateran Palace. The light of twin candles was all that illuminated the chapel this evening, but Gregory took solace in the dim light of this sacred place. Although his headaches and chills had worsened, he did not pray here for his health. He prayed for the success of Gerbert's mission.

The idea of an actual angel in Rome seemed as impossible tonight as it did yesterday. Yet Gerbert's conviction in the truth of Solomon's words had troubled him all day, for what if this seemingly impossible theory might actually be real? He made the sign of the cross and whispered another prayer, then he heard the scrape of a panel opening to his left. A chill rushed down Greggory's spine. "Who's there?"

"Just me, Your Holiness." The slap of sandals echoed in the chapel as Rumeus emerged from the hidden door, which concealed one of the palace's many secret passageways.

Gregory breathed a relieved sigh and rose to his feet. "What is it? Have you heard from Gerbert?"

"No." Rumeus shook his head, clasping his hands at his chest. "Seeing you here reminds me of the night two years ago when we took sanctuary in this chapel. Crescentius and his forces had gathered outside the palace, and I swear you could hear their threats even through these walls."

Gregory remembered the night vividly, for the cries of "Down with the Saxon pope!" had echoed through the palace halls. "I'll never forget that night, but why does it matter? Because of it, Crescentius lost his head, and Philagathos has been punished. The Crescentii remain, but I fear there are more important things to worry about tonight."

"Perhaps," Rumeus said. "But the Romans have never forgotten that night. In their minds, that was the night a once proud people stood up to a foreign invader. The Romans, you see, used to elect their popes from among their own kind until Otto the First arrived. He impressed his authority over the Holy See until the papacy was reduced to little more than a German bishopric. At least in the eyes of many proud Romans."

Gregory furrowed his brow. "Why are you telling me this?"

"So you might understand. You came into your papacy so very young. Just twenty-four years old. How could you be expected to understand how the Romans would perceive you? I, for one, felt great empathy for your situation, which is why I worked so hard on that night to spirit you away to safety, through the passageway in this very chapel. I sent you off to Pavia, where you would be safe." Rumeus's lips pressed into a thin line. "But then you had the gall to come back."

Gregory shook his head. "Why are you saying these things?"

Rumeus narrowed his gaze. "Because the thousand years are ending, and when the Savior returns, no foreigner shall sit on Saint Peter's throne."

Gregory felt a sudden coldness in his core. As he gaped at his archdeacon, a towering figure emerged from the passageway, followed by men in dark cloaks.

Naberus da Roma pursed his lips. "Every reign, Your Holiness, has an end."

5 6

THE TEMPLE

Theodora stared at the Saxon pope bound and gagged in the stern of the narrow skiff. The pope glared back, defiance simmering in his eyes. It was the type of look she longed to see, one she thought would bring her immense joy. Yet as she sat in the skiff, with her cloak pulled tight around her pale dress, she felt on edge.

On the bench across from her, Naberus seemed obsessed with his secret plan, one she knew involved her, but he refused to tell her how. Or why. There was a tinge to his gaze. One of madness, perhaps, though she could not tell. He had promised her vengeance would be had this night, that the pope would die for his crimes. Though where or when the execution would occur remained a mystery. She imagined it happening before a seething mob of Romans shouting "Down with the Saxon pope!" Instead, it appeared the pope would die in the dark of night, in the ruins of the ancient Forum. Nothing like she desired.

Naberus had also warned her the pope's men would come for them in skiffs. Theodora had not believed him at the time, because it seemed impossible the papal guard would so quickly have learned of the pope's abduction. But when she heard the roar of Greek fire, she knew Naberus's prediction proved true, for his trap had been sprung.

The inferno lit up the Forum, billowing smoke into the storm-filled sky. Rumeus, the papal archdeacon who had served as her confessor and spy within the Lateran Palace, nearly jumped from the skiff when he saw the wall of fire.

"What in God's name is that?" Rumeus asked, his face ashen.

"The end of Gerbert of Aurillac," Naberus told him, "as well as that Irishman and the Danes who arrived the day before."

Rumeus swallowed hard and made the sign of the cross. Beside him, the pope closed his eyes, as if mourning their loss.

Soon, the bell tower of the Basilica of Santa Maria Nova came into view, looming over an island rising from the floodwaters. Members of the Brotherhood of the Messiah awaited their arrival outside the basilica, whose stone walls and tower took on a hellish hue, bathed in the light of the inferno that stretched from the Coliseum to the Palatine Hill.

As the skiff neared the steps, Father Ugo and three of the brethren waited to moor the craft. Naberus disembarked first and helped Theodora from the skiff. She glanced back, only to realize no one else was leaving the vessel. "You're not taking the pope?"

"I need him elsewhere," Naberus said. "Though I need you here."

She shook her head. "After all this time, you'd rob me of my vengeance?"

Naberus swallowed her in his embrace. She tried to push away, but her resistance only tightened his viselike grip.

A tear stung her eye. "Why?"

"Because something glorious is about to happen here." He pulled a small vial from a pocket in his robes and held it to her lips. A bitter smell rose from the vial. "I need you to drink this, to be prepared."

"No."

"You must open your mind," he hissed. "This elixir of belladonna and henbane oil will help you do that. It's time you remembered the lives you've lived throughout the eons, so you may understand who —and what—you truly are."

His lips brushed against her ear, and Theodora found herself short of breath. "I think you'll find," he continued, "that inside you there's a gift." He pressed the vial to her lips, forcing a splash of the liquid into her mouth. An acidic taste washed across her tongue. As she swallowed the elixir, her head became suddenly light. Her will to resist began to fade.

"Tonight, you shall offer that gift to one greater than us," he promised as he drained the rest of the elixir down her throat. The liquid burned, its heat spreading from her throat to her lungs. Beneath her feet, the ground felt unsteady. Naberus's voice sounded like an echo in a cave.

"And then," she heard him say, "we shall have our salvation."

~

BILE ROSE IN ALAIS' THROAT AS SHE GAZED AT THE SHEER NUMBER OF foes amassed in front of the Temple of Venus and Roma. "They're Crescentii loyalists and a brotherhood of fanatics," Gerbert remarked.

Alais shook her head. "They outnumber us nearly ten to one." And they looked ready for a fight. Among the enemy ranks stood Roman warriors in mail hauberks, gleaming orange in the firelight. Many drew longswords and raised shields painted with the image of a marble horse. Others were common ruffians in leather tunics, wielding axes and clubs. And a full quarter of the men wore monkish robes with pointed cowls, gripping tall staves crowned with spikes.

The skiff full of Danes rowed up beside Alais'. The seven men inside drummed their swords against their wooden shields. Next to Alais, Breda drew her own blade. Ewin gripped the Holy Lance, while the hair on Rosta's back stood on end, a guttural growl forming in his mouth.

Overhead, the skies rumbled, but the sound gave way to a Danish roar. Alais craned her neck to see another skiff of Danes rounding the Coliseum.

"Our odds just improved," Gerbert said, "but not by much."

Alais clutched the crystal in her palm. "We'll need to even those odds. Have you ever used the light to blind a man?"

"No." Gerbert shook his head.

"I haven't either, but it's time we tried."

As the skiffs neared the shore, Gerbert removed his own crystal from his cassock, and Ciarán raised Caladbolg to his lips. "That will even the odds, too," she said.

Ciarán blew on the sword's pommel and uttered the Fae word, followed by an Irish battle cry. *"Columcille!"*

Fire and light flared from the blade. Alais had to shield her eyes, while panicked cries rose from the temple's shore.

The skiff rocked violently as Ciarán and Holger leaped ashore, along with the Danes in the second skiff. Shouts of "Odi-i-i-n-n-n!" filled the air, joined by Rosta's savage barks as the boarhound bounded into the fray.

The Danes crashed into the enemy line, and in a breath, the shore erupted in the chaos of battle. Steel clanged against steel, swords clattered on shields, and men screamed when steel found flesh. Amid a press of foemen, Ciarán swung Caladbolg in wide, fiery arcs, driving the enemy back, while Holger and his Danes towered over the Crescentii, hammering down blows. Yet for every man they felled, another took his place, and the number of foes threatened to envelop the Danes.

Alais' heart pounded in her chest as she and Gerbert clambered from the skiff, followed by Ewin, still gripping the lance. The frigid water rose to her knees. "We have to get inside the temple!"

Gerbert pointed to a half-dozen ruffians and fanatics rushing toward them. "Then we'll have to get by them first!"

Ewin met the first attacker, driving the Lance of Constantine straight through a leather breastplate into the man's chest. Alais drew in a breath, then whispered a string of Fae words. Within the crystal, light flared, and Alais focused all her will on projecting her soul light at the men charging toward her with axes and spiked staves. Light exploded from her palm. As it faded, a trio of attackers staggered back, clutching their hands to their eyes. Gerbert followed her lead, blinding two more with a burst of light from his own crystal, while Ewin swung the lance like a scythe, clean through another's neck.

In the glow of the fire still burning on the floodwaters, the temple ruins stood two hundred feet away. *I could make it in a sprint,* Alais figured, as thunder pealed overhead. The problem was the Crescentii. Even as Ewin skewered another, a roaring horde burst from the enemy's ranks to avenge their blind and fallen brethren. With another blast of light, Alais blinded two attackers, but a score still threatened. Six men, bearing shields with marble horses, overwhelmed Ewin, even as Gerbert blinded half of them.

A burly fanatic charged Alais, raising a spiked staff over his head. Her light seared his eyes, forcing him off course, but five more charged behind him. *We'll never stop them!* Her breath felt short as she blinded another; the fatigue of using the power weighed heavy on her limbs. *Can't keep this up.* She scurried ashore, struggling to summon more power, as four fanatics rushed toward her.

Before she could finish another Fae verse, a spiked staff smashed into her shoulder. The blow knocked her back into the floodwaters, her shoulder screaming from the bloody gash. As she clutched the wound, the fanatic raised his weapon for a second strike.

Just as Rosta flashed before her eyes.

The boarhound barreled into the man, sending him tumbling sideways before Rosta ripped out his throat. The next thing Alais knew, Breda was there, engaging the other three attackers. Quick as a hare, she parried staff blows with her shield while cutting her blade through the nearest man's jaw. Rosta grabbed the next fanatic by the leg, before Breda buried her sword in the third man's chest.

She glanced at Alais. "Go where you must. We'll keep 'em off you!"

Alais rose gingerly to her feet, her palm slick with blood. Short of breath, she nodded back.

As Breda and Rosta engaged the enemy surrounding Gerbert and Ewin, Alais started toward the temple. Her legs moved slowly at first, still suffering from the fatigue of wielding her soul light, but with each step, her strength grew, and soon she broke into a run.

She scrambled up a set of crumbling steps and made for the gap between the two sides of the temple. To her left, the side that once held a great statue to the goddess Roma was hollow and stripped of any ornament other than the crisscross pattern in the remnant of the apse, aglow with firelight. The side that honored Venus remained in the shadows, and she knew that was where she must go.

Drawing a deep breath, Alais entered the vault. Fireflies danced above the marble and porphyry floor of the rectangular chamber, just as they did in her dreams. Though absent was the moonlight and the haunting song, replaced now by the rumble of storm clouds and the clangor of battle raging on the shore. She peered into the alcoves on the far wall, flanked by the broken porphyry columns. Noting stirred in their shadows except the fireflies flitting and winking, oblivious to the chaos beyond the ruined walls.

A shiver shimmied across her skin as she stepped onto the patterned floor, and then gasped. From the passageway that led to the Basilica of Santa Maria Nova, a figure emerged. A woman, tall and slender, with long hair that looked silver in the glow of the firefly light. The woman swayed as she walked, clad in a pale dress. Her face was flawless, with high cheeks and full lips, but her glassy eyes stared through Alais as if she was not there.

A roar of thunder shook the ruins beneath their feet, and the woman staggered forward. She struggled to regain her balance, moving nothing like the dancer in Alais' dreams. Alais reached out her hand. "Sirra?"

The woman tilted her head to the side. *"Sirra?"*

She lunged forward, stretching a shaky hand toward Alais as lightning exploded from the sky. It struck the ground like the God's wrath, blasting Alais off her feet, enveloping her in its heat. All she could see was a searing, white light, then her head struck the marble floor. The light burst into a thousand stars expanding to fill the night sky. The stars began to flicker and fade like the fireflies' light until nothing was left but darkness.

And Alais found herself lost within its void.

JÖTNAR!

L ightning seared through the night sky. As the bolt struck the Temple of Venus and Roma, thunder rocked the ground beneath Ciarán's feet. For a heartbeat, the battle ceased. Something had happened, though Ciarán was nowhere near the temple to see what it was.

The Crescentii swordsman confronting Ciarán blinked twice, then swung his sword wildly toward Ciarán's chest. Ciarán jumped back to avoid the blade, before Caladbolg, still hissing with white fire, severed the swordsman's arm below the elbow. The swordsman staggered backward, and Ciarán let him go, while Holger thrust Curtana through another swordsman's gut.

The jarl glanced at Ciarán. Around them, smoke wafted through the temple grounds where a dozen attackers lay dead, as many felled by Caladbolg as by Curtana. Nearby, Magnus and Jorundr finished off two more swordsmen, while Strong Bjorn and a trio of Danes dealt with their remaining foes. A third of the enemy had fled at the sight of Caladbolg's fire, while the fierce Danes overwhelmed those who stood their ground, many reeking of drink. Wine may have fueled their courage, but it rendered them reckless and lacking against the battle-hardened Danes.

Holger pointed his bloodied sword toward the fight raging near the last of the columns lining the shore. "There!" Through the drifting smoke, swordsmen and fanatics clashed with three Danes from the second skiff, and Breda fought furiously alongside them. The enemy outnumbered them three to one.

"Right," Ciarán huffed. Raising Caladbolg in the air, he followed Holger into the fray.

A swordsman met Ciarán's charge, raising his shield painted with the image of the marble horse. Caladbolg shattered it as if it were made of willow weed. The frantic swordsman answered with a desperate swing that glanced off Ciarán's mailed shoulder, a breath before Caladbolg cleaved through the man's neck, sending his head careening across the temple grounds. *Forgive me, Father,* Ciarán prayed, *but our cause is more important than my vows.*

Around him, blades hammered on shields and mail, while Holger and his Danes plunged into the enemy line like reapers scything wheat. Amid the chaos of clanging blades and dying men, Ciarán spied Gerbert. The archbishop clutched the Holy Lance, holding off a trio of fanatics.

Ciarán rushed to Gerbert's aid, cutting past a ruffian who blocked his way. He spun toward the nearest fanatic, who gaped wide-eyed as Caladbolg sheared through his chest. Seeing their comrades fall to the flaming blade, the remaining attackers scattered in panic.

"Are you all right?" Ciarán asked Gerbert between breaths.

Gerbert nodded. "But Ewin's gone with God."

"Where's Alais?"

Gerbert swallowed hard. "She stole into the temple before the bolt struck."

Ciarán sucked in a deep breath. Only dying men lay between him and the temple's entrance. He bolted toward the temple and bound through a gap in the ruins. Broken columns framed half the vault, but Alais was gone. A soot-blackened scar marred the center of the porphyry floor.

Ciarán's heart fluttered in his chest. *I have to find her!* He called out from the temple, "Keep one of them alive!"

A moment later, one of the black-robed fanatics flew through the gap and thudded on the floor. Judging by his tonsure, Ciarán took him to be a monk, not much older than himself. The monk's once handsome face was red and swollen, and he clutched the bloody stump where his left forearm should have been. The monk let out a deep groan as Jorundr strode through the gap, followed by Holger and Gerbert. "Will this wretch do?" Jorundr asked.

"He'll have to." Ciarán knelt beside the monk. "Where is Naberus da Roma?"

The monk winced. "On the Palatine Hill," he said through labored breaths.

"Did he take a woman there?"

The man's head lolled from side to side. "You're too late."

Ciarán grabbed the monk by his robes. "Answer me!"

"You can't stop him . . ." the monk sighed. His eyes fluttered before his head slumped to the side, though his chest still rose with breath.

"He's succumbed to the pain," Gerbert said.

Ciarán couldn't care less. "What's on the Palatine Hill?"

"The ruins of the imperial palaces," Gerbert replied. "But why would Naberus go there?"

"I don't know," Ciarán said, "but he must have Alais, and maybe Sirra, too." He glanced outside the temple, where seven more Danes still stood. Strong Bjorn and Magnus were among them, alongside Gunnar Boar's Head and Breda. At her side padded Rosta, his fur matted with blood, though if the boarhound was wounded, he showed no sign of it.

"Wherever Naberus has gone," Ciarán told Holger, "we should expect more men."

"Then they'll die like the rest of them." Holger called to his crew. "To the skiffs!"

Ciarán and Gerbert joined Holger, along with Magnus, Breda, and Rosta, in one of the skiffs, while Jorundr and the remaining five Danes manned another. They embarked from the temple grounds and rowed through the smoky haze left by the Greek fire. Only patches of flames still burned on the floodwaters. "Any idea, Irish, what you're getting us into?" Magnus asked.

"Nothing you can't handle."

"Tell that to the five of our crew lying dead at that temple," Magnus snapped.

Holger scowled at his hirdman. "They died with swords in their hands. Right now, Alais is our concern."

Clenching his jaw, Ciarán ignored Magnus's glare as they rowed past the Arch of Titus, half submerged in the flooded Forum. Across the channel loomed the Palatine Hill. Near a cypress grove where the hillside met the water, four skiffs had been beached. "We'll land here," Ciarán said.

They pulled the skiffs ashore and Ciarán rushed to the hilltop. His companions followed. Atop the Palatine Hill, the shadowy silhouettes of cypress trees and the remains of ruined buildings rose like titanic gravestones in the night. In the distance, two motes of light flickered. *Torchlight.* "What's over there?" he asked Gerbert.

The archbishop pursed his lips. "If my bearings are correct, that's near the House of Augustus."

"Anything else?"

"The house is close to the hut of Romulus," Gerbert said, "and a temple to Apollo that Augustus built over an old Etruscan shrine."

Beside Ciarán, Rosta peered in the direction of the torchlight. A guttural growl formed in his throat; the hair stood on his back.

"He sees something over there," Breda said.

Ciarán slid Caladbolg from its sheath. "Aye, but what?"

They skulked through the darkness, crossing a meadow that had grown between the crumbling walls of a roofless building the size of a great hall. Ahead stood the ruins of what might have been an imperial garden with a fountain in its center.

With each step, Rosta's growls grew louder. Breda hissed to quiet the boarhound.

Beyond the garden, the silhouettes of seven columns began to take shape. "That's not right," Gerbert said. "There shouldn't be columns there." Then one of the columns moved.

Rosta barked fiercely at the shapes, spittle flying from his jaw.

As the shapes became more distinct, Ciarán realized they were not columns at all, but seven men, each one immensely tall.

"They're bigger than you," Magnus said dryly to Strong Bjorn, who stood a forehead taller than Jorundr.

"They look like Jötnar," Bjorn admitted.

Ciarán recognized the word—*giants*. The last time he had seen men this tall was at Rosefleur. Except those were not men, but Nephilim. He glanced at Gerbert. "Remember what I wrote about the battle at Rosefleur?"

Gerbert swallowed hard. "You think those are . . ."

"Aye."

"Dear God." Gerbert made the sign of the cross. "As soon as we breach their line, you need to go. Save Alais and find Sirra." He turned to Holger and offered him the Holy Lance. "I believe you may find this weapon more effective against what stands before us. Use it well in the name of God."

Holger gave Gerbert a curious look as he took the lance. "The Christ-god?"

"The one true God," Gerbert said. "May He guide your hand."

Ciarán's muscles tensed as they crept toward their new enemy. "Move on my signal, when I show them the power of Enoch's device. And pray that they fear it."

Metal scraped as the Danes unsheathed their swords. Ciarán drew in a breath, then whispered into Caladbolg's gemstone. *"Eoh."* He thrust forth the sword, light exploding from its blade.

The warriors stepped back a pace, then leveled their spears, each one the length of a longship's oar. Caladbolg's light gleamed off the polished helms that hid their faces, illuminating the steel of their breastplates and the armor fitted to their limbs, as if the warriors themselves were made of metal. The one in the center called out in Greek. "Begone!"

Ciarán sighed. "So much for them fearing the light."

"The numbers favor us," Holger said. "Use shields to deflect those spears. Now onward, to battle!"

Holger aimed the Holy Lance at the warrior in the center, and charged. The Danish lord batted away the warrior's spear and thrust the lance into the central warrior's gut. Ciarán rushed forward, without a shield, hoping Caladbolg might shear the enemy spears in two. Yet before he reached the nearest warrior, Rosta rushed past him. The warrior hesitated between Ciarán and the boarhound, just long enough for Rosta to dart past the spear's tip and seize the warrior's left leg in his jaws. Ciarán swung at the spear, and Caladbolg splintered the shaft. The warrior reached for a massive sword strapped to his side, but could not grip the hilt before Caladbolg tore through the steel plate over the warrior's thigh, fire hissing into the wound.

Flailing violently, the warrior knocked Ciarán away with a steel-sheathed forearm. He tumbled onto the muddy ground and watched the warrior swat away Rosta, sending the boarhound barrel-rolling across the turf. But Holger took his place and hacked at Ciarán's attacker with Curtana, while cries of battle, both Danish and Greek, filled the air.

His greatsword free of its sheath, the towering warrior returned Holger's blows, shearing the top off the Danish lord's shield. Ciarán climbed back on his feet and aimed for the wound on the warrior's thigh. This time, Caladbolg cut straight through the giant's leg. The warrior let out an unearthly scream, a breath before Curtana sliced into his exposed neck, misting the air with blood. The warrior crashed to the ground, beside his comrade clutching the Holy Lance in his gut.

"Now, Ciarán," Gerbert called from behind. "Go!"

Ciarán glanced back at the battle. Five of the giant warriors engaged the Danes, though some of his crewmates had fallen. *Alais and Sirra matter more.* Ciarán sprinted toward the torchlight. When he reached the burning brands, he found they had been wedged into a pile of bricks, the remains of a much larger structure that once claimed these grounds. Nearby, a well of crumbling stairs descended into darkness. Pairs of muddied footprints marred each step. *The ruins of Apollo's temple. Gerbert said it was built over an Etruscan shrine.*

Using Caladbolg like a torch, Ciarán started down the stairs. He

450

descended scores of steps before the blade's dancing flames illuminated an archway shaped like the mouth of a gaping giant. The sculpture was carved into the rock, its hollow eyes staring back like a raving devil. As he passed through the archway, a chill crawled down his flesh.

He took a deep breath and continued down the stairs until they ended in a narrow cavern. Something large and dark was lying at the base of the steps. His muscles tensed. Creeping forward, the light from Caladbolg's blade illuminated the shape. It was the body of a man dressed in black robes. Ciarán shuffled toward the corpse, whose head twisted a bit too far to the side. He tipped up the head with the toe of his shoe. The face of Rumeus, the papal archdeacon, stared back, his eyes frozen in death. *What in bloody hell is he doing here?*

As he stepped over the corpse into the cave, Ciarán noticed a thrum in the air. And when he saw the far wall, he knew why. A crude alcove had been carved into the rock, and within its archway a smoky mist writhed and swirled. *A gateway, just like the mists that surrounded Rosefleur.* He did not know what he would find when he passed through those mists, but on the other side, he knew he would stand in the Otherworld.

And every fiber of his being told him Alais was already there.

THE CHAINED WOMAN

A lais awoke from what seemed a lifetime of dreams.
Dreams of Rome, and vast deserts, and haunting waste-lands. Of sandstone pyramids, and a great city of soaring towers, and the vastness of the night sky, and a light brighter than the sun. Of a shower of stars falling to earth and the sky turning black, and of deafening winds and unending rain. She dreamed of days of joy and nights of sorrow. Of living in the splendor of royalty, and in the bleakness of poverty, and in the village of Selles-sur-Cher. Or was it some other place, familiar but not, with cottages, and haystacks, and fields of wheat? As she blinked the sleep from her eyes, she realized she was in none of those places now.

She found herself lying in the damp hull of a skiff. Iron manacles bound her wrists and ankles, and a chain attached above her right foot secured her to someone else: the platinum-haired woman. Clutching her head with her manacled hands, the woman let out a faint groan. Beyond her, two huge mastiffs slept in the stern, with a fat raven nestled between them.

Alais' skull ached as she lifted her head to look around. She was underground in a massive cavern, its ceiling shrouded in darkness.

Bronze torches burned along the cavern's walls, where gigantic human faces had been crudely carved into the limestone. Each face bore a visage of madness or despair, bathed in the hellish glow of the torchlight. Beneath the skiff, water filled the cavern, similar to Avalon's subterranean lake, though the water was not luminescent like the Lethe, but dark like cuttlefish ink. She had seen such water before, but she could not remember when.

The skiff was moored to a pier that appeared older than any structure in Rome. Rectangular columns, etched with familiar hieroglyphs, rose from the water, each flanked by standing bronze braziers burning like cook fires. Near the skiff, an immensely tall man clad in armor from shoulder to foot stood sentry on the dock's timeworn flagstones. A long black braid dangled from the back of his polished helm as he watched something happening on a squat stone pier that jutted into the water.

From the pier echoed a voice, chanting a verse in an ancient tongue. She sensed a faint thrum with each spoken syllable, and from the recesses of her memory, she recognized the words.

> *Spirits of the ancient world, souls of gods and men,*
> *Prepare me for this sacrifice, to break the bonds again.*
> *Imbue me with your sacred power, to take the soul within,*
> *The sacrifice required, for salvation to begin . . .*

A chill washed through Alais' veins as she craned her neck. On the pier, Naberus da Roma stood naked to his full, towering height. Runes covered his glistening skin while he gestured before the sacrifice that hung between a pair of square columns at the pier's end: a naked man, chained at the wrists, his arms spread like a cross. As he lifted his head, Alais gasped. Pope Gregory grimaced, his body convulsing with the power of Naberus's words.

As more memories rushed forth, she understood the meaning of those words, and how the pope's soul would fuel their purpose. Her mind screamed. *We're almost out of time!*

Frantic, she tugged on the chains. The manacles bit into her wrists, summoning a trickle of blood. Her heart began to pound. Then a voice called through the cavern. *"Alais!"*

From an archway beyond the pier, Ciarán emerged through a curtain of smoky mists, with Caladbolg in his grasp.

"Ciarán," Alais screamed, "stop Naberus!"

His gaze darted between her and Naberus da Roma, who turned toward Alais. His face bore a look of pure malice.

"Listen to me," she cried, "you cannot let him kill the pope!"

Ciarán hesitated, then gave her a nod.

As he rushed toward the pier, Alais finally understood the meaning of Orionde's words and the role she must play. But if Ciarán did not save the pope, it might all be for naught. For beneath the black waters, she knew what was coming. And the thought of it sent a pang of terror through her soul.

CIARÁN'S HEART WAS RACING. AT THE END OF THE ANCIENT STONE PIER, the pope hung chained between two pillars, his face contorted in agony. Before him, Naberus da Roma raised his hands, uttering words Ciarán could not understand. But somehow, he knew, they were killing the pope.

Naberus glanced back, his gaze boring into Ciarán, a breath before an enormous figure eclipsed Ciarán's view. It emerged from behind one of the square columns, a warrior a head and a half taller than the ones Ciarán had battled outside Apollo's temple, and nearly twice as broad. An iron breastplate protected his massive chest, and more plates adorned his arms and legs, revealing only hints of pale white flesh. A great helm covered his head, its crown shaped like a gaping lion, with a steel visor forged like a man's face, masking his own. In his hands, which looked large enough to crush a man's skull, he gripped an iron-shafted poleax tipped with a brutal spike and curved blade.

Ciarán stepped back. *He's a yard taller than me, and as large as an ox. But I still have Caladbolg.* He clutched its hilt with both hands. Fire hissed from the sword's blade.

With a grunt, the giant lunged forward, swinging his poleax in a wide arc. The blade glanced off Caladbolg, but the force of the blow hurled Ciarán off his feet. He landed hard near the mist-filled archway, clambering away a breath before the ax blade crashed into the flagstone.

He darted toward the pier, but the giant caught him in two massive strides. Ciarán ducked beneath the poleax a hair before it smashed into one of the ancient columns, sending a hail of stone into the water. Gritting his teeth, Ciarán countered with a sword-strike that sheared through an iron plate on the giant's thigh. The giant howled, but kicked back with rage. His boot caught Ciarán in the chest, forcing the air from his lungs. He flew ten feet across the dock before crashing to the ground. The impact jolted Caladbolg from his grasp. To his horror, the weapon clattered across the flagstones.

He scrambled for the sword. Then, from the pier, Pope Gregory let out a bloodcurdling cry.

As HE UTTERED THE NECROMANTIC VERSE, POWER SURGED THROUGH Naberus's veins. The energy was unlike anything he had ever experienced, as if his blood, his flesh, his whole being had transformed into something divine. He touched his hands to the pope's bare chest and could sense the man's soul brushing against his fingertips. "Your sacrifice shall seal my salvation."

The pope wailed as the tendrils of his soul wrapped around Naberus's fingers. "You cannot win . . ." the pope groaned.

"I already have," Naberus said.

"No . . . Daniel's prophecy still stands."

Naberus grimaced. "The last empire fell five hundred years ago."

Sweat drenching his skin, Gregory shook his head. "You're wrong .

. . it lives through Constantine's heir." He glared at Naberus. "Through *Pontifex Maximus.* So long as the Church stands, so does the prophecy . . ."

Rage welled within Naberus. "Blasphemer!" Power surging within him, he seized hold of Gregory's soul and ripped it from his chest.

WHEN SHE HEARD GREGORY'S DYING SCREAM, ALAIS KNEW THEIR situation could not be more urgent. Somewhere in the shadows of the dock, Ciarán was fighting that monstrous warrior. Yet even if he prevailed, they would not survive what was coming.

She glanced at the shackles on her wrists. *With my crystal, I could break those chains.* She fumbled for her pouch, but the crystal was gone. With a sigh, she recalled Nimue's teachings. The crystal, the chalice, the sword—all were but tools to help mortals focus the power. *What if I don't need those tools anymore?* She concentrated on the chain between her wrists. The iron was made of thousands of particles, like grains of sand held together by an energy forged through the power of creation. But with the right Fae words, that energy could be manipulated and the particles could be rearranged. She let the words flow off her tongue. With each syllable, she felt the power pulse through the metal. An ash-gray stain spread across the links.

Praying it worked, she jerked her wrists. The links snapped as if they were made of glass. She spoke the verse again, breaking the chains that bound her ankles and tethered her to the woman with the platinum hair.

The woman's head swayed; she opened her eyes. They were glassy and unfocused. "What's happening?"

Whoever this woman was, she was in no condition to move. "If you believe in God," Alais told her, "start praying to Him now." She turned toward the dock, only to look up at the towering sentinel. The man glared down through the slits in his helm, the braziers' light reflecting off its polished crown. Her eyes darted between the pair of standing braziers blazing with fire.

456

Plenty of fire.

She uttered another Fae verse and sensed a thrum of energy as the braziers flared. The sentinel reeled back, but was helpless when the flames leaped from the braziers onto his torso. Three more Fae words caused the fire to spread as if burning dry straw. As the inferno engulfed him, the sentinel let out a terrified howl. He staggered toward the edge of the dock, flailing while the flames consumed his flesh. At the edge, he leaped into the black waters. The liquid doused the fire, but did nothing to quell his panic as his heavy armor dragged him beneath the surface.

Her path free, Alais clambered onto the dock. The fight, she knew, had robbed them of precious time. For at the end of the pier, Naberus da Roma stood triumphant, drawing a luminescent vapor from the dead pope's lungs. She watched in horror as he uttered another Nephilim verse:

> *Master, with this sacrifice, shatter your bonds,*
> *For your servant longs to see your light.*

With each word, the luminous vapor wisped into the lake as if being devoured by the dark water. As the last hint of vapor disappeared, a chill rushed through Alais. For she knew nothing could stop him now.

CIARÁN GRABBED CALADBOLG BY ITS HILT AND LOOKED UP. TEN PACES away, the giant was sauntering toward him, laughing under his breath. Ciarán glanced to his left, where one of the standing braziers crackled with flames. Without a second thought, he threw his shoulder into the brazier, and heaved. Its blazing fuel spilled onto the flagstones, hissing with smoke before erupting into a hedge of fire.

The fire stood between him and the giant, and for an instant Ciarán stopped to catch his breath. But his eyes grew wide as the giant continued onward, walking straight through the flames. With a roar, the giant thrust his poleax. Ciarán leaped to the side as its spiked tip buried deep into a flagstone. As the giant pulled it free, Ciarán charged. With all his strength, he swung Caladbolg at the giant's waist, just below the breastplate. The giant twisted away from the blow, but the blade grazed his flesh, leaving a streak of white fire across the wound.

The giant yowled in pain, dropping his poleax but lashing out with his enormous hands. Ciarán tried to spin away, but the giant caught hold of the back of his mail coat. The giant hefted him off the ground before hurling him toward one of the faces carved on the cavern wall. He smashed into the limestone; his vision exploded with a thousand stars.

Blood filled his mouth as he thudded onto the ground. He shook his head to clear his vision, fearing nothing would slow his attacker down. The blurred form of the giant lumbered forward, poleax in hand. Yet behind the giant, something flickered. Ciarán gaped in disbelief, for the fire from the toppled torch had formed into a serpentlike shape, reared and ready to strike. The giant turned his head toward the serpentine flames, just as they lunged.

Fire surged into the eyeholes of his mask, then an inhuman roar burst from the giant's lungs. He tore the helmet from his head. His pale, hairless face contorted with rage as smoke hissed from his eye sockets.

"Ciarán—*now!*" Alais cried. She stood ten paces away, her arms outstretched. A faint flicker of light danced from her fingertips.

Ciarán rose to his feet. His limbs ached, but Caladbolg felt warm in his hands. He lumbered toward the roaring giant, and hollered, "*Columcille!*" Caladbolg plunged through the giant's breastplate, ripping through flesh and bone while the blade's fire flooded the gash. As he tore the sword free, the giant fell to a knee. Then with a groan, he slumped onto the flagstones.

"Well done!" Naberus boomed from the pier, "but it won't save you." He turned toward Alais. "I underestimated you, my dear. Badly, it seems. But the master will still get what he needs."

Beyond the pier, the lake churned like a seething cauldron. Steam billowed from its surface, rising behind Naberus and obscuring the faces on the wall. Ciarán rushed to Alais' side. From the corner of his eye, he glimpsed the mists swirling in the archway to the Etruscan shrine. From the vapors, Gerbert stepped into the cavern, his eyes wide. Holger followed, gripping the Holy Lance. "Dear Lord," Gerbert gasped. *"The pope—"*

"Is dead," Naberus said. "His life was the final sacrifice needed to finish what began at Rosefleur. The bonds then were weakened, but with the pope's death, they've been broken!"

Ciarán's blood went cold; the demon's words raged through his mind. *The Morning Star awakens . . . the sacrifice is ready . . .*

Naberus raised his rune-covered arms as a torrent of water erupted from the center of the lake. "Behold, *salvation!*"

Within the blasting torrent emerged a searing light. As the water cascaded back into the lake, the glowing form remained and took on a vaguely human shape. Around the cavern, the torches flared. Their flames rushed toward the glowing figure as if being summoned. Blazing fire enveloped the man-shaped apparition, which was growing in size. The cavern descended into darkness, save for the fiery figure floating in the center. Its arms broadened into wings and its legs twisted like serpents; its neck grew and curved, while its head took on a heron shape. The flames faded into embers, covering the being's flesh like glowing scales.

Ciarán's limbs began to shake as the being expanded in size. Its wings stretched thirty feet on each side, and its torso was larger than an auroch. "Blessed Mother of God," Ciarán exhaled.

Fully formed, the Dragon let out a triumphant roar. Its eyes glowed like molten slits in its massive skull. Its jaws opened wide, filled with swordlike teeth. Fire gathered in its throat.

Ciarán felt rooted in place, unable to take his eyes off the terrifying creature burning with unimaginable power—the ancient enemy, older than time itself. As its jaws filled with fire, Ciarán knew that Naberus had won.

"Holy Jesus," Gerbert prayed.

With a roar like Greek fire, the Dragon's breath exploded from its jaws. Ciarán braced for the searing pain, but it never came. Instead, the air thrummed as Alais raised her arms. From the lake, a wall of water blasted skyward to meet the flames. Fire hissed into steam as Alais stood defiant against the enemy of God.

"I won't be able to keep this up long," she stressed to Ciarán as the wall of water collapsed.

The Dragon glared down on them, beating its wings while flickers of flames flared deep within its mouth. Ciarán felt the weight of the beast's gaze, though he sensed it was not focused on him, but on Caladbolg. *He knows this weapon,* Ciarán realized, *and he hates it.* Though what good was it against him in midair? It was not like an arrow—*or a spear!*

He turned to Holger, who gripped the Holy Lance of Constantine. "Aim true, my lord," Ciarán said.

A grim smile spread across Holger's face, the smile of a battle lord. He cocked the lance and charged. Halfway down the pier, he hurled the weapon, putting all his weight into the throw. *"In the one God's name!"*

The Dragon reared back its head, fire filling its jaws as the lance sped through the air. With a beat of its wings, the beast twisted away, but not before the lance plunged deep into its side. The roar that followed shook the cavern. Fire blasted from its mouth across the limestone walls. Its tail whipped across the lake, while its wings shed their emberlike scales, hissing as they pelted the water.

Ciarán watched in awe as the beast thrashed against the cavern walls. More scales fell from its torso, and the fire within its jaws was now consuming its head. Its glowing hide was crumbling into the lake, but beneath the bestial form, something remained. Its beating wings had withered to half their original size, and its body was becoming more manlike. As the scales cascaded into the black waters, luminous flesh emerged to form a muscular man, as large as one of the Nephilim, with a perfect face, both beautiful and terrifying. His eyes smoldered with a mix of rage and anguish, for the Holy Lance still pierced his side, its tip protruding from his back.

Breathless, Ciarán waited for the angel to plunge into the lake, or dive toward them to inflict his wrath. If he did, Caladbolg would be there to meet him. Ciarán raised the sword high, light gleaming from the fire on its blade. With two beats of its dragonlike wings, the angel flew toward a tunnel at the cavern's far side. As it disappeared into the darkness, a voice echoed like thunder. *"THIS IS NOT THE END . . . THE PILLAR WILL BE BROKEN, MY PEOPLE SHALL BE FREE . . ."*

Ciarán staggered back, overwhelmed by what he had witnessed. Beside him, Gerbert shook his head in disbelief, while Alais let out a long sigh. Holger crouched on the pier, holding a hand over his chest. On the surface of the lake, a skiff glided toward the tunnel. Ciarán had almost forgotten about Naberus da Roma, having lost track of the necromancer the moment the Dragon arrived. Though there he was, manning the skiff's oars. Naberus shot Ciarán an expressionless glance, while from the stern, an ashen-faced woman with long platinum hair gazed in horror.

As Ciarán watched them go, a terrible thought struck. "Was that Sirra?"

Alais shook her head. "No."

"Then you didn't find her?"

"I know where she is." Alais smiled weakly. "And I know what Orionde meant when she said I had another role to play."

Ciarán cocked his head. "What do you mean?"

"I'll explain, but first, let's leave this place."

Ciarán nodded. "Aye."

"We cannot leave him like that." Gerbert stared at Pope Gregory, hanging lifelessly between the two pillars at the end of the pier.

"He deserved better," Ciarán said.

Gerbert gave a heavy sigh. "I'm sorry I ever doubted you, Brother Ciarán."

"No need to say it," Ciarán replied. "You're part of this now. We may have driven the enemy away, but it's not defeated. And you heard its words. This is not the end."

"Whatever may come," Gerbert swore, "you'll have my aid."

After they unbound Pope Gregory from his chains, Holger carried his body from the pier. When they reached the archway, still swirling with smoky mist, Ciarán summoned Caladbolg's light. In its brightness, the mists began to part.

Once Holger and Gerbert walked through the archway, Ciarán took Alais' hand. And together, they stepped back into Rome.

THE JOURNEY'S END

They emerged from the Etruscan shrine beneath a dawn-red sky.

Near the top of the steps, Rosta waited, his tail wagging and his tongue lolling out of his mouth. Beside the boarhound stood Breda. Blood stained her mail vest and her face looked haggard from the night's battle, but her green eyes grew bright the moment she saw her husband's face. As she and Holger embraced, Ciarán squeezed Alais' hand. She returned his gesture with a smile that warmed his heart, despite the winter chill in the air.

"Where are the others?" Holger glanced around.

"Tending to the wounded," Breda said solemnly, "and the dead. We lost Gunnar and Taft, and his brother Oddr. Sigarr fell, too."

Holger furrowed his brow. "What about Magnus?"

"Oh, that one fared just fine. Fought like a berserker, he did. Jorundr as well, though he took a mean cut across his ribs."

Holger bowed his head. "Take me to them."

"Can I help?" Gerbert asked, trying to follow the Danish conversation.

"Several of the Danes are wounded," Ciarán told him in Latin.

"Dónall swore you taught him Arabic medicine, so they could use your aid. And the ones who fell could use your prayers."

"Of course." Gerbert nodded. "Are you coming, Brother Ciarán?"

"I'll be there soon." Ciarán watched Gerbert depart with Breda and Holger, then he followed Alais. She headed for the ruins of the House of Augustus and stopped at the edge of the cliff. She glanced back, before gazing out at the flooded bowl that was once Circus Maximus during the glory of ancient Rome.

"A dozen times, I dreamed I lived in this house," Alais told him, a wistful look on her face. "We would watch the chariot races from this very hill. In those dreams, I was the adopted daughter of Livia and Augustus, and friend to their daughter, Julia Caesaris. I often wondered how the dreams could seem so real. But now I know. They were not dreams, but memories of a life I've lived before."

Ciarán shook his head. "The Church doesn't believe in past lives."

"Who knows how many things the Church has gotten wrong?" Alais mused. "When I was in Avalon, Nimue told me how Lilith sought to kill Sirra to claim the power to free the fallen angels. Sirra knew that as long as she lived, the enemy would try to seize the power, for it is the Key to the bottomless pit. So she forged a solution with the aid of the archangel Michael. Nimue said Sirra surrendered her beauty in order to change her skin, so that she would never appear the same from age to age, making it nearly impossible for the enemy to find her. But that's not precisely what happened."

"What do you mean?"

"Sirra's solution was not some glamour to make her appear as someone else. It was far more permanent. She sacrificed her physical form so her spirit could be free to live another life. And when that mortal shell died, her spirit moved on again. With each life and each death, she became reborn, but recalled nothing of her past lives or the terrible power within her. Until the time came in each millennium, when she would have to know, when her memories would awaken at the journeys' end, as they did last night."

As Ciarán listened, he remembered something Blind Mikkel had told him. *After Ragnarok, Freya was reborn as Lifthrasir . . .* What if Sirra and Lifthrasir were one and the same, simply different names for different myths, each derived from a universal origin? The implication sent a chill up his neck. "You believe you've lived past lives?"

"I know I have," she said. "And one of them was Sirra's."

"Which means . . ."

"That in my veins flows the Key to the Abyss." She put her hand on his. "The understanding came to me when the bolt struck the Temple of Venus and Roma. That's why I can wield the power without a staff or a sword. For I have Sirra's spirit to draw upon."

Ciarán felt a lightness in his head. Never would he have imagined what she was saying could be true. Despite this, he believed her. "You think Orionde knew this too?"

Alais nodded. "I don't know how, but I believe she did. She knew I had another role to play—the same one Sirra played three thousand years ago. To protect the Key so that the fallen angels remain in their prison."

Ciarán gave a long sigh. "I don't suppose from your past lives you remember what we're supposed to do next?"

Alais shook her head. "It doesn't work that way. All I know of those lives is what I recall in my dreams. Though I feel certain it ends in Dudael."

"I was afraid of that."

"I think it's always ended there. But I know one more thing." She wrapped an arm around him and rested her head on his shoulder. "Wherever the next journey takes us, we'll go there together."

BY THE END OF THE WEEK, THE FLOODWATERS HAD SUBSIDED AND THE city of Rome began to return to everyday life. Through muddied streets and alleyways, rumors quickly spread about Pope Gregory's demise. Some claimed he was poisoned by the Crescentii, with his eyes ripped out for what he did to John Philagathos. Others clung to a rumor Gerbert had spread the morning after the pope's death: that the pontiff had succumbed in his sleep to the Roman fever. While this became the official position of the Church, Ciarán found it ironic there were hints of truth to both lies.

At the Lateran Palace, Gerbert took it upon himself to run the Curia in Rumeus's absence until Emperor Otto could return and name a new pope. Gerbert soon learned his temporary position put him in control of the Holy See's vast web of spies, and Ciarán made him promise to have them search for the Varangian, and discover where he sold his slaves. If Josua and the rest of *La Margerie's* crew still lived, Ciarán swore he would find them and make sure they were set free.

As for *Lindworm's* crew, Jorundr, Strong Bjorn, and the other injured Danes soldiered through their recovery. Meanwhile, Jarl Holger announced an unexpected decision—that he would be baptized a Christian. And so, on the last Sunday of February, Anno Domini 999, in the baptistery of the Basilica of Saint Peter, Jarl Holger Horiksson of Denmark dressed in a plain white tunic and stood waist-high in the baptismal pool. There, Gerbert immersed the jarl three times, once for each day Christ spent in the tomb. When it was over, Holger wrapped the diminutive archbishop in a bear hug, much to Gerbert's chagrin. Though it was clear to Ciarán the two men now shared a bond, forged by their ordeal in that ancient cavern. One that would last a lifetime.

After the ceremony, under the protection of a score of mounted papal guardsmen, Ciarán rode from the basilica beside Gerbert and Alais, followed by Holger, Breda, and the rest of the Danes. Merchants and pilgrims stood to watch the procession as it ambled down the street from Saint Peter's Square. As Castel Sant'Angelo came into view, Alais leaned toward Gerbert. "Your Excellency, I've been meaning to ask. Have you any word about Father Michele?"

"Ah, my lady," Gerbert replied. "I almost forgot. Unfortunately, the Holy See has no record of a Father Michele at the Basilica of Santa Maria Nova. In fact, that basilica's been under the care of a young priest named Father Antonius da Pavia for the past three years."

"That's not possible," she said. "I've spoken to Father Michele there. Ciarán's seen him, too."

"I have," Ciarán agreed. "He even helped save us from Naberus's men outside the Pantheon."

Gerbert shrugged in his saddle. "Well, I don't know what to tell you, but if there had been a priest by that name at Santa Maria Nova, the Holy See would know of it. They keep meticulous records, you know."

Alais frowned. "I was looking so forward to speaking with him again. He always said the most prescient things, as if I needed to hear them. He once told me that sometimes people see what they were meant to see. Strangely, he was right."

Ciarán blinked. "That's odd. When I was in Uppsala, a gothi named Blind Mikkel told me the same thing."

"How curious," Gerbert said. "Though I suppose they do share something in common. Both Mikkel and Michele are derivations of the name Michael."

That is strange, Ciarán thought as they neared Castel Sant'Angelo. He glanced up the sheer walls of the central keep, where the emperor's huge banner fluttered in the breeze. The banner depicted a winged Saint Michael holding a flaming sword over a dragon at his feet, an image drawn straight from the Book of Revelation: "And war broke out in Heaven; Michael and his angels fought against the dragon, and the dragon and his angels fought back." It reminded Ciarán of the Dragon's eyes when it saw Enoch's device. *He feared that sword because he had known it before . . .* The possibilities whirred through Ciarán's mind.

"You know," he told his companions, "maybe we're not alone in this. Perhaps there's a higher power watching our backs."

"We could certainly use one," Gerbert said with a slight grin.

Alais shot Ciarán a curious look. He nodded toward the banner flying above the castle. She stared at it for a moment, then her eyes flew wide, her mouth falling open in wonder.

When they reached the Ponte Sant'Angelo, the bridge that crossed the Tiber into Rome, Alais pursed her lips. "I suppose it's good to know that if a demon's words can lead a man astray, there's always an angel around to put him back on the right path."

"Indeed it is," Ciarán said. "And now I know I have another one at my side."

She smiled back, her face as beautiful as ever. "Not quite, but I'll have to do."

"We Irish are stubborn," he said with a wink. "We need all the help we can get."

HISTORICAL NOTE

O ne of the reasons I love historical fantasy as a genre is the history aspect of it all. I've found that history can often be more fascinating than anything I could invent in my head. And for *The Key to the Abyss,* history provided much of the story's backbone.

Until the final chapters, most of the events concerning Pope Gregory, Emperor Otto, and Crescentius are historically accurate. In October of 996, Crescentius II, the head of the old Roman families and self-styled Prince of Rome, broke his oath to Otto III and chased Otto's twenty-four-year-old cousin, Pope Gregory V, from the Lateran Palace. In his place, and with the backing of the Byzantine emperor Basil II, Crescentius put John Philagathos on Saint Peter's throne, anointing him Pope John XVI. Those events compelled Otto III in December 997 to embark on his revenge expedition to Rome.

Carrying the Holy Lance of Constantine, the seventeen-year-old Otto and his army arrived at Rome in February of 998, though in the novel I pushed this back a month to align it with the events in *Enoch's Device.* Along with his host of Germans, Tuscans, and Lombards rode Pope Gregory V and Gerbert of Aurillac, Otto's mentor and counselor, and one of the most remarkable men of the late tenth century.

In the face of Otto's massive army, Crescentius took refuge in his ancestral home of Castel Sant'Angelo, which resulted in the siege depicted in the book, led by Margrave Eckard of Meissen. Following the victory, Otto had Crescentius beheaded and thrown from the walls of Castel Sant'Angelo, after which the Roman mob dragged his corpse through the Leonine City until his body was hung upside down on the Vatican Hill. Around the same time, Otto's men, led by Count Berthold of Breisgau, captured and mutilated John Philagathos, who was taken to Rome and defrocked outside the Lateran Palace by Gregory V. That humiliation caused Nilus da Rossano—who was considered a living saint in his day—to travel to Rome, where he condemned both Otto and Gregory for their treatment of Phila-gathos. Otto was so shaken by Nilus's judgment that he left Rome for Monte Gargano to prostrate himself before the hermit and beg for forgiveness. During the emperor's absence, Gregory V died on February 18, 999. By most historical accounts, the pope fell victim to malaria (known then as the Roman fever), though there were rumors he had been poisoned and had his eyes plucked out in revenge for what he had done to John the Greek.

Otto's and Gregory's beliefs about the Apocalypse are also based on history. While many European Christians in the late tenth century believed the end times would begin upon the millennium, one thousand years after the birth of Christ, not everyone shared this view. One of those was a Benedictine monk named Adso of Montier-en-Der (a contemporary and friend of Gerbert of Aurillac), who believed the prophecy in chapter two of the Book of Daniel meant the end times would be forestalled so long as the fourth of four empires—the Roman Empire—lived on. This theory relied on the belief that the Roman Empire had transferred to the Franks under Charlemagne, eventually passing to Otto I. So it was not a stretch to imagine that Otto III and his cousin Gregory would share this view of the end times.

Other aspects of the Roman plotline, such as Naberus da Roma and Countess Theodora, are clearly fictional, though Theodora was inspired by her famous ancestors in the book, Marozia and Theodora.

The two daughters of Senatrix Theodora effectively ruled Rome in the early tenth century during an era deemed the "pornocracy" by some historians, one of the most scandalous periods in the history of the papacy.

Naberus's tome, however, the Book of Giants, is real, and a copy of it was found in Qumran among the Dead Sea Scrolls. The ancient text covers the same events written of in the Book of Enoch (also a real text), and hinted at in Genesis 6:1-4, but it tells the story from a Nephilim point of view. Any connection between the Nephilim and Stonehenge is pure speculation on my part, though according to the twelfth-century British historian Geoffrey of Monmouth, the famous monolith was built by giants and even referred to as the Giant's Ring.

Geoffrey of Monmouth was also a source of many of the legends about Merlin, King Arthur, and the Isle of Avalon. Nimue, the Lady of the Lake, appears as a character in Sir Thomas Malory's fifteenth-century work *Le Morte d'Arthur,* and remained a prominent figure in the Arthurian legends of Avalon, many of which center around the former island of Glastonbury Tor. Home of two medieval monasteries, Glastonbury Tor is one of the most mythically rich places in England, and was even believed to be a gateway to the Otherworld in Celtic mythology. Those myths inspired Avalon in the novel, but the rest of the events set in England are based on history.

On the night he became king of Denmark, a drunken Svein Forkbeard vowed to conquer England within three winters. It took a bit more time, but in the year 991 the Danes attacked England in the Battle of Maldon, which Magnus recounts for Ciarán in the book. The English king, known today as Ethelred the Unready, responded by paying the Danes a ransom to go away. That ransom, which was funded by a tax called the Danegeld, had the opposite effect of inspiring even more Viking raids, and for a time the Danes carried out those raids from a settlement on the Isle of Wight (called Vette in the old Nordic tongue, and Vectis in Latin). The raid on Dorsetshire depicted in the novel occurred in the year 998 according to the *Anglo-Saxon Chronicle,* though the battle of Poole is fictional, as are all the Viking characters except for Svein. In 1013, Svein would finally realize his dream of conquering England and become the kingdom's first Danish king. Svein's son, Cnut the Great, and Svein's grandsons, would go on rule England for the next quarter century.

One of the things that made Viking raiders so fearsome was their dragon-prowed longships. The sleek vessels could cross oceans and row up shallow rivers, allowing the Vikings to raid farther inland. For this reason, a longship would have been ideal for maneuvering through a flooded Rome. The Eternal City experienced terrible floods during the Middle Ages, and while I've found no historical account of the Tiber overflowing its banks in February of 999, the ruins of the ancient Forum, which lies in a valley between four of Rome's seven hills, almost certainly would have succumbed to the floodwaters. The Lateran Palace on the Caelian Hill would have been spared.

Built by Emperor Constantine, the Lateran Palace served as the seat of the popes until the Holy See was moved to the Vatican in the fourteenth century. The palace would have contained the precursor to the Vatican Secret Archives, and it's not hard to speculate that a copy of the Testament of Solomon would have existed among its treasures. Based on the oldest surviving copy of the scroll, scholars believe the Testament of Solomon was written in the first century A.D., as opposed to by King Solomon himself. But the scroll does describe how Solomon, using a magic ring given to him by the archangel Michael, commanded demons during the construction of the temple in Jerusalem. There is even a prophecy by one demon about a pillar whose fall would herald the end of the world, though the reference to Sirra is my own creation. The name Sirra is associated with the constellation Andromeda, the chained woman. Yet under Brother Dónall's theory of a universal origin of myths, I suppose she could have been Freya, or even Venus.

Any connection between Sirra and Saint Michael is purely fictional, though the archangel does have a significant connection to Rome. In fact, Michael is the angel after which Castel Sant'Angelo takes its name, based on a supposed miracle in the year 590 when Pope Gregory the Great prayed for God's intercession as a deadly plague ravaged Rome. According to legend, Michael appeared atop the Mausoleum of Hadrian and used his power to end the plague. Today, a statue of Michael stands atop Castel Sant'Angelo, so it only seemed fitting to hint at his presence in the novel. After all, chapter twelve of the Book of Daniel states that Michael will return at the end times. So perhaps both he and Sirra still have a role to play before the tale of Ciarán and Alais reaches its end.

BOOKS BY JOSEPH FINLEY

The Dragon-Myth Cycle

Enoch's Device

The Key to the Abyss

Dragon-Myth Prequels

Hela's Bane

The Fae Dealings

Other Tales

Mava's Echo: A Short Story of Celtic Myth and Magic

ABOUT THE AUTHOR

Joseph Finley is a writer of historical fantasy fiction. Following a tour as an officer in the U.S. Navy Judge Advocate General's Corps, he returned to Atlanta where he lives with his wife, daughter, and two mischievous rescue dogs. A lifelong love of medieval history, vintage fantasy, and historical mysteries helped inspire his writing, along with a penchant for European travel. Joseph is a member of the Science Fiction and Fantasy Writers of America, and posts frequently about historical and fantasy fiction on his blog. He can be found most nights enjoying a hearty glass of wine, and in the wee hours of most mornings surrounded by history books and plugging away on his next story.

To receive a **free novella**, as well as emails with updates on Joseph's next novel and special offers, join his Reader List by signing up **here** or at his website, below:

www.authorjosephfinley.com

Lastly, if you enjoyed this book, please consider leaving a review (even if it's only a line or two) at Amazon or Goodreads. Word-of-mouth is essential to an author's success, so your input is greatly appreciated!

facebook.com/AuthorJosephFinley
twitter.com/joseph_finley
instagram.com/josephfinley

Printed in Great Britain
by Amazon

85432114R00278